DESERT VENGEANCE
The Ninth Lena Jones Mystery

"Former cop Lena has a fine sense of justice, which she achieves in this ninth entry of a series that features a vivid sense of place, an indomitable protagonist, and a sensitivity to painful social issues."

—Michele Leber, *Booklist*

"Webb offers fans the profound pleasure of watching Lena mature as she comes one step closer to understanding and accepting her difficult past, while providing new readers with an introduction to this strong and genuinely likable character."

—*Publishers Weekly*

"Webb, no stranger to hot-button issues, takes on child molestation in a page-turner that presents both her flawed heroine and the reader with plenty of challenges to their moral codes."

—*Kirkus Reviews*

"Webb's pithy first-person narration cuts to the chase without a lot of filler, making *Desert Vengeance* a pleasure to read....Lena Jones is tough yet vulnerable, irreverent and sarcastic, yet dead serious at times...The Arizona desert and its touristy towns offer up a strange bonanza of desert tropes, and Webb mines them with enough restraint to strengthen, rather than overshoot, her themes of loss and retribution."

—*Shelf Awareness*

DESERT RAGE
The Eighth Lena Jones Mystery

"The Lena Jones series is notable for its persistent protagonist and vivid southwestern setting; this eighth entry, centered on a gruesome crime, also is particularly sensitive to the issues of foster children and what really makes a mother."

—*Booklist*

"Several red herrings arise along the road to a surprising and satisfying ending."

—*Publishers Weekly*

DESERT WIND
The Seventh Lena Jones Mystery

"Webb uses her expert journalistic skills to explore a shocking topic that private investigator Lena Jones uncovers with masterly resolve....a must-read."

—David Morrell, *New York Times* bestselling author of
The Protector

"Webb pulls no punches in exploring another human rights issue in her excellent seventh mystery starring Arizona PI Lena Jones."

—*Publishers Weekly* (starred review)

"Webb's compelling exposé of the damage done to nuclear fallout victims (known as downwinders), accompanied by research notes and bibliography, makes for fascinating reading...Sue Grafton's alphabet series is a prime read-alike for this series; also consider Pari Noskin Taichert and Steven Havill for Tony Hillerman influences."

—*Library Journal*

DESERT LOST
The Sixth Lena Jones Mystery

Winner of *Library Journal*'s Best Mysteries of 2009

"Richly researched and reeking with authenticity—a wicked exposé."

—Paul Giblin, Winner of the 2009 Pulitzer Prize for Journalism

"Webb's Scottsdale PI Lena Jones continues to mix southwestern history with crime in her latest investigation...This is a complex, exciting entry in a first-class series, and it makes an excellent read-alike for Sue Grafton fans."

—Barbara Bibel, *Booklist* (starred review)

"Webb's sobering sixth mystery to feature PI Lena Jones further explores the abuses of polygamy first exposed in 2003's *Desert Wives*...Clear-cut characterizations help a complicated plot flow smoothly. As Webb points out in a note, polygamy still spawns many social ills, despite the recent, well-publicized conviction of Mormon fundamentalist prophet Warren Jeffs."

—*Publishers Weekly*

DESERT CUT
The Fifth Lena Jones Mystery

"Mysteries don't get more hard-hitting than this...Readers will be talking about *Desert Cut* for a long time to come."

—David Morrell, *New York Times* bestselling author of *The Brotherhood of the Rose* and *Creepers*

"...a compelling story that will appeal to a broad range of mystery readers—and may bring increased attention to a too-little-known series."

—*Booklist* (starred review)

"Webb's dark tale of a clash of cultures is emotionally draining and intellectually challenging."

—*Kirkus Reviews*

"This Southwestern series has a depth that enhances the reader's pleasure."

—*Library Journal*

"As in Webb's earlier adventures—particularly *Desert Wives*, with its critically praised exposé of contemporary polygamy—the long-time journalist manages to fuel her plot from the starkest of news stories without compromising the fast-paced action."

—*Publishers Weekly*

DESERT RUN
The Fourth Lena Jones Mystery

"This thought-provoking novel is a gem."

—*The Denver Post*

"Webb bases her latest Lena Jones adventure on a real episode in Arizona history: the great escape of 25 Germans from Camp Papago, a POW camp located between Phoenix and Scottsdale... As in the preceding episodes in the series, Webb effectively evokes the beauty of the Arizona desert."

—Jenny McLarin, *Booklist*

"Webb combines evocative descriptions of place with fine historical research in a plot packed with twists."

—*Publishers Weekly*

DESERT SHADOWS
The Third Lena Jones Mystery

"This third in Webb's series makes good use of both tony Scottsdale and the small-press publishing scene. Lena makes a refreshing heroine; being raised by nine different foster families gives her unusual depth. Solid series fare."

—Mary Frances Wilkens, *Booklist*

"As the suspense builds, the author touches on such issues as consolidation in the book industry, the plight of foster children, mother-daughter relationships, animal rescue programs and more. The glorious Southwest landscape once again provides the perfect setting for Webb's courageous heroine."

—*Publishers Weekly*

DESERT WIVES
The Second Lena Jones Mystery

2004 WILLA Literary Award finalist

"Reading *Desert Wives* is like peering into a microscope at a seething culture of toxic microbes."
—Diana Gabaldon, author of the Outlander series

"If Betty Webb had gone undercover and written *Desert Wives* as a piece of investigative journalism, she'd probably be up for a Pulitzer..."
—*The New York Times*

"Stark desert surroundings underscore the provocative subject matter, the outspoken protagonist, and the 'insider' look at polygamist life. Webb's second Lena Jones mystery, after *Desert Noir*, is recommended for most collections."
—*Library Journal*

"Dark humor and thrilling action inform Webb's second Lena Jones mystery...The beauty of the Southwestern backdrop belies the harshness of life, the corrupt officials, brutal men and frightened women depicted in this arresting novel brimming with moral outrage."
—*Publishers Weekly*

DESERT NOIR
The First Lena Jones Mystery

2002 *Book Sense* Top Ten Mystery

"Another mystery strong on atmosphere and insight."
—Connie Fletcher, *Booklist*

"A must read for any fan of the modern female PI novel."
—*Publishers Weekly*

Desert Redemption

Books by Betty Webb

The Lena Jones Mysteries
Desert Noir
Desert Wives
Desert Shadows
Desert Run
Desert Cut
Desert Lost
Desert Wind
Desert Rage
Desert Vengeance
Desert Redemption

The Gunn Zoo Mysteries
The Anteater of Death
The Koala of Death
The Llama of Death
The Puffin of Death
The Otter of Death

Desert Redemption

A Lena Jones Mystery

Betty Webb

Poisoned Pen
PRESS

Published by Poisoned Pen Press, an imprint of Sourcebooks, Inc.
P.O. Box 4410, Naperville, Illinois 60563-4410
(630) 961-3900
Fax: (630) 961-2168
sourcebooks.com

Library of Congress Cataloging 2018959448

Printed and bound in the United States of America.
SB 10 9 8 7 6 5 4 3 2 1

To my "new" brother, Ron Corbin, and his/our family

"[No] matter what a waste one has made of one's life, it is ever possible to find some path to redemption, however partial."

—Charles Frazier, *Cold Mountain*

35 years earlier

Screams in the distance. Gunshots. Angry voices.

Helen is halfway through the meadow, almost to the trees, but Christina has no trouble keeping up with her, even though the four-year-old is dragging a younger child by the hand.

"The ranger station isn't far," Helen whispers to her husband. "I think we can make it."

Liam's face is white against the night, but a narrow strip of moonglow through the clouds reveals his green eyes.

Running with them are the other children, white, black, Hispanic, Asian. Most are having trouble navigating the uneven ground, but little Christina provides a steady guide. They'll be fine as long as no one cries.

They have almost reached the tree line when the child running alongside Christina slows and begins to whimper.

"Quiet, Morningstar!" Christina admonishes. "Or the bad men will hear you."

Morningstar falls silent at the same moment a lighter-haired girl, not as obedient, begins to wail.

"No, Louisa!" Liam hisses.

Louisa, more frightened of the big red-headed man than of their pursuers, wails even louder. Startled, the babies Liam is carrying join in. Their screams blend with hers.

"Hush, children, please," Helen begs.

Louisa gulps to a stop, but it is too late.

The men behind them are closer now, and one shouts, "I hear them!"

Christina opens her mouth to scream, but no sound comes out.

Chapter One

Present day

My screams echoed those in my nightmare until Jimmy rolled over in bed and put his arms around me.

"Shhhh. It's just a dream, Lena. Just a dream."

"Not a dream," I rasped, my throat raw from screaming. "A memory."

"You need to start seeing someone again. How about that anger management therapist you used to go to?"

"She moved to Tucson. Besides, I'm not angry anymore."

"And I'm the Queen of Sheba."

"That line wasn't funny the first time I heard it."

Silence.

As Jimmy continued to hold me, caressing the old bullet scar on my forehead, I caught my breath. Finally able to speak normally, I said, "The cats are traumatized. Again."

"They'll get over it."

Snowball and Mama Snowball were huddled together in the far corner of the Airstream's bedroom, their fear-fluffed coats making them look twice their size. At least we had delivered the last of the litter to their adoptive homes yesterday, so only two white flame-point Siamese remained behind to listen to my nightmares.

"I'm sorry, cats. It won't happen again."

But I knew it would.

It was a brisk October morning, a mere seventy-two degrees—freezing temps for this part of Arizona—as we headed from the trailer to the corral to feed the horses. Big Boy, Jimmy's pinto gelding, trotted over immediately, while Adila, my Appaloosa mare looked as spooked as the cats. Living out here on the wild expanse of the Salt River Pima/Maricopa Indian Reservation for two months should have calmed her some, but no, she showed me the whites of her eyes and switched her tail as she approached in a sidling walk. When she got close enough to touch, she flattened her ears and bared her teeth.

"You phony," I said.

She shook her head, making her snowy mane ripple.

"Nothing but a drama queen."

She vented a threatening squeal and shook her head again.

"You're a liar, too, but I brought you a treat anyway."

When I produced the carrot pieces hidden behind me, her ears, curved like two halves of a crescent moon, flicked forward. Smiling, I thrust my flat palm through the slats of the fence so she wouldn't be tempted to bite my fingers.

"Careful," I warned.

Black velvet lips brushed against my palm, picking up carrot pieces with the delicacy of a neurosurgeon. After crunching them down she flattened her ears again and backed away from the fence. Then with a squeal, she wheeled, kicked up her heels, and thundered around the corral, completing three circuits. As I watched my misbehaving horse, I admired her white coat with its dappling of quarter-sized black spots. My beauty. My equal. My spirit animal.

"That horse is going to kill you," Jimmy said, as he stroked Big Boy's gentle muzzle.

"Adila? It's all theater with her. She wouldn't purposely harm a hair on my head."

"Maybe not purposely, but with horses like her, accidents happen."

"I can handle every accident she throws my way."

Jimmy muttered something I couldn't hear, then smiled. A full-blooded Pima, his russet skin glistened in the rising sun, making the curved tribal tattoo on his temple look darker in contrast. "You want to ride first or work?"

"Work," in this case, meant finishing construction on the three-bedroom house he had begun in the spring, months before I'd semi-moved from my apartment in Old Town Scottsdale to join him on the Rez. The early-morning beauty out here was still new to me. Around us orange and violet mesas thrust upwards into the clear blue sky. A bright red cardinal sang from a nearby patch of prickly pear cactus, while a family of top-knotted Gambel's quail scratched for breakfast under a yellow-bloomed creosote bush.

"Let's ride first," I said.

"That's got my vote."

We were just saddling up when we spotted Harold Slow Horse's Ford Bronco coming up the dirt road, leaving a rooster tail of dust behind him.

"Here comes trouble," Jimmy said.

"What makes you say that?"

"Something tells me Chelsea's taken off again."

"Took off? I thought she divorced him last August, split with some guy from Texas."

"She changed her mind and came back."

"And Harold let her?"

"You know Harold."

Indeed I did. Harold Slow Horse, a fierce-looking Pima-Kiowa, was even more forgiving than Jimmy, which made him a patsy for users of the female persuasion. In Chelsea's case, "user" also meant the oxycodone addiction that had led her into treatment at the clinic next door to the convenience store Harold had once managed. She had come in one day for a Coke, the legal kind, and they'd begun chatting. Despite Chelsea's white bread upbringing, she had a yen for all things Indian, so one thing led to another, and as soon as the clinic declared her clean, she moved onto the Rez with him. That had been three years, one divorce, and two après-divorce kiss-and-make-ups ago. Chelsea Cooper-Slow Horse was nothing if not changeable.

"*Ya ta hey*," Harold called, jumping down from his truck, followed by Doofus, his yellow Lab. Thanks to so many years of living indoors, Harold's round face wasn't as deeply grooved as most Indians in their fifties. His eyes were those of a much younger man.

"*Ya ta hey*, yourself," Jimmy said. "So what's up, cousin?"

Jimmy was related to just about everyone on the Rez in one way or another. When we had first gotten together I'd tried to track his actual family tree, but soon gave up. It was too complicated, what with members of various tribes moving here and there, intermarrying and having multi-tribal children. Harold himself was the product of a Kiowa father who'd met his Pima mother at a local pow-wow thirty-eight years earlier. As for Chelsea, she claimed a Cherokee great-great grandmother, not that she looked it with her porcelain skin, streaked blond hair, and blue eyes. Harold bore her claim with patience.

"Got a minute?" Harold said, as Doofus bounded back and forth from the corral to us, yipping excitedly. Doofus couldn't understand why the horses didn't like him as much as he liked them.

"Maybe I should go on ahead," I said to Jimmy, sensing some man-to-man time was in the offing. "Let you two talk, then you can catch up with me. It won't kill Big Boy to travel faster than a walk for once."

Harold shook his head. "This concerns you, too, Lena, since you're the licensed PI."

Apprehensive, I led Adila back into the corral. Sensing my

mood, her ears flattened again. When I walked away she gave me a disgusted snort.

At Jimmy's suggestion, we ordered Doofus back into the truck, and went into the Airstream, where Harold nodded his approval at Jimmy's carpentry—the coffee table constructed from saguaro cactus skeletons and studded with turquoise; the wooden cabinets covered with paintings of Pima gods, Earth Doctor, Elder Brother, and the entire traditional panoply. You'd think an artist lived here, not an IT expert.

After we made ourselves comfortable on the sofa, Jimmy served up steaming mugs of Jamaican Blue Mountain coffee, his favorite.

"So, okay, what's the problem?" I asked Harold, after taking a sip. Super strong, unsweetened, just how I liked it.

Harold pretended to study the Navajo rug draped across the back of the sofa. He sat so still that Snowball jumped into his lap, followed immediately by Ma Snowball. As he stroked the cats, I saw the skinned knuckles on his right hand. Maybe he was back to sculpting again. Or not.

"C'mon, Harold, tell me. I'm not a mind-reader."

He looked up at me and sighed. "It's Chelsea."

When Jimmy snorted he sounded so much like my horse that in other circumstances I would have laughed, but, aware of what might have happened between Harold and his ex-wife, I didn't. Their relationship had been going from bad to awful of late. "Please don't tell me she's left you again and you want me to talk her into coming back." Waving at his injured hand, I added, "And just to clear the air, you haven't hurt her, have you?"

His mouth dropped in shock. "Hurt Chelsea? You've got to be kidding!"

"Pretend I don't know you and answer the question."

Harold and Chelsea had married too soon after meeting, and they had divorced even sooner when she left him for a Texas boot-maker. Then she came back, but a few months later left again, thus establishing an oft-repeated pattern. Her erratic behavior was fueled by her drug dependency, and Harold had been trying to get her back into rehab ever since I'd known him. But that didn't mean helping her had come without an emotional cost, and given the stress she had put him through lately....

"Rest easy, Lena, I would never hurt that woman. It's...it's something else."

"Is she using?"

He scratched Snowball behind his ears, and repeated the process with Ma Snowball. Purrs abounded. "A couple of months ago I caught her with a stash of OxyContin she'd been hiding. I flushed it and told her she had to get clean or move out, so she hunted around some and found this rehab place down by Ironwood Canyon, and checked herself in a month ago."

"Well, that's good news, anyway." Jimmy, ever the optimist, looked hopeful.

I didn't, sensing there was more to Harold's story.

"That place, it's called the Kanati Spiritual Center. After three weeks went by and I hadn't heard anything from her, no texts, no emails, no new Facebook posts, I started calling. All I ever got was voice mail. And before you ask, I tried Kanati's 800-number, too, and after a few transfers, finally got to talk to some woman with a French accent who cited 'patient confidentiality,' and wouldn't tell me zip. A couple of hours after that, I did get a phone call from Chelsea, but it was weird, so yesterday I drove down there to see what was going on. That's when I really got worried. The place is operating out of that abandoned movie set used for *Wagon Trails West*. You ever see it?"

As a movie, *Wagon Trails West* had been fun; as a historical artifact, it was ridiculous, with olive-skinned Arabs and Italians pretending to be Indians, their costumes ranging all the way from Apache to Zuni. Some of them could barely stay on their horses.

"Now it's surrounded by a stockade fence and there's some mean-looking dude sitting at a guard shack in front," Harold continued. "He wouldn't let me in, wouldn't tell me anything, not even if Chelsea was still there. When I raised a fuss he called the office, and a few minutes later, the French woman I'd talked to on the eight hundred number came out and told me there was nothing to worry about, that everything was fine. But she wouldn't let me in the place or send Chelsea out to talk to me, saying that as Chelsea's ex-husband, I had no say in whatever type of treatment she may or may not be undergoing."

Knowing what the flighty Chelsea was like, I wasn't worried yet. "You say she 'hunted around' for a detox place. Why didn't she ask her father for a referral? Being a physician, he would know the best clinics."

"Because he'd picked the detox center she'd been in when I met her, and she'd hated it."

"*Kanati*. That's a Cherokee word, isn't it?"

"Yeah, their name for God. Earth Doctor, as we Pimas call him. Chelsea's still convinced she has Cherokee blood a few generations back, and if that's what makes her happy, I'm not going to burst her bubble. That's why she chose this Kanati place, because of the name and the fact that they have a 'Native American'..." his hands made quotes in the air, "...detox program. But nobody I saw there—the guy at the guard shack, the French gal I talked to, and a couple of people clearing brush away from the fence—looked Cherokee. They looked more like you."

Harold's reference to my appearance—pale skin, blond hair, green eyes—meant he had doubts about the rehab center's Native American bona fides.

"Maybe whoever runs the place thought 'Kanati' just sounded pretty," I offered.

"Maybe. But the more I think about it, I'm afraid she may have gotten herself mixed up with some kind of cult."

At the word "cult," I raised my hands. "Whoa, there, pardner. You don't know that. Settle down and tell us more about Chelsea's phone call, the one you described as weird."

Harold looked uncomfortable. "She told me that part of Kanati's program was to help their guests 'gain independence from codependents.' Is that all I am to her now? A *codependent?*"

To answer his question truthfully would be to insult him because Harold, regardless of what he believed, exhibited many traits of codependency. He not only acted as Chelsea's amateur therapist, but he took care of her to the detriment of taking care of himself. Witness his frowsy hair, his old clothes which had degenerated way beyond "retro," his inability to hold any kind of conversation without referring to her, and his constant fear of losing her. Which—Chelsea being Chelsea—he was bound to do.

"Let's just say you're overly invested in her welfare," I replied.

"But I love her!"

Said every codependent ever. Deciding to ease away from the touchy codependency issue, I said, "Some rehab programs think a temporary separation from a partner is a good idea, and from what I've seen with some of our clients, it can work. Then again, you know what Chelsea's like better than anyone. This place she's found might just be an excuse to try something new and exciting. Remember the last time she left you? She rented an apartment over in Phoenix with Joy Tolinski, that friend of hers from ASU. They were planning on setting up some kind export business in Thailand. So who knows? Maybe she's left this rehab place or cult or whatever it is and has already moved in with Joy. She could have asked the Kanati folks to provide cover for her."

"That's the first thing I thought of, too, so I called Joy, but she told me she hadn't seen Chelsea in almost a year, and that the whole Thai thing had been a bust from the get-go. She said Chelsea couldn't stay focused long enough to be of any help."

"Did you get in touch with her father?"

Dr. Orville Cooper, a Paradise Valley widower who had raised Chelsea with the aid of live-in nannies and maids, was not known for his geniality toward his daughter's mostly temporary partners. Harold was the only one he had even been halfway civil to, and that was because Cooper was an art collector and a couple of Harold's bronzes were part of his collection. He'd demanded a "friend" discount, and received it.

"Her dad hasn't heard from her, either. They don't get along, you know."

Chelsea and her father, both mule-headed people, were always at odds, if not over her choice of lovers, then her choice of drugs. But it would take a psychiatrist's couch to solve those problems, not a PI. "This French woman you talked to at Kanati. Do you remember her name?"

Instead of answering, Harold dug in his pocket and pulled out a business card. Printed on expensive cream-colored stock, it stated in burnished gold letters, KANATI SPIRITUAL CENTER. Underneath was an illustration of a blissed-out cartoon Indian in the lotus position. Next to the Indian was the name Gabrielle Halberd, Facilitator.

"You realize this says nothing about rehab," I pointed out.

"Ms. Halberd told me they don't use that word."

I reached down and scratched Ma Snowball's ears; she hadn't cared for the card search and had deserted Harold's lap for mine. "A rehab center that doesn't use the word rehab. That's odd, don't you think?"

"She gave me some blather about Kanati's spiritual experience 'elevating the soul,' making traditional rehab unnecessary." Harold closed his eyes, and in a sing-song voice, mimicked the Halberd woman's French accent. "*Reehab is zee false trail, trod only by zee unbelievair.*"

Jimmy grunted. "An old Cherokee saying, not."

"Did this woman mention any kind of medical staff?" I asked.

"Nope."

Alarm bells were ringing now. It was possible Harold wasn't overreacting. "Arizona law doesn't allow rehab centers to operate without certified medical staff on the premises."

Harold's expression was rueful. "Not being uneducated on

the subject of addiction and rehab, I brought that up, but Ms. Frenchie said theirs was a 'spiritual program,' not a medical one."

When Jimmy frowns, the tattoo on his temple appears to contract into two thin lines instead of three. "You thinking what I'm thinking, Lena?"

"Probably." In calling Kanati a cult, Harold might not be as far off base as I'd first suspected.

For decades, Arizona had been home to numerous ersatz-American Indian groups which promised—for a hefty price—spiritual, physical, and financial growth. Few were connected to recognized Native American beliefs, and even fewer offered medical advice other than the ritual burning of sage bundles. For the most part these groups were harmless, and in some instances even beneficial in that they offered a way out of the uptightness which had sometimes caused the participant's problems to begin with.

Some groups, though, were dangerous, such as James Arthur Ray's former Spiritual Warrior program. In 2009, three participants in the program died of heat stroke and eighteen more were hospitalized after an ill-advised sweat lodge ritual supposedly based on the sweat lodges used by some Native American tribes. No Native Americans were involved in Ray's ceremony, even as advisors, and that had turned out to be a fatal mistake. The tribal medicine men contacted afterwards by the press were highly critical of Ray's amateurish copy-catting of their traditions, and especially alarmed by Ray's comment to his soon-to-die followers, "You will get to a point where you surrender and it's okay to die." The state of Arizona hadn't thought it was "okay to die." In 2011, after a four-month trial, a jury found Ray guilty of negligent homicide. The judge sentenced him to two years in Arizona State Prison, and ordered him to pay upwards of fifty-seven thousand dollars in restitution, thirty-six thousand in fines, plus various financial awards to the decedents' families.

As I pondered the vagaries of Arizona's ever-expanding Native

American spiritual industry, Jimmy stood up, a determined look on his face. "You folks excuse me for a minute. I'm going to find out who's the brains behind Kanati. I smell a rat, and its name just might be James Arthur Ray." With that he vanished into the Airstream's add-on, another single-wide trailer that served as a dedicated computer room.

Harold grunted in agreement. As for myself, I doubted Ray's connection to the Kanati group. Since the Spiritual Warrior deaths, he had lost the bulk of his multimillion-dollar fortune and now lived on book sales and speakers' fees. Having learned his lesson, he had never held another sweat lodge ceremony.

I pointed to Harold's empty cup. "How about some more coffee while we're waiting?"

"If I have any more of this stuff, my hands'll be shaking so much I won't be able to work on my newest piece. I promised to deliver a fourth bronze to the Heard Museum by noon tomorrow." He managed an uneasy laugh. "And I've still got about two square feet to go on one of my canvasses. All pointillism, and you know how slow that goes."

Harold Slow Horse was one of Arizona's leading artists, and the Heard Museum in downtown Phoenix was doing a retrospective on his work. In fame, he was right up there with Fritz Scholder and R.C. Gorman. His bronze pieces were fairly literal. Kiowa men hunting buffalo, Pimas praying to Earth Doctor, Apache women weaving burden baskets—that sort of thing. But his painting style, hyper-realism interspersed with his own brand of dot-intensive pointillism, was unique. One of his paintings, *Crazy Horse Laughing*, hung in the conference room at Desert Investigations. Another, *Geronimo's Last Sunrise*, hung in Chelsea's father's living room between a Warhol and a Lichtenstein.

While we waited for Jimmy to do his IT magic, Harold and I discussed the weather, which was warm and sunny. The cats purred along in accompaniment. We were just getting to the commentary on last year's monsoon season—it had been wicked—when Jimmy returned.

Handing out two sets of printouts, he explained, "As you can see, the Kanati Spiritual Center, established in Arizona two years ago, is run by a company titled Arneault, Pichard, and Theron, which was founded in 1962 by Maurice Arneault. They're head-quartered in Quaydon, a suburb of Paris. The one in France, not Texas."

"France?!" Harold and I chorused as one.

"*Oui, mes amies.* As I said, Kanati—that's their satellite group—has been operating here for the past two years, led by Adam Arneault, Maurice's son, who was born in Oklahoma. Apparently his father was doing some business there at the time."

"What the hell is a group of woo-woo Parisians doing in Arizona?" I asked.

Jimmy grinned, his white teeth flashing from his dark face. "Spreading peace, health, and prosperity through spiritual enlightenment. At least that's what their brochure says. But there's one thing you need to know, Harold. Since Kanati opened, there haven't been any complaints, and believe me, I checked. But there were a lot of accolades from people who swore that Kanati had changed their lives for the better."

Harold didn't look relieved. "But they're doing business as a rehab."

"They merely say they're a center devoted to spiritual enlight-enment."

Unsettled by the surprising international connection, I said, "No promises, but I'll take a drive down there tomorrow and see what's going on. Jimmy's been hinting that I could use some spiritual enlightenment myself."

I'd meant that as a joke, but it was close to being true.

Jimmy, the most patient of men, was aware of how much trouble I was having getting used to our new relationship. Not that I didn't love him, I did, but when you've led a life like mine, allowing yourself to grow close to someone wasn't easy.

We'd been business partners at Desert Investigations for more than a decade. Over the years we'd grown so close that I began calling him my "Almost Brother." Despite our different blood-lines—he was one hundred percent Pima Indian and I was one hundred percent European mongrel—our backgrounds were oddly similar in one important respect. His parents had died soon after his birth, and he had been adopted by a white family in Utah, and had grown up yearning to be reunited with his Pima kin.

I was an orphan, too, or at least the social workers had believed I was. I'd been found comatose on a Phoenix street at the age four with a bullet in my head. No one came forward to claim me. The social workers had attempted to find a good placement for me, but it hadn't worked out, and so I'd spent the rest of my childhood being tossed from one place to another. One of those places had been horrific.

So let's just say I had trust issues, where Jimmy had none. He accepted the world as it was, whereas I was always trying to change it.

"Want me to drive down to that Kanati place with you?" Jimmy asked. "That's some pretty territory."

"Nah, I'll go it alone."

After all, wasn't that what I'd always done?

Chapter Two

The next morning, after my four-times-weekly workout at Scottsdale Karate, I pulled into my parking space at Desert Investigations in Old Town Scottsdale almost an hour after Jimmy.

We had started our company as equal partners, with Internet-savvy Jimmy manning the online investigations and me following up with the footwork. Most of our clients were from the Scottsdale area, especially the Indian-arts-and-artifacts neighborhood our office was in, but the footwork sometimes took me out of state while Jimmy manned the fort.

While walking toward the office, I heard someone call, "Lena Jones! Just the person I've been meaning to talk to." I turned around to see Sharona Gavala, who owned the prestigious art gallery three doors away from Desert Investigations, standing in front of her gallery door, keys in hand. She looked immaculate with her trim black suit, raven-colored hair bobbed in a neo-Twenties cut, and kohl-rimmed gray eyes. Very New York, but I knew she was born in Tucson. "If you get a chance, could you come see me today?"

"How about now?" I asked. "I have time."

A phone rang. "Damn. The phone's ringing, and I've got this out-of-state buyer…"

"Later, then."

With a final wave she unlocked the door and dashed in.

When I walked into Desert Investigations, Jimmy gestured toward the conference room. "Your nine-thirty appointment has arrived."

"I don't have a nine-thirty appointment."

"You do now."

Opening the door to the conference room, I saw my fifteen-year-old goddaughter sitting at the long table. She was grasping a handful of tissues and her face was a blurry mess. Alison Cameron-Thorsson wasn't a crier, so my mind immediately flew to that forbidden place in my nightmares where children screamed, fathers died, and the world turned dark. Sitting in the chair next to her, I took her hand in mine.

"What's wrong, kiddo?"

Her lower lip quivered. "Kyle's parents are moving to Oregon and I want to go with them."

This was bad news indeed, although not quite the horror show my mind had summoned up. Like Jimmy and me, Ali and Kyle Etheridge shared a unique bond. A year earlier, Alison's birth mother, father, and younger brother had been found murdered in their plush Scottsdale home. Ali and her boyfriend, Kyle—who had his own troubled past—each believed the other had committed the crime, and so confessed separately to the murders. Only after they had been shuttled off to different juvenile facilities had I discovered the truth and brought the real killers to justice.

But life can be complicated, and thanks to advances in reproductive science, it was becoming even more complicated. Ali had two biological mothers. The first was Juliana Thorsson, who as a cash-strapped college student, had sold the eggs that were implanted into the uterus of Alexandra Cameron, Ali's second biological mother. Following Alexandra's murder last year, Juliana had then adopted her own biological child.

Juliana was doing her best to be a good mother, but since her own life as a member of the U.S. House of Representatives was time-consuming, she had asked me to pick up the slack by becoming the girl's godmother. Feeling honored, I had accepted, but over the past year I had learned that "godmother" wasn't simply a title.

Trying to maintain my equilibrium, I asked Ali, "Does your mother know about this?"

Sniffling, she answered, "She knows they're moving, that's all. I need you to help me talk her into letting me move with them."

I took a deep breath. "Um, are Kyle's parents are on board with this?"

She wouldn't meet my eyes. "You'll have to talk to them, too."

"Ali, does your mom know you're here instead of in school?"

"She will as soon as the school reports me absent. Oh, Lena, Kyle means everything to me, and if I can't be with him I'll just die!" A fresh gush of tears.

I wouldn't be a teenager again for all the money in the world. Everything was now or never, black or white, ecstasy or sorrow. "Look, why don't we call…?"

A woman's voice from the front office alerted me that Ali's mother had already learned she'd skipped school and who she was probably with. Juliana Thorsson stormed into the conference room, prepared to deliver a scathing speech about truancy. Upon seeing the tearful girl, her stern face softened. "What's wrong, Ali? Did someone hurt you?"

Juliana's pale blond hair looked hardly brushed, and her makeup was even more hurried. Up until recently she had always been circumspect about her appearance, but now, only a month before the election, her campaign for the U.S. Senate was in crisis. Her numbers had declined sharply when Gerald Simpson, her opponent, unearthed the information about her personal involvement in the still-controversial in-vitro fertilization process, and had leaked the story to the media. Now her daughter was having a meltdown, too.

"Nobody hurt me, Mom," Ali told her.

"Then why…?"

Before Juliana could cross-examine the girl, I murmured to her, "Let's you and me talk in the other room." To Ali, I said, "Jimmy will bring you a 7-Up. Want some Cheetos, too?"

She sniffed. "I don't eat Cheetos."

"They're good for you."

"Godmothers aren't supposed to lie." She managed a weak smile.

Jimmy, who had entered the conference room with Juliana, turned around and headed for the small refrigerator we kept in the office. Juliana and I followed.

"What's going on, Lena?" Juliana, too wound up to sit in the client chair beside my desk, paced back and forth while I struggled to plead Ali's case. Not that I agreed with it.

"It's complicated, so…"

She didn't let me finish. "Ali's not the truant type. If she's being bullied because of that damned Simpson thug, he can…"

"This has nothing to do with Simpson's IVF slanders, Juliana. It's something else entirely. Did you know that the Etheridges are moving to Oregon?"

"Ali's been carrying on about it all week. She's miserable, and I'm none too happy, myself. Escrow just closed on that condo down the street from the Etheridge house, the one she wanted me to buy so she and Kyle could remain close even if I win the election. Not that I regret buying into that neighborhood, it's a great one, but what with all this fuss about the IVF thing and my opponent's other smears…" She stopped. Paled. Slumped into a chair. "Oh, hell. Is Ali *pregnant?*"

"You can rest easy about that."

Ali couldn't be pregnant, not with all the birth control advice she had received from me. I had even bought her a box of condoms to sneak to Kyle, just in case. When a girl is fifteen and sexually active, a godmother needs to be watchful.

"At least I don't think she's pregnant," I amended, "but here's the deal. She wants to move to Oregon with the Etheridges."

Juliana's face hardened. "Over my dead body."

"Probably over theirs, too, but that's why she's here, to get me to talk you into letting her go. Then I'm supposed to talk the Etheridges into it."

"She's crazy."

"No, she's fifteen."

"This is all my fault."

"Said by every mother about every problem every child ever suffered."

When Juliana brushed her white-blond hair away from her eyes I noticed that her mascara was running, but from sweat, not tears. If she didn't curb her emotions, she would not only lose the election, but Ali's respect at the very time she needed it most.

Oblivious to my concern, she continued her self-castigation. "Considering everything she's been through—her family being murdered, the court cases, the adoption problems—I knew I should have spent more time with her. Hell, I should have dropped this entire senate race and stayed home and just been a good mom."

"So said every mother, etcetera, which is why we have so many asshole males running the country. You wanted to change that, remember."

"What am I supposed to do? Chain the brat to the bedpost?"

"I've heard worse ideas, but they're all illegal. For now, dumb as this may sound, take her over to the Sugar Bowl for something full of endorphins. Hot fudge sundaes are packed with them. You have a sundae, too, because you need it as much as she does. Then go on home and spend the rest of the day playing Happy Families. Let her talk while you *listen*. Then call me tomorrow and we'll discuss the situation further."

A bleak smile. "In other words, take two aspirin and call me in the morning."

"Doctor Jones' best advice."

"Asshole males, huh?" Jimmy said, after mother and daughter had left for the ice cream parlor.

"You know what I meant."

"Uh huh. By the way, while you were in there practicing medicine without a license, we received a call from Harold Slow Horse. He's in a frenzy because the morning news reported that the body of a Caucasian woman matching Chelsea's description was found near Talking Stick. The authorities are calling it a suspicious death, so Harold's on his way up there to see what he can find out."

It took a moment for my shock to ebb. Talking Stick was a huge, upscale resort, casino, and entertainment complex that offered everything from high-stakes poker, to fine dining, to indoor skydiving, to animatronic dinosaurs, to a dolphinarium where you could swim with friendly dolphins. Not only was Talking Stick the last place you'd expect a suspicious death, but it was on Indian land, which meant any serious crime there would bring in the Feds, something criminals with any intelligence at all avoid at all costs. There was another oddity, too. The complex was a full ninety miles from that so-called spiritual center Chelsea was staying in.

"We might be looking at a case of mistaken identity," I told Jimmy. "Because why in the world would Chelsea drive all the way from that Kanati place to Talking Stick?" I said. "Gambling was never her thing."

When Jimmy shrugged, his ebony hair rippled across his broad shoulders, making me wonder once again how I could have blocked out his physical beauty for so many years. But love is blind in more ways than one.

Unaware of my thoughts, he said, "I caught the tail end of the same newscast, and the woman they found was said to be in her early twenties, five-six, slender, with light-colored hair. Could be her."

"It doesn't make sense."

"Neither did Harold when he called. You know what he's like."

People who think Indians are all about stoicism haven't known any. Like most artists, Harold had his highs and his lows (usually Chelsea-related), and he was impulsive. For him to hear part of a news broadcast and project it onto his still-beloved ex-wife was exactly the sort of thing he would do, especially since Talking Stick was only a couple of miles from his house. He might even have thought Chelsea had died while trying to make her way back to him. If Harold hadn't been a successful artist, he probably could have made it as a romance novelist.

I reached for the landline. "I'm calling Sylvie and getting the straight scoop."

Detective Sylvie Perrins of the Scottsdale Police was an old frenemy of mine. The all-sting-and-no-smile Sylvie seldom had a good word for anyone, the exception being her current partner, the ever-patient Bob Grossman. Years ago, when I'd put in my time with the Scottsdale PD, she and I had worked a few cases together, but although she remained quick with an insult, that kind of partnership tends to be long-lasting.

She answered on the second ring. "What the hell do you want this time, Lena?"

"That body out near Talking Stick. You hear anything about identifying jewelry or tattoos?"

"Bob and I didn't catch the case. Yarnell and Telez did."

That stumped me for a second, since Scottsdale PD doesn't handle reservation crime. "Why would Yarnell and Telez be working a body found on Indian land?"

"It wasn't on Indian land. You know the El Mesquite Business Park, the one next door to the Rez? That's where she was found, half-hidden under some damned mesquite tree. Nobody noticed her until the buzzards moved in."

"I meant the tattoo, Sylvie. Did she have any?"

"Just to shut you up, yeah, a unicorn tattoo, and for further identification, not that you asked, a thin gold wedding ring. A cheap one."

"Where?"

"Third finger, left hand."

"The tattoo, Sylvie."

"Ass."

"No tattoo on either arm?" Chelsea had a butterfly on her left arm, and she'd stopped wearing her wedding ring even before divorcing Harold.

"Nada."

"Thanks."

"Quit bothering me." Dial tone.

Next, I called Harold. "It's not her."

"How do you know?" His anxiety leaked through the phone.

"I talked to a friend who heard it from another friend. The dead woman has a unicorn tattoo on her rear, so unless Chelsea had one inked there recently to keep her butterfly company, the body is someone else."

"You sure?"

"My source never lies." Other than to her boyfriends.

A relieved sigh. "Thank you."

"Any time, Harold. Go home and paint. Or sculpt. Do whatever you need to be doing. I told you I'd check out the Kanati Spiritual Center, and I'm headed to Ironwood Canyon right now."

The ruler-straight drive down I-10 from the Phoenix area to Tucson is one of the most tiresome drives in the world. The scenery isn't much, just miles and miles of flat, monochromatic desert broken occasionally by a scraggly creosote bush. One hour into the drive you're in danger of dozing off from sheer boredom. Fortunately, I wasn't going all the way to Tucson, but taking the Ironwood Canyon turnoff near the Pinal County airplane boneyard, where hundreds of out-of-service commercial airliners have gone to die. Watching airplanes rot away in a desert was about as interesting as watching paint dry, or continuing on the boring drive to Tucson. Once I caught sight of a coyote loping along the median, going God knows where. This was unusual because coyotes are night hunters, but as urbanization spreads its nasty way into the desert, wildlife has had to adapt. In the coyotes' case, it often meant daytime hunting.

Halfway to the Ironwood Canyon turnoff, and unable to stand the boredom anymore, I stopped at one of the souvenir shops, used the restroom, then bought a liter of water and a cheap key-chain with a picture of a cactus on it—not that I needed either. As a life-long desert dweller, I've learned to never leave home without at least a gallon of some kind of potable liquid—water, Gatorade, whatever. But there are just so many miles of flat beige desert you can face before overpriced trinkets made in China start looking pretty good to your color-starved eyes.

During the drive, something had been niggling at me, and while returning to my rented Chevy Malibu, I finally figured out what it was. I had meant to stop by the Gavalan Art Gallery to find out what Sharona Gavalan wanted to talk to me about, but forgot. Well, no biggie. I probably wouldn't be at Kanati all that long, and should have time to see Sharona before she closed the gallery for the evening.

After downing the bottle of water and throwing the Chinese keychain into my tote, I pulled back onto the highway. Several more stupefying miles later I heaved a sigh of relief when the Ironwood Canyon turnoff came into view. Not that the scenery on the long gravel road leading to Chelsea's new digs was any more interesting than the scenery along I-10. But whereas the highway was perfectly maintained, the same couldn't be said for the rutted gravel road I shortly found myself enduring. It had been washed out in several places, and the Malibu had a hard time dealing with the potholes. I longed for my 1945 Jeep, which ate roads like this for breakfast, but the Jeep was also an unforgettable vehicle, and much too easily traced back to Desert Investigations. I planned to go in as a mere truth-seeker, not a suspicious PI.

From Harold's description, I had imagined the Kanati Spiritual Center would be depressing, but it when it appeared on the horizon I had to smile. The one-time movie set had been expanded to around twenty acres, which now included a large entertainment complex I could see through the open gate. This Xanadu in the desert was surrounded by the log walls of a Geronimo-era U.S. Cavalry fort—two-story guard posts and all. On the eastern side, most of the same structures which had appeared in *Wagon Trails West* remained intact. Rustler's Roundup Saloon, the site of so many gunfights in the film, still sat between a hotel humorously named the Hotel OK Corral, and the rather uncreatively named General Store. Across the dirt street from those stalwart businesses sat the Sheriff's Office, the jail, and several other old-timey shops. Nothing new there, except fresh coats of paint.

Things got funky on the western half of the complex, where five rows of pioneer-type log cabins existed peacefully along with a wigwam-ed Indian village. Capping off this section of the Old West was a huge teepee which looked large enough to house a goodly portion of the Mormon Tabernacle Choir. It almost, but not quite, eclipsed the three-story log lodge tucked into the corner of the complex. All this frontier-era wackiness appeared wildly out of place next to an Olympic-sized swimming pool and tennis courts. One more modern oddity made me laugh outright: the bright pink Porta Potty sitting between the outer stockade wall and the paved parking lot. For the guard? Or a courtesy for pioneers who couldn't make it to the next wagon stop?

In front of the massive teepee a co-ed group of people wearing chinos and white golf shirts were playing hacky sack. Some wore beaded, faux-Indian headbands. The cartoonish Western setup displayed one more modern oddity: The guard shack Harold Slow Horse had referred to turned out to be a cheap lawn chair placed under a green awning, the kind you see at craft fairs. As I rolled to a stop, the thin, redhaired gatekeeper greeted me with a smile. When he John Wayne-ambled up to my window, I saw bruising around his lower jaw.

"Welcome to Kanati, ma'am. Didn't know they was expecting anybody new today."

I shut off the ignition and stepped out of the Malibu. Having already decided on my approach, I said in a hesitant voice, "Uh, I'm not exactly checking in, at least not yet, but a friend was telling me about this place and it sounded like it could help me with my, um, problem. I just want to take a look before I make a commitment."

Red Head's smile grew broader. "No problem with that, ma'am. Check it out, see if it's right for ya, 'cause Kanati sure ain't right for everyone. Some folks leave after a few days, but the smart ones tough it out. From what I hear, ya gotta be serious about this spiritual growth thing, not just pussy-foot around. Tell ya what. You just relax for a couple of minutes while I get Gabrielle down here to give ya the grand tour."

After a quick call and a few muttered words, he returned his attention to me. "I'm Ernie." He was more muscular than I originally thought, but I sensed no menace in him.

I stuck my hand out. "Pleased to meet you, Ernie. I'm Lena."

His handshake was firm but jovial. "You from outta state? A lot of the folks here are."

"Local."

"Good. Good. And how about…?"

He stopped when a beautiful woman in her late thirties walked through the gate. Although definitely Caucasian, with her chestnut-colored hair and dark eyes, the beaded headband wrapped around her sophisticated chignon lent her a slight resemblance to the Disney version of Pocahontas. But she wasn't wearing the Disney Pocahontas fringed mini-dress, just khakis and a white golf shirt emblazoned with the Kanati logo.

She stretched out a professionally manicured hand. "I am Gabrielle, Lena, and I hear you seek spiritual growth." A warm contralto, possibly stage-trained. And a heavy French accent.

I stretched out my own hand, purposely making it tremble. "I've been having some, uh, problems lately and I thought spirituality would…" I trailed off.

Gabrielle gave me a look of compassion. "Kanati welcomes all distressed souls." Pointing to the parking lot, she said, "Park there, and I shall give you a tour of our facility."

I pretended hesitancy. "Um, how much is it? I don't have…"

Her smile didn't waver. "Do not concern yourself with monetary issues for now. Simply observe what we have to offer. Kanati is a community dedicated to peace and harmony, not financial gain. Our business is to bring light to this world, not take advantage of any pain our friends may be suffering."

She almost made me believe it. But from past cases, I knew that cults—if Kanati turned out to actually *be* a cult—tended to strip their followers of every penny they had.

Unaware of my skepticism, Gabrielle escalated the sales pitch. "First, allow me to show you where we hold group meditations three times a day."

"That's a lot of meditating."

A graceful nod. "If you decide to make Kanati part of your life, you will find that you enjoy it so much you will want to meditate five times, six times a day. But we do not encourage such puritanical rigor. One of our teachings is that it is of utmost importance to maintain balance in every area of our lives." She gestured toward the hacky sack players. "Elevated mind. Elevated body. These are the keys to health and happiness, even when it includes such silliness. May I ask what your particular problems are? Alcohol? Drugs? Sexual abuse? Or simply the sense of aimlessness and hopelessness that afflicts so many un-Elevated souls these days?"

Every time she used the word "Elevated" it came capitalized.

"I suffered trauma in my youth." No lie there. The specifics included starvation, beatings, and rape in foster homes, all by the time I was nine. Then there were my years as a Scottsdale police officer when I'd been shot, then... But it would be foolish to open up to this woman. Her very slickness hinted at a painless past.

My vague generalization warmed her contralto further. "So many of us have suffered, yet I promise you that with adherence to the Kanati program, you will rise from the ashes of your past like the legendary Phoenix. You will become Elevated."

There was that word again.

Like all successful salespeople, the woman had her routine down pat. Meekly obeying her instructions, I parked at the end of a row comprised mainly of Mercedes and BMWs, and a couple of newer model white passenger vans embellished with the Kanati logo. Such automotive luxury made me wonder how much seeking spirituality at Kanati might cost. But now wasn't the time to ask.

Once I returned to the gate, Gabrielle led me through the compound, all the while extolling Kanati's virtues, which appeared to be many. Although it did look a bit on the wacky side, what with its Old West folderol, the place came across as better organized than some of the high-end retreat facilities I'd found in Sedona. The log cabins, although sparsely furnished with eight bunks per, were spotless, their beds neatly made and covered with Indian-print blankets. No one was in them, probably because they were out enjoying the fresh air. Same with the small teepees.

"Do all the members of Kanati live on the premises?" I asked Gabrielle. I was having a hard time accepting that the owners of those Beemers and Benzes I'd seen in the parking lot would submit to summer camp-type lodgings.

"At the start of their spiritual journey, many maintain their outside homes," she explained, "but as they grow to love us, almost all of them choose to live with us. Why remain in the cold and uncaring world when Kanati offers so much warmth?"

Cults were good at separating initiates from their family and friends, so this was a bad sign. My suspicions grew.

Behind the hacky sack players, a team of doubles batted a tennis ball around on a clay court, while off to the side, several people in modest bathing suits cavorted in the pool. Opposite them, ten slightly overweight individuals wearing khakis and white Kanati-logoed golf shirts performed calisthenics led by an instructor wearing a seriously beaded headband. Nearby, a group of morbidly obese folks enjoyed a game of croquet on a patch of artificial turf.

As we toured, Gabrielle introduced me to several Kanatians, which is what they called themselves. Most wore beaded headbands and were friendly to a fault. Everyone wanted to shake my hand, to tell me how beautiful I was—no one mentioned the bullet scar on my forehead—and what an asset I could become for the Kanati community.

Such behavior was called "love-bombing," but this place was so loosey-goosey I still wasn't convinced Kanati qualified for cult status. In my days as an investigator, I had seen a great many cults, including several of the polygamist kind, and none had appeared as free-wheeling as this goofy place. True cults were all about brainwashing and control, especially of women. Here, the opposite seemed to be true, with most of the group leaders being female. The Kanatians' ages ranged mostly from twenty-somethings to fifties, but as we walked around, I did see one man so elderly he was bent almost double over the two canes he used to support himself. He looked so frail that when we passed him, which wasn't difficult, given that he moved so slowly, I found myself surprised at the sharp awareness in his eyes.

As the old man made his creaky way toward the big lodge, I asked Gabrielle, "What's with those headbands? And the beads? Do they mean anything in particular?"

The facilitator beamed. "Most certainly. A new bead is awarded each time a Kanatian reaches a new level of Elevation. They begin with no beads, then work their way toward ten."

"Kind of a status thing, then."

"We are all equal here at Kanati." Gabrielle gestured toward the Hotel OK Corral. "That building houses not only a sauna and accredited masseuses, but also a fully furnished gym with the latest Nautilus equipment. If you prefer to exercise with a group, we have classes in aerobics, dance, skip-rope, and cycling."

"Skip-rope?"

"A simple exercise, but effective. Both the arms and the feet are constantly in motion. Would you like to see the facility?"

Having already spent much of the morning smelling sweaty martial arts practitioners, I gave it a pass. "Maybe later. Right now I'd like a closer look at that teepee. I've never seen anything like it before." I had, though, at several highway souvenir stands, although their teepees weren't as large.

This particular teepee turned out to be built of reinforced fiberglass painted a buckskin color and decorated with an inter-tribal jumble of American Indian pictographs. Inuit ravens flew over Pima mazes, Hopi kokopellis danced under Zuni zias. The buckskin-painted cement floor was made less sterile by a large assortment of pillows covered in even more faux-Indian patterns. After a quick count of the pillows, I realized the space housed up to eighty people at a time. This worried me.

James Ray's fire circle celebrants had suffered life-threatening health problems because their so-called kiva had inadequate circulation. But as I examined the architecture of the teepee, I saw a large opening in the ceiling where the lodge poles came together. Added to the teepee's front and back doorways, the circulation would have been fine, especially since there was no fire pit. Instead, the teepee sported a raised circular dais in its center, where I imagined Kanati's spiritual head honcho, whoever he or she was, led the meditation meet-ups.

While Gabrielle showed me around, her hands caressed the pictographs on the teepee's walls. "Are these drawings not lovely?"

Tired of lies—I had told so many during the last half hour—I answered, "They're certainly colorful."

"Here in this holy place is where you will be doing the bulk of your work."

"Work, did you say?" My voice rose in alarm.

In a true cult, "work" was used as a method of control by the leader. Possibly the most infamous use of cult "work" occurred in the indoctrination methods of Heaven's Gate. In order to work toward a "higher level," the cultists were ordered to put away all Earthly sensual behavior, including the enjoyment of food and sex. To keep his followers from enjoying food, cult leader Marshall Applewhite not only fed his fellow cultists a tasteless diet, but even dictated the number of times they had to chew their food before swallowing. To wean them away from sex, Applewhite instituted an even more extreme solution: castration. His followers' lives became so joyless that thirty-nine of them—including the Castrato in Chief—committed suicide.

Not knowing my background in cult investigations, Gabrielle's smile held a hint of condescension. "Elevation of the spirit never comes without serious work, Lena. But we at Kanati prefer the term 'education.' Work has such a negative context, do you not think? Even Ernie is aware of the value of work."

"Ernie's a member, too?" The gateman had come across as a down-to-earth guy.

"*Non, non,* but we have been working on the dear man. He smokes, and we love him so much we wish him to live a long, long time."

This wish for Ernie's long life made some of my unease diminish, if not vanish entirely. Despite Kanati's pseudo-Indian trappings, it appeared to be just another high-priced health spa with a few woo-woo frills. But my discomfort level rose again when I neared the teepee's rear exit and scanned the old movie set buildings. None bore a sign reading SAWBONES.

"Where's your medical facility?"

A bright smile. "The Tucson Medical Center is less than a half hour away. But rest assured, several of us are trained in First

Aid, although our skills have yet to be needed. Our meditation program eases the stressors that cause most physical emergencies."

As we exited and started across the wide plaza toward the big lodge, I took note of the fancy-dancy way Gabrielle had sloughed off my question. According to Harold, Chelsea was using this place for rehab, and bad physical things can happen to a person during rehab. Pop singer Amy Winehouse had died while attempting to detox on her own, as had many others. Besides, stress was seldom the cause of broken bones, cancer, or even AIDs, so, as far as I was concerned, her explanation earned Kanati another negative mark.

Deciding that it was time to tell the truth, I said, "I have a friend here, name of Chelsea Cooper-Slow Horse, and she has an oxycodone addiction. How does meditation without medical care help a person withdraw from opioids?"

Gabrielle halted at the steps to the lodge. She tilted her head, and the many-colored beads in her headband sparkled in the sun. "I do not remember that you gave me your last name, Lena."

"It's Jones."

"Lena *Jones?*" Doubt clouded her face, and she whipped a wine-colored iPhone from her pocket. Tapped it several times. Ran her finger along the screen. Stopped. Tapped once more. Used her thumb and forefinger to enlarge the image.

"You are Lena Jones of Desert Investigations, in Scottsdale," she said, the contralto warmth gone from her voice. "It says here, a private detective." She pronounced detective like it was a four letter word.

"We call ourselves investigators, but *oui*, Madame Halberd." I wanted her to know she wasn't the only one familiar with Google.

Her eyes were such a dark brown they were almost black. Like Jimmy's eyes, only colder. "It's *Mademoiselle* Halberd, actually. I have no husband. Are you investigating us?"

"Just checking on the welfare of a friend. Is that a problem?"

"I see. Then I wish for you to get out…"

Before she could finish, a gust of wind came up and blew my hair away from my face. Then it died down, but not before she saw. She raised her manicured hand, and with a light finger, traced the scar on my forehead. Her eyes, as well as her voice, softened. "Someone has shot you."

"My mother."

A wince. "But your *maman* did not mean to, Lena Jones."

Surprised, I said, "No, she didn't. How…?"

Her voice became a whisper. "There was truth among your many lies. You did suffer trauma in the past and it has scarred you more deeply than your skin. Let Kanati help you, like it has helped me." She turned her beautiful hands over so I could see the long vertical scars on her slender wrists. At some time in the past she had tried to kill herself, and unlike many would-be suicides, had known the proper way to cut. Yet she had survived.

Resisting the urge to touch my three decades-old scar, I said, "I'm over it."

The smile she gave me then was tender. "Ah, another lie. But the truth lies in *les cauchemars*, your nightmares."

I pretended to study the cedar lodge we were nearing. It was as perfectly cared-for as everything else in the Kanati compound. Blue asters bloomed in its flowerboxes, seemingly out of place among the growths of prickly pear cacti that hid the lodge's cement foundation. A wide porch wrapped around three sides of the building, much of its length occupied by rocking chairs. No one was currently sitting in them.

When I had recovered my equilibrium, I said firmly, "I want to see Chelsea Cooper-Slow Horse."

Instead of fending me off with the standard refusal of not being able to discuss whether someone was a resident or not, she nodded and said, "*Certainement*, since you are not one of the proscribed names on her guest list. I only ask that you not upset her in any way. Ms. Slow Horse remains fragile, but with our treatment she has become well enough to assist in serving lunch today. Are you hungry? Our chef is most excellent, and we promise not to poison you."

What was it with this woman? She was a slick-talking salesperson for just another woo-woo group, yet her empathy came across as sincere.

Maybe that's why she was so good at her job.

Chapter Three

The great room of the three-story lodge reminded me of a millionaire's hunting getaway I had once visited in northern Arizona while on a case. Except for a lack of taxidermied animals, Kanati's massive living area/dining hall could have been designed by the same architect. Groupings of Indian-printed easy chairs arced around the huge rock fireplaces that stood at each end of the room. The glowing embers in the hearths added to the visual warmth, giving the room a cozy, homey feel despite its size. A sea of white linen-covered tables stretched across the middle of the room, each decorated by large bouquets of flowers. Large wicker baskets filled with more flowers hung from the rafters above. But what caught my attention was the professional-looking cafeteria station where the Kanatians had lined up.

"Is it not lovely?" Gabrielle asked.

"It's stunning."

So was the room's aroma, a combination of cedar, flowers, wood smoke, and fresh bread. These heady scents were joined by something just as wonderful wafting from the food line. No wonder the rocking chairs on the lodge's porch had been deserted, as were the chairs surrounding the double fireplaces. Whatever Kanati's religious belief—I had yet to learn the details—it certainly didn't include the self-denying asceticism of Heaven's Gate.

My stomach growled. Loudly.

A sly grin teased at the corner of Gabrielle's mouth. "Ah, a woman of healthy appetites, I see. Excellent, because to achieve optimum Elevation, the enjoyment of good food is of the essence."

"One of Kanati's teachings, I presume." Hint, hint.

She winked. "*Mais oui.* Shall we?"

Chelsea spotted me the minute we entered the serving line, where she was working the salad section. To my relief, Harold's ex-wife looked healthier than I'd ever seen her. She wore no makeup, yet her lips and cheeks were pink, her eyes clear. Always an attractive woman, she now verged on beautiful. She wasn't as happy to see me as I was to see her.

"Harold hired you to check up on me!" she snarled.

"I'm doing it gratis," I said sweetly. "What's that you're ladling out?"

A frown. "Cucumber Canapés with Lemon Dill Sauce."

"Then I'll have two scoops, please."

"But…"

"Chelsea, *mon amie,*" Gabrielle interjected, "why do not you find someone to take your station so we will not be holding up the line? Then you may join us at the small table in the corner we reserve for our very special guests."

While Chelsea grumbled an assent and called over to a group of Kanatians working in the corner, I got busy choosing other selections. By the time I made it to the table Gabrielle had pointed out, I'd added a Grilled Portabella Mushroom on Herbed Polenta, and for dessert, Baked Brie and Blackberries in Puff Pastry crowned with raspberry sauce. Kanati's chef hadn't been hired away from some school's lunchroom, unless the school was Le Cordon Bleu.

For my beverage, a server delivered a *café au lait* to the little corner table, although I noticed he brought Gabrielle a bottle of Evian.

"Is good?" Gabrielle asked, as I sampled the polenta and made a moaning sound.

"Is scrumptious."

"Food is not only supposed to give life, it is one of those things which Elevates our senses, like a Beethoven symphony, a perfume by Chanel, a painting by a great master, or a caress by a gentle lover. Properly prepared food Elevates the soul."

After gulping down another bite of portabella, I said, "You sound quite the sensualist, Gabrielle."

"No one should be so foolish as to turn down the gifts of the senses."

"If this is what you guys mean by Elevation, I'm all for it," I said, attacking the Brie.

"Ah, here comes your good friend Chelsea. I will leave you two alone to talk, so that you can ease your mind about her welfare."

With that, she pushed herself away from the table and wandered away to chat with other Kanati truth-seekers, apparently unconcerned about anything critical Chelsea might say rc Elevated life on an old movie set.

"Damn that Harold," Chelsea grumped, pulling up a chair. "Gabrielle told me he showed up here yesterday and tried to beat the crap out of Ernie, but Ernie's tougher than he looks. Gabrielle came this close to calling the sheriff." She used her thumb and forefinger to illustrate.

Like the rest of the Kanatians, she wore chinos and the standard logoed golf shirt. No headband, though.

"He's worried about you, Chelsea." But I was almost as worried about Harold as I was Chelsea. He hadn't said anything about slugging the gate man, but I remembered seeing his skinned knuckles. Slugging someone these days, even when warranted, could get you locked up. And sued.

"Then tell him to stop worrying, Lena, and for God's sake, make him stop sending people up here looking for me! I don't want him interfering with what I'm working toward."

"What exactly are you working toward? World peace?"

She gave me a sour look. "Let the Moonies worry about that, and good luck to them. As for me, I want to become Elevated."

"Gabrielle keeps using that word, too, but I have no idea what it means."

"It means living life on a higher plain."

"Isn't that what everyone is trying to do? But without all this…" I gestured toward the pictograph-covered teepee, visible through the lodge's picture window "…without all this phony Indian hoo-hah. You're a native Arizonan, Chelsea, and you know that the tribes don't worship one homogenous God. The Apaches have Usen, the Pimas have Earth Doctor, and so on and so on. Each tribe walks its own unique path, and often their deities don't even resemble each other."

Rather than refute what she knew to be true, she turned up her surgically snubbed nose. "Don't knock what you don't understand."

I suppressed a sigh. "Then help me understand. Those headbands, for instance. Some of the people here have them, and others, including you, don't. And why do some headbands have only a few beads, but others are loaded with them? What's up with that? Oh, and those log cabins and the teepee village. Do people actually live in those dinky little things?"

My questions earned me a lecture.

"We live in the place that matches our level of Elevation, just like you lived in a 'dinky little' one-bedroom apartment for fifteen years," she replied, her tone snarky. "As for the headbands…"

As she explained it, the headbands designated a person's status, or lack thereof, in the community. In keeping with the compound's Cherokee pretensions (although she didn't actually use that word), the number of beads ascended through the Cherokee numbering system. No headband meant you were *sowo* or *tali*, lowly recruits like herself. A plain headband meant you were *tsoi*, not quite so lowly, but beginning to move up. Four beads, and you were *nvgi*, well on the way to becoming Elevated. Near the end of the Elevation ladder, you could claim the title of *sonela*, or Highly Elevated One, such as Gabrielle and only a few others

I had seen. Since *sonela* meant "nine" in Cherokee—as Chelsea explained—my interest was piqued.

"No number ten?"

Chelsea smiled. "That would be Adam, the Most Elevated One. And a couple of others."

"I take it he runs this joint."

"Nobody actually *runs* Kanati, Lena. We're all equal here."

"Then why the caste-denoting headbands?"

"None are so blind as those who will not see."

I smiled at the attempted insult. "Nice to know you've kept up on your Bible studies, Chelsea." Years earlier, her father, having given up on controlling his wild child, had sent her to an Anglican boarding school where daily Bible reading was part of the curriculum. It hadn't worked. Only a few years later, as soon as she had come into the inheritance bequeathed by her mother, she left her Arts major in college to major in Street Life.

In an attempt to placate her, I said, "You know, I think I'd like to meet this Adam. He sounds like a special guy."

"Adam only meets with the Highly Elevated."

I couldn't help myself. "That sounds pretty secretive."

You ever meet the President of the United States?"

"No, but he's on CNN all the time, talking up his agenda."

"Reading from a prepared script."

Well, she had me there. The U.S. of A's Most Elevated One seldom spoke off the cuff, but whenever he did, uproar was certain to follow.

Chelsea crossed her arms over her augmented chest. "Thanks to big-mouth Harold accusing Kanati of being a cult, you've been given a skewed view of what's going on here. If I wasn't so busy, I'd show you around, not that it would change your mind."

"Gabrielle's already given me the guided tour."

"Then you see? No one's hiding anything. Honestly, Lena, this place is on the up and up. Granted, Kanati's not the Anglicans or even the Buddhists, but the program works. Look at me, for instance. Do I look like I'm in withdrawal? Am I puking? Am I shaking? Am I huddled in a corner, clawing at my skin? After only a few weeks here I'm regaining my health, and becoming a productive member of society." She stood up. "On that note, I need to get back to work. As for you, while I appreciate your concern, stop worrying about me. This is the best thing I've ever done for myself. And tell Harold to back off. His codependency is embarrassing."

With that, she walked back behind the serving line and began ladling out more cucumber canapés with lemon dill sauce.

And I'd missed my chance to ask her how much it cost to become Elevated.

Chapter Four

"If you want to hire a de-programmer, that's up to you, Harold, but they're expensive and can embroil you in serious legal difficulties. Like I said, Kanati doesn't look all that cultish to me. It's just another Arizona woo woo joint with Native American trappings."

Yesterday, I had arrived back at Desert Investigations from my fact-finding drive to Kanati. By then, Sharona had closed her art gallery for the day and my calls to Harold had rolled over to voice mail. But he'd been waiting in front of Desert Investigations when Jimmy and I arrived this morning. When I'd told him Kanati didn't seem all that dangerous, just expensive and goofy, he refused to listen.

"Just because something looks goofy doesn't mean it's not dangerous." Too irate to sit down, he paced back and forth behind our big plate-glass window while he sipped at a cup of Jimmy's Jamaican Blue Mountain coffee. His shadow moved along with him in eerie pantomime, making a few passersby look at him in alarm. He ignored them. "I'm sick of white people—I don't mean you, Lena—co-opting Indian culture. Wearing headbands, running around pretending to be Cherokee? Worshipping the White Buffalo? Oh, please. The Cherokees aren't even one of the Southwestern tribes. Their hunting grounds were in the Southeast until that damned Andrew Jackson made them walk the Trail of Tears to Oklahoma."

None of this shocked me because white people had been co-opting Native American culture for years. What did shock me was Harold's use of a curse word. Like most Indians, he rarely cursed.

"I'm on your side, Harold. Adam Arneault—you know, Kanati's grand pooh bah—probably picked up the Cherokee stuff while he was living in Oklahoma."

"But I'll bet you didn't see one Cherokee while you were in Kanati, did you?"

"Cherokees have better sense."

Harold had come up with what he thought was a brilliant a plan to "rescue" Chelsea from the evil clutches of Kanati, and so far, nothing Jimmy nor I said was making an impact.

But I kept trying. "I'm telling you, Harold, I saw nothing alarming there, just a bunch of people walking around wearing ugly headbands. But they're eating well and Chelsea looks healthier than I've ever seen her. And happy. Could you sit down, please? You're making the tourists nervous. And I'm begging you, *please* forget this idea of using that deprogrammer."

A friend of a friend had once used famed deprogrammer Clint Moran to "extract" his twenty-three-year-old daughter from the Children of the Universal Gods, a group in New Mexico led by a married couple who claimed to be from one of the planets in the Alpha Centauri star system. As someone with more than a passing interest in cults, I was familiar with the group, and while Harold talked, I was aware that he was glossing over several pertinent points. Point number one: at the time of the daughter's "extraction," the Children of the Universal Gods had yet to commit a crime, although they did later. Point number two: the "extracted" daughter was forced at gunpoint to spend a month in a mountain cabin with the deprogrammer and her father as the helpless subject of their anti-religious rants. Point number three: the father and the deprogrammer were eventually found guilty of kidnapping and torture—a stun gun was involved—and were sentenced to prison terms of several years. The daughter promptly returned to the Children of the Universal Gods, and was anxiously awaiting the return of the Alpha Centauri starship fleet to beam them all up, Scotty.

When I reminded Harold of this, he said, "I know, I know, but Clint Moran's been released from prison. After learning a few hard lessons, he's come up with a less extreme method."

"Meaning he's come up with a new word for kidnapping?"

"Stop being so cynical, Lena."

Harold might as well have told me to stop breathing.

Jimmy, less of a cynic than I, asked the question I would have asked if I'd been less irritated. "How do you propose to pay for that Moran guy? I heard he charges several hundred a day for his services. You don't have that kind of money."

"I'd be paying for it in artwork."

Jimmy groaned. "You're talking thousands of dollars!"

"Chelsea's worth it."

It was my turn to groan. "The woman's left you three times, Harold. Four, if you count this time. She wouldn't do the same for you."

In a voice hardly louder than a whisper, he replied, "I know."

The rest of the day went more smoothly.

Between the time Harold left and we locked up for the evening, Desert Investigations closed three inventory theft cases: a costume jewelry store, an upscale steak house, and a retro clothing shop. We also located a deadbeat dad. The last case was the most satisfying, the deadbeat owing more than two hundred and forty thousand dollars to his four children. They were living with their three-jobs mom in an apartment in a sketchy Phoenix neighborhood while their father lolled on a La Jolla beach with his mistress. We'd done that one gratis.

"Think we have time for an evening ride?" Jimmy asked, as we finally headed back to the Rez.

I checked my watch. Five-thirty-five. The sun was flirting with the horizon, painting the desert an array of soft pinks and lavenders. Beautiful, but by the time we saddled up, it would be dark. "Why don't we get up early tomorrow and ride before we head to work?"

"Sounds good to me."

That was Jimmy, ever affable. When I woke up screaming in the middle of the night, he never minded, just held me close. The man was so patient, so loving, that by contrast, I often found myself wondering what I had to offer him in return. Damned little, it seemed. Love was a mystery.

Our evening remained peaceful until the ten o'clock news came on. After giving us the weather forecast—clear, low eighties tomorrow, breezes topped at ten miles per—local broadcast affiliate reporter Polly Yamaguchi led off with an update on the body found near Talking Stick. Yamaguchi looked perky in a pink dress with charcoal gray trim, but her demeanor was all seriousness.

"Sources tell us that the deceased woman found at the El Mesquite Business Park near Talking Stick had been dead for several days, but due to the low-hanging mesquite tree limb covering her body, its presence wasn't noted until, ah, wildlife became attracted to the site. Preliminary autopsy results suggest the woman died of heart failure due to extreme malnutrition." Yamaguchi, on the thin side herself, blinked several times before continuing. "She has not yet been identified, but an artist at the Medical Examiner's office is currently preparing a sketch in hopes it will aid in her identification. Because of the condition of her body and clothing, authorities believe she may have been part of the Valley's homeless population, and wandered into the area while searching for the homeless encampment a mile south on the Salt River Pima/Maricopa Reservation. We will give you updates as they come in."

Polly's expression morphed into a bright smile. "And now for some fun! My colleague, Chip Fonseca, is here to tell us about the Miss U.S.A. Model Teen Competition Finals being held at the Phoenix Convention Center this weekend. Are the girls excited, Chip? I know I am!"

The camera switched to a lineup of teenage girls, all as thin as Yamaguchi, some even thinner.

Then the screen went blank.

"Hey!"

Jimmy had the remote in his hand. "We don't need to watch that dreck."

I didn't want to see that dreck, either, but since we were still in the early stages of establishing our own turf, I grabbed the remote and clicked the TV back on. A snub-nosed brunette was telling Steve Fonseca how honored she felt to have made it to the finals.

"Being crowned Miss U.S.A. Teen Model would be the most wonderful thing to ever happen to me in my whole life," Miss Teen Model New Hampshire squeaked.

Jimmy shot me a look. "Your punishment for being grabby will be watching this in order to make a point." Smirking, he decamped to the computer room, leaving me to learn more than I'd ever wanted about the difficulties of applying eyeliner while riding in a tour bus.

I decided making a point wasn't worth it, so I clicked off the "news" program and joined Jimmy in the computer room. He had a topographical map up on his computer.

"What are you doing?" I asked.

"Flying the flag of territorial independence."

"Smart mouth." I gestured at the monitor. "That shape looks like the Pima Rez."

"It should, because it is. I'm looking for the homeless encampment Yamaguchi was talking about."

"Hardly a live feed you've got there."

"We Pimas don't have CCTV cameras stuck on every cactus. At least not yet, we don't. She described the homeless encampment as being a mile south of Talking Stick, and from what I can see here, that would put it somewhere near Wolf Ramirez's place. Except for a couple of arroyos, that's flat terrain over there, and the horizon line is, what, something like ten miles away in that area? If there's a homeless camp where Yamaguchi says it is, Wolf should be able to see it from his kitchen window. I'll call him tomorrow and see if he knows anything."

The next day was supposed to begin with a short horseback ride across the desert, but when Jimmy and I entered the corral, we discovered Big Boy had lost a shoe. There being no point in calling the farrier at six a.m., Jimmy suggested I take Adila out alone.

"She's more desperate for a run than he is," he said. "Take your cell and handgun in case there's any trouble."

"Bad guys aren't known for being early risers."

"I wasn't talking about bad guys, I was talking about wildlife. Wolf thinks he spotted a mountain lion near the Beeline Highway the other day."

"Mountain lions don't bother you unless you bother them."

"Ever hear of rabies?"

That stopped me. A couple of aggressive coyotes had been shot in a Scottsdale subdivision the week earlier, and the subsequent autopsies confirmed both carried the rabies virus. When coyotes get rabies, they lose all fear of humans and other animals, and a nip from them could turn even a normally shy mountain lion into a human-stalker. This was a part of desert living the chamber of commerce never told you about.

After returning to the trailer and sliding my .38 into its holster and buckling it around my waist, I finished saddling Adila and headed out into the desert alone.

Riding a horse into the sunrise is a unique pleasure few people are lucky enough to experience. As the desert comes alive, your troubles recede. You feel the wind on your face, smell the sage and earth, hear the cardinal's call, feel the rocking motion of your horse as she weaves between the blooming creosote bushes and mesquite. When you are this aware of your surroundings, you become less aware of yourself. It's something like meditation, only better, because instead of escaping the world, you enter into it more fully.

For an hour, Adila and I were one with the awakening desert until I was jarred back into the mess we humans call life. As we cantered up a gentle rise, Adila shied at something that lay half-hidden behind a stand of barrel cactus. Once my mare had calmed, I urged her forward until I could more fully see the thing that had disturbed her.

A woman's body.

She hadn't been dead long because her filmy but intact eyes still gazed at the sky. The rising sun caressed her pale skin and light brown hair, proving she wasn't Pima. Caucasian, and young. Early twenties? Her ankle-length blue dress revealed stick-thin arms flung outwards in a pose reminiscent of crucifixion. No shoes, no purse, and no jewelry other than a simple gold band on the spindly ring finger of her left hand. No nail polish.

Dismounting, I studied the ground around her, taking note of the tire tracks stopping just short of the cactus stand, the faint impression of shoeprints too large to be hers. Besides, she was barefoot, and her feet were clean.

Body dump.

Was the crucifixion pose purposeful, or simply the result of the way she'd landed?

I took out my cell phone, snapped several pictures, then carefully retraced my own footsteps in order not to further disturb the site. My first call was to Jimmy to tell him what happened, to go ahead and open the office without me. My next call was to the Salt River Police Department.

Adila nudged me with her soft muzzle. She was impatient, wanting to go return to the paddock. But I had to disappoint her.

There was no way I could leave the woman alone. I had to stand watch, to bear witness.

"I'm so sorry," I whispered, not certain who I was apologizing to—my horse or the dead woman.

"How bad was it?" Jimmy asked, when I finally made it in to Desert Investigations.

"Could have been worse. There were no marks of violence that I could see. It looked like she had just…well, just died." I stopped there, not being able to get those thin arms out of my mind.

Reservation Woman, as I would call her until she was identified, had been the second woman found dead on or near the Rez in a week, and both were white. People died in our desert all the time, especially in the summers when the temperatures could get up to 123 Fahrenheit. Entranced by the area's beauty, tourists wandered into it without enough water, then became disoriented and died of heatstroke. But this was October, and the temps hadn't risen past the low eighties in weeks. Besides, the woman had been barefoot, and no sane person entered the snake-friendly desert without sturdy boots or shoes.

"What did the cops say?"

"Not much. You know how careful they are. The case might wind up with the FBI. Caucasian woman, reservation dump, possible homicide."

"Possible?"

"Probable, actually. Someone dies naturally at home, you don't drive their body all the way out to the Pima Rez to dump them. You call 9-1-1."

He grunted agreement. "Cops treat you okay?"

"Norm Jakupi was the first one there." No further explanation was necessary, since Lieutenant Jakupi and Jimmy were old friends. Given the situation, he'd been solicitous as possible. Haunted, still seeing Reservation Woman's soul-emptied face, I knew I needed to stop talking about death or I'd be worthless for the rest of the day.

Horses. Talk about horses. Forcing away my sadness, I said,

"When I was putting Adila away, I noticed you'd had the farrier out."

Quick on the uptake, Jimmy responded, "He stopped by on the way to Wolf Ramirez's place."

"I didn't know Wolf had horses."

"He's taking care of his niece and nephew's animals while they're visiting a cousin in Wind River."

"Hope they dressed warmly enough. I hear October can be a bitch in Wyoming."

From there the conversation segued into the fall weather in various parts of the U.S., pushing the image of Reservation Woman's filmy eyes into the recesses of my mind, as I had hoped. After returning a few calls, I asked Jimmy, "Did you call Wolf?"

He looked at me over the top of his computer. "About what? The horses?"

"About the possibility of a homeless camp up by him."

When he shook his head, I picked up the phone, dialed, and when Wolf answered, put him on speaker.

"Homeless camp?" the tribal elder said. "Out by me? Not that I'm aware, but since you've brought it up, maybe I'll drive around today and see if I can spot what looks like a camp, but after that mess a few years ago, the tribal police have been pretty strict about that sort of thing."

Wolf was referring to an incident when a homeless camp comprised mainly of veterans had occupied a portion of the Rez near the Salt River. Since a couple of the residents were Indian, although not Pima, the tribe had allowed it for a while, but once the camp tripled in size and the area surrounding it became a sanitation problem, tribal officials clamped down. The camp was relocated to vacant land held by the Arizona Department of Transportation, underneath a freeway overpass.

"Let us know if you see anything," Jimmy told Wolf.

"Oh, don't worry, I will. I sure won't tell that Yamaguchi woman. Last thing our tribe needs is more bad publicity. Our casinos are already being blamed for the rise in gambling problems. Hmph. That's like blaming grapes for alcoholism."

The third person to walk into Desert Investigations that morning, after an elderly woman looking for her lost dog, and a twenty-something man looking for his lost girlfriend, was Clint Moran, the cult deprogrammer who had "extracted" a young heiress from Children of the Universal Gods. After serving less than three years at Arizona State Prison, Moran was out and about, still doing business.

He handed me his card, which I took with two fingers. God knows where it had been. "Nice seeing you again, Lena."

"Wish I could say likewise."

Those years behind bars hadn't changed Clint much. He was still the same self-righteous boor I'd met years earlier at a convention held by the National Council of Investigation and Security Services. Only his hair had changed. Instead of the thick brown pompadour he used to rock, he was currently bald, and he hadn't yet recovered from his prison pallor. Women inexperienced with the type often found him attractive, but I had never trusted those squinty eyes or baby-pout mouth.

Oblivious of physical boundaries, he lolled back in the client chair, his left leg outstretched so far I had to move mine back several inches to avoid contact. "Harold Slow Horse tells me you've been out to Kanati," he smarmed. "What's it like?"

"Do your own research."

"I tried, Lena, but the rent-a-cop at the gate wouldn't let me in."

"Your reputation must precede you."

"But you got in. Maybe he was overcome by your beauty. May I say you're looking particularly fine today, Lena?"

Jimmy, busy working the computers, took time to scowl.

I made a great show of looking at my watch, a cheap Timex. "A new client will be arriving in a couple of minutes."

"You always were a bad liar, Lena."

Ever notice how a salesman keeps using your name over and over? They're trying to establish intimacy.

"Get lost, Clint." I could play the game, too.

"Don't be like that, Lena."

"Listen, you sack of..."

Miraculously, the phone rang. The display panel showed a Pima Rez number, so I answered before Jimmy could grab it. I held the receiver close so the caller's end of the conversation wouldn't leak out and alert Clint, who hadn't yet taken the hint.

"What'd you find out?" I asked Wolf Ramirez.

"If there's a homeless camp out here on the Rez where Yamaguchi said it was, it's led by the Invisible Man and his invisible followers."

"That's what I figured. Thanks for checking."

"No prob. I love hanging out by Talking Stick. Saw a red-tailed hawk take a rabbit, and a Mercedes rear-end a Rolls. Good times."

We chatted aimlessly for a couple of more minutes, and long before I rang off, I heard the front door shut. Clint was history.

"Need some air freshener over there?" Jimmy called.

"I'll live. That was Wolf on the phone just now. He says there's no homeless camp anywhere near him."

"It's not like Yamaguchi to get things wrong. Wonder what happened?"

I wondered, too. Placing a call to the television station, I left a message for Yamaguchi. I'd helped her on a couple of stories and hoped she remembered.

My next call was to Harold Slow Horse.

"Guess who just dropped by," I said, when he picked up.

"Clint Moran, right?"

"How much is he charging you?"

"I'm paying in art, remember."

"Which he'll promptly sell. Paintings? Sculpture? Which and how many?"

"That's between me and Clint. If he gets Chelsea out of that place, no price is too high."

Ever notice that men in love act dumber than women? I motioned to Jimmy, and mouthed, "Harold."

Jimmy picked up the extension. "My man!"

The conversation switched to Pima, and I went back to work. Jimmy didn't want me to hear him begging Harold to fire the deprogrammer, and I didn't want to hear it, either. Especially when the phone rang again and it was my goddaughter Ali on line two, calling me between classes. She sounded considerably more upbeat than yesterday.

"You watch the morning news? Mom's dropped three points in the polls!"

Yes, I had watched. "The only polls that matter are in the voting booths on election day."

"If she loses, I won't have to go to D.C. with her."

So there we were. After months of mere grumbling, Juliana's daughter had officially come out against her mother's U.S. Senate run. "Ali, I don't see how your mom losing the election would help you with the Kyle situation. Either way, I doubt she'll let you move away with the Etheridges. Speaking of, have you talked to them about it yet?"

Her silence told me everything I needed to know. The Etheridge family wasn't any more thrilled about Ali's plan than was Juliana.

Poor Ali. Poor young love.

The day continued to be busy, with new clients across the Valley wanting Desert Investigations to put out various fires, none of which helped dim the memory of the dead woman I'd found that morning. Reservation Woman had appeared peaceful, but past experience with murder victims taught me that appearances could be deceptive. Sometimes that "peaceful" look arrived after hours, even days, of agony.

An elderly widow from Tempe hired us to run surveillance on her grandson, whom she feared was selling drugs to Arizona State University students. If it turned out to be true, she wanted us to warn him that if he didn't stop, she was not only going to disinherit him in favor of the Halo No-Kill Animal Shelter, but she'd also narc him off to the DEA. Closer to home, I finally made contact with gallery owner Sharona Gavalan. She was worried about Megan Unruh, one of her artists, and wondered if I could find out why she wasn't answering her phone calls. Megan had dropped off the radar and Sharona needed her to sign some release forms.

"I must have called her a dozen times this past couple of months, and left a message each time, but never got a call-back," Sharona explained, when I'd dropped into her nearby gallery. Her latest exhibit seemed to be doing well, with a lot of SOLD signs tacked up beside the paintings. Instead of looking gratified, Sharona's immaculately made-up face was tight with anxiety.

Although I was busy, I told her I'd check around, just as soon as I got a few things out of the way.

Late afternoon found me on Mill Avenue only three blocks from ASU, taking a video of a blatant drug deal going down on Mill and University between an angel-faced dealer, and a scraggly student who looked like he hadn't eaten in days. As soon as money changed hands, I walked up to Angel Face, flashed my ID, and showed him the video. When I delivered Grandma's warning, he spit at me. I'm quick on my feet, so he missed, but his grandmother wasn't pleased with his churlish behavior—which I'd also videoed. Angel Face's loss would be the doggies' and kitties' gain.

I was less successful at running down Sharona Gavalan's missing artist. The other two artists Megan Unruh shared studio space with hadn't seen her in a couple of months, which they declared odd, since she normally came in several times a week. When I dropped by her low-rent apartment in an industrial section of

Tempe, the manager, a woman whose gray hair looked like it had exploded outward, said she hadn't seen Megan in a while, and her rent was two weeks past due.

"Did she pay last month's rent on time?"

The landlady's mouth compressed into a thin, mean line. "Yeah, but that was then, this is now. I'm not running a Salvation Army here, so if she doesn't turn up at my door by the end of the week with money in hand, I'll initiate eviction proceedings."

"After only two weeks? For all you know, she could be dead in there." Unbidden, the vision of Reservation Woman's face returned. I pushed it away. You'd think that after being in the business for so many years I'd be inured to death and sorrow, but I wasn't. Something about her touched me deeply.

Maybe concern is catching. After some hemming and hawing, the landlady backtracked and agreed to enter the artist's apartment for a look-see. For legal reasons, I wasn't invited along. During the next few minutes I cooled my heels in the dark hallway, and when she finally came back out, she announced, "Okay, she's not dead in there, but Jesus, it does look like a funeral parlor with all that black. Black sofa, black throw rugs, black bedspread, every damned thing black, even the walls. It'll take four coats of Navajo white to cover that. Damned artists. I got three of 'em living here. Talk about a bunch of weirdos. The stories I could tell you…"

I didn't have time to hear them. "Did you see her purse? Cell phone?"

She shook her head. "Wherever she went off to, she musta took them with her, but I can tell you this, I even checked the screen on her landline and she's got eleven messages. That's kinda worrying."

I thought so, too.

Megan Unruh's mother lived in Wildwood Heights, a North Scottsdale community so far north it was almost in Fountain

Hills. It nestled against the side of a hill overlooking the Valley, and as soon I pulled my Jeep in front of her house, I took a moment to enjoy the million-dollar view. It was a clear day, and from here I could see the high-rises of downtown Phoenix, the lower rises of Scottsdale, and the no-rise Pima Reservation, its only exception being the big Talking Stick Resort and Casino. The desert wasn't fully concreted over yet. Some more natural landmarks remained, such as the red sandstone Papago Buttes, Camelback Mountain, and Piestewa Peak, named for Lori Piestewa, the first American Indian woman killed in combat while serving in the U.S. military. Looking into the distance, I thought could even see the creosote grove where I had found Reservation Woman. Do spirits inhabit the places of their death? Or do they go home, wherever home was?

Turning my mind to more easily answered questions, I walked up the drive to Dorothea Unruh's two-story house. It was one of those pretend-Mediterraneans, its outsized grandeur meant to telegraph the inhabitant's financial status. Large enough to contain a family of polygamists, its sole inhabitant was Megan Unruh's widowed mother.

The doorbell chimed to the tune of "You Are So Beautiful," so when the door opened and I was confronted by an astoundingly beautiful woman, I wasn't surprised. Dorothea Unruh stood almost six feet tall, and her expensively streaked hair framed a flawless face. Her eyes were such a pale blue they looked almost colorless. She was dressed as if on her way to a formal high tea: lavender silk shantung sheath, pearl necklace and earrings, bone-colored backless heels. When she invited me in, I saw that her beam-vaulted living room matched her shoes, with a bone-colored carpet, sofas, and chairs. Even the walls had been painted a soft bone. Some people may have considered the decor as beautiful as its owner, but the color scheme made me feel that I had just stepped into an ossuary.

Mrs. Unruh showed little alarm when I told her Megan hadn't been seen in two months.

"My daughter hasn't contacted me in some time, but that isn't unusual." Her voice was as chilly as the room's décor.

"Did you try calling her?"

"What for? We have nothing in common."

I asked if she could give me a photograph of her daughter. She tilted her head. "Why?"

Exasperated, I tried again. "Her art dealer is worried about her, so I'm checking around to see if anyone's seen her lately. A photograph would help."

With all the regality of a queen bestowing a favor on an unworthy subject, Mrs. Unruh stood and walked down the long hallway. After a few minutes she returned with a ten-year-old high school yearbook. Megan's picture was near the back, where she'd been voted Most Creative. It showed a plump brunette with a glum expression on her round face. Her bangs were so long they cast a deep shadow over her brown eyes.

"You don't have anything more recent?"

"Megan didn't like to be photographed. Said cameras made her look fat, which they did. Because she was."

As I scanned the bone-colored living room, I didn't see one picture of Megan, although the far wall displayed a large photo montage of her mother. From what I could deduce from the shots, Mrs. Unruh used to be a model.

She was still stick thin.

When I arrived back at Desert Investigations, I found several phone messages, one of them from TV anchorwoman Polly Yamaguchi stating that she was currently off-air, and to call her back quick because she would be unreachable after four.

Since it was already three-thirty-five, I returned her call first. "My sources say there are no homeless encampments on the Pima Rez near the El Mesquite Business Park where that body was found. In fact, they say there are none at all in or on the Rez since the authorities moved that old one onto ADOT property."

"Who are your sources?"

"A Pima who lives less than a mile from El Mesquite Business Park."

"Wolf Ramirez, then."

"I never said that."

"I didn't say you did."

"If you're acquainted with Wolf Ramirez and know where he lives, then you already knew all this. Heck, every one of those Pima bungalows are so neat and tidy they could fit right into a Scottsdale suburb, so why'd you report there was a camp nearby?"

Just as I was beginning to think she wasn't going to answer, she grumped, "In the old days we journalists researched and wrote our own stories, but today we read from scripts prepared by someone else."

"You're telling me you reported something you knew wasn't true?"

"I pointed out the misinformation in the morning's story meeting, but was overruled."

"The newsroom holds a vote on whether a story is accurate or not?"

"I'd love to say you're wrong."

"But…"

"Say, Lena, you're living on the Rez, aren't you? With that hunky Pima guy? Jimmy Sisser?"

"Sisiwan. I still have my apartment on Main Street." Because I was having trouble letting go of my independence.

"But he's building a house for you, right?"

"He's building a house, yes, but not necessarily for me. He has his own life."

"Don't we all, but I'll bet you spent last night there. And I hear you like to ride around the Rez in the morning on that fabulous spotted horse of yours."

"Appaloosa. Polly, could you please get to the point?" Like all reporters, she didn't give two hoots where anyone lived unless it had to do with a story, so I didn't trust all this friendly chatter.

"I also hear you're the person who found that woman's body."

So that's why she was being so chatty. "Where'd you hear that?"

A chuckle. "You didn't immediately deny it, so thanks for confirming what I'd already guessed. What did she look like? Same age, maybe, as that woman found up at the business park? Do you think they were both murder victims? I mean, do we have a serial killer on our hands?"

God bless the Press. Leaping to conclusions was their stock in trade. It would have been pathetic, if they weren't so often right. "Polly, I never saw the body found in the business park, just the, ah, woman found on the reservation proper. And before you go to town on this, no, I didn't see any blood or any other sign of violence. For all I know it was a natural death. The other one, too. Hey, are you taping me?"

"Of course I am. Tell me, Lena Jones, well-known private investigator, how within a couple of days two women of about the same age wound up dying of natural causes on or near the Salt River Pima-Maricopa Indian Reservation."

"I haven't a clue. And you can quote me on that."

"I will. Okay, gotta go. Places to go, producers to argue with."

Dial tone.

"Interesting day," Jimmy said later that evening while we roasted hot dogs over the outdoor fire ring.

We hadn't closed the office until six, too late for Jimmy to cook one of his gourmet meals, but as far as I was concerned, there was nothing like an al fresco dinner eaten while listening to the music of the desert. Across from us, the horses munched on fresh alfalfa hay, and from inside the Airstream, Snowball and his mother were yowling for another can of Gourmet Feast. In the distance, a coyote tuned up for his nightly serenade.

"Polly was right about one thing," I said, cuddling against Jimmy. "Two Caucasian women in their twenties dead in or near the Rez within the same week. They have to be connected."

He nibbled at my ear. "Makes sense to me."

"And that thing with Polly Yamaguchi? I'm having trouble wrapping my mind around it. She knew there was no homeless camp where she said there was, yet she went ahead and reported a false story. Doesn't anyone care about the truth anymore?"

Jimmy's white teeth glistened in the moonlight. "As Pilate said, 'What is truth?'"

The evening was balmier than usual for an October night, almost sixty degrees. Overhead, stars sparkled through a deep indigo sky, and the full moon glowed so bright it cast shadows. Scenting the sizzling hot dogs, the coyote yipped closer.

After eating, we stayed cuddled by the fire until the cuddles turned into something more.

35 years earlier

When Abraham tells them to gather by the fire ring near the old mine shaft, Helen is as eager as the others to hear the wisdom he will impart. Pure in his white robe, smiling in the firelight, his first words are soft as an angel's while he shares his latest Revelation.

"God spoke to me last night."

"Glory be!" Helen and her friends shout. Liam remains silent, and she almost hates him for his stubbornness. Doesn't he realize they are in the presence of God's Anointed One?

"Our Holy Father told me what we must do to regain his favor!"

"Glory be!"

"What did the first Abraham do?" their Prophet asks.

They stand in confused silence. Only last week, Abraham had taken away their Bibles, leaving only one left in the camp: his. But that was his right, wasn't it? Only their Abraham knew the true nature of God, and was the only person among them qualified to interpret that holy but confusing book. Only their Abraham understood every passage. He was the Anointed One, their very own prophet.

As Abraham reminds them of this, his smile is gentle. "The first Abraham, my namesake, knew there could be no salvation until we learned to obey God's commands." Now his voice rises. "Every! Single! Command! There must be no doubting, no looking back! No care for self, only the Lord's Commandments!" His voice lowered. "That first Abraham walked the difficult path of pure obedience, and so he and his followers found salvation. That's what this is all about. We, who are striving to be true servants of God, must throw down our earthly desires to walk that same glorious path."

"Glory be!" Helen's voice has always been the loudest, something she took pride in.

Out of the corner of her eye, she sees Liam frown. He alone of the other men has refused to obey Abraham's latest Revelation.

Liam leans toward her, whispers in her ear. "We need to get out of here."

"Don't overreact. Abraham's just testing us." Her husband means well, but he is wrong.

Liam whispers again. "Helen, two days ago Abraham ordered Dale to turn his wife over to him. And yesterday he started looking at Francine."

Helen laughs. "Francine's beautiful. No wonder he was looking."

"I hear he did more than look last night."

"You need to stop listening to rumors." Helen knows that her husband doesn't understand Abraham like she does, and that hurts her. Abraham only wants the best for everyone.

But that night Abraham sends for Helen.

Chapter Five

Polly Yamaguchi might not have had a problem with inaccuracies, but I did. The next morning I drove up to El Mesquite Business Park. The first body dump—the newspapers had been calling her Unicorn Woman because of her tattoo—had been found fifty yards beyond the well-lit parking lot, hidden by a stand of creosote and mesquite. Unicorn Woman's body was long gone, but pieces of yellow police tape still fluttered from the low-hanging branches of a dying tree.

Another hundred yards to the east, cars rushed unconcernedly by on Loop 101. A mile to the south rose the fifteen-stories-high Talking Stick Resort and Casino. Theoretically, this entire area would have been a bad place to get rid of a body, because during the day, the nearby parking lot was heavily trafficked and bristled with CCTV cameras.

But at night...

Studying the area, I began to wonder if the first woman had been a body dump, too, and if we had another serial killer on the loose. Our most recent serial killer—yes, the Valley had suffered through an entire string of them—had been dubbed the Serial Street Shooter because of his practice of driving around the city until he found someone he thought would be fun to shoot. By the time his killing spree ended, he had killed nine people and wounded several others. Therein lay a coincident, if it truly was a coincidence. Before the Serial Street Shooter's reign of terror, a man known as the Baseline Rapist had also murdered nine people before he'd been caught.

Nine.

Both serial killers used firearms to dispatch their victims, whereas neither Reservation Woman nor Unicorn Woman had been shot.

Another call to Sylvie was in order.

"You again." Sylvie didn't sound happy to hear my voice.

"Yep, me again. This morning I drove up to El Mesquite Business Park, where Unicorn Woman's body was found."

"Of course you did."

"Anything new on the autopsy?"

"Nope." Sylvie was a woman of few words.

"The woman had light-colored hair, right?"

"Yep."

"Blond? Or light brown?"

"Blond," she huffed. "Don't go mixing up your bodies. The gal on the Rez had light brown hair; our body's hair was frigging daisy-yellow."

I remembered Reservation Woman's stick-thin arms and legs. "Was Unicorn Woman malnourished?"

"Nothing but bones. Well, in a manner of speaking. She still had most of her skin."

"Any sign of violence?"

"Nope. Except for the coyote bites."

"What age?"

"Twentyish. Same as your gal."

"Have any twentyish Caucasian women been reported missing in Maricopa County in the last month or so?"

"First thing we looked for, and nope."

"Any fresh leads on her ID?"

"Nope."

"Has the Medical Examiner's artist finished the sketch?"

"Yep."

"When's it going to be released to the media?"

"Today sometime. Or maybe next year."

"There are no homeless camps anywhere near that office complex, Sylvie."

"I know that."

"Are Yarnell and Telez still working that case?"

"Yeah, and they don't like you any more than I do."

"Could you switch me over to one of them?"

"They're busy."

"Doing what?"

"Breathing."

The conversation being no longer fun, I said, "Well, thanks a million for your help."

"We at Scottsdale PD always aim to please."

Dial tone.

As Sylvie had promised in her own sweet way, the ME artist's sketch was released in time to make the noon news, which I watched on my office computer. The sketch showed a bland-featured Caucasian woman with hollow cheeks, and short daisy-yellow hair swept back from her face. She bore a passing resemblance, at least in type, to Reservation Woman, which meant she could have been anyone.

Something about Unicorn Woman's gaunt face, though...

"What?" Jimmy said, turning away from his computer.

"What do you mean 'what'?"

"You were making a weird noise."

"I was?"

"Not quite a grumble, but definitely not a coo."

I gestured to the picture on my monitor. "Come over here and take a look. Ever see her before?"

After studying the face on the screen—the station kept the

sketch up in the left hand corner throughout the news seg-
ment—Jimmy shook his head. "Never met her, at least not that
I can remember. I don't recall her showing up in any of our other
investigations, either. Didn't the Medical Examiner say she died
from malnutrition?"

"'Coronary brought about by malnutrition' is the way it was
worded."

"Well, my first thought is that she looks a lot like those
anorexic teens we've been reading about lately."

He was right. Encouraged by a host of pro-ana—or pro-
anorexia—websites and blogs, Maricopa County had recently
seen several teenage girls die from what could best be described
as starvation. Attempts to shut the websites down had been
unsuccessful. These sites, most often run by other troubled teens,
offered young girls exercise advice, purging advice, and diet advice
of the food-makes-you-fat-so-don't-eat-it kind.

"The ME described Unicorn Woman as twentyish," I reminded
him. "Around the same age as the woman I found."

"Teens aren't the only people afflicted with anorexia nervosa.
Or even only females. I knew a guy…" Jimmy went on to tell
me about a college friend who had almost died from the com-
plications of anorexia nervosa before his family could organize
an intervention. After several months of treatment, he fought his
way back to health, but at six-foot-two, weighing one hundred
and ten, he'd still had a long way to go. Then, not quite a year
after his hospitalization, he began starving himself again. "He
died at nineteen from a coronary brought on by malnutrition.
Just like Unicorn Woman. So, see? Her death could be natural
causes."

"If you can call anorexia 'natural.'" I looked at my watch.
"Hey, it's fifteen to one. Let's grab some lunch. I'm starved."

After a pig-out of Thai food at Malee's On Main, I didn't feel like
returning to the office, but as I drank a fill-up of ice tea, I saw

Harold Slow Horse walking down the street with Clint Moran. Clint's bald head gleamed in the midday sun, and he lugged an expensive-looking computer satchel.

"Here comes trouble," I said to Jimmy.

He looked out the restaurant window and scowled. "Let's play hooky. Maybe the staff will let us sneak out the kitchen door." His face lit up. "It's a beautiful day to go riding. Big Boy was saying to me just the other day that he wasn't getting enough exercise."

"My horse doesn't talk to me."

"Considering Adila's temperament, you should probably be happy about that."

"Don't insult my horse."

While we defended our respective equines, Harold and Clint stopped at Desert Investigations and peered through the closed glass door.

"Thank God we turned off the lights," I said.

"Uh, sorry to tell you, but I left a note on the front door saying we'd be back at one-thirty."

"What time is it?"

"One-thirty."

Being grown-ups, we paid our check and walked across the street.

"*Ya ta hay*, you two," Harold said.

"Hi, Harold," Jimmy said. "Clint."

Jimmy is friendlier than I am, so I only nodded at Harold, cutting the deprogrammer out of the gesture. While the computers were waking up, the two sat down: Harold by Jimmy's desk, Clint by mine.

"I have nothing to say to you, Clint."

"You will when you hear what I've found out, Lena."

I pretended to be engrossed by the icons on my monitor.

"Don't you want to know?"

If I ignored him, maybe he'd go away.

As Jimmy and Harold settled into a friendly chat, Clint

continued to badger me by asking questions I had no intention of answering. Didn't I want to know about the former-Phoenix Suns forward who'd just joined Kanati? Didn't I want to know about Kanati's mind-control methods? Didn't I want to know about *yadda yadda* this, *yadda yadda* that?

I was getting pretty good at ignoring his listing of Kanati's supposed recruits until he mentioned Roger Gorsky. A year earlier, Marie Gorsky, Roger's wife, had hired Desert Investigations to locate him. As was so often the case in marital disappearances, the CEO of Neptune Computing Solutions had gone out to buy a pack of cigarettes and never returned. We'd urged her to file a police report, but even the combined resources of Scottsdale PD and Desert Investigations hadn't been enough to track him down. It wasn't a money situation. Marie, the heiress to a soft drink company, had considerable financial resources of her own, but she was worried about her husband's welfare. Although her calls to Desert Investigations had tapered off, every month or so she still called to ask if there had been any sightings. My answer had always been in the negative.

The icons on my monitor not being all that interesting, I eventually caved. "Are you going to tell me Roger Gorsky is part of that Kanati group?"

"Thought that would get ya."

"Spit it out, Clint."

"Yes, the famously missing Roger Gorsky, one-time high muckety-muck of Neptune Computing Solutions, has surfaced in Kanati. He's looking terrific, believe it or not."

Besides the fact that Marie still cared for her errant husband, the main reason she was concerned about Roger's welfare was that he had been in poor health. Although suffering from Type 2 diabetes, he'd smoked too much, drank too much, and despite being only five-eight, tipped the scales at almost three-fifty.

Clint had never been a stickler for the truth, but ever-hopeful, I attempted to get it out of him via a little flattery. "As infamous as you've become these days, I know you'd never make it past the guard, so how'd you find out Gorsky was hiding out down there?"

He pulled a manila folder out of the case and handed it to me. Inside was a series of aerial photographs of the compound. In one I saw a man who looked like a thinner Roger Gorsky playing a game of croquet with a sexy, headband-wearing redhead. He was looking straight up at the camera.

"Drone," Clint explained. "Gotta love those things."

"You're aching to go back to prison, aren't you? Miss the food?" I handed the manila folder back. "Your drone's photography skills need work. This photo is blurry."

"Not blurry enough you can't recognize Mr. Gorsky. When you took his case, you pretty much littered the state of Arizona with missing person fliers. One of them wound up in my hot little hands, and while I was figuring out a way to extract another missing person, Chelsea Cooper-Slow Horse, of course, I happened to spot your guy. Being the enterprising man that I am, I turned the drone around and took these beauties." He waved the folder at me.

"So what do you want me to do? Stand up and sing the 'Star-Spangled Banner'?"

That smarmy smile again. "I've been contracted to help Chelsea see the error of her ways. As for Gorsky, his wife is your client, not mine. I'm giving you this photograph out of the goodness of my heart."

I felt torn. I was duty-bound to let the poor woman know her husband was alive and well, but feared that as soon as I did, Clint would show up on her doorstep singing songs about expensive "extractions."

"Forcibly extracting an adult from a cult—if that's what Kanati is, although I doubt it—is still kidnapping. This is a free country, Clint, and people are allowed to make their own choices about how they want to live. As long as they're of legal age and their lifestyle choices don't result in violence or holding by force, there's nothing anyone can do about it." I finished my lecture by giving Harold Slow Horse a stern look.

Which he ignored.

"See you later," I told Jimmy, when we locked up at the end of the day. "I'm driving over to Marie Gorsky's to give her the news about Roger."

"Let's hope she shows better sense than Harold does."

People don't always react the way you think they will. Before Harold had begged us to get Chelsea out of Kanati, I would have sworn he wasn't dumb enough to hire a convicted felon to perform another felony. That belief was now blown. So who knew how Marie Gorsky would take the news of Roger's whereabouts? Tears of joy? Curses? Whatever, she deserved to know her husband was alive and well, although playing croquet with a hot redhead.

"Why, doesn't Roger look wonderful!" Marie enthused, when I showed her the photographs.

Compared to the three-hundred-plus pound behemoth he had been before his disappearing act, Roger did look wonderful. But why wasn't Marie expressing outrage at him for putting her through an entire year of pain, of not knowing if her husband was dead or alive? When she had hired us, she'd been so overwhelmed I had talked her into joining a grief counseling group.

We were sitting in her decorator-appointed living room at her hilltop Paradise Valley estate. Like the exterior of the house, it was done up in Territorial Modern, which meant that a house less than two years old was trying hard to look more than two hundred. The only thing giving it away was the peach-colored lighting glowing across the peach leather sofas, a sound system playing an R. Carlos Nakai's flute composition, and the four rescued greyhounds ticking their silver-painted nails back and forth on the white-and-peach marble flooring. Then there was the turquoise pool in the xeriscaped backyard being tended to by a yummy, bathing-suited pool boy, and twin blue-eyed Siamese cats sneering at me from Mrs. Gorsky's lap while she smiled fondly at the photograph.

"You're not, ah, angry with your husband?"

Like her husband, Marie had lost considerable weight since we'd last met and no longer looked like the sweet-faced grandma she'd earlier resembled. Giving a teenage-ish wriggle, she piped, "Oh, no, I'm thrilled! I can divorce him now, instead of waiting seven years to have him declared dead."

One of the cats turned its sneer away from me and up toward Marie in irritation. Thinking only of itself, as Siamese are prone to do, it wanted her to stop wriggling.

"You're going to divorce him." My voice sounded as flat as I felt.

"Of course I am. Wait just a second." With admirable delicacy, she sat the two cats aside on the peach sofa, where they immediately began clawing at it, and walked briskly through the sliding glass doors that led to the backyard. She called out to the person I'd thought was a pool boy, who was netting stray bougainvillea petals out of the pool. "Glen, could you come in here a moment, please?"

Seconds later a fit, still-handsome man somewhere in his fifties, wearing a wowser of a Speedo, strolled in and gave my client a less-than-platonic hug. I received a brief nod of acknowledgment.

"What's up, Hot Stuff?" he asked her.

"Lena's found Roger."

"Still alive, I hope."

Grinning ear to ear, she showed him the photographs.

"Yup, that's him all right. The dog! Oh well, his loss is my gain." With that, he patted her on the rump and returned to his pool cleaning.

"We met in that grief-counseling group you told me about," Mrs. Gorsky explained, setting the cats back on her lap, where they went to work destroying her peach crepe de chine dress. "He wanted to hold up on moving in here until we cleared up my legal situation, but this means he's free to put his house on the market. Since it's a four-bed, five-bath in Biltmore Estates, it should move quickly. We'd invite you to the wedding, but we're just going to shack up."

I covered my guffaw with a pretend coughing fit.

She looked at the pictures again and sighed. "I hope that redhead likes Roger as much as he so obviously likes her."

More pretend coughing.

For some reason, a mantra I'd once heard during a New Age church service had been running through my mind recently, and here it came again. *"All shall be well, and all shall be well and all manner of things shall be well."*

All things being pretty damned well at the Gorsky residence, I bid my former client farewell and headed home to a man who would never leave to get a pack of cigarettes and not come back. First of all, because he didn't smoke.

And because Jimmy wasn't that kind of man.

Chapter Six

On my way in to Desert Investigations the next morning, my cell phone yelped the first few bars of Howlin' Wolf's "Smokestack Lightnin'" and Juliana Thorsson's name popped up on the display screen. Ordinarily I would have let the call roll over to voice mail, but this time I answered.

"Make it quick, because I'm hemmed in between two semis and a Ferrari," I told her.

"Ali ran away. That quick enough for you? I'm at home. Get here as soon as you can."

She hung up.

Feeling sick, I called Jimmy's cell and alerted him, finishing with, "...so cancel all my appointments. I have no idea when I'll make it to the office."

A sigh. "Guess I'll see you when I see you."

By the time I made it to Juliana's condo, I had conquered my nausea, only to find the U.S. senatorial candidate looking like something Snowball had barfed up. Her eyes and nose were red, and she was wearing a red paisley-print shirt with brown corduroy slacks and pink house slippers. Compared to her, I was overdressed in my black tee-shirt and jeans.

"Calm down," I told her when she began to pick at her cuticles.

"Haven't you ever noticed that when you tell someone to

calm down they get even more upset?" Juliana pulled at a piece of loose skin, making the cuticle bleed onto the white piece of paper she handed me. "She left this note."

MOM –
SINCE YOU DON'T CARE ABOUT OUR HAPPINESS, KYLE AND I ARE MAKING OUR OWN PLANS. SEE YOU AGAIN SOME TIME, MAYBE.
ALI
P.S. WE BORROWED SOME MONEY BUT WE PROMISE TO PAY YOU BACK. P.P. S. PLEASE TAKE CARE OF MISTY FOR ME.

The mixed-breed mutt in question lay snoring on a blue armchair in the corner of the living room. At least someone around here wasn't borderline hysterical.

"Oh, Lena, the little brat couldn't even sign it '*Love*, Ali,'" she wept. "But she worries about her dog!"

I tried being the voice of reason, a challenge for hot-tempered me. "Ali's not so little anymore, and she's not actually a brat. You know how she feels about Kyle. She thinks the world's going to end if they get separated. Have you talked to his parents yet?"

She blew her nose. "First thing I did after the school called to report she didn't show up again this morning."

"And?"

"The Etheridges got a note, too. Not only that, they're missing the money they kept under the towels in the linen cabinet. And some credit cards."

This was actually good news since credit cards could be tracked unless the Etheridges had already cancelled them. "How much in cash?"

"About two hundred."

"Did Kyle skip school yesterday, by any chance?"

"That's what his mother said."

Kyle's background was as tragic as Ali's. After being removed from his biological mother's home because of extreme abuse,

CPS had fostered him out to the Etheridges. This arrangement lasted for several years until they received the good news that his troubled mother had signed away her parental rights. They immediately adopted him, yet this was how he'd repaid them. Not that I could judge. I had been a fostered teenager too, and my own behavior had often been every bit as shortsighted.

Skipping school probably meant that Kyle had been delegated to take care of the details of the duo's upcoming escape, but he was only a few months older than Ali, and, given his weedy build, he looked younger. With all the standard methods of escape—planes, trains, buses, etc.—demanding several forms of ID these days, their choice would be limited to "borrowed" automobiles.

"Are the Etheridges missing a car?" I asked.

Juliana blew her nose again. "Some old Hyundai, white, I think."

I'd been hoping for something more noticeable, like a purple Kia Soul, but because of Arizona's paint-fading sun, most cars here were white, and every other car was a Hyundai. "I take it your own car is still in the garage?"

She nodded.

"Wherever you've stashed your emergency cash, better go check so we can see how much they've got on them. Make sure you still have all your credit cards."

While she was searching, I phoned the Etheridges and told them not to cancel their cards yet, because those were easy to track. For the meantime, they agreed. "But if those kids rack up too many bills, we'll be forced to," Glen Etheridge told me. "We're not millionaires."

After getting their Hyundai's license plate number, I hung up, leaving Kyle's parents to comfort each other. From where I stood in the living room, I could see Juliana as she rummaged through a hollowed-out book in the bookcase, a coffee can in the kitchen, and an old shoe in her bedroom closet. The expression on her face when she returned told me she'd been cleaned out.

"Four hundred and fifty-something gone," she said. "But at least my credit cards are still in my handbag."

"That means they've got something like six hundred and fifty in cash between them for the moment, and some cards, but I'm betting they already hit the ATM. Okay, here's what we need to do. First, clean yourself up and change clothes. We're going to drive around for a quick search of the obvious places, and if anyone recognizes us, I don't want them to think their senatorial candidate is on a bender."

We hadn't yet called the police. Despite Juliana's genuine maternal love, she was still a political animal, and knew it would not be wise to give Gerald Simpson, her opponent for U.S. Senate, more ammunition to use against her. As cynical as it sounded, she was right.

The first place we looked was the abandoned house the two had once holed up in during the hunt for Ali's family's killers. The windows and doors had once been poorly secured with cheap plywood, but these days the house was ringed by chain-link fencing, and the plywood replaced by stout wooden panels. The sign in front said SOLD. Probably for another flip.

"There's one more place we need to check," I said.

"You don't mean…?"

"Kids in trouble almost always run home, Juliana. Or to a place that once felt like home."

"But *that* house…" She didn't finish the sentence, her horrified expression speaking for her.

A year earlier, Dr. Arthur Cameron, his wife Alexandra, and their son Alec—Ali's brother—had been found slaughtered in their house in an upscale Scottsdale enclave. After the crime had been solved and Ali was adopted by Juliana, her other biological mother, I hadn't bothered to keep tabs on the murder house. Part of me hoped it had been abandoned, but the group of college-age boys shooting baskets at the hoop attached to its garage showed me the house was very much lived in. No white Hyundais were visible on the street. This was Mercedes country.

Because of the Pima symbols painted all over my Jeep, it has always drawn an admiring male crowd, so I didn't have to knock on the door to ask my questions. "Any of you guys see a couple of fifteen-year-olds, blond girl named Ali, and a dark-haired boy named Kyle?" I asked, once they'd converged on the Jeep. "They're driving a white Hyundai."

A sandy-haired string bean wearing a maroon ASU sweat shirt, said, "Nope. Just a couple of Jehovah's Witnesses hawking *The Watchtower*. We told them we were all Satanists." When his buddies laughed, he grinned. "Say, that Jeep a '48?"

"Part of it. Mostly a '45, and some '46, with contemporary upgrades."

"Sick paint job."

In ever-confusing teen parlance, "sick" currently meant "terrific," so I thanked him for the compliment. Handing him my business card, I said, "Do me a favor. If you see anyone matching their description, give me a call."

He studied the card. "Desert Investigations. You're a detective?"

"Something like that."

In an instant, his face changed. "Does this have anything to do with what happened in this house before?"

The Cameron murder case had made headlines around the country. The murder of a beautiful woman, her young son, and her famed physician husband were guaranteed fodder for the local newspapers. But when the national press got wind that the suspected murderess—Ali—was the product of eggs sold to a fertilization clinic by a one-time Olympic medalist and currently rising politician, CNN, MSNBC, and FOX NEWS had had orgasms over the story, as did all the syndicated talk shows. Therefore, it came as no surprise that Mr. ASU knew his house's history.

"The girl lived here," I told him.

"And she's gone missing?"

"Afraid so. We're trying to find her."

He switched his gaze from me to Juliana. "You're her, uh, mom?"

Juliana nodded and waited for the barb; there had been so many. But none came. For a moment the boy hung his head, apparently thinking about something he didn't want to make us privy to, but when he looked back up, his eyes were grave. "If I see her, I'll call."

"That was interesting," I said to Juliana as we drove out of the cul-de-sac, leaving the boy staring after us. "You know what we have to do now."

"Tell the authorities." From the expression on her face, I could see she was kissing the U.S. senatorial seat goodbye.

Being a political high flier, however temporary, does have its benefits. Rather than wait for Juliana to complete reams of paperwork, the officer in charge at Scottsdale PD headquarters immediately issued a BOLO on the Etheridges' white 2009 Hyundai Elantra.

That done, he said, "Last time seen?"

"This morning," Juliana said. "I thought she was on her way to school, but a couple of hours later they called and told me she'd never shown up."

Having sat through similar statements with other clients, I knew I wasn't needed, so I gave Juliana a pat on the shoulder and went back to the reception area to wait. On the way out, I passed Detective Sylvie Perrins. When I blew her a kiss, she stuck out her tongue.

I took a seat in reception and prepared myself for a long wait.

Instead, Sylvie showed up bearing a cup of coffee.

"For little ol' me?" I asked.

"You think I drink this shit?"

I took a sip and found the coffee strong enough to run for its own election. "Mmm. Just the way I like it."

"What're you doing here with the Princess?" Like most cops, Sylvie didn't like politicians.

"Her daughter ran away."

"I hate kids," she lied.

"So do I," I lied back.

Sylvie allowed a rare look of compassion onto her sharp-featured face. "Not that the poor thing doesn't have a reason. First her birth mother gets murdered, then she winds up in juvie, then she gets adopted by her supposed real mother—a politician, for fuck's sake—then learns that every move she makes for the rest of her life will be put under a microscope. If I were that kid, I'd run away, too."

"Same here." Actually, I had run away several times during my years under the kind auspices of CPS.

"How you holding up, Lena? I know you're her godmother."

"I'm fine."

"You are such a liar."

"Takes one to know one."

"I'm never having kids." Despite being single, Sylvie had been trying to get pregnant for the last three years. Of late she'd been talking about IVF, the very procedure that had ushered Ali into the world.

"I'll never have kids, either." I told her, not knowing if that was a lie or not.

"All they do is rip out your heart." This statement was so self-evident it needed no reply.

Sylvie's glum face tightened. "Hear anything else about that body you found on the Rez yesterday?"

"I was about to ask you the same thing."

"Well?"

"The answer's nada, Sylvie. But just think. Reservation Woman has the same general description of Unicorn Woman—the gal at the office park. That's around two miles away, right? Woman in her twenties, light brown hair, wearing a blue dress. The only difference is that my gal was a fresh dump and hadn't been dined on yet."

"Why, thank you, Lena, for that lovely image."

"You're welcome."

"So what the hell you think's going on?"

"I haven't the…"

The door to the squad room opened and Juliana came out, looking drained.

Sylvie gave me a quick goodbye and headed back to her desk.

"Take me home," Juliana said. "Or to the nearest dive bar. My career's shot, anyway."

No dive bars being close by, I dropped Juliana off at her place. Then I headed to Desert Investigations to pull up the old Cameron file.

I was just about to enter my office when I spotted Sharona Gavalan ushering a well-dressed couple out of the Gavalan Gallery. The man had a large wrapped package under his arm. As soon as they climbed inside the silver Ferrari parked at the curb, Sharona motioned me over.

"Hear anything from Megan?" I asked.

"Nada." Although as sleek as ever with her bobbed black hair and vampire-white face, the skin around her eyes was creased with worry. "I just want to talk."

I followed her inside her gallery, which was bereft of furniture, save for a knock-off Louis Quatorze desk. And the paintings, of course. An abstract oil took up most of one wall. The title card next to it didn't reveal much—just *Sunday: I-17* and a red SOLD stamp—but I immediately recognized the painting as one of Megan Unruh's. It was mainly grays and blacks, interspersed with a few barely recognizable shapes, such as an automobile tire and a severed hand (a smear of alizarin crimson in that area), but mostly blurs and swatches of whatevers. The artist had managed to turn her dark outlook on life into art. Her work was grim, but it captured how I felt at the moment. *Was my goddaughter safe?*

Sharona turned away from the painting. "You look as chipper as me, Lena. Learn anything yet about Megan's whereabouts?"

"I've talked to several people, including her mother. No one seems to have seen her for weeks, and they're all a little blurry about the exact day. Or even the week."

"Artists. Half the time they don't even know what century they're living in. I read a report one time, supposedly scientific, which said that of all areas of the arts, painters tended to have the highest IQs. You sure couldn't prove it by me." She gestured around the gallery. "Every one of her paintings has sold. Given the subject matter, that's a major miracle. You ever see so many amputations gathered together in one room, other than at a field hospital in a war zone? Maybe people are so damned depressed these days they want to be looking at something that looks more stricken than they feel. As for me, I prefer a little more escapism."

"Paintings of puppies and clowns?"

"Serial killer John Wayne Gacy painted clowns."

Regardless of artists' often questionable subject matter, I've always been drawn to art galleries. Like Sharona's gallery, they are almost always pure white—none of this "eggshell" or "oyster" business—yet they never came across as sterile. Their paintings and sculptures throb with life and with ideas. Sometimes I could relate, sometimes I couldn't, but I was never bored. In this partic-ular case, I found a soul mate in Megan Unruh's work. We both took a dim view of the world. She had ten big oils on display, all mainly blacks and grays, each sprinkled with assorted body parts. The most cheerful items in the exhibit were five watercolor studies, two of them of Gothic-looking graveyards, yet every one of them had a SOLD card next to it.

"How much money are we talking about here?" I asked Sharona.

Sharona closed her kohl-rimmed eyes for a few seconds, run-ning figures. When she opened them, she said, "Enough that I'm not about to put that kind of check in the mail. If Megan stays disappeared, I don't even want to think about the legal ramifications."

"Tell me what you know about her personal life."

She vented a bitter laugh. "It's pretty much what you'd expect of someone who uses fatal car wrecks for subject matter. Can't keep friends, and God knows she can't keep lovers. Drifts from man to man, all of them punks. Over the years she's dragged a few in here, and Christ almighty, what losers. She tried gals for a while, but that didn't work out any better, so she went back to shitty guys."

Remembering the severed hand in one of Megan's grislier paintings, I asked, "Were her relationships abusive?"

"You mean did she ever show up covered in bruises? Nah. She was more into emotional abuse, always going for guys who kept finding fault with her. You know the drill. 'You're too fat. I don't like your hair. You look like hell in that dress. Your skin's like an alligator's. I don't know what I ever saw in you.' On and on with the 'you're not good enough for me' routine until the woman breaks."

Yeah, I knew the drill, having been subjected to it several times. "You think maybe that's what happened to Megan? She broke?"

"Something's going on, because she's never been out of sight this long before. In fact, she…"

The gallery door opened and a less-expensively dressed couple walked in. They took a horrified look around and left. "Looks like they're more into escapism, too," Sharona said, a wry smile lifting the corner of her maroon-lipsticked mouth.

"Different strokes for different folks. Do you have any recent photographs of her, maybe on publicity brochures or photos from her last show? Her mother gave me an old one, but Megan was in high school when it was taken." I showed Sharona the photo.

She curled her lip. "I'm not surprised. I met Dorothea Unruh once. She came in here with Megan, and couldn't bring herself to say anything nice about her own daughter's work. I tried talking to her but gave up. Hell, she didn't have anything nice to say about her daughter, either. Cold bitch, that one."

She opened a drawer of the Louis Quatorze desk and took out a brochure. When she handed it to me, I saw a much more recent photograph. Megan had dropped some of her baby fat—not all—but still wasn't smiling. Deep stress lines mapped her brow and led downward from the corners of her mouth to her chin. Her hair was bright blue.

"Quite the transformation," I said

"The month before that, it was pink. I think she liked to use color on herself because there's so little of it in her paintings."

Or her apartment, I remembered. What had the landlady said it looked like? *A funeral parlor, with all that black.*

Sharona's face, already tight from a recent facelift, grew even tighter. "How much do you charge for your services, Lena? I'm willing to pay you, but please remember that I'm not as wealthy as my clients."

Despite the unhappiness of the day, I had to smile. Crafty Sharona had already managed to wring a couple of days' work from me for free. "Don't worry about it. Consider what I can come up with to be my contribution to the Scottsdale art scene."

As concerned as I felt about Megan, the first thing I said to Jimmy when I walked into Desert Investigations was, "Hear anything from Ali yet?"

"She hasn't called. Say, you want to try lunch at that new French place over on Miller?"

"No can do. I only stopped in to pull the old Cameron file."

While investigating that old case, I'd had the occasion to talk to Ali's and Kyle's friends, and like any decent detective, I'd saved their phone numbers because, as every cop knows, if you want to spread news around, telephone, television, and tell-a-teenager. It was just past noon, and the chances were good that they'd either be scarfing up cafeteria food or on their way to the closest McDonald's, so I started calling.

My first three calls rolled over to voice mail, but I got lucky on the fourth. Dido Emmett, Ali's best friend, had just finished lunch and was looking for better entertainment than the gossips at her lunchroom table. "Hey, you're the detective, right?"

"Right."

"OMG! So, it's true then, that she really did it! Ran off!"

Puzzled by her reaction, I said, "You being her best friend, I thought you'd be the first to know."

"We're not besties anymore."

"What happened?"

When she started whispering, I had to hold the phone closer to my ear.

"Uh, could we put this off 'til I leave school? I've got an early day today, outta here at two-ten. But for God's sake, don't meet me anywhere near the school."

"Your house? I remember where you live."

A screech. "Are you crazy?" She lowered her voice again. "Two-thirty, the Starbucks in the Safeway at Hayden and Chaparral. You're buying."

While we'd been talking I'd received another call, this one from Eli Pressler, a friend of Kyle's. The message he left was: "I'm not telling you anything, so don't waste your dime."

Don't waste your dime? What century was this kid living in? Then I got it. The new video game *Detective Dick*, a homage to the old film noirs, was filled with lines like that. Unless I remembered wrong, Eli was a gamer. The fact that he had memorized some of Detective Dick's dialogue made me feel hopeful. It meant he liked mysteries, and regardless of his snippy message, he liked detectives. I called him back and left my own message, one calculated to pique his curiosity.

I bade farewell to Jimmy, and for the next two hours drove around Scottsdale, checking out every abandoned house I could find, which weren't that many since we'd mostly recovered from the housing slump. I also drove by Eldorado Skate Park, a popular teen hangout, but had no luck there, either.

By two-fifteen I was already sitting in a chair at the Safeway Starbucks, waiting on Dido. She was fashionably late, and when she finally drifted in, she looked like the cover of *Seventeen*, dressed in a pink-and-gray miniskirt, a gray cashmere sweater, pink tights, gray fleecy Uggs, and enough jangly costume jewelry to set up its own table at a craft fair. I hoped Dido's brain would prove as sharp as her wardrobe.

It didn't.

"Vanilla latte venti, double shot of espresso," she announced, jerking her head toward the Orders line.

I obeyed, but ground my teeth as I did.

The little snot refused to speak further until she got her drink, and when she finally began gabbing, it was easy to understand why she had descended to *former* best friend status.

"Ali's, like, stupid, you know. Majorly stupid. That freaky egg mom of hers, for instance, always squawking on and on in those TV commercials about running for this or that, like, does anybody care? And that Kyle thing for a boyfriend? With Ali's looks and her super-fantastic Snapchat following, she could, like, have anyone, even the captain of the football team or maybe even that sexy economics teacher, but no, she hangs onto dumb old Kyle, like he's even in her league."

Only three minutes into our conversation and I was, like, so bored. "Did you know she and Kyle were planning to run off together?"

"Like, *yeah*! The whole school knew!"

"Did they say where they were going?"

She waved her bejeweled arms around. "Like, who listens?"

"You, I hope."

"Do I look like I have time to care about the Deadly Duo?"

"Deadly Duo?"

"That's what they're called because they, like, killed her whole family."

At this point, several nearby latte-sippers looked up in alarm.

One of them, a waspish-looking woman sitting close to us, picked up her drink and moved to a table farther away.

"Lower your voice, Dido," I said. "As for that 'killed her whole family' thing, both Ali and Kyle were absolved when the Camerons' real killers were brought to justice. It was in all the papers."

She gave me a smug smile. "Don't believe everything you read."

Time for a little shock treatment. I made a big show of putting the to-go lid on my tall Americano, then stood up. "You're useless to me."

Dido gaped. "What?!"

"You know nothing."

She actually plucked at my sleeve as I started to pass by her. "No! Wait! I know everything!"

Squinting my eyes, I snapped, "Prove it."

"Sit down! Sit down! I'll tell you what I know!"

I sat back down. "Get right to it or I'm leaving. *Where did Ali and Kyle say they were going?*"

Trying desperately to regain her former demeanor, she snooted, "Somewhere out in the desert. They bought all this camping stuff, but first they were going to, like, stop by his bio mother's place. Euwww. As if anyone in his right mind would want to have anything to do with that slag."

Her nose wrinkled, she grabbed her vanilla latte venti, double shot of espresso, and fled.

The news could have been worse, but not by much. Kyle's biological mother, from whose home Child Protection Services had forcibly removed him, was a crack addict who had twice tried to kill him.

Fiona and Glen Etheridge, Kyle's adoptive parents, were sitting on their front porch watching three of their current foster children pedal Big Wheels along the sidewalk. The kids look great;

the Etheridges didn't. Their house, a generic split level, had a big
FOR SALE sign in the front yard.

"You know why I'm here," I said, climbing out of my Jeep.
"And I'd like to start by looking through his room."

"I hope you can make more sense out of this mess than we
can," Glen muttered. The big man was hollowed-eyed with
worry, his voice husky.

Fiona Etheridge looked no better. Her dark hair was in dis-
array, and her sweater had been buttoned up wrong. "Want one
of us to go up there with you?" she asked.

Before I could answer, one of the Big Wheel kids, a little
redhead, aimed her bike at the street, making Glen rush to the
rescue.

"On second thought," Fiona said, "you'd better go it alone.
These three are a handful. Your friend loved them, though. Even
played with them for a while."

"Friend?"

"You know, Detective Sylvie Perrin. She stopped by earlier to
ask a few questions about Kyle. Such a sweet person! Oh. Almost
forgot to tell you. When you get to Kyle's room, watch out for
the parrot. It asks for a kiss, then bites your lip."

Sylvie? *Sweet?*

I let myself in the house, which they hadn't bothered to lock.
The Etheridges had already started packing for their move to
Oregon, and the living room was filled with sealed boxes. The
walls, which over the years had featured photographs of every
one of the children they had fostered, were bare. Feeling more
than a little sadness about Arizona's loss to the foster care community once they moved, I headed up the stairs to Kyle's room.

Except for the menagerie, it was a typical teen boy's room.
Posters of rock bands and an ASU Sun Devil pennant were taped
to the wall above his bed. In the bookcases, heavy tomes about
zoology sat next to manga comics. Kyle had left all his rescued
pets behind with detailed notes telling his adoptive parents how

to take care of them. His collection included a tank full of tropical fish, a salamander, three gerbils, six kittens and their mother, two puppies—one with only three legs—and the infamous parrot. Ignoring its plea for kisses, I prowled through the room, pawing through drawer after drawer. I got lucky when I spotted an old pair of jeans on the floor of his closet.

In the back pocket I found a receipt from Big 5 Sporting Goods. The day before he and Ali disappeared, Kyle had purchased a tent, two sleeping bags, a camp stove, a rod and reel with an assortment of lures, and enough ready-to-eat meals to last at least two weeks. He'd paid for the haul via Visa.

Two weeks.

I said goodbye to the parrot, who was still begging for kisses, and headed back downstairs.

"When were you supposed to move?" I asked the Etheridges.

While holding the redheaded toddler in her lap, Fiona answered, "Monday. The social worker is coming to pick up the kids…" she gulped, "…tomorrow."

"You've put that off, right? Until you find Kyle?"

Twin nods.

"May I ask why you've decided to move?"

It was Glen's turn to answer. "Job offer. About twice the amount I've been making."

"I thought you owned a print shop."

"Put it up for sale last month."

Kyle, being bright as well as in love, had correctly calculated that by disappearing, the Etheridges would at least reschedule their move. Maybe he even believed if he and Ali managed to stay gone long enough, the Oregon job offer would be rescinded, and everyone would live happily ever after.

Now the two were out there in the dangerous Arizona wilderness.

Chapter Seven

Kyle's aunt lived in a single-wide trailer in a downscale Apache Junction neighborhood. I didn't bother to call ahead, knowing that with her poor health she wouldn't be out hiking the majestic Superstition Mountains, which were visible from her driveway. Whispering Pines Mobile Home Park wasn't much, just a collection of aged trailers that attested to their inhabitants' dire financial straits. Having run into past trouble with the young meth crowd, the park was now listed as Seniors Only, but as I drove up, I saw several children playing on a rusting swing set. Grandchildren, probably, their conscripted caregivers stepping in when their parents' stepped out.

The BEWARE OF PIT BULL sign was still taped to Edith Daggett's rusty screen door, and my knock evoked a hideous roar. Like his owner, Pit Bull—an elderly golden retriever mix—was still alive.

"Well, if it ain't the famous private detective," Edith said, opening the door. "What crime you tryin' to pin on Kyle this time?"

"I need some information."

"So did the cops. I didn't tell them a damned thing, same as I'm not doin' for you."

A convicted felon herself, Edith was well-acquainted with crime. She had served five years in Perryville, the women's prison on the far west side of Phoenix, but the rumor mill whispered she'd committed many more felonies than the one she'd done time for. She was not to be trusted, but I had no choice. I needed to find those kids before someone with a motive other than love found them.

"Edith, may I come in?"

"Who's stopping ya?"

I weaseled my way around the partly open door, only to be met by a blond blur. I cringed back against the trailer's tin wall.

"Ha!" Edith snorted. Evidently, her health hadn't improved since an earlier case we'd discussed, because she was still wearing a cannula in her nose, still dragging around an oxygen tank. "You're scared of Pit Bull."

"Last time I was here he slobbered all over my new black jeans. I had to wash them, and you know how much I hate laundromats." I had hardly finished my sentence when Pit Bull launched himself at me again, dewlaps dripping. There being no escape, I let the toothless hound gum me from ankle to knee. Once he'd wetted down my jeans, he gave a satisfied huff and staggered off to the corner.

"Sit down, Ms. Detective. Take a load off."

As I lowered myself into an afghan-covered chair, I thought it might be easier to simply throw these jeans away. My hatred of laundromats had never died, but the washer/dryer install Jimmy planned for the new house wouldn't happen for another month.

"Where's Kyle's birth mother living these days?" I asked.

"Nowhere you or the cops are gonna find out. She needs more grief like that chair you're sitting on needs more dog hair."

"Kyle and Ali have run away and word is, they're headed for her house."

"House?" She cackled. "In your dreams."

"Or whatever squat she's staying in."

Although old and frail, Edith Daggett had plenty of fight left in her, and was quick to use it in what she believed was a threat to her nearest and dearest, despite their police records. "Why the hell should I tell you anything?"

"Because it was my investigation that got Kyle released from juvie."

She scratched at her left nostril, where the cannula irritated her. While she did, Pit Bull emitted a loud fart.

"This trouble Kyle's in, is it bad?" Edith asked.

"It will be if he and Ali run into the wrong people." Such as his crack-addicted mother, and whatever new acquaintance she might have added to her retinue of users and usees. Although I try to give people—especially mothers—a break when they screw up, the break-cutting ends when they re-offend. Kyle's mother had tried to kill him twice, so as far as I was concerned, she'd earned my undying enmity.

"You gotta understand, I feel for that girl."

"Ali?"

"Miss Little Rich Bitch?" she snorted. "She can go hang, for all I care. My concern's for my niece."

"I'm worried about her, too." Worried that she might try to kill Kyle for the *third* time.

Edith gave me a sly look. "I know what you're thinking, but she's better now."

The stench from Pit Bull's fart finally reached me. Waving it away, I said, "I'm happy to hear that."

"She's off the stuff she was using and has turned things around."

"Sounds like she might have been to rehab, then." Kanati, maybe? On second thought, no. Jimmy had done some further research on Kanati, reinforcing my suspicion that their "spiritual growth" program targeted the wealthy, not the down-and-out. One week there cost several thousand dollars, and in the case of longer stays, property transfers were not uncommon.

Edith wiggled her cannula around until she found a more comfortable place. "Tricia Ann's been in rehab several times, but this last one stuck."

"Good news."

"If I tell ya where she is, you can't let her know you heard it from me."

I raised my right hand. "Scout's honor."

"No Girl Scout troop would ever take you."

"They wouldn't take either of us."

She liked that. Grinning a gray-dentured grin, she said, "Shadow Hills Mobile Home Park, Glendale. Not far from Luke Air Force Base. She's at space two-forty-two."

I stood up. "It's been a pleasure doing business with you again." Turning toward the mound of yellow fluff in the corner, I added, "You, too, Pit Bull."

He farted his reply.

The October sun was low in the sky when I reached the Glendale trailer park where Tricia Ann Gibbs lived. Despite my hopes, no white Hyundai was in evidence among a collection of battered pickup trucks and elderly sedans. I knocked on the door anyway, dreading this first meeting with a woman whose history revealed more tragedy than I wanted to be reminded of. At the age of fourteen, her mother's live-in boyfriend had raped her; the product of the rape was Kyle. When the boyfriend was ultimately released from prison, Tricia Ann's mother took him back.

The first time Tricia Ann had tried to kill her son was just after his homebirth in a filthy apartment. She had wrapped the umbilical cord around his neck and pulled it tight before her mother stopped her. The second time was during Kyle's third birthday party, when she'd given him a glass of chocolate milk containing drain cleaner. Only at that point had Child Protective Services stepped in and removed him from the home.

While I waited for this wannabe child killer to answer the door, I surveyed the grounds. The mobile home park was in better shape than Edith Daggett's, which surprised me. Tall eucalyptus trees shaded the trailers, and there was even a water-spewing fountain in the small greenbelt that ran through the middle of the park. The trailers were less dilapidated, too—some looked almost new.

While I stood there wondering how Tricia Ann could afford her improved digs, the trailer door opened. The neatly dressed woman who stood there had Kyle's dark blue eyes and his thick black hair, but not his innocence. "Hi! So glad to see you!" Her big smile was a tip-off that she'd been expecting someone else. A new dealer?

I flashed my ID. "Tricia Ann Gibbs?"

Her smile faded. "And you're here because?"

"I want to talk to you about your son."

The expression on her face reflected a world of hurt. "Kyle isn't my son anymore."

"Correct. You lost your parental rights the second time you tried to kill him."

She flinched, but didn't deny it. At least that was something. "Kyle's run away," I told her, "and I figure there's a good chance he ran to you first."

"So?"

"So where is he?"

It took a moment for her to answer that one, but when she did, her voice was devoid of emotion. "I told him to go back home, that I couldn't help him, that it was all I could do to help myself."

"Help yourself. You mean rehab style?"

"Twelve Step style."

I noticed she hadn't told me to get lost nor invited me in, just stood there blocking the doorway as if shielding me from who or what was inside. The reason became self-evident when a small child's gurgling laugh sounded from inside the trailer.

Alarmed, I asked, "You had another child?"

She shook her head. "Giving birth to Kyle, it...I can't have children anymore."

"Then who's in there?"

"Is it any business of yours?"

"A child's welfare is the business of every responsible citizen." I hated the self-righteous way that sounded, but it was also the truth. Too many children are injured every day because people don't want to be told to mind their own business. As if any expectation of privacy mattered when a child's welfare was concerned.

"Meaning I'm not a responsible citizen?" Tricia Ann's voice took on a hard edge, revealing the kind of woman she actually was.

So I shoved her aside and barged into the trailer. Let her charge me with unlawful entry; I didn't care. Whatever child she had in there needed to be in protective custody. As I grew accustomed to the darker interior, I lifted my phone from my tote, prepared to call 9-1-1.

Instead, I found myself in the middle of a child-friendly Narcotics Anonymous meeting.

"Oh, won't you please come in?" one of the women said, sarcasm heavy in her voice. She was in the process of passing out what appeared to be a meetings list.

"Uh…"

Tricia Ann put a hand on my arm. Her fingernails were clean, unpolished but well cared-for. "Let's continue this conversation outside."

As I followed her out, I heard the beginning of the Serenity Prayer. "God grant me the serenity to accept the things I cannot change, courage to change…"

She led me over to a nearby picnic table. "You should have called before dropping by."

"A funny thing happens when I call ahead. People disappear."

"My disappearing days are over."

Having heard this sort of thing many times before, I tried not to let my cynicism show. "How long have you been clean?"

"Nine months."

The length of a pregnancy, the rigors of which would never be thrust upon her again. A blessing for some, a heartache for others. "Tell me more about Kyle and Ali's visit."

We sat underneath two paloverde trees, their bare limbs offering only intermittent shade. No matter. Octobers in the Valley are mild, though this late in the day the temperature had fallen into the brisk sixties. As we talked, a group of starlings roosting in one of the trees squawked their own conversation. It sounded friendlier than ours.

"I told Kyle I wouldn't discuss what they told me with anyone," Tricia Ann said.

"Sounds like you're prepared to do nothing while two fifteen-year-olds are driving around out there, neither of them with a driver's license, neither of them knowing diddly-squat about the ugliness that can happen to two attractive runaways. Get real, Tricia Ann. We live in a world where sex traffickers lurk on every corner and behind every friggin' cactus. And in case you've already forgotten, the last part of that prayer your friends were saying includes, 'the courage to change the things I can…'"

"…and the wisdom to know the difference," she finished.

"Well, this is something you *can* change, so I suggest you do a little work on the 'wisdom' part."

She didn't say anything for a while, just stared at the sign in front of a nearby iron gate, which announced, CHILDREN NOT ALLOWED IN POOL AREA WITHOUT SUPERVISION. She wasn't quite thirty, but out here in the late afternoon light she looked fifty. Living *la vida loca* will do that to a woman.

"Tricia Ann?" I prodded.

Tearing her eyes away from the sign, she finally spoke. "The way you put it, my choice is between breaking a promise to Kyle or…"

"Or keeping him alive."

Another long silence. Just when I was ready to give up on her, she blurted, "They're headed south."

"South? Such as South Phoenix? Tucson? Yuma?"

Before she could answer, an enormous roar from above made us duck our heads in fright; it sounded as if the entire sky was tearing apart. Before my heart charged into full panic mode, I identified the source of the noise: six F/A-18 Hornets streaking across the sky in tight formation. Then I remembered hearing that Luke Air Force Base, less than a mile from the trailer park, was hosting an air show this coming weekend. The jets making that terrific noise were the U.S. Navy's Blue Angels practicing for the show.

"It's not always that loud around here," Tricia Ann said apologetically. "Just an F-35A or some other fighter jet every now and then. The Blue Angels, they fly low."

"You know aircraft?" For some reason, her knowledge surprised me.

"Living around here, you soon learn."

The busy Air Force base and its low-flying aircraft explained why she'd probably received a good deal on her trailer rental. When planes are almost landing in your backyard, landlords tend to be reasonable. "As I was asking before I was interrupted, what exactly do you mean by 'south'?"

"I'm not sure, but it might be Nogales. They were talking about camping out for a while—they had all this camping stuff with them—then maybe crossing the border to get married in Mexico. Kyle said they've got enough money to rent a little house down there, buy a couple of horses, and go for sunset rides on the beach."

Oh, the unformed brains of fifteen-year-olds. Scientists tell us that the prefrontal cortex, the *reasoning* part of the brain, doesn't fully form until people reach their twenties. Up until that time, teens live on impulse alone, heedless of whatever consequences may apply.

"Didn't you try to talk them out of it? Hell, there's not even any beach in Nogales. It's miles inland."

"I talked until my throat was sore. They wouldn't listen."

"How about calling Kyle's new parents? That didn't occur to you? They're worried sick."

"I thought about calling, but in the end, I just gave the kids some money." She looked down at the ground, but not before I saw the flush on her face.

Scientists also tell us that prolonged, heavy drug use can damage an adult's prefrontal cortex, returning an adult to an almost teenage state. Here was the perfect example.

But at least, thanks to the god of the Serenity Prayer, she was trying to grow up.

35 years earlier

Some of the children are weeping. Helen is all cried out.

The old mine is lit by torches and incense fills the air as Abraham sweeps by, followed by his acolytes. He wears his priestly robes this night, and the light of God shines on him.

"Those who follow the Lord, draw nigh!" Abraham commands, his voice that of the angels.

Liam, holding baby Jamie, tries to comfort Helen, but she has been shocked into silence by last night's rape and can no longer speak. Or move.

Her daughter Christina leaves her side and moves forward with the rest of Abraham's flock. She wants to watch the fancy ceremony Abraham has prepared for them. Abraham's oldest son is dressed in nothing but a breechclout and is lying on a stone altar. His smile is the empty smile of someone on drugs. The rest of the group—everyone except Helen and Liam—smiles. Abraham's smile is the brightest of all.

"How do we show our love for the Lord?" Abraham asks.

"By following His commands!" choruses the flock.

"Does the Lord command sacrifice?"

The flock responds, "The Lord commands sacrifice!"

"What does the Lord command us to sacrifice?"

"Our firstborn!"

Helen hears her husband's tortured groan before it is drowned out by the voices of the hundred-strong flock. *"We do as the Lord bids us!"*

Only then does Helen notice the knife in Abraham's upraised hand. Before she can force her mouth to move, to shriek a warning, he plunges the knife into his son's chest.

"Great are the works of the Lord!" Abraham cries, as blood rolls down the side of the altar to pool on the mine's dirt floor.

"Great are the works of the Lord!" the flock responds.

Confused, Christina runs back to her mother. "I don't understand, Mommy. Why did Abraham do that? And why isn't Isaac getting up?"

Getting no answer from Helen, the child—curious, always too curious—turns to her father and asks the same questions.

But Liam can't answer because of the blood in his mouth.

Chapter Eight

The horses hadn't been treated to a good long ride for more than a week, so Saturday morning, before we resumed work on the house, Jimmy and I saddled up and braved the murky light on the trail paralleling the Beeline Highway. Adila celebrated the occasion by throwing in a few bucks before finally settling down to a gentle canter. Big Boy, thrilled to be out of the corral, followed gamely, but the tranquil pinto skipped the bucking part.

"How far do you want to ride?" Jimmy asked when Big Boy caught up to us. "All the way to the McDowell foothills?"

Nowhere near the place I'd found Reservation Woman, I thought. "Just along the canal. We've still got the house to worry about, remember. Two rooms left. And plumbing."

Adila, having bucked the kinks out of her system, cantered along peacefully with Big Boy while the rising sun rolled a sheet of golden light across the desert's grays and browns. Every now and then we came upon a rock covered in graffiti. Yes, there are taggers on the Rez, but their artwork leans toward the traditional: spray-painted pictographs of Earth Doctor, Elder Brother, and Spider Woman—images less disturbing than gang signs.

Mother Nature's wild citizens, wilder even than the local teens, greeted the day's glory with joy and trepidation. Ground squirrels, jackrabbits, and deer mice scurried between various kinds of cacti, while a chorale of birds sang from mesquite and ironwood trees.

In the lightening sky above, a bald eagle drifted along a thermal, deciding which scurrying creature to kill first. As we approached the canal, a small band of wild horses galloped along, oblivious of the life-and-death drama about to happen. Just as we arrived at the canal bank, the eagle struck. After a dust-raising flurry, it rose again, carrying away a struggling jackrabbit.

It happened too close for Adila's comfort, and she shied to the left, almost bumping us all into the canal.

"I thought you said she'd settled down," Jimmy groused.

It took me a while to bring my mare under control, but once I did, I threw him a dirty look. "This is what we get for not riding every day."

"Pretty hard to work a full-time job, build a house, entertain the cats, and keep the horses exercised."

"Especially when each succeeding day is shorter than the last."

"We can do something about that, Lena."

His serious tone made me suspicious. "Like what?"

"You don't have to go to the office every day. A lot of the stuff we do, you can do from home."

"Like finding missing goddaughters?"

"The police are working the case."

"The Scottsdale PD is because Juliana's got juice, but if Kyle's birth mother is right, those kids are headed to Nogales, where the authorities are eyeball-deep in drug runners and God-knows-what all. I should be there helping, not poking along enjoying the scenery."

"Has it ever occurred to you that you can't do everything?"

"Every single day. But I can try."

With that, I wheeled Adila around and headed back. We had already covered ten miles of desert, and by the time we made it to the trailer, the accumulated twenty miles should be enough to satisfy the horses for a while. Other good news? Tomorrow was a Sunday, which meant no office hours. That should have made me happy, but it didn't. Downtime can be dangerous time for me, because when I have nothing to do, my mind acts up. It always wants to take me on a forced march down Memory Lane, where monsters dwelled.

When we walked into the Airstream, the landline was ringing. The screen said WOLF RAMIREZ, so I picked it up and hit the speaker button. Wolf had unexpectedly good news: he was bringing over a team of Pima teens to help with the house-raising.

"I know you two have a lot going on, what with your god-daughter running off and the Chelsea thing for Harold. So I told some kids I've been mentoring about your situation, and they've volunteered to help lighten your load."

Before I could say it wasn't necessary, Jimmy thanked the tribal elder and said we'd be waiting with gallons of iced tea and snacks.

"Why'd you do that?" I asked when he hung up. "We're doing fine by ourselves."

"It's the Pima Way. Better get used to it."

"But not everything needs to be a group effort!"

"Pretend we're Amish and we're building a barn." His smile made me smile, too.

Jimmy was only half joking. After so many years of operating solo, of solving my own problems and shouldering my own sorrows, I was having trouble viewing life as a shared experience. Yet, as Jimmy kept repeating, sharing was the Pima Way, especially when it came to building houses on the Rez.

Ten minutes later Wolf drove up with a truckbed full of raven-haired Pima teens, all eager to get to work. Because diabetes on the Rez had left so many kids parentless, mentoring was a much-needed stopgap. Pima farmers mentored, Pima carpenters mentored, electricians mentored, plumbers mentored, and in some cases, Pima doctors, attorneys, and teachers mentored. Such guidance by successful adults had done a lot to deflect the drug and alcohol problems that had derailed so many young lives. I knew I shouldn't be nervous about letting Wolf's team work on the house, but I wasn't Amish. I was a go-it-aloner who was already having trouble living with another person for the first time since age eighteen, when I'd aged out of Child Protective Services' oversight. In our last meeting, my social worker had warned me I might have trouble adjusting to a "normal" lifestyle, and I'd pooh-poohed her. A mistake.

Unsettled at the thought of watching others work on a house I would live in—and my own carpentry skills being haphazard at best—I did the one thing I was truly qualified to do: Saturday notwithstanding, I climbed into my Jeep and drove to Desert Investigations.

At eight on Saturday morning, the Arts District is fairly dead. Because the nightlife in Old Town Scottsdale is fierce on Fridays, tourists tend to stay in bed for a while, nursing their hangovers. Well, to be honest, the same goes for some shopkeepers, too, especially the art gallery crowd. With everything being so quiet, I was able to get a lot done. I spent the first couple of hours catching up on bookkeeping, rejoicing that so many of our clients paid their bills without having to be hassled. Among them was Marie Gorsky, the soon-to-be ex-wife of Roger the Runaway. Pleased, I called her.

"My attorney's already drawn up the divorce papers," she said, "but you know what I've been thinking?"

I felt a moment of alarm. "Don't tell me you want him back, not after he walked out on you like he did."

"I'm not that foolish. Besides, I've got Glen now, and he's twice the man…" She cleared her throat. "Whatever. This whole thing with that goofy Kanati group, it's driving me crazy trying to figure out why he'd leave me for something like that. Roger was never the religious type. When we first married I tried to get him to go to church with me, and he absolutely refused. Seems he had a bad experience with religion when he was younger, so I just let sleeping dogs lie and attended church myself. Now, all of a sudden, he's attending Native American church services when he doesn't have a drop of Indian blood? That makes no sense."

"Actually, I'm not sure Kanati is a religious group. When I was out there it came across as more of a New Age-type thing, but with better food."

"What do you mean, 'better food?"

"The group originated in France, so…" I spread my hands.

She chuckled. "Roger always did have a big appetite. Um, I'd been thinking about driving up to talk to him, find out what was so lacking in our marriage that he chose them over me. But when I mentioned my idea to Glen, he had a fit. Maybe he's afraid that seeing Roger might rekindle the flame, or the Kanati people might suck me in, too. I don't want to make the same mistake twice, but to avoid that, I need to find out where I went wrong in the first place. I'm sure you can understand."

I did. Many of my own past relationships had gone south— Dusty, Warren, and several others—but unlike Marie Gorsky, I'd never tried to find out why. I'd just chalked it all up to Life with a capital L.

"Are you asking me to do what I think you're asking?"

"I need to know why Roger left me, Lena."

By noon herds of tourists were streaming along Main Street and I'd finished the bookkeeping. I'd also checked in with Juliana to find out if Ali and Kyle had been spotted, and received the expected negative answer. After a quick visit to Micky D's for a quarter-pounder, I made one more call, this time to Detective Sylvie Perrins, who professed herself undelighted to hear from me.

"You must think I have nothing better to do than talk to you."

"But I can't get through the day without hearing the lilting sound of your voice. One thing, then I'll let you get back to doing what you're doing. That dead woman by the office park. She get ID'd yet?"

"You mean Unicorn Woman? We hoped the artist's rendering would spark some public interest but it hasn't yet."

"No calls at all?"

"Plenty of calls, but turns out nobody's looking for a blonde with a unicorn tattoo on her ass. Hey, Lena, you have any ink?"

"Nope."

"Me neither. I've thought about it, though. Maybe a pretty Glock, or my own name and D.O.B., just in case. Don't want my scraggly, unidentified ass to end up in the White Tanks."

A gravel lot near the White Tank Mountains on Phoenix's far west side was where unidentified and unclaimed bodies were buried by a team of volunteers from the city jail. No one wanted to end up there, but unless someone identified Unicorn Woman, that's where she was headed. Same with Reservation Woman. When I wasn't busy, I kept seeing her filmy eyes, her matchstick arms stretched out as if attached to a cross. After all the dead people I'd seen in my life—most of them by the time I was five years old—I didn't know why these two women haunted me so, but they did.

"You have any new info from the Medical Examiner's office on Unicorn Woman's cause of death?" I asked Sylvie. "Or Reservation Woman's?"

"Not yet. Well, this has been boring. You need to step up your game, Lena."

Dial tone.

I had a contact at the Medical Examiner's office, so I put in a call to Pete Ventarro, but wound up on that other morgue, voice mail, which didn't surprise me. After a booze-and-drug-fueled Friday night, the Maricopa County Forensic Science Center would be overflowing with shot, stabbed, strangled, and mangled bodies needing a pathologist's kind attentions. I left Pete a message, stating that if at all possible, I needed to view a couple of bodies.

Putting the body ID situation on hold momentarily, I made a quick trip up to Marie Gorsky's house to collect some papers. After stashing them in my tote, I stopped at a gas station and fueled up the Jeep so I wouldn't run out of gas on the way to Kanati. Just as I was pulling away from the pump, Pete Ventarro returned my call. As much as I hate yakking on the phone while driving, I made an exception in his case.

"*Hola*, Lena. Sorry, but us being a secure facility and all, you can't view anyone's body, but I do have a photo of what's left of 18-3271's face, the one everyone's calling Unicorn Woman," he said. "I've also got a picture of the ink on her butt, and of both her hands. She's got a ring, plain silver band on her right forefinger, and a gold band on her left, so there's probably a spouse out there somewhere. If you want the pic, meet me in the parking garage in thirty."

"Be right there, Pete. *Muchas gracias*. And what…?"

He hung up before I could ask him about Reservation Woman.

Twenty-eight minutes later I pulled into the Forensic Science Center's underground parking lot on West Jefferson. Pete had no business showing me the photos, but Desert Investigations had once helped his mother out of a bad spot with an ex-husband, and he owed me.

I knew the Medical Examiner had already fingerprinted Unicorn Woman—I couldn't bring myself to use the county's corpse-numbering system—and obtained dental and full body X-rays, plus taken a DNA sample, and entered everything into the CODIS national database. Same with Reservation Woman. The two women had made their premiere appearance on the ME's website, but in Unicorn Woman's case, the decision had been made to use an artist's sketch instead of her disturbing photograph. There had been no hits on her yet, which meant that a pauper's burial in the White Tanks Mountains could be the ultimate fate of both women.

As soon as I pulled into a parking space in the underground garage, Pete appeared at my door, grasping a manila folder. "Be careful who you show these to, and for God's sake don't mention my name. My job may be grim, but it pays the rent."

I nodded agreement. "I appreciate it."

He gave me a quick wave, then disappeared behind a panel van.

Underground garage lighting not being optimum for viewing photographs, I drove out into the daylight and kept driving until I found a half-empty lot behind a florist shop. I removed the photos from the envelope.

Unicorn Woman hadn't been as fortunate as Reservation Woman. The former had lain under that mesquite tree near the business park for at least two days, and animals had visited. Both eyes were gone from her too-gaunt face, along with most of her nose and lips. But the close-up showed me two things the artist's sketch hadn't. Unicorn Woman's bright, daisy-blond hair had black roots. In a different close-up, the red smear that crossed the cuticle on her left forefinger wasn't dried blood, but a vivid alizarin crimson. Oil paint.

Putting off my trip to Kanati, I headed back to Scottsdale, where I found Sharona Gavalan talking to a customer when I entered her art gallery. I bided my time studying Megan Unruh's mainly black-and-gray paintings of carnage. Walking from painting to painting, I counted a dislocated jaw here, a broken ankle there, and on one canvas, a screaming face. When I reached the painting of the severed hand, I saw a splash of the same alizarin crimson I'd seen on Unicorn Woman's forefinger.

Sharona's customer finally left with a framed Unruh sketch tucked under his arm. Happy to have made a sale, she smiled her way over to me. "So nice to see you again, Lena. What's up?"

"Did Megan wear any jewelry?"

She shook her head. "Like most artists, she preferred to keep her hands free, but I remember seeing her wearing a silver ring once. Not some fancy Navajo silverwork, just a plain band that wouldn't bother her while she was working."

"Did she get married recently, kept it on the down-low?"

"Not her." There was an edge to her voice I couldn't quite identify, but I let it pass.

"Do you know if she had any tattoos?"

Her frown deepened. "Why are you asking me that?"

"Let's just say I may have a lead on her whereabouts."

The frown morphed into a slight smile. "A unicorn. One day she came in here all excited and flashed it at me. Said she got it at that tattoo parlor down the street. Scottsdale Ink."

"Where?"

"I just told you. Scottsdale Ink."

"I meant on her body."

"Oh. On her ass."

Thanking Sharona for her help, I took the Medical Examiner's photograph to Nils Quaid, one of the artists Megan shared studio space with. I asked him to do a pastel drawing of the face, making it rounder, with eyes and nose intact, and with brunette hair, instead of bright daisy yellow.

After one brief look at the photograph, a single tear slid down his cheek. Artists had excellent facial recognition skills.

"You're certain?" I asked.

"Let me show you."

Ten minutes later, Nils had produced a non-maimed version of the face in the photograph. As a finishing touch, he put warm brown eyes into the empty sockets.

There could be no mistake.

Mysterious wedding band notwithstanding, Unicorn Woman was Megan Unruh.

Chapter Nine

When I emailed the new sketch and Unicorn Woman's likely ID to Sylvie Perrins, she immediately called me.

"Where'd you get this?"

"Acting on a hunch, I had an artist friend re-envision it from the sketch you guys released," I lied.

"What 'artist friend'?"

"There are so many artists in Scottsdale I can't remember."

"Every day in every way I hate you more and more."

"The feeling's mutual, Dahling." '

In a different tone of voice, she said, "God, I hope you're right about the ID. I've been thinking about that pauper's cemetery…"

Concerned that she was about to lose it, I said, "Oh, and before you take that sketch over to Megan's mother, you need to know she's a cold-hearted bitch."

"Like you, huh?"

"And you."

A laugh. "Let's not be strangers."

"That'll never happen."

As I put my cell away, I felt a certain amount of satisfaction, but it was fleeting. Unicorn Woman may have been identified, but who was Reservation Woman?

On Saturdays, the I-10 traffic to Ironwood Canyon isn't heavy, so I arrived at Kanati's front gate little more than an hour later. Ernie was in his usual spot, lounging under the sun umbrella. When I leaned over to show him my ID, he didn't bother looking at it.

"Word's come down to let you in anytime you feel like dropping by," he said. "Sorry you missed lunch. They had Coq au Vin, Fondue Savoyarde, and Pear Tarte Tatin. Working here's gonna get me fat."

Considering the extraordinary lunch I'd enjoyed during my first visit, I was sorry I'd missed lunch, too. "Why, Ernie, are you planning on joining Kanati? Becoming a Believer?" I kept it light, not wanting him to be alerted to my ongoing concerns about the place. My job had taught me that whenever something appeared too good to be true, it usually was.

Ernie chuckled. "I don't have enough money to join this place. Besides, that New Agey 'Elevated' stuff's not my thing. Phony Indian headbands and plastic beads and all? That shit's Amateur Night. Pay's good, though, not to mention the food. So who you looking for this time?"

When I told him, his laugh took on a mean edge. "Good luck with him. That guy's a jerk."

With those encouraging words, he waved me through the gate.

Tracking down Roger Gorsky wasn't difficult once I enlisted the help of Gabrielle Halberd. She informed me that the runaway husband was in the movie set part of the complex, where he spent two hours a week throwing clay pots in the building named Past Times. As we walked along the old movie set's raised board sidewalk, I passed the elderly man I had noticed during my first trip here. Not only was he the oldest person I'd seen in Kanati, he was also the crankiest. He didn't even acknowledge my greeting. Maybe the arthritis that kept him doubled over his two canes was hurting him. Then again, maybe something in Kanati had made him unhappy. I made a mental note to have a private talk with him before I left.

Past Times was divided into two different areas: one for painters and one for potters. Instead of the standard Kanati golf shirts,
smocks were the order of the day. Gabrielle and I made our way
through a group of people painting watercolors of a flower-stuffed
vase, then an even larger group which had confined their artistic
urges to charcoal sketches. Since I was used to the more pro-
fessional products displayed in the Scottsdale galleries, I found
myself less than impressed. Maybe Roger Gorsky's work would
be better. After all, he had once been a big-time CEO, which
to my way of thinking, proved that he had a drive to succeed at
anything he tried. At least that was the theory.

I discovered the flaw in my theory when Gabrielle and I
reached the back of the long room, where I saw five men hunched
over potters' wheels. Unlike everyone else, Roger wore no artist's
smock, just a clay-spattered tee-shirt that proclaimed SPIRI-
TUAL GANGSTA. A few examples of his pottery skills were
lined up on the table in front of him, ready to join other cre-
ations to be fired in the kiln on the building's outdoor patio. I
saw lopsided pots unusable as flower vases, and mugs guaranteed
to leak any liquid poured into them. Looking at his collection
of talentless handiwork I wondered how, given Kanati's French
origins, its artistic standards could be so low. None of those
pieces deserved firing. The most charitable thing that could be
said about Roger Gorsky's pots was that he was relatively new
to the world of creative expression. The least charitable? That
he had no talent.

As if reading my mind, Gabrielle leaned over and murmured,
"It is only those things which flow from the spirit that count,
not the outer shell."

Talk about bullshit. "You're kidding, right? Where did you
say you were from?"

Still whispering, she replied, "Paris. Sixth Arrondissement.
But if abusing lumps of clay makes him happy, the clay has not
been wasted." In a more conversational tone, she said, "And so!

I will now leave you to speak with your friend. Afterwards, if you wish, I will give you a more detailed tour of Kanati's other offerings, such as the delights of our sauna. It is located in the Hotel OK Corral, which I believe is named after a famous place, am I correct?"

"Yep, famous. A few people had a big shootout there once."

Brown eyes danced. "Oh, you Americans and your guns! *Our* OK Corral celebrates more soothing times than gunfights. Massages. Saunas. Rejuvenating skin treatments. Even mani-pedis, which I suggest you take advantage of, my treat." She winced as she looked at my hands.

Karate practice can be hell on a woman's fingernails. "Thanks, but I'll take a raincheck."

She frowned. "You believe it is going to rain? I have seen no clouds during this day."

After I'd explained that particular Americanism, she laughed. "Ah, well. Live and be educated, as your people say." With that, she left to talk to a group of watercolorists, few of whom showed any actual talent. Kanati might not have had rigid artistic standards, but so far the group hadn't shown signs of secrecy, one of the hallmarks of a cult. Aside from the light woo-woo stuff I'd seen, the place might make for a pleasant weekend getaway. Craft rooms. Tennis. Croquet. Sauna. Heated pool. Four-star cafeteria...

But it was time to do what I'd come to do: find out why a man had walked out on his wife.

Roger, whose headband had accumulated three beads of various colors, didn't act pleased to see me, but it may have had something to do with the way I introduced myself.

"Hi, Roger, I'm Lena Jones, private investigator, and your wife wanted me to give you this." I handed him the papers I'd been carrying in my tote. "You've been served."

He stood up, anger flaring in his eyes. "You bitch!" Then the anger died, as suddenly as if it had been switched off. He sat back down, put his hands together in a prayerful pose, and took a couple of deep breaths. "I beg your forgiveness, Miss Jones. As an Elevated person, I accept whatever happens to me as a result of my actions."

Although he sounded a bit robotic, I appreciated the apology. "Your soon-to-be ex-wife also wanted me to ask why you left her, and why you never took the time to let her know whether you were dead or alive."

He looked over at the lump of clay he'd been manhandling. "I don't think you'd understand."

"Try me." Looming over someone is never a good way to get them to open up, so I settled myself into the chair next to him and tried to look sympathetic—not always easy when you've just handed them a summons.

Roger Gorsky may not have been a handsome man, but even after vacating his CEO chair two years earlier, he still maintained an air of power. The weight loss helped, too, as did the toned arms and chest that filled out his tee-shirt.

"I felt empty," he said.

"Why? You'd done well in business, had a great house, a wife who loved you, a…"

He waved away the rest of my sentence. "Material things that count for nothing."

Not noticing my usage of the past tense on the "love" word, he continued. "What the average person calls love is nothing more than a combination of lust and fear. Wanting the sexual release, fearful you either won't get it, or if you do, you won't be able to keep it. Here I've learned to live life on an Elevated level, not that you'd understand."

I'd heard such reductionism before, but it surprised me to hear it coming from a Kanatian. "I may not be an expert on all things spiritual, Roger, but I believe the average person has greater depth than the shallowness you just described. I won't bore you with examples of men dying on battlefields for love of country, or parents running into burning houses to save their children, or people endangering their own lives to save total strangers. Those things happen every day."

"You have no idea what you're talking about, Miss Jones. Or is it Mizzzz?" With a sneer, he emphasized the Z.

It was probably useless to argue with him, but the guy got my back up—which, I guess, just goes to show what a low level of spirituality I've attained. But then I remembered something Reverend Giblin, one my foster fathers, had told me. After failing to convert my little pagan heart, he and his wife had backed off and just loved me. Not that I'd dismissed everything he said. In fact, one lesson in particular remained with me.

Stating the Reverend's words as best I could, I said to Roger, "A preacher, a man I greatly respected, once told me there are four kinds of love: *eros*, the erotic form of love, which is the form you were talking about; *philia*, the kind of love we have for our friends; *storge*, empathy—think Mother Theresa living among the lepers and homeless; and *agape*, the supposed unconditional love of God for humankind." As an added jab, due to my own lowly spiritual state, I said, "You weren't doing so great with the *philia* kind of love when you left your friends behind, were you?"

It took him a minute to get over his shock, but when he did, he reverted to his I'm-more-Elevated-than-you-are tone. "My so-called 'friends' were mere business associates, not soul partners, the kind I've developed here."

I looked at the long line of ill-shaped pots, each one of them made by a supposedly Elevated Kenatian. "Soul partners, hmm?"

He made a contemptuous sound, somewhere between a grunt and a sniff. "Look, Mizzzz Jones, despite the teachings of your preacher friend—and all preachers are frauds, as far as I'm concerned—I doubt you can understand what I'm about to say, but here goes. Having soul partners means being at one with others on a deeper level than someone like you, with your superficial legalistic life, can ever realize is possible."

Superficial legalistic life. Well, that's telling me.

"I am now Elevated, Mizzzz Jones. Out there, in what un-Elevated people such as yourself perceive as the physical world, my life was meaningless. I didn't know who I was or what the hell I was doing, other than taking one breath after another for no particular reason. As for me lying to my wife about going out for a pack of cigarettes, that was no lie. I did need cigarettes. And booze. I needed a lot of things to fill up my emptiness, so I headed off to the Circle K and bought a carton of the best cancer sticks they had. While I was at it, I bought a bottle of Cutty, too, but on the way home, a weird thing happened. I can't explain it. I just…"

He paused a moment to reflect, then continued. "I just passed my house and kept on driving. I didn't know where I was headed or what I was going to do when I got there. Next thing I knew I was on the I-10 headed for Tucson, but when I stopped for gas at one of those tourist traps you always see on the interstates, I noticed this other road, so I got on that, and then I saw a gravel road so I took that road, too. It was like I was on automatic pilot. When I spotted this place, I was curious so I parked my car and walked in…" His face took on a beatific look, like a haloed angel had just appeared before him. "…and changed my life."

"That's what you want me to tell your wife?"

"I don't care what you tell her. She's nothing to me anymore." With that, he returned to torturing clay.

Gabrielle had finished talking to the watercolorists and was waiting for me at the door. "How was your friend Roger?" she asked, as we strolled across the wide plaza. Nearby, Kanatians frolicked in the pool or hit tennis balls back and forth. Supposedly a perfect day in a perfect place, regardless of your level of Elevation.

Answering Gabrielle's question, I said, "I'm thinking he wasn't awarded any of those beads for humility."

She averted her face, but not before I saw the grin. "He received the beads for keeping the pink Porta Potty clean, which is supposed to be a humbling experience." Once she had her facial expressions under control, she looked back up at me, with a wicked gleam in her eyes. "As you have discovered, he was awarded the beads anyway."

"Kind of like getting a spiritual E for Effort, then."

A snicker, which she also tried to hide.

As we ambled toward the tennis courts, one of the players, a burly woman, aced a serve that had her male opponent falling on his face as he tried to return it. Instead of feeling humiliated, the man stood up and applauded her. Apparently, some people were paying attention to Kanati's lessons about humility.

Gabrielle called out, "Excellent, Ruby! You show your Elevation more each day. Also you, Arnold."

Watching her unclouded happiness, I was once again struck by how beautiful she was, with her lithe body, fine-featured face, and smoothly coiffed chestnut hair. Such physical perfection made me wonder why she had left Paris to take up residence in the middle of the Arizona desert. Had she, like Roger Gorsky, felt empty inside, or was it something else? Taking a chance, I asked, "In your life before…" I waved my hand around, "…before you joined up with all this, did you ever feel it was meaningless?"

To my relief, the question didn't bother her. "I have been part of *all this*, as you call it, for many years, but yes, there was a 'before' time. You see, in Paris, I was part of the fashion industry, charged with putting together fashion shows, *tres haute monde*. One of the most beloved models at the time was Isabelle Caro. Is it possible you are familiar with her?"

The name sounded vaguely familiar, but I shook my head.

"Isabelle appeared in the American video, *The Price of Beauty*, and I am so sorry to tell you that soon afterwards she died of anorexia."

Now I remembered. The former beauty had starved herself to death.

"Isabelle was a dear friend, and with her death my heart was broken. In that brokenness, the scales fell from my eyes and I saw that the young girls I hired for our runways were getting thinner with each passing season. And I was, as you Americans say, part of the problem. But how had I allowed such an outrage to happen? How could I have been blind to the girls' suffering? I became so filled with self-loathing that I walked away from the fashion industry and began a search for a deeper calling in life, a different way of looking at my place in the world. Like most of my countrymen, I was raised Catholic, but I found no answers in the Church, just dictates to accept an event that supposedly happened two thousand years ago. So I began searching for something more contemporary, something illuminated by modern scientific discoveries. This led me to Scientology, but I found it too controlling, and…"

She searched for the phrase. "…and too filled with what you Americans call 'junk science.' I am a graduate of Ecole Polytechnique, you understand, and would never listen to such amateur foolishness. Then one beautiful day, while I was at a Buddhist retreat, someone mentioned the work being done by Adam Arneault. I investigated, and…" A bright smile. "Here I am!"

It sounded nice, and I knew that the Ecole Polytechnique was one of the highest-rated universities in the world, so Gabrielle was no dummy. Still…

"But let us have no more talk of young girls and death," she said. "Kanati is not only about life, it is about a life well-lived. Here, follow me to our massage room. It is time you learn to relax."

Ten minutes later I was in the Hotel OK Corral, lying on a thickly padded massage table. As I inhaled the aroma of burning sage and listened to a recording of Enya cooing about Irish rivers, a heavily muscled woman pounded on me. Gabrielle lay on the table next to mine, her face a repository of bliss.

Once the pounding was finished, and we'd showered and

dressed, she said, "That was lovely, *non*? And now would you like another treat? I invite you to go with us to see either *Black Panther* or *Raw Life*, the new documentary."

"Kanati has an on-site theater?" This so-called "cult" was full of surprises.

Brushing her hair back into its normal perfection, she said, "Unfortunately, no, but perhaps in the future. For now, every Saturday, our vans ferry those interested in film to the Tucson CinePlex, where our members can watch any film of their choosing. I myself have seen *Black Panther* twice, and now that it has been re-released, I wish to see it again. The title character is an exquisite black man, and the African costumes put Paris designers to shame." She paused as we went back outside, where the lowering sun had begun to streak the blue sky with rose and orange. "But you being an investigator, you might prefer that student documentary, *Raw Life*. It is also showing at the CinePlex, only on the smallest screen. I have seen it and found it shocking."

At the thought of a film shocking a Parisian, I had to smile. "A movie about nudists?" As we left the Old West enclave and headed toward the recreation area, I saw people forming a line in front of the large teepee. Among them was Chelsea, who gave me a surprisingly friendly wave. It was meditation time. And then, dinner.

My stomach growled at the thought.

This time Gabrielle ignored my stomach's complaint. "Not nudism, although walking barefoot is encouraged in that foolish EarthWay. I suggested the film to you because of your obvious fear of cults." Her face changed, and her former bliss was replaced by a frown. "Portions of the movie were filmed at EarthWay, and although the film is of only of student quality—the sound is garbled and the editing uneven—I found its message to be quite alarming. EarthWay's lifestyle is…" She paused for a moment, fishing for the right word. "Barbaric."

Her choice of the word piqued my interest. "Are they polygamists, by any chance?"

Arizona had numerous polygamist cults in the barren northern end of the state, all headed by self-proclaimed "prophets." Some of those "prophets" forced little girls into fraudulent "spiritual" marriages to men decades older in an ugly combination of child sexual abuse and modern-day slavery. Despite the imprisonment of one of their leaders—"Prophet" Warren Jeffs after his child rape conviction—the polygamy compounds still thrived, protected by the high-desert barrenness of their surroundings.

"If the people at EarthWay are polygamists, it was not spoken of in the documentary," Gabrielle answered. "But I very much doubt that they are, because the group was established by a woman called Mother Eve." Here she vented an un-ladylike snort. "More foolishness, do you not think? I suspect the name is not her own. But I am sorely troubled by EarthWay's health issues, which seem to be many. And, oh, the poor children! While I was speaking to Adam this morning, he suggested I invite you to come with us and see this film. Like me, Adam is very concerned about EarthWay's babies."

"Adam?" I looked over at the big lodge, where Kanati's administrative offices were located. "He saw it?"

"Most certainly. Adam is very much the cinephile and often accompanies us to the CinePlex. Especially when they are showing the French movies. I believe he sometimes feels homesick."

"But I heard he was American-born." At least that's what Jimmy's research had shown.

"Quite so, in the state called Oklahoma. But he and his father spent much of their young years near Paris, where the Arneault family originated. The Arneaults are a *très* respected family, descended from pre-Revolution aristocracy."

I'd been under the impression most of the "pre-Revolution" aristocracy had lost their heads via the guillotine, although a few of them had managed to escape. Why would their descendants care about whatever was happening to EarthWay's children?

When I asked, Gabrielle spouted more spiritual mishmash,

finishing with, "Adam Arneault very much loves children. Wherever children suffer in this world, his concerns are with them. This is why he would like you to see *Raw Life*. He believes the viewing will lead you into action."

I had first heard about EarthWay two years ago when it moved into its location forty miles north of Scottsdale, but knew little about its beliefs other than its stated wish to return to a less complicated agrarian life off the grid. I had certainly heard nothing about EarthWay having problems with children, or I would have been up there in a heartbeat. Yet here Adam Arneault, whom I had not met, was sounding the alarm. As for the "very much loves children" bit, I had noticed there were no children at Kanati, just adults. It seemed more likely that Adam was worried EarthWay might start poaching Kanati's own wealthy members. Places like this were expensive to keep up, and I had no doubt that any threat to Kanati's financial well-being would be dealt with in whatever way possible, including siccing a PI on a rival organization.

But I had also noticed the way Gabrielle's eyes sparkled when speaking about Adam. Unless I was wrong, she was in love with her boss in an un-Elevated way. "While I appreciate the information about EarthWay, I'm not certain..."

I was cut short by a shriek coming from the direction of the fiberglass teepee, where the line had been forming for afternoon meditation. I turned to see a scuffle between two men, one of whom was face-pounding the other. What once had been an orderly group had degenerated into chaos, with people scattering in all directions. Without thinking, I ran toward the fighters, only to be cut off by two muscular men wearing multi-beaded headbands and carrying two-way radios. Within seconds, the larger of them had grabbed the face-pounder around the waist and hauled him away from his bleeding victim.

"Okay, Leo, you've gone and done this after Adam himself gave you your third and final warning," the big man said, while his just-as-big friend rendered aid to the victim.

"But the guy took cuts in line, Jerry!" Leo bleated. Unlike most of the members of Kanati, he wore no headband at all, just the official Kanati golf shirt. Not a good sign.

Jerry wasn't moved by his protest. "Whatever the provocation, it makes no difference. Now let's go pack your things. You're going home."

"But…"

Jerry flexed his huge muscles. "Violence is not allowed at Kanati under any circumstances. You were told that on your first day and you signed an agreement to that effect."

"But…"

Without further ado, Jerry hustled him toward one of the log cabins at the rear of the compound.

"Then I want a refund," the Kanati reject whined, attempting without success to pull away. "I paid for three months!"

"You should have read the fine print."

As the two disappeared, I turned my attention to Leo's bleeding victim. I couldn't tell if his nose was broken or not, but it was a gusher. "This is why you need a medical staff," I told Gabrielle.

"Noah was a medic in Afghanistan," she replied, gesturing to the man attending to the victim. Despite her reassuring tone, she appeared shaken. "If he feels poor Walter needs further treatment, he will drive him to Tucson Medical Center."

"Does that kind of thing happen often here?" I expected Gabrielle to go into full whitewash mode, during which I might learn even more about the way Kanati operated.

She surprised me by answering, "It happens more often than we would wish. We take in troubled people, and some of them have backgrounds in violence, especially the recovering addicts. Not, you understand, that I am saying Leo is or was an addict. We observe our newcomers carefully during their first few weeks among us, and structure their days in such a way that they seldom experience stressful situations. But with Leo…" She shrugged. "Even standing peacefully in line has proven too much for him."

"Jerry and Noah, the guys who broke it up, their headbands had beading all over the place, even more beads than yours. Which means?"

"They have reached a higher state of Elevation than I."

Her admission shocked me. "May I ask what's holding you back?"

She stopped smiling. "You may ask, but the best answer is another quaint Americanism, 'It's complicated.'"

Behind her, the line in front of the large teepee began to form again. I looked around, hoping to see the elderly man again, but he was nowhere to be found.

Upon leaving Kanati, I drove straight to Marie Gorsky's house and told her what I'd learned. At first she had trouble believing it.

"Nobody disappears just because they get up one day feeling empty."

"His words, not mine, Marie."

"If feeling empty on occasion was reason enough to disappear, every new mother experiencing postpartum depression would hit the road."

"That sometimes happens." And worse. I remembered Kyle's mother. And my own. After shooting me, however accidentally, she had never shown up at the hospital to claim me. Why not? Was she dead?

"What did Roger say when you served him the divorce papers?" Marie's question jolted me out of the memory.

I gave her a weak smile. "Well, at first he called me a bitch, then kind of backtracked, saying, 'I accept whatever happens to me as a result of my actions.' It's part of the Kanati teachings, apparently."

Glen, who had been lifting weights on the patio when I arrived, laughed. "Accept? That's rich!"

Marie didn't find it quite so humorous. With a worried look, she turned to him and said, "You don't feel empty, do you?"

The big man put a comforting arm around her. "Only when you're not around."

"Nothing Roger said makes sense."

He hugged her tighter. "Does it have to? It's just life, honey, and life doesn't always make sense."

On that, Glen and I were in agreement. I didn't think life—especially the love part—made any sense whatsoever.

Chapter Ten

"But it's Sunday!" Jimmy still hadn't reconciled himself to my schedule, and made his unhappiness known when we put the horses away after a too-short morning ride.

"I'll only be gone an hour or two."

"It'll take you an hour to get to EarthWay, at least an hour to look around, then another hour to get back. I thought you were going to help on the house. The plumbing's about to go in, and you know what that's like."

Thanks to the aid of Wolf Ramirez's teen mentorees, the new house was coming along nicely, while my own contributions continued to fall short. Other work, especially the Desert Investigations kind, kept getting in the way. Maybe EarthWay wasn't officially our case, but if the information Gabrielle had given me proved correct, I might need to tip off the Department of Child Safety, the new name for Child Protective Services.

"I promise to help as soon as I get back," I assured Jimmy.

He harrumphed. "You're overloading yourself again. Remember me warning you that you can't do everything?"

"Yeah, and I remember my comeback: I'll always try, especially when children are involved."

It took only forty minutes to get to EarthWay, which was located in Hopi County just off the Beeline Highway. At an elevation of

fifteen hundred feet, the mile-long Orange Valley didn't experience the blistering summers of Scottsdale, which decades earlier
had allowed it to gain fame for the orange orchards specializing
in Arizona Sweets. Twenty years ago most of the trees died during
a prolonged drought, almost bankrupting the orchard owner,
who then sold out to a thoroughbred training stable which also
went bust. The valley was then parceled off to four back-to-the-
land-type communes, two of which coalesced into EarthWay.
Perhaps thirty of the original orange trees remained, and as my
Jeep nimbly navigated the rutted dirt road, I could still detect
their citrusy aroma.

Gaining access to EarthWay proved easy. Unlike Kanati, there
was no gate and no Ernie, just a sign announcing HANDMADE
FURNITURE, QUILTS AND GIFTS. FREE PARKING!!!
EarthWay did have one thing in common with Kanati, though.
Its members had moved lock and stock into pre-existing buildings, which in this case meant sharing three houses, two barns,
and a long row of horse stables turned into living quarters. All the
structures were more ramshackle than Kanati's well-maintained
buildings, and the wooden privies—located alarmingly near a
large vegetable garden—smelled very much in use. At the other
side of the garden grazed a small herd of goats and milk cows.
They shared their space with a flock of molting red chickens
and several collarless dogs. The only sign of modern technology
was a neglected-looking water tower looming at the end of the
property, where the words ORANGE VALLEY STABLES were
fading away.

After parking (FREE!!!), I bypassed the hut with the FRESH
UNPASTURIZED MILK & EGGS sign, circumvented a group
of runny-nosed children playing hopscotch, and headed for a
general store that boasted a HANDICRAFTS sign above its
open door. Once across a porch lined with wooden rockers,
each bearing a price tag, I entered a large, gloomy room lit only
by three kerosene lanterns. For effect? Or did EarthWay have

no electricity? While driving down the dirt road I had noticed power lines leading to the compound, but they might not have been operational. Electricity costs money, and EarthWay was no Kanati.

"May I help you?"

In the dim light I could see a fifty-something woman behind the counter. She wore her graying hair pulled back into a school-marm bun, and the ankle-length dress she wore was a loose weave of unevenly dyed blue cotton. It hung loosely on her too-thin frame, making me wonder if she'd recently lost weight. Her soiled white apron added to her bedraggled appearance, as did the angry red rash along her arms.

I had decided that the easiest way to check out the commune would be to act like a fat-pursed tourist, and so I wasn't averse to spending a little money out of Desert Investigation's petty cash. The coverlet on Jimmy's bed had already proven too light for the season, which was growing cooler as we headed into November.

"I'd like to see some quilts," I said.

The woman's smile revealed yellow teeth flecked with small cavities, and her breath when she neared, had a sour smell. "Oh, we have lovely quilts, all handmade on site. Are you looking for any particular pattern or color family?"

I knew nothing about quilts, only that many of them qualified as works of art, thus the popular quilt competition at the Arizona State Fair. I'd yearned for the prize-winner one year, but its price turned out to be not much less than a new motor for my Jeep. I hoped the prices here were more affordable.

"Maybe something with a lot of blue." Blue was Jimmy's favorite color.

"We have a nice selection of blues. I'm Sally White Flower. And you?"

"Lena Jones."

As Sally White Flower led me past a pottery display table where the offerings were considerably more accomplished than any of those I'd seen at Kanati, I noticed she was barefoot. "You don't get splinters?" I pointed to the rough-hewn floor.

She chuckled. "After a while your feet toughen up so much you don't even feel it. Besides, going barefoot is Nature's way."

Bubonic plague was Nature's way, too. And malaria. And more to the point, hookworms, a parasite you could contract by walking barefoot over ground where animals had defecated. Sally White Flower's rash was one symptom of hookworm infestation, making me wonder what other symptoms she might have: abdominal pain, cramping, fever, loss of appetite? Judging by her condition alone, I could understand Adam Arneault's concerns about EarthWay.

Health issues aside, the store was a treasure trove of highly skilled handmade crafts. A display of sweet-scented soaps and candles stood next to a rack offering handmade jewelry, all the pieces quite beautiful. At the back of the room, a pile of quilts was stacked waist-high beneath an open window through which I could hear children playing and chickens clucking.

After a brief flip through the quilts, Sally pulled one out. "How about this? The pattern's called Steeplechase, and as you can see, it's a lovely blue on white."

While the blue was a lovely shade, all those squares cocked at angles made it look like an Escher drawing. Hardly restful. "Perhaps you have something a little less eye-crossing?"

"Then how about this Sunbonnet Sue?" The quilt she held up was covered by little girls in blue dresses and matching bonnets.

"Pretty, but it's a gift for a man."

"Straight or gay?"

The question, coming from a woman who looked like something out of a nineteenth-century photograph, made me chuckle. "Very straight."

"Would you describe him as bold?"

That gave me pause. Jimmy was one of the gentlest men I'd ever known, but he had a backbone of steel. And he'd certainly been bold enough to take me on. "Very bold."

She nodded, flipped through the stack some more, then pulled out a multi-colored quilt that could have been put together by Pablo Picasso, if the artist had ever dropped acid at a quilting bee. Blue was the predominant color, but I also saw splashes of red, yellow, green, purple—the entire color spectrum. It was such a wild-looking thing I could already see it on Jimmy's bed. He had a wild side, too.

"What's this pattern called?"

"Foundation Pieced Crazy Quilt."

Crazy Quilt? I fell further in love. "How much?"

Her answer made me gulp, but I fished for my wallet. Then stopped. Everything about EarthWay telegraphed its back-to-basics philosophy. "Um, how do I pay you? Personal check? I never carry that much cash."

"We don't take checks, but how about this?" She reached into her pocket and pulled out a smartphone with an attached card reader. "Visa, MasterCard, or American Express, we take them all."

Well, of course. No matter how back-to-basics a commune proclaimed itself, it still needed to make money. I handed over my Visa, and within seconds, Jimmy was the proud possessor of a handmade Crazy Quilt. Instead of a plastic bag, Sally wrapped it up in a long sheet of butcher paper.

"This'll keep the dust off," she explained. "Would you like me to hang on to it while you look around the store? Maybe sit in one of the rocking chairs? They're handmade, too, as is our one-of-a-kind jewelry. Our artisans find and polish the stones themselves. We also offer a nice line of handmade dresses and aprons, like what I'm wearing."

Bless Sally White Flower. She had given me the perfect opening. "I'm full up on dresses." A lie there, I didn't even own a dress, much less an apron. "Same with jewelry, but I might as well do a little grocery shopping while I'm here. Since I can see chickens right out your window, the eggs have to be fresher than anything I can get at the supermarket. Your produce is guaranteed organic, right?"

"Absolutely. Everything here is homegrown and pesticide-free. No GMOs, of course." She actually shuddered. Recovering, she motioned to my tote bag. "If you can't fit everything in there, the produce stand has a nice collection of reusable cloth bags. All handmade, and very attractive."

After seeing those beautiful quilts, I had no doubt of that.

From the general store I ambled over to the produce stand run by a man who introduced himself as Jeremiah Blue Sky. Thin, pushing fifty, he was ruddy-complexioned and had eyes that matched his name. Like the other men I'd seen walking around the compound, he wore a long-sleeved lumberjack shirt underneath his bib overalls, and his blond hair hung in foot-long dreads. While he filled my new handmade grocery bag with an expensive selection of guaranteed no-GMO carrots, salad greens, oranges, and apples, he chattered away.

"We've been wholly organic for three years, but we've only been doing the raw water thing for one." His nasal accent placed him from the southern Midwest, Arkansas or Missouri. "When we found out about the chemicals getting flushed into people's water systems—Xanax, Librium, Premarin, and a whole witches' brew of painkillers—we decided raw *everything* was the only way to go. With raw water you cut the processed crap and stay with the Earth's own natural bounty."

"My thinking exactly," I lied. "But where do you get your water? I didn't see any streams on my way in."

"There's a nice little stream in the woods back there," he gestured toward a stand of pine trees, "but it's a little risky. I mean, you never know if something has died upstream somewhere and fallen into water, do you? Microbe City, baby. One of the reasons we moved here was because there's an artesian well on the property. Some of the best-tasting water you've ever had, guaranteed pollutant- and chemical-free."

"I wouldn't mind tasting that."

He thought for a moment. "Selling you water would be illegal, and since that damned documentary and last month's incident with the marijuana patch, the Feds have been keeping a close eye on us. So, here, take this." He handed me an empty but recapped Coke bottle that appeared clean. "Just take it to the well behind the big barn and haul up the water yourself. We always recommend that our produce be eaten raw. Just wash everything down with a vegetable scrubber, blot dry, and you're all set. Within a week you'll start seeing a change. Stay raw and you'll drop a few pounds, not that you need to, because you look super-fine, if you don't mind me saying so, but lean and mean is the way we roll."

After paying a king's ransom for the produce, I bid Jeremiah Blue Sky goodbye and set out for the artisan well. As I crossed the compound, I took note of the children. They wore home-made clothes and all were barefoot. More worrying was the fact that every child I saw appeared underweight. Instead of the pink cheeks you might expect from children who spent so much of their lives outdoors, most were paler than I would like. Almost all of them had runny noses, but they seemed happy. No bruises that I could see, no broken bones.

Like the general store manager, the women wore ankle-length dresses similar to those I'd seen in polygamy compounds at the northern end of the state. Although they were as thin as their children, they looked considerably more cheerful than the polygamists' beaten-down "sister wives." As I studied them, I realized their long dresses reminded me of the dress worn by Reservation Woman. Hers had had a similar pattern: long, short-sleeved, but high-necked. And she'd been thin, too. Overly so.

As I rounded the compound's barn, I was so deep in thought that I almost collided with a young woman carrying a bucket of water in one hand, a baby in her other arm. Both were red-heads. She also wore an ankle-length dress, but unlike most of the others', hers had a lower neckline and a row of buttons down the front. A nursing mother, I guessed.

"Oops," I said, side-stepping out of her way.

"My fault. I should've watched where I was going. Hey, are you the lady who bought my Crazy Quilt? I was up at the store a few minutes ago and saw it sitting on the counter. Sally told me some blond woman bought it."

"You're the quilter?"

"Yep, that's me. Born Sara Jenks, but my artist's name is Sunflower. I sew it into each of my quilts on the lower right border. I've got five more quilts in the store, in case you're doing some early Christmas shopping. Handmade quilts make lovely gifts, and even become heirlooms. They're one-of-a-kind, not the products of some soulless production line."

Her infant made a kitten-like mewl, shifting Sunflower's attention from sales to the little redhead. She put the bucket down, unbuttoned the front of her dress, and hauled out a vein-marbled breast. Little Red latched on.

"Sally displays my pottery, too," she said, ignoring the snuffling and smacking noises. "Mugs, vases, even complete place settings, each piece signed. Natural earth colors, browns and soft greens. They go with any décor."

Impressed by the young mother's lack of self-consciousness, I smiled. "That's some sales pitch you've got there. May I ask what you did for a living before you wound up in EarthWay?"

"I tended a cosmetics counter at Nordstrom. Made other women beautiful while I was dying inside." A brief shadow of sadness crossed her face. "You ever feel like that?"

I had a brief flashback to some of the more abusive foster homes I'd lived in as a child. "Not lately."

"Same here. Since moving to EarthWay, I've been able to lead a more peaceful and creative life." Still holding Little Red to her bared breast, she hauled the water bucket back up. "Well, I gotta get back to the kitchen and help prepare lunch. It's a special celebration. Sister Claire delivered her baby last night and it's a healthy little girl, so we're having one of our rare cooked meals. Brown rice with mushrooms, sautéed veggies, spiced pumpkin custard for dessert with real whipped cream. We're serving home-made wine, too, legal, as long as we don't sell it. Say, as a valued customer…" here a laugh, "…you're welcome to eat with us today if you want. No charge, although small love offerings are always appreciated. Oh, and when you pick up your quilt, don't forget to check out my dinnerware. And my hand-milled soaps."

With that, she walked away, Little Red still sucking mightily.

The artisan well was shaded by a large stand of pine trees abuzz with birdsong. As the morning sun filtered through the branches, I poured sparkling clear water into the Coke bottle Jeremiah Blue Sky had given me. Snapping the cap back on, I couldn't help but feel guilty. Private investigators were trained to see the worst in people, but everyone I had met so far at EarthWay had been friendly, yet here I was, looking for evidence that might ruin their Eden-esque lifestyle.

Well water collected, I followed a dirt trail through the pines until I came to the stream. Although clear, the water appeared less than a foot deep, which meant that it probably ran dry during Arizona's long, hot summers. Today the stream burbled merrily along, washing around granite boulders and leaching away at its bank. I hadn't needed the Coke bottle Jeremiah Blue Sky had given me because I had brought several glass vials I'd pulled from Desert Investigations' supply closet, but the more the merrier, right? Satisfied no one was watching, I took out two vials and filled them with stream water. Firmly stoppering them, I tucked them into my tote.

As I turned to go back, I found myself facing a tall, stern-faced woman with flowing, waist-length silver hair. At five-foot-eight I'm not short, but this woman had at least four inches on me. Her sunburnt skin was furrowed with deep creases, and her gray eyes missed nothing.

"What are you doing?" she asked, her voice a deep alto. Her biceps, revealed by the shirtless bib overalls she wore, looked as toned as a gymnast's. No Skinny Minnie, she.

She was blocking the pathway to my Jeep.

"Just, ah, getting some water." I tried to sidle around her, but she sidled with me.

"Why?"

"I want it tested for purity."

"Why?"

Since I couldn't think up a believable lie at the moment, I fell back on the truth. Well, partial truth. "There've been rumors that the water around here is unsafe, and since this stream crosses some land I'm, ah, thinking of buying…" I shrugged. "Since I was already doing some vegetable shopping here, I thought I might as well kill two birds with one stone." Oops. Probably not the wisest metaphor to use in a vegetarian commune.

Now she looked even less friendly. "Are you with some government agency?"

"No."

"So you're doing this on your own." She moved closer. Put her hand in her pocket. Grasped something there.

Just because these people were vegetarians didn't mean they couldn't be dangerous, so the motion alarmed me. But considering that I'd already been caught with the vials, there was no further point in lying.

"A friend of mine, a government chemist, knows where I am today," I said, "and he'll worry if I'm late getting back. So if you don't mind, move aside so I can pick up the quilt I bought at your lovely general store and head on back to town. As I'm sure you realize, vegetables are best eaten freshly picked."

She didn't move. "What's your name?"

More irritated than alarmed, I asked a question of my own. "What's yours? As they say, with whom do I have the pleasure of speaking?"

Another hard look. "I'm known as Mother Eve."

"And I'm known as Lena."

"Lena who?"

"Eve who?"

"Think you're smart, don't you, Lena?"

"If you'd be so kind as to let me pass…"

She finally moved aside, but she kept her hand in her pocket. Knife? Glock?

Mother Eve followed me all the way back to the general store, and from there, to my Jeep.

"Don't come back, Lena."

I gave her my best smile. "Thanks for the hospitality."

35 years earlier

Because of his broken jaw, delivered the day before when he tried to keep Abraham from taking Helen, Liam can barely speak.

But Helen has found her voice.

"Abraham has gone crazy, and so have the rest of them," she whispers, as the others dance in the firelight, still celebrating Abraham's supreme sacrifice. "We can't let this go on. And… and Christina is our firstborn. He'll kill her, too. He's already killed his own son!"

The look in Liam's eyes shows he understands.

Helen looks down at baby Jamie, nursing at her breast. "It's starting with firstborn sons, so Jamie's in danger. And later it could even be firstborn daughters, and we'd lose Christina, too. Abraham has changed, Liam! Did all those drugs he's been taking do this to him, or has he always been like this, just better at hiding it?"

Liam shrugs, then turns his hands palm-up in a hopeless gesture. He has no answer for her, not even if he could speak.

"We have to help the other children, too," Helen tells her husband. "I've been counting the kids who're left, and I've come up with seven babies, nine toddlers, and fourteen children old enough to run on their own. We could…"

Liam grunts, shakes his head furiously. His injuries garble his words, but she can make them out. "Uhnee too ands." *Only two hands.*

"Four," she corrects, holding up her own.

His eyes are anguished. "Ow do choose hu lih?" *How do we choose who lives?*

"We can't. We can only grab the babies we can reach and put them in our backpacks. I'll put Jamie in yours, and I'll put Oriana's new baby in mine. I can carry at least one more, maybe two, if they're really small. The older kids can help, so I'll get extra backpacks for them." Helen's bruised face turns bitter. "At least now I know where Abraham stashed everyone's stuff."

She looks down at her daughter. At only four, Christina is too young to carry a baby, but she can run, oh, can she run. Helen has never seen a child so swift. Christina can help lead the toddlers to safety.

"In?" Liam asks. *When?*

"Tonight, after everyone is in bed. They're drugged out of their minds now and they'll be sleeping it off.

"Un air?" *Run where?*

"Remember that logging road we saw just before we pulled in here? I'm pretty sure it ends at the ranger station, and they'll have guns and radios and stuff."

They wait until the bonfire burns down before beginning to round up the children, but it doesn't go the way they hoped. Snatching the infants is easy since their parents are more unconscious than sleeping, but several of the toddlers resist when they try to pull them away from the drugged adults. So Helen and Liam leave them. Most of the other children are old enough to be afraid of the dark; they refuse, too.

By Helen's new count, they have twenty-one children, including Christina and Jamie, to usher through the woods to the ranger station. Twenty-one lives to save.

They set off into the dark.

But less than ten minutes away from camp a toddler trips over something and begins to wail. Up until then the night has been silent, broken only by nature sounds: wind whispering through the pines, coyotes' yips, owls flapping toward their prey. With the toddler's fall—her name is Louisa, and she is five months short of four—the silence is broken. As if Louisa's pain is contagious, the other children join in, and the soft night comes alive with wails.

Chapter Eleven

The drive from EarthWay to Scottsdale took longer than planned because DPS had shut down the Beeline seven miles north of Shea Boulevard. Probably another wreck. The Beeline was notorious for pileups on hard-drinking weekends. Whatever the cause, I found myself in a line of cars detoured onto a barely there gravel road.

I was still muttering in frustration when I dropped off the produce and water samples at Rudy Foreman's lab. An old friend of mine from my days at Arizona State University, Rudy headed up GESKO, a company that provided testing for everything from DNA to HIV. Nearsighted and rotund, Rudy was a workaholic who thought days off were for chumps. His only exercise was playing video games, so although the rest of him was at least seventy-five pounds overweight, his fingers and thumbs were in great shape.

"You looking for anything in particular?" he asked, taking the bag of veggies from me. "Oooh, pretty tote!"

"Look for anything that could make people sick. I picked this stuff up at one of those retro-hippie communes north of here."

He eyed the Coke bottle and vials. "Raw water?"

"The bottle's from an artisan well, the vials from a nearby creek."

"The veggies?"

"Watered from the well. Or the creek. Maybe both."

His round face split into a grin. "Oh, this is gonna be fun!"

Jimmy loved his new quilt, and took it into the Airstream while I checked to see how the building was coming along. Wolf and the teens had already finished installing two bathroom sinks and two commodes. In keeping with the times, the kitchen, which they were currently working on, was a galley-type overlooking the living room/dining room combination. The space was large enough that we could even invite the horses over for dinner.

"The cats love the quilt, too," Jimmy said, returning from remaking the bed. "Come to think of it, in two weeks, three at most, we can start moving the rest of your stuff over to the new house."

"That's, um, great." A dull ache throbbed behind my eyes.

The headaches had begun when Jimmy asked me to move in with him, saying there was no point in all this driving back and forth from the Rez to Scottsdale, from Scottsdale to the Rez. Ever budget-conscious, he'd pointed out that given current rental rates, renting out my apartment above Desert Investigations could bring me a tidy profit. A couple of Excedrin had made that first headache disappear, but since then, every time the subject of me moving everything came up, another headache rolled in.

"My apartment's a disaster area. Snowball ripped the living room drapes and shower curtains to shreds, and…" Tsk-tsking, I shook my head. "I can't see anyone renting such a shambles."

"All fixable."

"It'll take weeks."

"Two days at the most, you pessimist. I'll help." He flexed his impressive biceps. "Get some use out of these things."

My headache, worsened by all the banging and clanging, intensified. "Do we have any Excedrin left?"

"You took the last one yesterday."

I inwardly cursed myself for forgetting to restock, but that's what happens when you have too much to do, and too little time to do it in. "Tell you what. I'll run down to the Walgreen's on McDowell, and once I've dosed myself, I'll stop by the apartment and make a list of whatever needs to be fixed or replaced for possible renters. It won't take long, so I should be back in time for dinner."

I headed for my Jeep, pretending not to see the disappointment on Jimmy's face.

I'd planned on talking to Sharona, but when I drove by, I saw that her art gallery hadn't opened. No matter, I could catch her tomorrow. In a way I was relieved the gallery was closed, because now I could concentrate on packing. My headache went away the minute I entered my apartment above Desert Investigations. It could have been due to the efficacy of Excedrin or my relief at returning to the three small rooms that had served as my home for the past decade. Like most former foster kids, I didn't handle change well, even when the change was for the better.

Snowball had left his imprint on the place, however.

As I'd explained to Jimmy, the beige living room drapes hung in shreds, and the sunlight poured through painted piebald splashes of gold on the off-white walls. Shaking my head, I took the ruined drapes down and stuffed them into a black garbage bag. Across the Navajo-print sofa, white stuffing oozed out of several throw pillows, spilling onto the beige carpet, making it look like a cotton crop ready for harvest. The cotton crop joined the drapes.

By some miracle, Snowball had spared the black satin pillow embroidered with the words, WELCOME TO THE PHILIP-PINES. I'd stolen it from one of my nicer foster families so I could have something to remember them by. Smiling, I picked up the pillow, gave it a brief hug, then gently put it back on the sofa.

The bedroom appeared untouched. My Roy Rogers and Trigger bedspread remained pristine, as did the spare Lone Ranger and Tonto coverlet. Snowball hadn't knocked over my chartreuse ceramic horsehead lamp, either, and when I flipped the wall switch, creamy light illuminated the room. But on the floor I found another of the cat's victims: a Hopi clown Kachina doll he'd drug in from the living room windowsill. Snowball had chewed off its head.

Sighing, I picked up the doll and threw it into a black garbage bag. Then, remembering that Wolf Ramirez knew how to fix damaged Kachinas, I hauled it back out, wrapped it in a clean tee-shirt, and stuffed it into my tote. Returning to the living room I decided that the damage wasn't all that bad. An otherwise neat little kitty, Snowball had faithfully used the kitty litter boxes, as had his mother and siblings. And since I, just as faithfully, had cleaned out the boxes as soon as they were used, the apartment didn't smell too gamey.

Still, I opened the windows and let the cool October air rush in. To the west I saw a bank of storm clouds rolling in from California. Realizing that it might rain by sundown and that I had left my Jeep uncovered, I hurried up my inventory, and within minutes, a job I'd thought would take at least an hour was finished. All I needed to do now was replace some curtains, then pack up my clothes and other personal items. Once that was finished, I would hire Merry Maids for a deep clean, but my part was done.

As was my life here.

I was ready to head for my Jeep when I noticed the cardboard banker's box of childhood memories I'd temporarily shoved under the coffee table.

Oh.

Sitting down on the sofa, I took a deep breath. It would be wiser to throw the damned thing away, but fueled by the magnetism of the forbidden, I opened the box with none-too-steady hands. When I moved the packing tissues aside I could see that everything was still there. The police photo of my bloodied blue dress, a child's size four, and the age-yellowed newspapers with the horrific headlines.

CHILD SHOT IN HEAD REMAINS UNIDENTIFIED

SHOT CHILD AWAKENS FROM COMA

SHOT CHILD RELEASED TO CPS

Five years afterwards, another headline:

CHILD STABS FOSTER FATHER
WITH KITCHEN KNIFE

The week after that:

FOSTER FATHER CHARGED WITH
SERIAL CHILD ABUSE

I'd also saved the newspapers that covered every day of the
trial, until midway through, Brian Wykoff, the foster father from
Hell, had suddenly pled guilty to multiple child rapes. I had
been his last victim until I'd stopped him with the now-famous
kitchen knife.

I didn't bother looking at the more recent newspaper clippings
announcing Papa Brian's grisly murder earlier this year. The less
I thought about that, the better off I'd be.

In the midst of repacking the box, my cell phone rang.
Detective Sylvie Perrins, Scottsdale Police. "You watching the
six o'clock news?" she asked, puffing like she'd been running.

"No. Why?"

"Yamaguchi's covering something you might find interesting.
By the way, you were right about that dead artist's mother. When
we delivered the news, she didn't bat an eye. Talk about a stone
cold bitch."

Empty air.

Turning on the TV, I saw a swooping helicopter shot of a
miles-long traffic jam on the Beeline Highway, the same one
I'd been caught in while returning from EarthWay. Since Sylvie
wasn't given to casual TV programming advice, I kept watching
until the helicopter veered away from the highway and followed
along a low ridge to a spot where at least a dozen DPS cruisers

and a crime scene van were parked near a crime scene tent. The feed then switched to a close-up of newswoman Polly Yamaguchi. A fierce wind blew her long black hair around while she stood in front of a DPS vehicle.

"I'm here at the scene of yet another mysterious death," she yelled into her mike. "A couple hours ago, a trooper from the Department of Public Safety discovered a body lying a few yards off the Beeline Highway. One of my sources claims that the condition of the body is similar to the bodies of the two women found earlier this week. Caucasian, emaciated, no immediate signs of violence. The only difference is that this victim—if 'victim' is what we're talking about here—is a male in his late twenties or early thirties. This is Polly Yamaguchi, with 'Eye on the Valley,' reporting to you live from the Beeline Highway, just a few miles north of the Pima Indian Reservation. We will have updates at ten, so stay tuned."

That made three emaciated bodies in one week, each found near or in the northern end of the Rez. Artist Megan Unruh, found under a tree near a business park, and the still-unidentified Reservation Woman I'd discovered during my morning ride. I looked over at the banker's box, which held the photo of a dress the same color as hers.

Reservation Woman and I had something else in common: I had never been identified, either. Thirty-five years after I'd been found comatose on a Phoenix street, I still didn't know my real name. I didn't want that to happen to her. I wanted to give Reservation Woman a name and a decent place to rest, even if I had to pay for it out of my own pocket.

Picking up my cell, I punched in Rudy Foreman's number at GESKO.

"Put a rush on those tests," I told him.

"There's a double sci-fi feature tonight at Harkins Valley Art, and I've planned to…"

"I'll pay double."

"Make it triple."

"Rudy."

A brief silence, then, "Hell, I've already seen them both dozens of times."

Chapter Twelve

Jimmy and I had long ago noticed that Mondays were always Desert Investigations' busiest days because of the weekend's general lack of structure. Friday nights, Saturdays, and Sundays, drunks indulged in barroom brawls; ex-husbands hung around their former wives' homes, making threats; and teens shop-lifted from Target. The bill for all this mischief came due every Monday, when some people rethought their messy lives and simply vanished.

After fielding a host of calls about missing mothers, fathers, and teens, I took a break by turning on the office TV to watch U.S. Senatorial Candidate Juliana Thorsson deliver a rousing speech at the Scottsdale City Council's annual prayer breakfast. Ignoring Jimmy's cynical laughter, I listened to her promise prosperity for all, an end to sexual trafficking, and a return to the religion of your choice—as long as it was Christianity, I thought. Juliana lied even better than I did.

To the uninformed viewer, Juliana looked great, with her sleek blond hair and skillfully made-up face. But when the camera zoomed in on her, I could see shadows underneath her blue eyes and deep lines bracketing her mouth. She and I had spent half of Sunday night searching more of Ali's and Kyle's former hangouts, always coming up empty. The kids had even had the good sense to leave their cell phones behind so they couldn't be tracked.

There being nothing I could do about them for the present, I listened to Juliana's speech all the way through, turning the TV off only when the council members rose as one in loud applause.

People can be so gullible.

"I don't see how you can listen to that," Jimmy said, a scowl on his normally pleasant face. Like most Indians, he disliked politicians, regardless of which side of the political fence they were on. Politicians had never served his people well.

"I used to be a cop," I reminded him, "and thus have a high tolerance for bullshit."

"At least you're not as bad as your pal Sylvie."

"Cynics like her are just brokenhearted idealists."

The phone rang. Juliana's private number.

"Everybody done praying?" I asked.

"Damned if I know. I'm calling from a ladies' room stall. You hear anything about the kids?"

"Nope."

"No update from the cops?"

"Nope."

She made a noise that sounded somewhere between a cough and a sob. "At noon I'll be over in Phoenix speaking at Victims of Violence, and after that maybe we could drive around some more. We might get lucky and spot them."

I looked at the clock—it was eight forty-five a.m.—and did some quick math. "It's only been ten hours since we cased the neighborhood for them."

"Nothing wrong with double-checking."

Remembering those receipts for camping gear, I knew that sticking close to their old stamping ground would not be fruitful, but worry makes even the smartest among us lose our minds. I could have parroted the standard platitudes—the authorities are on it, the kids are smart enough to keep safe, they'd eventually come home on their own—but I didn't. Regardless of our differences, Juliana was a friend, and you don't desert your friends just because they've gone crazy.

"See you when you get here," I sighed, hanging up.

From across the room, Jimmy called, "Sucker!"

"You heard that conversation?"

"They could probably hear her in Tucson. Guess this means you'll be late for dinner again."

I gave him a don't-judge-me-just-pity-me look. "Guess so."

He grunted, whether from irritation or sympathy, I couldn't tell.

At ten, Rudy Foreman called with the results on EarthWay's produce and water.

"Haven't seen so much coliform bacteria since 2010, when I was a volunteer in Haiti after Hurricane Matthew," he said before rolling out of list of the creepy-crawlies he'd found in the samples. "The well water wasn't too bad, if you discount its high arsenic levels and a scattering of *cryptosporidium parvum*, but the creek water is a veritable nightmare of *giardia lamblia*. Some animal's been shitting in that creek." He paused. "Or died in it."

"Translate what you just told me into English."

"Arsenic and *cryptosporidium*, bad. *Giardia lamblia*, worse. The giardia might not kill you unless you're very old or very young or have a compromised immune system, but it'll give you the runs, maybe even Hep A. Talk about a sure-fire diet aid. One more thing. Judging from the amount of giardia I found floating around in the veggies you brought in, those 'raw water' idiots must have been using the creek water to irrigate their gardens, and since they practice 'raw food,' too..."

"The giardia wouldn't be boiled away." I remembered Sunflower's red-headed baby and the too-thin children I'd seen at EarthWay. "Can tainted water be transferable by nursing?"

"If Mommy has bugs, baby will, too. Look, Lena, this needs to be reported to the Arizona Department of Environmental Quality, and if kids are involved, as you say they are, probably to the Department of Child Safety, too."

He promised to email the results to me within the next few

minutes, and was as good as his word. An hour later I was finally off the phone with ADEQ and DCS. Environmental Quality promised to send a team out to test the water, and Child Safety mumbled something about getting a social worker up as soon as possible. Like all government agencies, the resources of both were stretched ridiculously thin. Child Safety, for instance, received upwards of a thousand reported cases of child abuse *per week*, and because of budget cuts, didn't have enough caseworkers available to investigate them all. It was my guess that on the child abuse scale—yes, there was one—giardia poisoning didn't rate as highly as broken bones.

With growing concern, I placed a call to Pete Ventarro at the Medical Examiner's office.

"Make it quick," he said. "We just received two more uniden-tifieds."

"Megan Unruh and that other underweight unidentified female from last week. Were either of them afflicted with *giardia lamblia* or its friends?"

"I love it when you talk dirty to me."

"Quit screwing around, Pete."

"You're no fun. Okay, since you asked so sweetly, the answer's no and yes. The Unruh woman, no giardi. Barring the effects of a little decomp, her blood was clean as the proverbial whistle. But that unidentified from the Rez, different story. She was crawling with giardia and a whole bunch of other microscopic creepy-crawlies. The woman must have been drinking from a sewer."

"Why didn't you tell me?"

"Because you asked me for the cause of death, that's why. Cause of death was a coronary…"

I cut him off. "Caused by malnutrition."

"Exactly. What's this all about?"

"Don't know yet. But thanks."

After hanging up, I sat there for a few minutes, staring out the window, trying to put things together. Both Megan Unruh and Reservation Woman had died from malnutrition-related coronaries, but only one of them bore the signs of a possible visit to EarthWay or another place like it. While I was watching several tote bag-laden tourists exit Gilbert Ortega's Indian jewelry store, I noticed Sharona Gavalan walk by on the way to her art gallery.

Time to be the bearer of bad tidings.

When Juliana showed up at Desert Investigations a few minutes after eleven, I was still shaken over the way Sharona had taken the news about Megan. She'd become so pale that one of her customers, a lean whippet of a man with a New Jersey accent, asked if he should call 9-1-1. Hearing that, Sharona recovered enough to shoo out the customers before shutting down the gallery for the day.

"What's wrong!?" Juliana shrieked, the minute she saw me. "You hear something bad about the kids!?"

I shook my head. "Calm yourself. I just came back from delivering bad news to somebody. As it turns out, she and another person might have had a closer relationship than I'd believed, so I'm not feeling super-confident about my judgment right now."

"Join the club," she said, bitterly.

This time Juliana insisted we ignore Ali's and Kyle's regular haunts and hit the parking lots of local wilderness areas: South Mountain, McDowell Mountain Regional Park, McDowell Sonoran Preserve, and all entrances to the Superstitions. It turned out to be a waste of time because we found no eight-year-old white Hyundais with the right license plates. Of course, license plates can be changed, so when we were at the Superstitions' Peralta Trailhead lot and I spotted a car resembling the Etheridges' beat-up sedan, I peered through the window, only to see the passenger's seat filled with textbooks on urban design. Then I noticed a dust-covered ASU sticker on the window.

A little after four, we gave up, and joined the rush hour traffic on Highway 60.

"Well, it was worth a try," Juliana said.

"Hmmm."

"They could have been camping out in any one of those places."

"Hmmm."

"You think I'm a fool, don't you?"

"I never said that."

"You know what I found out Ali's friends call me?"

"I'm afraid to ask."

"They call me the 'egg mom.'"

I winced, only partially because a chromed-up Chevy Silverado swerved in front of me, causing me to slam on the Jeep's brakes. "I thought you didn't know."

"Ali was angry with me when I cut her TV time down to an hour, so in retaliation she told me that's what the kids were saying. How do you think it makes me feel?"

"Not great, I imagine."

"But they call the other one her birth mother."

"Technically, that's correct. And at least it isn't 'Vagina Mother.'"

But my attempt at a joke failed.

"I can't seem to do anything right," Juliana mourned.

I wasn't about to let that pass. "*This*, from the Honorable Juliana Thorsson, rising political star with two terms as a U.S. Congresswoman, currently the Republican candidate for the U.S. Senate?"

"Probably *failed* Republican candidate for the U.S. Senate," she muttered, looking out at the traffic.

"Your kid runs away so now everything in your life is a failure, even your career? C'mon, you know better than that, Juliana. You've accomplished amazing things. Medaled in the Olympics, won…" I rolled out a long list of her achievements over the years, but she was too mired in her full-on guilt trip to pay attention.

"I should have been nicer to her," she moaned. "Let her invite her friends over more often. Let her watch all the TV she wanted. I was so strict I drove her away."

"If you hadn't been strict, she would still have run off with Kyle, maybe even sooner. Teenagers…"

"I probably shouldn't have gotten involved in the IVF program to begin with."

I wasn't about to let that one go by. Steering my way through traffic over to the freeway's emergency lane, I stopped the Jeep and faced her. "If you hadn't donated your eggs, there wouldn't be any Ali at all. Is that the kind of world you'd prefer?"

Juliana stared back at me in shock. "Of course not!"

"Well, then?"

She looked out the window again, where a jackrabbit was hopping along the cement berm, a death wish, if there ever was one. "Am I ever going to stop feeling guilty about everything I do or don't do?"

"No. You're a mother."

Chapter Thirteen

Jimmy was still in the office when I made it back to Desert Investigations. Because of the afternoon sun streaming through the plate-glass window, his black hair was streaked with gold. God, he looked good. He smelled good, too, having taken time out for a visit to the gym, and a quick shower afterwards.

"From the expression on your face I take it you didn't find the kids."

"No, and I didn't expect to." I sat down and plopped my tote on the floor by my desk, savoring the comforting clunk of my .38. "They have more sense than to pitch their tent anywhere near Scottsdale, but Juliana wouldn't listen."

"Better be careful with her. Politicians have a way of using you, then dropping you."

"Tell me something I don't know. However, Ali's my god-daughter, so I'm stuck."

"Myself, I think they're headed for the border."

"I've heard rumors to that effect, and have been in touch with officials on both sides. No sightings."

"Kids can be sneaky, so don't rule it out. Onto other matters…I spent much of the afternoon researching those people at EarthWay, like you wanted, and I came up with some troubling stuff."

"More troubling than contaminated water?"

"I'll let you be the judge of that." He gestured toward my computer. "We were low on toner so I emailed you the files."

It seemed to take forever for my computer to warm up, time enough to remember that we were overdue for a new system. What with everything that had been going on—the new house, Ali, Chelsea, Megan Unruh, and the other emaciated body—we just hadn't gotten around to updating yet. When the computer finally came alive, I saw that Jimmy's handiwork took up more than twelve hundred KBs of info.

"What is this, *War and Peace*?"

"You wanted everything I could find, so there it is. Turns out EarthWay has been around for a while, operating in different places under different names, but always with the same…ah, leader."

"Mother Eve."

"You mean Priscilla Marie Heywood Stahl, oldest of the twelve Heywood children of White Bear, Minnesota; also known as Mother Priscilla in Madison, Wisconsin; inmate number 4768329 at Taycheedah Correctional Institution in Fond du Lac, Wisconsin; Mother Marie in Deer Lick, Kentucky; Mother Priscilla in Marengo, Indiana; Mother Elaine in Sparks, Nevada…"

My eyes wanted to bug out, but I don't like Jimmy to see me surprised by human villainy, so I shut them and took a deep breath.

Not noticing, he continued, "And most recently, Mother Eve of Orange Valley, Arizona."

A dull throb began above my right eye. "Just hit me with the highlights."

"Then here goes. Priscilla Heywood comes came from a long line of grifters, and when her parents died in a trailer fire—that's what all fourteen of them were living in—she took up the reins. One of the family's scams, taking 'advance money' to build new roofs that were never built, landed her a three-year stretch in Taycheedah. Upon release, she cut ties with her family and married Robert Stahl, who'd become one of her pen pals while she was serving time. For five years she stayed out of trouble, but then, oops, she allegedly tried to kill her husband via rat poison. She claimed it was an accident, and thanks to a lone jury hold-out, a male overwhelmed by her sincerity and then-beauty, she emerged from court with a Not Guilty verdict. She vanishes off the radar for a while, then reappears in Deer Lick, Kentucky, as Mother Marie, beloved organizer of People of the Earth, a small commune back in the piney woods. The commune went bust, as they so often do, and she next emerges in Marengo, Indiana, as Mother Priscilla, leader of yet another commune. This one developed serious problems when she forced stringent 'health practices' upon her followers, such as no meds of any kind for any illness, no ER or other hospital visits, home births for all, etcetera, etcetera. The commune shut down after a fatal breech birth, followed by a man dying of sepsis from untreated cuts and abrasions received while attempting to work a rocky field with a wooden plowshare."

"Any arrests out of that one?"

"Just lawsuits by the dead folks' parents. After the dust settled, she took off to Sparks, Nevada, where she changed her name to Mother Elaine and ran another failed commune. Now here she is, in the great state of Arizona, shepherding yet another flock, and preaching the fabuloso health benefits of raw food and raw water. Oh. One other thing I should have mentioned. 'Mother Eve' has no medical training. She lasted a year and a half at community college, and that's it. But..." He raised a forefinger and smiled. "...she does have a high six-figure bank account in her own legal name, mostly in long-term CDs. And where did she get the money? From the usual sources. Before being accepted as members of her communes, her followers must turn over any property they happened to have—inheritance, houses, cars, trailers, whatever—and she immediately liquidates it. Some of her followers have jobs, and they obediently turn their earnings over to her, too. Don't ask how I found that out, 'cause then you'll be an accomplice."

It would be easy to say that Mother Eve's gullible followers deserved to be fleeced, but I kept picturing sweet Sunflower and her red-headed baby. They didn't deserve to be the victims of a scam artist, but my head hurt too much to worry about that now. Question: What's the difference between a commune led by a grifter, and a cult? Answer: Damned if I know. The Branch Davidians in Waco, Texas, had started out as a peaceful, back-to-the-land religious commune, but ten years later they'd earned the cult designation with the fiery deaths of almost eighty men, women, and children who died proclaiming Koresh the Son of God.

I stared at the wall for a while, then asked, "What's for dinner?"

"Meaning you want to stop thinking about Mother Eve for a while. Okay, barbeque."

My gorge rose. "Maybe I'll pick up a salad on the way home."

Jimmy's face pantomimed shock. "Did you hear that, world? Lena Jones just turned down barbequed ribs."

My cell phone played a blues guitar riff, sparing me from reacting. It was Sylvie.

"We just got an ID on that Beeline Highway corpse, the male, if you're interested."

"Lay it on me."

"Ford J. Laumenthal, age twenty-six. Last known residence, Casper, Wyoming."

"He had a record then." Once a felon's in the system, his prints, blood type, and now even his DNA stay in the system, which makes ID-ing criminals a breeze.

"Nope, no record. Turns out he was wearing one of those medical alert bracelets. Type 2 diabetic. We've already contacted what's left of his family—early death by diabetes seems to be a problem with them—and his father's flying in tomorrow morning for the formal ID. Appears our Mr. Laumenthal was married, wife's name is Arlene or Darlene or Lurleene or something like that. The father can't be sure because he never met her or saw a picture of her. Apparently, Mr. Laumenthal and his son haven't spoken in something like eight years since he took off from home. The mother's dead, committed suicide not long after sonny boy left. Don't you just love these happy families?"

"They make my life worth living." I thought of Reservation Woman's vacant eyes, her spindly limbs, her sad blue dress. She'd been in her twenties, the right age to be married to Ford J. Laumenthal.

"Polly Yamaguchi said the Ford guy was emaciated, just like Megan Unruh and the woman I found on the Rez."

"Polly told you? That bitch! One of these days..."

"Sylvie. Answer me. Was Laumenthal emaciated?"

A tired sigh. "Poor guy was nothing but skin and bones."

Hours later we were sitting around the fire pit near Jimmy's trailer. The Rez having worked its magic, I had passed on the salad and was licking barbeque sauce off my fingers when my cell rang again.

"Your friend Chelsea is no more with us!" The coyotes yipping in the brush couldn't disguise the anxiety in Gabrielle's voice. It made her French accent stronger than ever. "A group of us, we drive to Tucson to view double films at the CinePlex, and between those she has excused herself to buy the popcorn. She never returned."

I put it on speaker so Jimmy could hear. "Did you mount a search?" A stupid question, but necessary.

"We have looked everywhere, *mon amie*. The theater, the restroom of the men, the mall, the streets, but she is but nowhere."

"Did you call the police?"

"The *gendarme* I spoke with said to me that since Chelsea is of age, they do not worry about adult people with such a short time missing, but they will be on the...the..."

"Lookout?"

"*Oui*, on the lookout. He said if she does not come back to us by tomorrow, to call them again and then they will do serious worry."

Serious worry. I threw a look at Jimmy. A neater eater than myself, he was cleaning his fingers off with a napkin, only partially listening to the conversation. "Have you contacted Harold Slow Horse?"

At the mention of his friend's name, Jimmy looked up.

A brief silence from Gabrielle as she took a breath. "We at Kanati have experienced problems with Mr. Slow Horse and we hoped that you would..."

"That I'd do your dirty work."

"*Oui*. Ah, yes. And I am sorry of this."

Not half as sorry as I was. Chelsea Cooper-Slow Horse had always been a wrecking ball of a woman. Chaos followed her everywhere she went. It followed her to the fancy school her father sent her to but which threw her out even before the first term was up, then followed her when she'd started her own jewelry line and wound up dealing in hot jewelry, and then had moved in with her when she'd discovered the joys of oxycodone. Just when I'd thought she was at least safe among the lousy potters of Kanati, here she was in trouble again. But maybe, just maybe, this time it wasn't her fault.

"Did she have her purse and phone with her?"

"*Certainement.*"

"Yet she hasn't called to tell you she's okay?"

"*Non*. We are worried, *mon amie*. Adam especially, who has grown quite fond of her, as have we all."

"Okay, I'll call the ex-husband, and let him know. I'll call her father, too, and her friends. Then I'll get back to you. In the meantime, relax, if you can."

After an assurance that she would "*je vaix me relaxer*," she ended the call.

"That didn't sound good," Jimmy said. "I hope it's just Chelsea being Chelsea."

Jimmy was concerned for Chelsea's safety, but I was more concerned for Harold's. Chelsea's disappearance from a planned trip to a movie theater had "cult extraction" written all over it. My suspicions deepened when Harold didn't answer his phone. Clint Moran didn't answer his, either. I wanted to be wrong, but what was the alternative? Chelsea kidnapped by a stranger? At least Moran had never raped or killed anyone—not that I'd heard, anyway—so if he had her, she was more or less safe. However, if he had her, she was about to be subjected to a form of deprogramming that sometimes included electroshock therapy.

After sharing my own fears with Jimmy, I cleaned the remaining smears of barbeque sauce off my face and got to my feet. "I'm driving over to Harold's."

Jimmy stood up, too. "Not alone, you're not."

"You think big bad Clint Moran can take me?"

He snorted. "Not even in his younger days. But I do think big bad Clint Moran won't be there, and neither will Harold. I plan on being with you when you go off on your next wild-ass search. I'm tired of being left behind."

Since Jimmy had never complained about my solo investigations before, I had thought he was content with his computers. Things appeared to be changing, but why? Surely not because I was living with him in his Airstream rather than in my own apartment.

"Are you sure coming with me is a good idea?"

"It probably isn't, but I'm doing it anyway."

That sounded so much like my own way of thinking I had to laugh. Maybe we were both changing. "Then saddle up, Pardner. We're going for a ride."

When Jimmy's pickup rolled onto Harold Slow Horse's property, the centerpiece of which was a three-bedroom adobe bungalow similar to the one Jimmy and I were building, Doofus, his yellow Lab trotted out to greet us. Behind Doofus came Barry

Tuukwi, Harold's fifty-something Hopi/Pima neighbor. He was brandishing a toilet plunger.

"Harold asked me if I'd fix his toilet while he was gone."

"He needs a new toilet, not the old one fixed," Jimmy said.

"You know Harold. He'd rather fix old stuff than buy something new and shiny, says older things have more character." He glanced at me. "*Ya ta hay*, Lena."

"*Ya ta hay*, Barry."

"It's a pretty night, isn't it?"

It never pays to be too direct with Hopis or Pimas; both tribes think it's rude, so I smiled and agreed. "Out here you can see every star in the sky."

Barry smiled. "I've always liked looking up at the stars."

"Me, too," Jimmy said.

"Earth Doctor's walking stick is bright tonight."

I was familiar enough with Pima legend to know that by this, Barry was referring to the Milky Way, which the world's creator had forged by rubbing his walking stick into a pile of glowing ashes, then drawing the ashes in a pattern across the sky.

"'*I have made the stars!*'" Jimmy quoted Earth Doctor's words. "'*Above the earth I threw them. All things above I have made, and placed them to make for my people a glowing highway.*'"

While all this chit chat about stars was nice, I couldn't stand it anymore. "Say, Barry, you wouldn't happen to know where Harold is, would you?"

Barry made a big show out of adjusting his bifocals, then smoothed his hair. Unlike Jimmy, he kept his hair short, which he believed better suited his work environment at Intel, where he'd been an electrical engineer for almost two decades. "Hmm. Where Harold is. That's something to ponder, isn't it?"

I wanted to sound Pima laid-back, but living with Jimmy hadn't relaxed me yet. "But here you are, fixing Harold's plumbing, and probably feeding his animals, right? And you did say he was gone, right?"

Still that serene smile. "Well, his Bronco not being here and all. Harold never lends it to anyone."

"He usually takes Doofus along wherever he goes," I pointed out. "Unless it's Walmart or some other ritzy place."

Barry chuckled politely. "I prefer Costco, myself."

Throughout this, Doofus kept looking back and forth at us, as if watching a tennis match. I felt like I was in one.

"So does Jimmy," I said. "Except for pastries. For those, he goes to AJ's."

Recognizing that this would go on forever, Jimmy said, "Their fruit tarts are killer. Say, Harold's ex-wife has disappeared under mysterious circumstances, and we're concerned."

"That pretty Chelsea?"

"Yeah. Her."

Barry studied the stars again. "Do you think that is a comet? Or a satellite. There are so many satellites in the sky these days, I sometimes have trouble distinguishing one from the other."

"We need to find Harold, Barry." I couldn't keep the edge out of my voice.

"Probably a satellite. At least I think so. Find Harold? Why would you need to find him when it is Chelsea who is missing?"

I was ready to scream, but Jimmy was used to reservation slow-talkers. "Where is he, Barry?"

Barry looked down at Doofus. "Did Harold tell you where he was going, boy? Because he didn't tell me."

Great. Now we were conversing through the dog.

Trying to move things along, I butted in again. "Harold can get in serious trouble if he and Clint Moran took Chelsea," I said. "Kidnapping's against the law. *Federal* law."

The mention of the Feds worked. Barry looked away from Doofus and straight at me. "I didn't know Clint Moran was involved in this, and so I didn't ask Harold anything, not where he was going or who he was going with. When he pulled up at my place in that Ford Bronco of his—nobody else was in there, except for Doofus—he asked if I'd take in his dog and feed his horses while he was gone. And that was it."

"Did he say when he was coming back?"

"Said his trip was open-ended, which is why Doofus is staying at my place. A dog gets lonely. Horses, not so much, because they have each other. Now, if you will excuse me, a stopped-up toilet awaits." Still brandishing the toilet plunger, he walked back into the house.

As we reached Jimmy's truck I recalled a conversation I'd overheard once between Harold and Jimmy, something about an old homestead.

I asked, "Didn't Harold's grandmother—the white one—leave him a place up in Yavapai County?"

"I remember him saying he was thinking of selling it."

"But it might be worth a drive."

He sighed. "Tomorrow, maybe."

"You can hold down the office while I make the trip."

He gave me the look I was beginning to know well. "That's not the way it's going to work, Lena."

Jimmy's memory being even better than mine, the first thing he did the next morning was run Evelyn Wheelright's name through the system, and after some hunting and pecking, discovered that her property, fifteen acres plus cabin, had indeed been transferred to her grandson after her death. Harold remained the legal owner.

"So what are we going to do if they are holding Chelsea prisoner up there?" Jimmy asked, as we drove north on I-17 toward the Prescott Valley turnoff. "Call the authorities? Crash through the front door, guns ablazin'?"

"Much as I'd enjoy that, the whole purpose of this operation is to get Chelsea released without anyone getting hurt."

"I still say we should contact the authorities."

"Did you not hear the 'without anyone getting hurt' part?"

He grunted. "Point taken."

Prescott Valley is little more than an hour's drive from Phoenix, but temperature-wise, at an elevation of five thousand feet, it's another world. When we'd left Scottsdale, the temps had been in the cool-but-comfortable sixties, but up here it was in the forties, and my thin desert blood didn't much like it. Especially not the autumnal wind. After making the turnoff to SR-69, we drove for another few miles, then took a side road that led us past the Fitzmaurice Ruins, a crumbling twenty-seven-room pueblo built by the Patayan people more than a thousand years ago. Evelyn Wheelright's own grandparents had homesteaded on the other side of the ruins, building a two-room cabin to house their family of eight.

Jimmy parked his Toyota at the bottom of the rise that separated the Patayan ruins from the old Wheelright property. After hiking up to the top, we could see down into the narrow valley, and noted that the original cabin had been added on to over the years. It had expanded to at least four rooms, and the big propane tank in the back signaled that it also had heat. Electric lines and a windmill boasted of further improvements. To complete these frilly mod-cons, Harold Slow Horse's Bronco sat in the driveway next to a plain white panel truck, the better to kidnap ex-wives in.

"Now what?" I asked, thankful for the dense brush that hid us from the house.

"I thought you were the one with all the plans."

"And I, you. Guns ablazin', then?" I patted the holster strapped to my thigh.

"This isn't the Wild West and you're not the sheriff."

"You think we're going to have a nice, civilized talk with those idiots?"

He shook his head. "But, granted, it would be nice."

"At least we've got the element of surprise."

Jimmy liked that, so continuing on foot, we circled around to the back of the cabin where a screen door flapped back and forth in the wind. Excellent. That would help cover any noise we might make during our approach to do whatever we were going to do. We weren't worried about Harold, nor about Clint; he was slime, but other than zapping "extracted" cultists with Tasers once in a while, he wasn't particularly violent.

"Now?" I asked.

"I guess so."

"You *guess* so?"

"This wasn't my idea, you know."

"Nobody forced you to come along. Let's go."

We stopped bickering and crept down the hill, making as little noise as possible. Upon reaching the house, Jimmy held the screen door back while I tried the doorknob.

They hadn't even bothered to lock it.

Treading softly, we entered what appeared to be a mud room. It was cluttered with several pairs of well-worn boots and a .32-40 Remington so old it could have been used by the original owners. I hoped Grandpa Remington was the only firearm in the house, but just in case, I drew my .38 Colt. The windows being small, the light was dim as we tiptoed down a short hallway, inhaling a century of dust overlaid with what smelled like bacon. We would have made it all the way into the main room without incident, but Jimmy—not the smallest man in the world—bumped into a clothes tree, knocking it to the ground in a great clatter.

With that, a door on the left side of the hall flew open, revealing Clint Moran brandishing a Taser. "What the hell are you two doing here?"

"Just happened to be in the neighborhood," I said, then kneed him in the balls and kicked the Taser aside.

"Help!" Chelsea's soprano made a fine counterpoint to Clint's basso howls as he writhed on the filthy floor. "Untie me and get me out of here! That man's crazy!"

Leaving Jimmy to deal with the cult extractor, I peeked into a tiny bedroom and saw her duct-taped to a chair. To my surprise, Harold sat duct-taped to a matching chair.

"He *tased* her!" he yelped. "He tased my wife!"

"Ex-wife," she snarled.

I felt like shooting them both, but contented myself by pulling out the knife I'd slipped into my jeans pocket before leaving the Rez. "Shut up, you two. This isn't the time for ex-marital spats."

"Me first!" Chelsea whined, as I sawed on Harold's bonds. He'd appeared the least hysterical, thus the least likely to cause further problems.

"Chelsea, did you not hear me tell you to shut up?"

"But he helped kidnap me!"

"Whine, whine."

Once freed, Harold rushed to his true love's side and fell on his knees. "Oh, baby, I'm so sorry!"

She tried to kick him, but due to her seated position, wasn't able to connect. Meanwhile, scufflings and grunts from the hallway revealed that Clint was recovering. I must not have kneed him hard enough.

"Harold, go help Jimmy," I snapped.

"But my wife…"

"Do it, by God, or I'll tase you myself!"

Muttering, Harold lumbered into the hall and joined the fray.

"If you'd hold still, this would go faster," I told Chelsea, whose constant wriggling threatened to pull the duct tape even tighter.

She obeyed, but not happily. "I've been in this chair for fucking forever. I even *slept* in it!"

The last of the tape finally fell away. "You can get up now."

"Those bastards are gonna pay for this."

"I *said*, you can get up."

She stood, but if I hadn't grabbed her arm, she would have fallen back into the chair. "There you go. Easy. Easy."

Shaking, she leaned against me. "I'm gonna fucking sue!"

Then she began to cry.

Chapter Fourteen

The next day, while at Desert Investigations fielding phone calls from the done-wrong Scottsdale citizenry, I reflected on the night's surprising turn of events.

After calming down, Chelsea had walked back her threat to sue. Not only that, but she also talked us out of calling in the authorities, pointing out that if Clint Moran was arrested, he would assuredly roll over on Harold, and as angry as she was, she didn't want to see her ex-husband behind bars. All she wanted was a ride back to Kanati, which we duly provided. Love was blind, even when it came to felony kidnapping.

"He's going to pull that stunt again, you know," Jimmy said, staring at his computer screen.

"Harold?"

"Oh, Harold's learned his lesson, I think. I meant Clint."

"But he'll have to buy a new Taser." I glanced at Desert Investigation's storeroom door, where Clint's small Taser temporarily resided. "If he does do it again, with luck it'll be somewhere far far away from Maricopa County. He'll have to wait until he heals, of course. That was some whupping you guys gave him."

Jimmy looked down at his sore knuckles. "Just a little love tap."

"You don't know your own strength. Speaking of, how are you coming along on your Kanati research? That place has to cost megabucks to keep going."

"I've hit so many walls I'm suspecting shell companies and Swiss bank accounts."

Since stumping Jimmy was almost impossible, I felt shocked. "Then how about Adam Arneault? You get anything there?"

"Only the usual. Birth, education—he's smarter than the average bear and attended Ecole Polytechnique…"

I broke in. "That's where Gabrielle went to school."

"Probably where they met, then."

If so, why hadn't she mentioned it? The story about the anorexic model may have been heart-wrenching, but it might also have been a convenient lie. "You know, I wonder if…"

The phone rang again and I picked it up. This time the caller was a Paradise Valley woman whose French bulldog had been dognapped and was being held for ransom. Having OD'd on kidnappings for the moment, I referred her to Cohen & Cohen. Stacey Cohen, an old friend of mine, was a retired FBI agent who, with her PI daughter, specialized in those kinds of cases. Their dog-retrieval rate neared one hundred percent.

As the morning passed, more calls rolled in and I put the mystery of Gabrielle's background on the back burner. Two cases sounded promising, but we referred the others. Our caseload was already dangerously full, but that didn't keep me from thinking about Reservation Woman. Who was she, and how did she wind up on the Pima Rez? Those filmy, empty eyes…

Not long after we'd finished lunch, takeout from Hasta El Burrito, I received a call from Pete Ventarro at the Medical Examiner's office. It was almost as if some sixth sense had let Pete know who I'd been thinking about.

"We just got an odd lab report on the guy found up on the Beeline the other day," he said. "You interested?"

I sat up straight. "Damn right I am."

"Our old friend *giardia lamblia* has shown up again, same strain as in that woman you found on the Rez."

"Same cause of death, then? Coronary brought about by extreme malnutrition?"

"Yep."

"Thanks," I whispered, after clearing my throat.

"Lena, you all right?"

"Never better." I hung up.

There are things you can let go, like a kidnap-happy friend, and things you can't, like three dumped bodies within one week, all dead from malnutrition, two of them crawling with the same microorganisms.

It was time to alert Sylvie about EarthWay.

"You shitting me?" she yelped, when I was finished. "Not only is this the craziest damn crap—gee, what a useful noun—I've ever heard, but it'll probably spread to at least three jurisdictions! Lena, why do you have to keep involving me in your messes?"

Still muttering imprecations, she killed the call.

At eleven thirty-eight that night, just as things were getting interesting under Sunflower's Crazy Quilt, Sylvie finally called me back.

"What, you been out jogging under the full moon?" she quipped, rather nastily, I thought.

"Do you know what time it is?"

"Who cares? Re EarthWay, turns out we got lucky with Stu Rizzo, the Hopi County Sheriff. Apparently, his oldest son has a doctorate in molecular chemistry and went to school with Rudy Foreman, your chemist buddy. Seems Rudy has been firing off emails to every bureaucrat in the state about that water, including to the Department of Child Safety. Long story short, having a chemist in the family makes Sheriff Rizzo more aware of certain, ah, problems, and he's been worried about EarthWay for some time. Anyway, collective concern about the EarthWay situation resulted in an emergency court order to take a look-see at the water those kids are drinking. It's going down at six a.m. tomorrow with Sheriff Rizzo, some test-tuber from the Hopi County Health Department, another one from Arizona Department of Environmental Quality, and a social worker for the kids, just in case. Oh, and yours truly."

"How'd you get invited to the party? EarthWay's not in your jurisdiction."

"Because I brought up the fact that one of those parasite-ridden bodies was found in Scottsdale, which is within my jurisdiction. But I'm only going as an observer, thus the reason for my obviously ill-timed call. Since you're the one who originally put two and two together, I'm inviting you along as Observer Number Two."

I sat up in bed, which didn't make Jimmy very happy. "I'll wear my best jeans."

Sunrise wouldn't come until six-thirty, but at six, a thin strip of pale gray spread across the hills on the eastern horizon. Adrenaline pumping, Sylvie and I sat in her personal vehicle, a 2018 black Camaro with red racing stripes, waiting for Sheriff Rizzo and his deputies to move into EarthWay. Two other cars huddled near the cruisers. The writing on one said HOPI COUNTY DEPARTMENT OF CHILD SAFETY; the other, ARIZONA DEPARTMENT OF ENVIRONMENTAL QUALITY.

"God, I love this shit," Sylvie said.

"Hmm."

"You don't sound excited."

"Too many things can go wrong." I couldn't help thinking about David Koresh and the other seventy-five Branch Davidians burning to death at Waco.

"Rizzo's cool, I talked to him earlier. So are his deputies. You must be worried about the social worker's reaction to the kids' bare feet."

She'd meant that as a joke, but as a former foster child, I'd had years-long experience with social workers; job-related meltdowns went with the territory. "I'm more worried about Mother Eve's reaction."

"You mean Priscilla Marie Heywood Stahl, a.k.a. Mother Eve? Have no fear. There's an outstanding warrant on her from

Deer Lick, Kentucky…something about missing church funds. If Arizona can't get big-time dirt on the bitch, we'll ship her back to Kentucky and let them deal."

"Just another reason to worry."

People like Mother Eve were all about control, and when that control was threatened in any way, they could erupt into violence. Besides Koresh, witness also Jim Jones, leader of the People's Temple; Joseph Di Mambro, leader of the Order of the Solar Temple; and Shoko Asahara, leader of Aum Shinrikyo. And then there was Abraham. His voice drifted up from my subconscious: *"Oh, great are the works of the Lord!"* Although I was wearing a jacket, I shivered. I already had pictures of Megan Unruh and Reservation Woman, but thanks to Sylvie, I now also had a photo of Ford Laumenthal's dumped body. Maybe someone at EarthWay could help tie all three together.

At six twenty-five, the cruisers rolled forward, blue and red flashers on, no sirens. The rest of us followed.

EarthWay was just waking up when we drove onto the compound. Several apron-wrapped women were walking to the dining hall while a girl in a long dress scattered ground corn for the chickens. When we exited the cars, they stopped and stared in amazement. Even the chickens stopped pecking long enough to cluck their irritation before returning to their breakfast. I did, however, notice that after giving us a startled look, a couple of bib-overalled men changed direction and disappeared into the forest. Outstanding warrants?

As more people emerged half-dressed from the buildings to see what was going on, a few children began to trickle out. The social worker, a middle-aged black woman with bright red beads on her dreds walked toward them with a big you-can-trust-me smile. Meanwhile, Sheriff Rizzo and his deputies stood by the arsenic-tainted well waiting for whatever trouble might arise. I looked around for Mother Eve, but saw no sign of her. Maybe she was a late sleeper. I hoped so, because that would allow the

ADEQ scientist, a spindly man wearing a neck brace, to take his water samples without being challenged.

No such luck. Just as Neck Brace Man set the valise carrying his collection of vials and bottles on the ground by the well, a voice shouted, *"What do you think you're doing?"* Then a silver-haired woman emerged from the largest house and headed straight for him.

The sheriff and his deputies closed ranks around Neck Brace Man, shielding him from Mother Eve's charge. Calm in the face of her fury, Sheriff Rizzo, a tall, muscular man, brandished the court order. "This gives us the right to take some water samples, Mrs., um, Eve. Then we'll get out of your hair." He didn't mention the social worker, who had already disappeared with the children into one of the other buildings. Sylvie followed, a concerned look on her face. Parents were known to get agitated when their own authority was threatened.

Mother Eve obeyed the sheriff long enough to read the first paragraph of legalese, then ducked around him and made a grab for the Neck Brace Man's valise. With a look of determination, he whisked the valise away from her and clasped it to his chest. "I'm just doing my job, ma'am."

"The fuck you will, fascist!" She lunged at him, hands open wide, claws ready.

"Ma'am…" He tripped and fell on his butt, the valise still clasped tightly to his chest.

Rizzo reached out a hand and grabbed Mother Eve by the wrist. "I'll have none of that!" In a measured voice, he said to a deputy, "Do the honors, Jeff."

Within seconds, Deputy Jeff had Mother Eve handcuffed and sitting in the squad car, as Rizzo helped Neck Brace Man to his feet.

"Neck okay, Dale?"

"More or less," Neck Brace Man muttered over the sound of Mother Eve's screeches. "First that damned Beemer, now the

Wicked Witch of the West. I'm gonna wind up on Worker's Comp." Still muttering, he cranked up a bucket of water out of the well.

Intrigued by the commotion, a small crowd had gathered to watch the action. Among them was Sunflower, the young woman who had sewn my quilt. Today she wore a yellow dress decorated with a cornflower-blue print, and it was unbuttoned down the front to allow her red-headed infant to nurse. The deputies blushed and looked away, but Sheriff Rizzo gave her and the baby a warm smile. I'd heard he was a grandfather.

Upon catching sight of me, Sunflower scowled and walked away. I followed.

"I'm not talking to you," she said, over her shoulder.

"You don't have to talk, just look at some pictures."

She slowed. "Pictures of what? Public hanging?"

"Not what. Who."

She wheeled around to face me, the baby whimpering at her abruptness. "If you think I'm going to rat out my friends just because you bought one of my quilts, you're sadly mistaken."

I waved the photos at her. "These people are dead."

"No one's died in EarthWay."

"One woman was found at the rear of a business park in Scottsdale, another on the Pima Indian Reservation. The man was discovered right off the Beeline Highway not far from here. Has anyone gone missing from EarthWay?"

"No." But her fury had dwindled.

"Anyone leave abruptly?" I was thinking about Mother Eve, her heft, her cold eyes, her swiftness in attacking the ADEQ worker.

"This is the best place I've ever lived." It sounded almost like a plea.

"You get diarrhea often? Does your baby?"

She curled a hand around the infants head, caressed the red hair. "No more than anyone else."

"No more than anyone else in EarthWay, you mean."

"I don't have any other place to go." This last was little more than a whisper.

"Do you have a husband? A boyfriend?"

"He left when I got pregnant. Mother Eve took me in and helped me give birth. She's a good woman. You just don't understand her, you want to think she's doing something wrong, but she isn't. We're all happy here."

"Arsenic-tainted water and all?" I pointed to the abandoned water tower looming over EarthWay. "With some work it could be usable again. But you've got to stop drinking water from that well. It's making you and everyone around here sick."

The scowl returned. "The purest water in the world won't do any good without Mother Eve to run things. She's our rock."

"Let me ask you this, Sunflower. When you and your husband, boyfriend, whatever first moved you here, did any money or property change hands?"

Her blush was enough answer, but she said, "Billy, my former husband, had this house he'd inherited from his grandmother down in Peoria. He signed it over to her."

"I'm certain there were similar instances among the other people here; it's the way she works. I can fix you up with an attorney who handles pro bono cases like this."

"What do you mean 'like this'?"

"Fraud cases. She's done it before, to other people in other states. As soon as she gets whatever amount she's decided to go for, she cashes out and blows town, leaving everyone in the lurch on the land she sold right out from under them. A good attorney could get that house back, or a settlement for its value, and since Arizona's a community property state, half that money would be yours. More, adding in child support, which you're probably not getting."

Her blush deepened. "My life here is based on how many quilts I sell. Most of that money goes to Mother Eve. I don't have anything of my own anymore."

"The others are probably in the same financial position, having turned over everything they owned. But the good thing here is that we didn't give her a chance to sell out yet, so you guys aren't as bad off as some of her past victims. In fact, if you can get some of that property back and pool your resources, you can repair that water tower, then truck in potable water until it's operational. Work together, fix up this entire place, and make it what you people wanted it to be. But for God's sake, stop irrigating your vegetables with water from that creek. It's a hotbed of a bacteria called—" I started to say *giardia lamblia*, but finished with, "It's crawling with some very nasty bugs, bugs that cause diarrhea and worse."

"You think we're stupid, don't you?" She'd caught my hesitation.

"I think you were looking for a better life than the one you had. In our own way, we're all doing the same thing."

A beam from the rising sun struggled through the surrounding pines and caressed Sunflower's hair, making it look like it was on fire. "Let me see those photographs," she said.

I handed over the drawing of Megan Unruh and the photograph of Ford Laumenthal, but after giving them a quick look she said, "Nope. Never saw either of them."

Disappointed, I started to take them back.

"Wait a minute," she said, holding on to the photo. "The group of moles above the guy's eyebrow…" Her face compressed into a worried frown. "It looks like a small turtle. See the oval? It's surrounded by five others, one where the head would be, the others, the legs? I've seen that before. Where…?" She shook her head. "But I've never seen the woman."

Despite her hesitation, I began to feel hopeful. If she could identify Reservation Woman as being a former resident of EarthWay, this case was close to getting solved. "Sunflower, who else have you run across who had a turtle-shaped birthmark?"

She swallowed. "The guy I'm thinking of, his name was Fred-something? No, not Fred, something else starting with an F, I think, but he was really obese, had to weigh close to three hundred pounds. This guy in the picture looks like something out of Buchenwald."

Something else starting with F. As in Ford.

"And how about this woman?" I still had the photograph of Reservation Woman I'd taken the morning I found her. I showed her my phone, enlarging the image with my thumb and forefinger.

She paled. "I…I…"

"Did you ever see the man with the turtle-shaped birthmark with her?"

"What happened to this woman?"

"The same thing that happened to the man and the other woman."

She had to take a deep breath before answering, but even then, her voice trembled. "When…when the turtle guy showed up, he was with a woman, her name was…it was Eileen? Alene? Doreen? Something like that. She was pretty heavy, too, so I don't see how this skinny gal could possibly have been her. Besides, the couple I'm thinking about only stayed with us for a couple of weeks. Then Mother Eve caught him slapping his wife around and threw him out. She told the woman she could stay, but that he had to go because she didn't allow violence in EarthWay, especially not violence against women or children. But the woman—she was totally under his thumb—left with him. That was the last any of us saw them."

"How long ago was this?"

"A year maybe? Yeah. About that long. Billy and I—he called himself Coyote—had been here for several months, and I was getting sick in the mornings. I remember Billy saying he didn't much like the guy, thought he was too bossy. Actually, Billy didn't much like anyone here, especially Mother Eve." She looked down. "But when he split, Mother Eve took care of me."

As if in sympathy, her red-headed infant began crying. Sunflower cooed at it, then flipped out the other breast and walked away.

When I got back to the well area, Sheriff Rizzo was addressing the crowd like an old-time politician on the stump. "What your leader has been telling you about the benefits of 'raw water' is pure bunkum, folks. Why, in Africa, where my son's been working, more than three hundred thousand kids die every year from contaminated water. Three hundred thousand! And more than a million are blinded. Is this what you want for your children? For yourselves?"

There was a great shuffling of feet and more than one incredulous face. Having been thoroughly indoctrinated by Mother Eve, they weren't buying it. But at least ADEQ might save them from their silly selves.

Recognizing their intransigence, Rizzo threw up his hands and escorted Neck Brace Man and his precious valise to his car.

"Well, that was fun, wasn't it?" Sylvie said, as we drove away in her flashy Camaro.

"Oodles. Watching Mother Eve leave in a squad car made my day."

She grinned. "And the social worker didn't have a meltdown after all."

I kept thinking about Sunflower and her baby, and about Ford Laumenthal's emaciated body riddled with *giardia lamblia*. I was almost certain that Reservation Woman was Laumenthal's wife, and that the two had been the couple Sunflower knew at EarthWay. But what had caused their transformation from obese to skeletal? And why had the woman been found on the Pima Rez, and her husband almost sixty miles away?

I filed away my concern about the Laumenthals when I walked into Desert Investigations and found the Honorable Juliana Thorsson waiting for me.

"What took you so long?" Without waiting for an answer, she said, "DPS spotted Ali and Kyle near Nogales last night."

Chapter Fifteen

The U.S./Mexico border city of Nogales, Arizona, is about one hundred and eighty miles south of Desert Investigations, and as luck would have it, there'd been an accident between three semis on I-19, so we had to crawl down one lane at about forty-five miles per hour all the way from Arivaca Junction to Rio Rico. After that, the pace picked up to a nifty sixty, and Juliana and I rolled into the desert-surrounded town almost four and a half hours after we left Scottsdale.

Although divided in half by the ugly border wall, Nogales is a pretty city. Its lush green hills harken back to the days when Americans, Mexicans, and the Tohono O'odham and Yaqui Indians could walk back and forth down International Street from one country to another without being stopped and frisked. These days, because of the border wall, the city was becoming best known for its infuriatingly long traffic backups at the crossing into Nogales, Mexico. Fortunately, we didn't have to head that way, just into the half-empty parking lot at 3030 Grand Avenue, where the Department of Public Safety was located.

Lieutenant Jaffrey, the DPS trooper who'd called in the sighting, had already gone home for the day—he'd spotted the kids' vehicle parked at an all-night McDonald's while working the graveyard shift—but Sergeant Gonzales said that if we wished, he could give him a call.

"Not that he'd be any help, because by the time he got turned around, they'd already left. He never spotted them again, but that's the way it goes, doesn't it?" A gray-haired man obviously nearing retirement, he exuded serenity and was soft-spoken to a fault.

Juliana wasn't. "Which McDonald's?" she snapped.

He hunt-and-pecked a few keys on his computer, making her huff with impatience. Leaning closer, he squinted through his bifocals and read, "The one on Mariposa Road. Not the Super Center."

"Where's that? Mariposa Road?" She was almost shouting.

I tugged at her sleeve. "Calm down. The Jeep's got GPS, remember?"

"I don't trust those things!" she snarled.

Behind her, Gonzales rolled his eyes, but when she turned back to him, his face had resumed its serene expression. "Well, turn left out of the parking lot…"

If you've seen one McDonald's, you've seen them all, but at the Mariposa Road McDonald's, there were more people enjoying Sausage McMuffins than at any Scottsdale McDonald's. In Scottsdale, late-day noshes tended towards breakfast burritos with plenty of hot sauce. After we made it through the serving line, the Yaqui woman behind the counter—her name tag said LILY—told me the shift manager who talked to the DPS trooper last night wouldn't be in until eight that evening, so we'd have to come back then.

"Do you know who waited on the kids?" I asked.

"Jeff. He's not here now, but he was talking to me earlier about how many yogurt parfaits they ordered. They must've had a cooler with them."

Lily started to add something, then noticed Juliana hovering behind me. "Hey, aren't you that woman's running for Senate?"

Oh, great. Juliana wasn't exactly running on the Vlad the

Impaler ticket, but close, which is why I'd told her to stay on the down-low in this Indian-friendly place.

Ignoring my warning, she said, "Yes, I am. And my daughter's missing and I'm scared to death for her. She may have been here with her boyfriend last night."

To which Lily said, "I'm a skeet shooter myself, and I'm tellin' you, you shoulda taken the Gold. The Silver, at the very least."

Her comment wasn't as odd as it seemed. While still in college, Juliana had been on the Olympic Skeet Shooting Team, and had returned home with a Bronze Medal. All these years later, she still enjoyed a loyal following of skeet shooting fans.

Juliana forced a smile. "Thank you. I tried hard for the Gold, but…" She shrugged her elegant shoulders. "You know how it is. Some days you're not your best when it counts the most."

"Don't I know it." Lily looked around, leaned forward over the counter, and whispered, "Try our night manager Maralita Simmons-Naquin. She works part-time at PreLoved, the resale shop next door. She's there right now."

Maralita Simmons-Naquin was not only at work, but when we showed her Ali's and Kyle's pictures, she remembered them. A sixty-something woman whose figure hinted at the enjoyment of too many Big Macs and Sausage McMuffins, her shoulder-length, silver hair was glorious enough to grace the cover of *American Salon*.

"I have grandkids about their age, and I would never allow them to be roaming around that late on a school night," Maralita said, explaining why she'd noticed the two. "We had a new cook working the shift, and he was having problems with the range, or I'd have paid more attention to them, maybe even called the police. They didn't stay long, just ate fast—Big Mac Meals for the both of them—ordered ten yogurt parfaits to go, and then took off. But as to which way they were headed, I couldn't tell you. Maybe the Border, not that they'd ever get across by themselves, being that young."

Therein lay another flaw in the kids' plans. With the tight-ened security at the Border, there was no way the guards would let two obvious runaways without parents or passports to cross into Mexico to fulfill their dream of buying a beachfront adobe hacienda complete with horses. Especially if the runaways didn't even have driver's licenses. Teenagers being teenagers, they hadn't thought that far ahead.

"Did they look okay?" I asked. "Healthy?"

"Oh, they looked fine. More than fine. You don't see kids that beautiful every day."

Her use of the word "beautiful" didn't make me as happy as it should have, because sex traffickers are always on the lookout for good-looking young teens. Before Juliana could think the same thing, I quickly asked another question. "Are there any camping grounds nearby?"

"You mean other than the parking lot at Walmart? Yeah, we've got a ton of them. Why? You think the kids are camping out?"

"It's a possibility."

The list she rattled off was lengthy, including Kino Springs, Patagonia Lake State Park, and the entirety of the Coronado National Forest. Searching for them would take more manpower than we had, and more bearish equipment than my tricked-out Jeep. At times like this I hated Arizonans' predilection for white cars. If the kids had been driving something purple or florescent green, they'd be more easily spotted by helicopter. As it was, from the air they'd be just one more white car amidst thousands.

After learning nothing else, we thanked her and left. We spent the next few hours talking to various local and state police officials, then cruising the streets of Nogales ourselves, but once the sun set and darkness crept across the lovely hills, we had to admit defeat. I needed to be at Desert Investigations first thing in the morning, and Juliana was scheduled to speak at another prayer breakfast. As soon as everyone said "Amen," though, she would return to Nogales on her own.

We were both quiet during the long drive back to Scottsdale, but as we passed another teepee-bedecked souvenir stand, she said, "You know, if I had been stricter with her, this would never have happened."

35 years earlier

The place Helen thought was Eden has turned into Hell.

Deep green forest surrounds the red-spattered bodies, and the pine-scented air is filled with moans from the dying. Liam, oh, beautiful Liam, is mortally wounded.

She hears more shots as the wounded are finished off.

But she can't move. Her arms are frozen, her voice nothing more than a dry whisper, so she can't even plead for their lives. Christina is silent, too, as body after body is tossed into the yawning mine shaft.

"You're a man now. Old enough to do a man's work."

Who said that?

Oh. Yes. Abraham.

He has finished telling the other men what to do, and is speaking to his son, the one Christina calls Golden Boy. And he is golden, he truly is, with his white-blond hair and sharp blue eyes. He looks like a young Apollo, almost as beautiful as…

Liam.

Oh, God. Her Liam.

Wait.

Is that an owl hooting? But how could it be, when the shots and the screams have flushed the birds out of their nests and into the night sky to seek refuge in a place outside of Hell?

No, not an owl.

It's Jaimie. Her baby boy still lives.

Abraham speaks to his son again, using that tone which must be obeyed.

"Finish it, according to God's Holy Word." He hands his rifle to Christina's twelve-year-old husband.

Golden Boy, happy to be accorded a man's status, smiles as he takes his father's rifle.

Shoulders it.

Aims.

Shoots.

Kills her baby boy. Then Liam.

Helen, finding her voice, begins to shriek.

Four-year-old Christina remains silent.

Chapter Sixteen

A half hour into our morning horseback ride across the Pima Rez the next morning, the scar on my temple began to throb. Always fortified against such an occurrence, I slid the packet of Excedrin out of my jeans pocket and gulped one down.

"Another headache?" Jimmy asked, pulling up beside me.

"Same old, same old."

"We can go back, if you want."

"Nah, the horses are having too much fun." No lie there, because my Adila pranced instead of walked, and even Big Boy champed at his bit. Despite my earlier concerns that the two would make poor stable mates, the high spirits of my leopard Appaloosa mare had been good for the stately pinto gelding, lending him a coltish gleam in his eyes.

Me, I felt less prancy. Last night's dream had been a bad one, and it had woken me, I hadn't been able to go back to sleep. So I just lay there awake in Jimmy's arms, fearing the worst for Ali and Kyle. Toward dawn I'd slipped off to sleep for a few minutes, just time enough to dream about the kids being kidnapped by career criminals who were holding them for a million-dollar ransom, and if Juliana didn't pay up, they'd send her a new body part (ear, finger, etc.) until she did. At least I didn't wake screaming from that one, just biting my tongue until it bled.

"I'm worried about Ali," I told Jimmy.

Jimmy reached across from Big Boy and patted my thigh. "Kyle will take care of her, Lena. Like most former foster kids…" He gave me a knowing look. "…that boy's got amazing survival skills."

"Such as riding horses across a Nogales beach?"

"Maybe his sense of geography could bear some improvement, but not his love for her." He smiled.

My Jimmy, always looking on the bright side. I still couldn't figure out why it had taken me so long to love him, why I'd taken so many side roads with so many men. Thank God—who maybe did exist, after all—I'd finally come to my senses.

No new emaciated corpses disturbed our ride today. Instead, a V-shaped gaggle of Canada geese honked above us as they headed for one of Scottsdale's lakes. Not far behind, and flying much more slowly, was a snowy egret, its white wings dazzling in the morning sun. The desert floor teemed with life, too: chuckwallas scurrying about on their lizardy business, a small family of javelinas grunting through the underbrush, and too many jackrabbits to count. At one point, we spotted a bobcat bounding along, carrying a still-wriggling black snake in its mouth.

With such a bounty of wildlife spread out before us, our ride lasted longer than planned. By the time we made it back to the trailer, Wolf Ramirez and his teen apprentices were hard at work. I waved at Wolf, which gave Adila another excuse to buck. It wasn't a serious one, though, and I barely had to shift my weight to stay in the saddle.

"You can do better than that," I said, patting her neck.

She snorted a reply, which I interpreted as, *Just you wait.*

An hour later Jimmy and I were taking phone calls at Desert Investigations.

One of the first was from Sylvie. "Can you believe that bitch was released on bail?"

"What bitch?"

"Priscilla Marie Heywood Stahl! Mother Fucking Eve! Didn't you watch last night's news? Or the morning's?"

I was so shocked, it took me a moment to answer. "I was busy. But how the hell did that happen?"

"She got old Griswold, who everybody knows should have retired from the bench twenty years ago. I'm sure the old fart's got Alzheimer's."

"But what about the outstanding warrant from Kentucky?"

"She told him it was all a mistake and that she would never embezzle money from a house of the Lord. Then she began to pray, and so help me, Griswold wound up praying with her. I'd watch my step if I were you. That woman is stone cold crazy."

Dial tone.

Three emaciated bodies, one—perhaps two—with links to EarthWay. According to the Medical Examiner's timetable, artist Megan Unruh has been the first to die, then Reservation Woman, and several days later, former EarthWay resident, Ford Laumenthal. They had all died the same way: heart attacks caused by extreme malnutrition.

What the hell was going on?

I would probably have stewed about the problem all day, but ten minutes later a phone call from a mother whose sixteen-year-old daughter had disappeared two months earlier put an end to my ruminations. No, Lorraine Gideon confided, she hadn't gone to the police. There'd been "family problems."

"This 'family problem,' Mrs. Gideon. Could you expound on that?"

"I'd rather not."

After years in the PI business, I recognized the hesitation. "Father? Brother? Stepfather? Uncle?"

"I'm divorced. But, ah, Nikki—everybody calls Nicola 'Nikki'—doesn't like my boyfriend."

"He molested her, right?"

"No! That's what she claimed, but she was always making up stuff to get him in trouble."

"What's his side of the story?"

"You mean Mike's? I, uh, I didn't ask."

Same old, same old. A mother more interested in her romantic attachments than in the welfare of her child. I had a pretty good idea how this story would end but hoped I was wrong.

I asked her a few more questions, mainly to get her to relax, then told her to email me the girl's picture. Fifteen minutes later—I guess she had to think about it first—the picture arrived. It revealed an angelic-featured girl who appeared closer to twelve than sixteen. Mike liked them young.

After hitting the speaker command, I signaled Jimmy, then called her back. "Okay, I'll check out the obvious places, then get back to you. But I strongly advise you to call the police and tell them about her daughter's claims against your boyfriend."

"Oh, I couldn't do that."

"Since she's only sixteen, her claim about sexual molestation should be taken seriously, and you should most definitely file a missing child report."

"No, no, I don't want any of this to get out. You know how people talk, and it's not worth getting Mike mad. Hey! I thought whatever you tell a PI was protected information"

"You're confusing us with lawyers."

She said something nasty, then hung up.

"Did you hear all that?" I asked Jimmy.

"And recorded it. Jeez, Lena. Sometimes I hate people."

Stifling my own fury, I sent out a series of emails to a couple dozen likely places, attaching Nicola "Nikki" Gideon's picture. Then I sat back and waited.

It only took ten minutes.

Wayfarer, a South Scottsdale shelter, had been started ten years earlier by ex-prostitute Wendy Janouzek, street name, DeeZee. Very much on the down-low, it catered to teens who had managed to escape from sex traffickers but who weren't yet ready to return home for one reason or another.

To the uneducated eye, Wayfarer looked like a private house, but I'd been here many times before and knew the secrets it held. Two stories high and badly needing a paint job, it sat between an RV storage yard and a doggie daycare center. When I pulled to the curb, a dozen Chihuahuas and Pekes rushed to the fence next door and gave me yips of welcome. I yipped back, which made several of the furballs dance in glee and turn up the volume.

"Please don't do that," DeeZee said, exiting the house. "Those little bastards are annoying enough as it is." She was forty-five, but like most women who'd spent decades working the streets, she looked at least sixty, with brittle, over-bleached hair, worry lines surrounding her eyes and mouth, a sagging jawline, and a chipped front tooth. The flowing caftan she wore completed her Frowsy Grandma chic.

"Point taken, DeeZee. So, what do you think?"

"It's her, all right."

Following her through the front door, I asked, "You file a report yet?"

"She's not ready. Won't even let me phone her mother."

Soon after her mom's new boyfriend moved into the house, Nikki had told DeeZee, he'd begun making less than subtle advances. At first the girl kept it to herself, but one afternoon when her mother was at work, the advances turned into rape. When she told her mother, she got slapped and called a liar. So Nikki ran away, only to wind up with a group of squatters in South Phoenix, one of whom was generous enough to share his heroin with her. Within days, he'd sold her to a trafficker, who then turned around a quick profit via resale. She got lucky when her third owner OD'd, and she was able to flee his apartment before another girl in his stable dialed 9-1-1. By then, Nikki had heard about Wayfarer.

She was sitting in the small dayroom reading a copy of *Better Homes & Gardens* when I walked in. Since she'd only been on the street for two months, she didn't look too bad, just tired.

There was a fading bruise under her left eye, but other than that, she appeared healthy. And, miraculously enough, she still looked innocent.

"Nikki, I'm Lena Jones, a private investigator. Your mother called and asked me to find you."

"That's rich." She didn't bother looking up.

"What are your plans?"

"What do you mean, plans?" Now she looked up.

"You know, after you leave Wayfarer. You can't live here the rest of your life."

"Who says?"

DeeZee, standing next to me, said, "Nikki, we've talked about this."

The girl snorted and turned the page of her magazine. "You're the one who did all the talking."

Annoyance wasn't evident in DeeZee's voice when she said, "As I said, you can stay here as long as you want, but you do need to start building a life. An independent life, one which doesn't include men who promise to rescue you."

"But it's okay if a woman says the same thing?"

"Most times."

The girl looked up. Her eyes were almost as green as mine. "That's sexist."

"Maybe so," I interjected, "but who's helping you right here and now?"

Nikki let the magazine fall into her lap. "What you gonna do, then, narc me off to the cops 'cause I been turning tricks and all? Send me to jail?" She looked like an angry ten-year-old.

"No, because you're the victim here," I told her. "Those guys, they're the criminals. You'd be doing a great service to other girls in your situation if you gave me some names. I have friends in high places…" I was thinking of Sylvie, who always had a hard-on for child traffickers "And they'd love to take those guys down."

"They'd kill me."

"Not from behind bars, they can't. Besides, didn't you go by a street name?"

The green eyes flashed. "Baby Sweetness."

I held my feelings at bay. "The squatter who gave you heroin. What was his name?"

She looked down and mumbled something.

"Sorry, I didn't hear that."

"Just Zach."

"Do you remember the squat's address?"

She mumbled again, but this time I could make it out. The house the squatters were living in was located right off Van Buren, near the Arizona State Hospital. I made a mental note and moved on. It wouldn't do for her to see me writing her answers down or, God forbid, recording them. "How about the name of the first guy who bought you?"

Her eyes dimmed. "Pink Floyd."

"Like the old rock group?"

"Was that a group? They call him that 'cause he had red hair and pink skin."

I made another mental note. "One more thing. I need the name of your last, ah, owner."

The light came back to her eyes. "He called himself Kit Carson, and I hope he was dead by the time the EMTs arrived!"

Once back in my Jeep I let myself shake with rage for a few minutes while the Chihuahuas and Pekes next door whined along in accompaniment. Then I called Sylvie to relate what I'd just heard, said goodbye to the yipping furballs, and headed for Nikki's mother's house. It took a while because she lived in the Paradise Valley hills, and those winding streets are always a bugger.

After a full five minutes of ringing the bell and pounding on the door—Lorraine hadn't answered my phone calls—the door finally opened. The woman standing there was exactly what I'd pictured after driving though the expensive neighborhood.

Tall, fit, auburn hair fashionably streaked with blond highlights, Lorraine Gideon wore an aqua linen pantsuit that probably cost more than Jimmy's Toyota pickup truck. The pantsuit needed to be cleaned, though.

"Who are you and why do you keep banging on my door? Go away before I call the police."

Talk about an empty threat. I gave her my best smile. "I'm Lena Jones, the private investigator you called about Nikki, and I just dropped by to tell you that she is safe and is staying with a friend. And I hate to be rude or anything, but you've got blood all over yourself."

A brief expression of joy crossed her face then faded when she looked down at the red-spattered pantsuit. "I'm, uh, uh, *cooking*. Roast beef. I got, I got this…I got all messy transferring it from the freezer to the stove. I, uh, buy in bulk. You need to go. Like, um, now. I have a lot, um, a lot of things to do, you know?" The longer she talked, the paler her face became.

"Not that I'm a kitchen-know-it-all or anything, Lorraine, but it looks like you must have butchered that cow yourself."

She attempted to shut the door, but I was stronger than she was. Also sneakier. Before she could do anything about it, I'd shoved my way into the entrance hall, from where I could see into a long, dark living room. She had closed the blinds against a perfect Arizona day. The living room wasn't so dark, though, that I couldn't see a man spread-eagled on the oak parquet floor. A glistening puddle surrounded his head.

I looked at her. "That's Mike, I take it."

No answer.

"Gun? Knife? Blunt instrument?"

Lorraine's eyes widened. Even in the dim light I could see they were the same color as her daughter's. "I don't know what you're talking about."

Amateurs often mistake the living for the dead, so I pushed by her and went over to see if Mike still had a pulse. But Mike was dead, all right. A few feet away from him lay a bronze bust of a Lakota warrior. There was a dent in the Indian's nose.

"Want me to call the police?"

"Oh, Jesus, no!" She all but fell on her knees in supplication.

"Then maybe you'd better tell me what happened."

She looked down at the rapidly cooling body. Even in October, she was running the air-conditioning, which in this case was probably a good thing. It would screw with the time of death.

"I...okay, but...I need to sit down. And not...not in here."

Taking her by the arm, I led her in a wide arc around the dead child rapist and into the *Architectural Digest* kitchen. White marble, black granite, money, money, money.

"How about there?" I pointed to a cunning little cabaret set-up nestled into a bay window.

She sat. Looked down at her bloodied pantsuit again. Wrung her hands.

"Tell me," I said, sitting across from her.

Her story had been duplicated on a thousand police reports. After our earlier phone conversation, she had done some hard thinking about good ol' Mike, and came to the belated conclusion that there might be truth in her daughter's claim. This morning she had confronted him, and it hadn't gone well. At first he'd denied Nikki's account, calling the girl a lying tease, but after repeated questioning, he said the "little slut" had "seduced" him.

She slapped him and ordered him out of the house.

He went.

Shaken, she'd opened a bottle of Chivas and poured herself a stiff one. Thought about what she should do next.

The ruminations stopped when Mike came back for his clothes, and the situation, lubricated by a half glass of Chivas, deteriorated.

"He...he threatened to kill me if I called the police."

"You told him you were going to call them?"

She nodded. "I...I think so. It's just that there was a lot of screaming back and forth and I can't remember everything I said. But I'm pretty sure I said that."

"Tell me about the bronze statue in the living room. When did you grab it?"

"After he told me he was going to cut my throat."

"He had a knife?"

"No, but he was on the way into the kitchen, and I thought…"

"So you actually killed him in self-defense!"

"Kind of." She wrung her bloodied hands some more. "But he didn't have the knife yet. He was just on the way to get it."

Her admission complicated things, because cops don't like it when only the perpetrator in a self-defense claim actually has a weapon. Same with judges and juries. "Does Mike have family here locally?" I asked.

"A younger sister. He told me they don't keep in touch."

I could guess why. "He have any friends you know about?"

She brushed her hair back, and in doing so, smeared blood on those expensive highlights. "He was what you'd call a loner."

"Nobody will miss him, then." Least of all, Nikki.

Lorraine tried to smile and failed.

Several years earlier, one of my former clients, a woman who had since become a good friend, had been faced with a problem similar to Lorraine's. I'd helped her solve it, so it was time for her to return the favor.

I picked up my cell and called DeeZee.

Two hours later, all existence of Michael Elias Bungeon—at least that's what his driver's license called him—had vanished from the Gideon residence, thanks to the two men I'd never seen before and would hopefully never see again. The house smelled of Mr. Clean, and Lorraine, having showered and shampooed, smelled like lilacs.

Chapter Seventeen

Emotionally drained from the day's work, I decided to kill three birds with one stone by continuing my research into Kanati's complicated organizational affairs, check on Chelsea's welfare, and at the same time, treat myself to a massage and maybe some French cuisine. So after phoning Jimmy and telling him where I was going, I practiced smiling while I drove out to Kanati to take Gabrielle up on her standing offer. Heck, as rattled as my nerves were, I might even attend the group meditation, the better to check out the mysterious Adam.

In Arizona, October can be an iffy month, and halfway there, it began to rain. Not much, just enough for raindrops to splash a polka dot pattern in the dust on the Jeep's hood. But when I finally arrived at Kanati, I saw that even this little drizzle had driven Ernie under the roof of his little shelter.

"If I'd wanted rain I would have stayed in Seattle," he complained, waving me to the parking lot.

Ernie appeared to be the only one bothered by the rain shower. When I walked through the stockade's gate, I saw several people looking up at the sky, arms outstretched. Chelsea was among them.

"Refreshing, isn't it?" she said, spotting me.

"Kinda. How are you doing?"

"You mean after being kidnapped and held for ransom?"

"No ransom was involved."

"Maybe not, but I'll never speak to Harold again."

I didn't believe her. Chelsea was one of those women who leave, return, leave again, return again. For her, the grass was not always just greener on the other side; once she was there, she decided it had actually been greener in the place she'd left. It was a dizzying way to live, but she needed a therapist to tell her that, not me.

"You never answered my question, Chelsea. How are you doing?"

"How's it look like I'm doing?" She laughed and twirled around in the rain. "I'm happy! Kanati is the place I've been looking for all my life." She stopped mid-whirl. "Hey, are you thinking about joining? Seems like you're here all the time these days."

"I wouldn't call it 'all the time.' Besides, I'm not much of a joiner." *Especially when I'm not sure I'm buying everything they're selling.* Then I noticed she was wearing a headband decorated with one blue bead. "Hey, how'd you get that?"

"Think I stole it?" At my expression, she began to laugh. "Adam said I've been doing so well after what happened that it proves I've moved up to a higher level. I've been *Elevating!*"

I pretended ignorance. "Who's Adam?"

"Only the guy who founded this place! He said I'm making great progress, and he would know."

Whatever was going on with the not-yet-seen Adam, he could have been right. I'd never seen Chelsea look so healthy and care-free, almost as if she was becoming the woman she was meant to be before drugs and neediness derailed her.

"Congratulations on the blue bead," I said, feeling slightly silly to be standing in the rain, congratulating a woman on her fake Indian headdress.

As quickly as the rain had begun, it stopped. Chelsea and the other twirlers kept looking into the sky for a few moments, and when no more rain was forthcoming, dropped their outstretched arms and walked away.

"You staying for dinner?" Chelsea asked, wiping the moisture off her face.

"I'm thinking about it." I wanted another talk with Gabrielle, too.

"Consider yourself invited."

"That's nice of you, but I thought Gabrielle Halberd was the only person who could issue invitations. Or your new friend Adam, of course."

Grinning, Chelsea tapped the blue bead on her headband. "Now that I've got this, I can invite anyone I want."

Power can be a heady thing.

The massage consisted of a half hour's kneading and pounding, but it drove away the memory of Mike Bungeon's untimely end, not that he was any great loss. But the deaths of Reservation Woman, Megan Unruh, and Ford Laumenthal still haunted me. No massage could fix them.

Forcing myself to think of pleasanter things, I joined the rest of the Kanati gang in the big dining hall. Outside, the setting sun had turned the sky orange, purple, and pink, and the light streaming through the lodge's windows spread its golden glow over everyone. Basking in that glow, I helped myself to small servings—no point in overdoing things—of Chicken Basquaise, Salmon Rillettes, Tomatoes Stuffed with Duck Confit, Mushroom Risotto, Potatoes Gratin Dauphinoise, and for desert, Almond Frangipane Tart with Cranberries and Honeyed Pistachios.

Gabrielle, who had seen me come in, steered Chelsea and me to her table. She asked how my day had been.

"I've had a pretty good day," I said, trying to forget about Michael Elias Bungeon's crushed skull.

"When you rushed into OK Corral you looked almost frantic.

Perhaps you should come see us more often. Perhaps even stay and become one of us. There are so many ways a woman with your energy could help around here."

Finally. A direct sales pitch. But it was odd in a way, because Jimmy's continued poking around in Kanati's financial affairs—those that he could get into, anyway—had revealed that most of its members were worth a million bucks up. Surely Gabrielle wasn't under the assumption I had that kind of money. So what made me so special?

Unaware of my suspicions, Chelsea stopped chomping on her Cruisses de Grenouilles long enough to say, "That's exactly what I've been telling Lena. Join Kanati and forget about that crazy world outside!"

Gabrielle gave her a brilliant smile. "It is a wonderful thing for you to encourage your friend so."

Chelsea flushed with pleasure.

Time to break up the love fest. "Gabrielle, I recognize that I don't know a lot about France, especially its educational system, but I was wondering exactly how you met Adam Arneault."

The brilliant smile dimmed somewhat. "As I told you, I was on a spiritual quest."

"You didn't go to school together?"

"Why would you wish to know such a thing?" No smile at all now.

Careful. Careful. "Because you're so intelligent, and I figured Adam would have to be super intelligent in order to conceive of a place like Kanati, so I…" I shrugged. "Don't all smart people in France go to the Ecole Polytechnique?"

"France has many schools for the gifted. But since you are so curious, yes, Adam also attended Ecole Polytechnique, but as he is a few years older than am I, we did not meet there."

"Too bad. It would have saved you years of fruitless searching, wouldn't it?"

She looked relieved. "You are correct, *mon amie*."

Careful to keep a convivial smile on my face, "Like you once said, Gabrielle, life is complicated. Look at my own. I have a business to run, a boyfriend to keep happy, and a house to help build. Not that I'd been doing much of that, lately."

At the mention of Jimmy, Chelsea's face lost its own smile. "Boyfriend? Love is a trap. It makes you do things you wouldn't ordinarily do."

Such as give up drugs, like Harold insisted? I didn't express the thought, because to a certain extent, she was right. Too many women had fallen into the drug life because of a man. But it could work the other way, and men could be fools for love, too.

Gabrielle flashed Chelsea a sympathetic look, then steered the conversation to a happier subject: food.

She and Chelsea were discussing which was the ideal flaming dessert—Cherries Jubilee or Bananas Foster—when I noticed a stir at the other end of the big room. A tall, blond man in his late forties had entered, flanked by two other men wearing headbands so loaded with muli-colored beads they looked top heavy. The blond man wore none; his handsome looks and the stunning Navajo blanket he was wrapped in lent him all the majesty he needed, although he was gaunt to the point of frailty.

The people around us stood up and burst into applause, followed by the chant, "Adam! Adam! Adam!"

Not being one for fawning over authority figures, I remained seated.

Adam raised one arm, the hand palm-up in a receiving gesture. For a moment, his piercing blue eyes met mine. Widened. Then he returned his attention to his flock.

"Dear friends, your good wishes sustain me." His mellifluous voice had no trouble making it all the way to our table at the opposite end of the room. Obviously a practiced orator, he had a slight French accent. "May they continue to do so."

With that, he gave a little bow, then left, still flanked by his top-heavy companions.

"Adam! Adam! Adam!"

The chant kept up long enough to become annoying. So much for Chelsea's comment about love being a trap; if she wasn't in love with the blond man, my name wasn't Lena Jones. As she continued to chant—along with Gabrielle, who I'd earlier believed had more business sense than to be caught up in idol worship—I began to worry. Had Chelsea given up one addiction for another?

It was only when I was driving up the gravel road to Jimmy's Airstream that I realized something. *I'd met Adam Arneault before.*

I just couldn't remember where.

Or when.

Chapter Eighteen

I was alone in the desert, walking toward a whirlwind. Overhead, buzzards circled, and I wondered if they were waiting for me.

"You won't get me yet," I told them, as I concentrated on putting one foot in front of the other. "I'm not ready to die."

One step.

Two.

Three.

The whirlwind grew closer, towering from the ground all the way to the sky. The suction from its maw was so strong that even the tallest saguaros leaned toward it, as if eager to join its dance across the desert. But I wasn't. No matter what I had to do, I would not let that whirlwind take me, would close my ears to its siren song.

Instead of growling or hissing, as whirlwinds are wont to do, this one was singing a high, sharp dirge.

Words?

Forgetting my determination not to listen, I cocked my head. Walked closer. Felt its pull. Leaned toward it like the saguaros.

"I'm lost," the whirlwind sang, its voice the sweet soprano of songbirds.

"How can you be lost?" I called back. "This is your home."

"So lost."

As I neared it, the whirlwind shrank and solidified from its former funnel shape to something vaguely woman-like. Whatever—who-ever—it was, she wore a blue dress.

"Help me," she sang, reaching out a writhing hand.
"Here!" I held out my own. Took hers. Recognized her.
Reservation Woman.
Now we were both lost.

I didn't stop screaming until Jimmy reached over and took me in his arms.

"Shhh, sweetheart. It was just a dream."

But I knew it wasn't.

Chapter Nineteen

Unable able to get Reservation Woman's face out of my head, the next morning I called Pete Ventarro at the Medical Examiner's office.

"Did you ever get an ID on that Caucasian woman I found on the Pima Rez?"

"Nope, she's still tagged as an Unknown." He sounded out of breath. "And I can't talk right now."

Ignoring him, I said, "I'm thinking I might have a lead on who she is. Could you—"

"Stop right there, Lena. I take it you haven't been watching the news this morning."

"I've been busy. Why?"

"Fire on an overturned bus on I-10. I'm sitting here with twenty-something crispy critters needing IDs, so I can't do a damned thing for you." Pete hung up, leaving me staring at the receiver and thinking how easily life can be snuffed out.

No matter how carefully you live your life, you're still going to die. Sometimes sooner, sometimes later. You can obey all the rules, mind your own business, stop at each stop sign, exercise regularly, and eat a balanced diet—but the Grim Reaper will find you wherever you are, even while sitting in a bus seat. Taking a deep breath, I went back to the business at hand—Googling the possible names Sunflower had given me for Ford Laumenthal's wife.

An hour later I'd worked my way through Eileen Laumenthal, Arlene Laumenthal, Alene Laumenthal, and was working on Doreen Laumenthal—the other possible names for Reservation Woman. There were three Doreens. The Doreen from Casper, Wyoming, held my interest for a while since Ford had once lived there, but when I found a picture of her on the obituary page and discovered that she'd died at ninety-six years of age, I kept going. The Doreen in Pontiac, Michigan, didn't work out, either: she was six, and was pictured receiving a Hero Award for helping rescue a kitten from a tree. For a short while I got excited over the Tallahassee, Florida, Doreen who was twenty-four and had five years earlier won the Florida State Lottery; my excitement died when I saw her picture. That Doreen Laumenthal was African American.

Then I remembered that Laumenthal would have been Doreen's *married* name.

"What's wrong?" Jimmy asked, startling me.

Brought back to the here and now, I looked at him over my shoulder. He had a spread sheet up on his computer, doing who-knows-what with it. "Nothing's wrong."

"You're muttering under your breath again," he told me.

"I wasn't muttering under my breath."

"Then who's Doreen Laumenthal and what did she do to make you so upset?"

"I'm not upset."

"If you're not upset, Lena, I'm Miss Mary Twinkletoes of the Moscow Ballet. Tell you what, how about I get you another cup of coffee since you've only had a pot and a half this morning?"

"Stop being cute and just let me concentrate over here, okay? I'm trying to figure something out."

Even Jimmy's sighs were melodic. "I'll do better than that. See you in another hour. I'm headed to the gym." With that, he grabbed his gym bag and headed out the door before I could apologize for my snappishness.

Why he puts up with me I'll never know, but I guess it had something to do with love. Not having time for that right now, I pulled my smartphone out of my tote and brought up Reservation Woman's picture again. Light-colored hair, not quite blond. Probable blue eyes, although when I found her, they'd been filmy in death. Blue dress that appeared to be three sizes too big. Barefoot. Thin arms flung outward in a crucifixion pose.

"*Tell me who you are*," I whispered.

I started at her death-emptied face until something new occurred to me. The Doreen Laumenthal in Wyoming who had died peacefully at age ninety-six may have been too old to be Ford's wife or even his mother, but maybe, just maybe, the Doreen in question had married the elder Doreen's grandson or great-grandson. So I tried again, going over the elderly Doreen's obituary, taking special note of her "survived bys." Unfortunately, the woman had twelve grandchildren, eighteen great-grandchildren, and nineteen great-great-grandchildren.

Once I'd finished muttering every curse word I ever knew, I grabbed the office phone and called the Casper Police Department.

After several transfers, I wound up with Sergeant Dewayne Kaplan, who sounded sympathetic. He told me he'd do what he could, so after sending him Reservation Woman's photograph, I hung up and returned to my Googling feeling more hopeful. But five minutes later, Kaplan called back and said she didn't look like any of their MisPers. He'd keep checking, though. Grateful, I gave him my personal cell number and email, then followed up that call with two more, one to Pontiac, the other to Tallahassee, getting the same results from both. Now I had three police departments who wanted to help, but for now, none of them recognized Reservation Woman's picture.

"You sure her first name was Doreen?" the cop in Pontiac asked.

"Not even sure of that. It could have been Eileen or even Alene."

"Then I wish you the best, but don't hold your breath."

"I'm not," I told him, but that was a lie. I knew I'd never have a good night's sleep again if Reservation Woman was buried without a name.

I was still running "Doreen" and "Laumenthal" through Google when Jimmy returned from the gym. He smelled wonderful, and to make up for my earlier churlish behavior, I lured him into the conference room and had my way with him.

I was in the middle of getting dressed when I heard Howlin' Wolf's "Smokestack Lightning" playing on my cell. It was either Juliana again, still frantic about her missing daughter, or one of the cops I'd recently talked to.

Tee-shirt and jeans back on but still barefoot, I grabbed the cell. "Lena Jones here."

"Found something that might work for you," said Sergeant Kaplan, in Casper, Wyoming. "I just emailed it. If it's a hit, get back to me, okay? I'm kinda interested in what happened to that gal. She has people up here who haven't given up hope. Her mother, God, I hate to even think about that poor woman. She goes my church, and this is going to hit her hard."

Promising Kaplan I'd let him know, I woke up my computer and checked my emails. In addition to several Nigerian princes wanting to let me in on a great stock buy, there was one from Casper PD. It had an attachment.

I opened it, only to be disappointed.

Alene Chambers, who went missing six years earlier when she'd been seventeen, had light brown hair and blue eyes, but she looked nothing like Reservation Woman. The Chambers woman had been severely overweight, and her double chin effectively disguised her jawline.

Since nothing about her looked like my "Doreen," I held off notifying Kaplan.

"Jimmy, could you do me a favor?" I called. He was still in the conference room getting his clothes back on.

"Anything in the world you want: diamonds, yachts, rare tropical plants," he replied. "But right this minute I'm having trouble moving."

"When you recover, could you use that new program you installed and run a cross-check on an Alene Chambers and Ford J. Laumenthal?"

A few minutes later he did.

Three years earlier, in Norcross, Georgia, Alene Chambers, of Casper, Wyoming, had married Ford J. Laumenthal, also from Casper. In their wedding picture she was wearing a white dress so large it could have been a muumuu. But the bride was still more slender than the groom.

Unable to bear looking at her in a happier time, I closed my eyes.

"Hello, Alene," I whispered.

Chapter Twenty

My arrival at EarthWay that afternoon was not greeted with glee by the few who were left. The day was a beautiful one—fleecy clouds tracking across a pure blue sky, a soft breeze, birds singing pretty songs in the trees—but from the expression on people's faces, you'd think they inhabited Hell.

Quilter Sara Jenks, a.k.a. "Sunflower," looked as if she'd rather spit on me than talk, but after considerable coaxing on my part as we stood by the boarded-up well, she relented. But not by much.

"You better not let Mother Eve see you coming round here again."

"She's back?"

"No thanks to you. You've not only destroyed everything we've built here, but two families've had their children taken away. And now we're having to drink that awful bottled water. It's full of chemicals!"

Sunflower only knew half the story, whereas I had been in touch with Sheriff Stu Rizzo, who had told me that the children who had been "taken away" were actually in the Hopi County Hospital being treated for *E.coli* infections. When I tried to explain the dangers of the compound's water supply, Sunflower shook her head.

"I don't believe you. There's nothing wrong with our water, but there's plenty wrong with forcing people to drink water that's been chemically treated. Our water is pure, but thanks to you again, the well's closed! Do you realize what a monster you are?"

While I had no patience with her ignorance of basic science, I did feel sorry for the pain she was enduring. However, the part of me that cared about the red-headed baby nursing at her breast knew that the child's health was more important than Sunflower's feelings. But I decided to throw her a bone. "Okay, I'll cop to being a monster and admit there's a chance those hospitalized kids might be suffering from psychosomatic diarrhea as long as you tell me more about the Laumenthal couple. The wife's name is Alene."

Ducking her head, she muttered, "I've already told you everything I know."

"Who did the Laumenthals spend the most time with while they were here?"

Before she could answer, three long-dressed women wandered by carrying gallon jugs of water. In a nasty counterpoint to the pretty birdsongs floating through the air, they told me what I could do with myself.

When Sunflower seconded their anatomically-difficult suggestion, I thought the conversation was over, but she surprised me. Looking me straight in the eyes, she said, "Alene was friendly with everyone, but Ford, not so much. He was the kind of guy who found it easier to make enemies. Snotty. Arrogant. That kind of thing doesn't do well around here, and in the end he got so many people's backs up that Mother Eve told Alene she was welcome to stay, but that her husband better start making other plans."

"Mother Eve was throwing him out?"

"It never came to that, because one morning neither of them showed up for breakfast—he was supposed to be one of the dishwashers that day. Mother Eve and I went looking for him, but they'd packed up and left."

"Okay, I can see he wasn't a popular guy, but surely he had to interact with people sometime. This is a commune, right?

You guys all do this and that together, dishwashing, gardening, whatever."

"He wasn't into gardening and couldn't tell a carrot from a radish. But come to think of it, I did see him talking to Jeremiah Blue Sky a couple of times. Jeremiah could get along with the Devil himself." She managed a faint smile.

I looked over at the closed produce stand. "Where would I find Jeremiah today?"

"Dunno. He might of cleared out last night with the rest of them." Finished with me, she walked away, her back stiff with rekindled anger.

The EarthWay General Store was still open, and with Mother Eve yet to be in evidence, I felt secure enough to lengthen my visit. After all, what could the woman do—shoot me?

When I entered the store, I found Sally White Flower packing her wares in cartons labeled SUNFLOWER, MARFA LIGHT, KRAFTWERK, NANNETTE, and even JEREMIAH BLUE SKY.

Pointing to Jeremiah's carton, I said, "He's still here?"

In the store's half-light, Sally's fifty-something face appeared careworn, and her schoolmarm bun had collapsed into tendrils. Recognizing me, her eyes lit up with hatred. "I'm surprised you have the gall to come back here after everything you've done."

I handed her the pictures I'd printed off my cell phone. "Alene and Ford Laumenthal. They're both dead. Ford's body was dumped not far from here, but Alene's was found further away, on the Pima Reservation. I hear Ford hung out with Jeremiah, and I want to know...."

"Who're you accusing me of murdering?" A male voice.

I spun around to see Jeremiah Blue Sky towering over me. For such a large man, he had entered the store so quietly I hadn't heard his approach. Today his ruddy face was even redder than the last time I'd seen him, and his blond dreads swung back and forth in agitation. Sandwiched between him and Sally White

Flower, I realized what a precarious position I'd put myself in. The General Store was dark. Half the commune had left during the night, and the few people still hanging around blamed me for destroying their Eden-esque way of life. I doubted any of them would mind if I ended up dead on the side of the road, just as long as it was far, far away from EarthWay.

"No, I'm not accusing you of murder," I answered Jeremiah. "I just want you to look at these." I thrust the photographs at him.

He looked down.

"Ah, shit, that's Ford and his wife." Raising his eyes to me, he asked, "What the hell happened to them?"

"I think they were murdered, but I don't know how or by whom. Please tell me anything you know about either one of them. It might help."

He shot a look at Sally, who shrugged and went back to putting the compound's handmade wares into the appropriate cartons. Maybe she was leaving, too. Despite everything I knew about water-borne illnesses, I did feel guilty. At least these people had tried to create a decent life.

Motioning me to follow, Jeremiah headed to the small bistro table by the open window and hauled his lofty frame into one of the spindly chairs. I sat across from him, waiting, as the chickens outside clucked cheerfully.

"Ford flat-out hated Mother Eve," he stated.

"Did he have good reason?"

He scratched his dreads. "We-ell, Mother Eve can be a bit bossy. And judging from the way that poor wife of Ford's was always cringing around, he liked his women submissive."

"Are you saying he beat Alene?"

"Don't put words in my mouth. *Beat* isn't the word I'd use, but one time I saw him slap her, and that was bad enough. I told him if I ever saw him hitting her again I'd whup his ass. So he stopped. But what he did to her in private, I can't testify to. Anyway, after that, it was more of a verbal bullying. Always with the 'you didn't make the bed right,' or 'you look fat in that stupid dress you made,' that kind of thing all the time. Frankly, I was glad when I heard Mother Eve was going to give him the heave-ho."

"I heard she offered to let Alene stay."

Hearing a series of loud squawks, Jeremiah looked out the window. "Stop that!" he yelled. The squawks duly stopped. When I looked out the window all I could see was a flock of chickens minding their own chicken business.

"Where were we?"

"With Mother Eve telling Alene she could stay."

"Oh, yeah. Fat lot of good that did. The woman was totally under his thumb. Wouldn't say 'boo' unless he told her to."

"Not a happy marriage, then."

He shook his head, sending those dreads flying. "Not my idea of one, that's for sure. And from what I could tell in the short time they were here, Ford was the restless kind. He'd dragged the poor woman from communes in Georgia, Kentucky, and New Mexico, always looking for a place that would appreciate his wonderful self."

"Sounds like a narcissist."

"Idiots frequently are. The guy was so full of his own imagined superiority he never bothered to check out the territory before making a move, so he kept getting disappointed. I'm betting that whoever told him about EarthWay, for instance, didn't bother to inform him it was run by a woman. Feeling the way he did about women, he'd never have moved here if he'd known."

"Is there anything else you can tell me about him, like where he and Alene might have headed when they left here?"

Another head shake. "He didn't say. There's places like this all over the country, you know, for some of us die-hards from the Seventies, and new back-to-the-landers who want to get the hell off the grid. Wherever the Laumenthals wound up, it would be whatever place rang Ford's chimes on that particular day."

"How do you feel about Mother Eve?"

"Remember when I sold you those vegetables? I told you to scrub them well before eating them, didn't I?"

"You didn't trust the water."

"Nope. Mother Eve was smart in some ways, ass-dumb in others. I've been hanging out here long enough to figure out that in some ways, women—especially women as hard-headed as that old woman—can be as rock-dumb as any man."

Despite the grim photographs lying on the table, I managed a smile. "So where are you headed next?"

Jeremiah Blue Sky sighed and leaned back in the spindly chair. "Dunno. Maybe that place he told me was so awful in New Mexico. If Ford hated it, it's probably great. Or maybe Twin Oaks, in Virginia. I read about that one in *The Atlantic*."

I studied his dreads, his bib overalls. "You read *The Atlantic*?"

"Judge not lest ye be judged. I read that in *The Atlantic*, too." He winked. "Wherever I wind up, it all depends on whichever way Elaine wants to go when we leave here."

"Your wife?"

"My van. I trust her more than I trust myself."

"She's named for?"

A snaggle-toothed grin. "My mother."

On the way back to Scottsdale I did some thinking; flat desert highway is good for that. First, oddly enough, I thought about chickens and their pecking orders. Although the birds were dim-witted animals, they were able to maintain their pecking order with little bloodshed, just a beak-jab every now and then. The chickens' pecking orders led me to the things humans do to maintain their own clan structures. Sometimes the method was as subtle and silly as Kanati's beaded headband hierarchy, but other times it was more malignant. From there my thoughts skewed back to a case when I'd been hired to free a thirteen-year-old girl from a forced marriage in a polygamy compound. She'd been pretty, and although the prophet already had numerous wives, constantly adding pretty girls to his flock was his own particular sign of status. Woe be to any pretty girl who resisted; she'd wind up dead in a canyon someplace.

Had Alene Chambers Laumenthal's submission boosted her husband's status, at least in his own eyes? And what would have happened if one day she'd defied him? Yet according to Jeremiah Blue Sky, Ford Laumenthal had never physically harmed her. She had died without a mark on her body, the same as her lout of a husband.

And as had artist Megan Unruh. Other than being a regular at the studio she shared with other artists, Megan had lived an isolated life. No enemies, no loutish husband. Try as I might, I couldn't come up with a connection between Megan and the Laumenthals. Well, other than the fact that all three had been overweight at some point in their lives, but at the time of their deaths, were starvation thin.

Health farms.

At this realization, I hit the brakes, thus sparing the life of the ground squirrel who had picked that moment to cross the highway.

There were several health farms in Arizona, their methods ranging all the way from the classic calorie-and-exercise programs led by board-certified physicians, to surgery performed by board-certified surgeons. But every PI knows that Arizona and its friendly neighbor, Mexico, teemed with unlicensed fat farms that promised, but seldom delivered, miracle cures for obesity. Then there were the private practitioners. One group I'd read about was accused of dosing its clients with large pills containing tapeworm larvae. According to the newspaper accounts, its clients had lost weight, all right, but some of them became deathly ill.

If only I could remember that particular "clinic's" name...

Using the Jeep's hands-free setup, I called Jimmy.

"You want to know *what?*" he asked.

"Crazy as it sounds, I want the name of that fat farm rumored to be feeding its clients tapeworms. It was all over the newspapers several years back, but I can't remember the place's name or where it was located."

A grunt. "Good thing I haven't had lunch yet."

"Oh, grumble, grumble," I teased.

"Okay, I've got an idea. Why don't we talk research over lunch? We can try that new Vietnamese restaurant down the street, order a couple of noodle dishes, which look like…?" A dramatic pause.

"Noodles," I finished for him.

Jimmy is fast, at least with computer work. When I walked through the door of Desert Investigations, he was sitting at his desk with a look of triumph on his face.

"Pray for a Miracle."

I frowned. "Jehovah's Witnesses stop by while I was gone?"

"Pray for a Miracle was the name of the fat farm that was supposedly dosing its clients with tapeworm eggs to help them lose weight. They were doing business in Apache County before the state shut them down."

"This was how long ago?"

Jimmy was nothing but thorough. "Twelve years. But I've got bad news for you, if you were thinking about dieting, and you better not, because you're already perfect. Anyway, there never were any tapeworms or tapeworm larvae, just big fat sugar pills. The whole thing was a scam. Read this."

He handed me an article he'd found on Snopes.com, the website that addressed fraudulent news stories and urban legends. Reading, I saw that tapeworm infestation was definitely a reality, but was caused by eating uncooked beef or pork. As for tapeworm eggs or larvae, they wouldn't survive long enough to be put into pills and stored for even a short amount of time before being ingested.

Feeling faintly nauseous, I asked Jimmy, "But if there were no tapeworms, why'd the state shut them down?"

"For fraud. Pray for a Miracle promised tapeworms and didn't deliver. Now let's go eat some noodles."

Chapter Twenty-one

As soon as we returned from lunch I called Nils Quaid, the artist who had helped me with the sketch of Megan Unruh. "Got another picture for you, and this time I want you to add a double chin," I said. "Make it look like the woman in the picture weighs at least a hundred pounds more than she does here."

At his agreement, I emailed him the photograph I'd taken of Reservation Woman, and less than an hour later, I had a retouched photograph of her in my hands. After studying her face for a few seconds, and allowing a fresh wave of grief to sweep over me, I forwarded the new version to Sergeant Dewayne Kaplan of the Casper Police Department. When I followed up with a phone call, the detective who picked up the phone told me Sergeant Kaplan had just left for Alene Laumenthal's mother's house.

"He told me to thank you," the detective added.

A couple of hours later I received Kaplan's call-back. "Mrs. Chambers is pretty sure the woman in that sketch is her daughter," he said. "Sure enough that she's flying down to Phoenix tomorrow to do a formal ID of the body."

Then I called Sylvie.

Mission accomplished, I sat there in Desert Investigations watching tourists pass by on Main Street. They looked so carefree, carrying their shopping bags and wrapped paintings, but I'd been in the detecting business long enough to be suspicious of appearances. Who knew which of them carried enough hate in his or her heart to commit murder?

While watching a particularly happy-looking couple walking along arm-in-arm, it occurred to me that if Megan Unruh and the Laumenthals had been intentionally starved to death, then their killer, or killers, may have committed the perfect crime. No murder weapon, and no known motive. Granted, none of the three had been poor. Megan had inherited money from her deceased father, a local attorney, and her art exhibit was doing well even before she disappeared. As for the Laumenthals, Sylvie had tipped me off that Ford was a trust fund baby whose grandfather had been CEO of a Fortune 500 company. Alene Chambers Laumenthal hadn't been poor, either. An only child, five years earlier she had inherited fifty percent of her sports team-owning father's estate when he'd dropped dead on a golf course in the Bahamas.

"But don't get all hot and bothered about some unknown perp enriching himself via their inheritances," Sylvie said, when she phoned me back with new information. "Upon proof of death, Ford Laumenthal's money reverts to the family trust. As for Alene Laumenthal, hers goes to her mother. Megan Unruh's goes to her mother, too."

Without thinking, I found myself rubbing the old bullet scar on my forehead, a reminder that mothers sometimes harmed their daughters, not always meaning to. Then again, sometimes they did. Another possibility occurred to me. It was rare, but cases have been found where multiple murders had been committed to provide camouflage for one suspicious death. Say, new bride Jane Doe wants to murder new hubby Richard in order to inherit his fortune, but Jane—clever girl that she is—knows that once Richard winds up on a coroner's slab, she'll be the most obvious suspect. So what does clever Jane do? Using the same method with which she kills Richard, she also kills Susan, Allan, Jennifer, Mark, and Carol. The police then suspect there's a serial killer at work, not a greedy bride, and clever Jane drives her new Rolls-Royce off into the sunset.

After switching the Jane Doe scenario to a Greedy Mama one, I decided that another visit to Megan Unruh's mother was long overdue.

The sun was setting when I arrived at Mrs. Unruh's house, and the shadows were long. But not long enough to obscure the note taped to the front door:

CALL THE POLICE

A quick glance up and down the street revealed no police cars, no nosy neighbors. How long had the note been there? Considering the neighborhood's large lots, with at least ten yards separating her house from the neighbors', the note could have gone unnoticed until the mailman came along.

Before following its instructions, I decided to see what I could see.

The front drapes were drawn but the back gate was unlocked, whether from forgetfulness or design. Entering the yard, I saw nothing suspicious other than a neglected swimming pool. Courtesy of the neighbor's acacia tree, the pool was littered with oval leaves and looked like it hadn't been cleaned in days.

When I crossed the lawn to the patio, I noticed that the arcadia doors were slightly open.

Taking a chance, something I would soon regret, I entered the house.

"Why did you enter the house?" asked the first police officer to arrive, once he'd seen what I had seen. His badge informed me his name was Brian Mulrooney.

I was still trying to explain my actions to Officer Mulrooney when an unmarked cruiser rolled up and detectives Sylvie Perrins and Bob Grossman climbed out.

"Fancy meeting you here," she snipped. "It's the mother?"

I nodded.

The "it" was the body I'd found hanging from a noose tied to one of the beams in the vaulted living room ceiling. Dorothea Unruh had climbed up there on a ladder, then kicked it over. The ladder had fallen on the glass coffee table, breaking it.

The note pinned to her dress said...

I AM WORTHLESS

"Just goes to show, doesn't it?" Sylvie.

"Yep, you never can tell." Bob.

"Looks like we pegged her wrong, didn't we?" Me.

Having depleted our collection of bereavement clichés, we stood there in silence, feeling awful about the things we'd thought, the things we'd said.

35 years earlier

Helen stands silently as twenty-three bodies—all but one of them children—are dragged to the mineshaft and thrown in. She can't move, can't speak, is unaware of the tiny hand gripping her own.

My fault.
My fault.
My fault.

Chapter Twenty-two

That afternoon I warned Jimmy I'd be working late at the office, then spending the night in my old apartment. He didn't like it, but understood. In my own way, I was grieving for Dorothea Unruh, a woman I hadn't even liked.

By nine, I'd typed up notes on a half-dozen cases, and after dumping out the remains of the coffeepot, I locked up. Outside, the night was beautiful, something I hadn't been able to appreciate while hunched over my computer. Although the stars weren't as dazzling as they were on the Rez—too much neon in Old Town Scottsdale—the full moon was bedecked with a bright halo, lending a silvery sheen to Main Street. To add to the evening's dreamlike quality, the tourists had abandoned the nearby art galleries for the bars on Scottsdale Road, leaving this block in peaceful silence.

I was halfway up the stairs to my second-story apartment above Desert Investigations when a shadow detached itself from the wall and rushed at me. Startled, I raised my left arm just in time to deflect a life-draining slash across my carotid. Instead, I sustained a less lethal cut on my forearm.

"Bitch!" Mother Eve screamed, lunging at me again.

With my uninjured right hand, I thrust the heel of my palm up against her nose. Blood gushed, but she ignored it. Silver moonlight danced across the knife's sharp edge as she jabbed it toward me, but this time I was ready. Grasping her wrist, I used her own weight against her by pulling her forward, thus sending her hurtling down the stairs.

"Bitch thinks she can ruin my life!" She babbled, hitting bottom with the knife still in her hand.

Before she had a chance to recover, I drew my .38 from its holster and bounded down the stairs after her. "I'll *end* your life if you don't drop that thing," I told her, the .38 aimed at the center of her forehead.

Although flat on her back and bleeding from a broken nose, she'd managed to land without stabbing herself. But the fight wasn't out of her yet. Waving the knife around, she hissed, "Gonna gut your sorry ass, bitch!"

"Lose the knife," I ordered.

"Make me!"

Happy to oblige, I shot her in the shoulder. She dropped the knife. What was that old saying? *Never bring a knife to a gunfight?*

As the knife clanged against the cement landing, Mother Eve yelped her favorite word again. Given her position—flat on her back, and oozing blood and snot—her rage was almost pathetic, but I wasn't in a sympathetic mood. My left arm burned, yet I was still able to use my left hand to speed-dial 9-1-1 on my cell while keeping the .38 leveled on her with my right.

Chapter Twenty-three

"Twenty-four stitches in a perfectly straight line," the ER doc said, admiring her handiwork.

"Lovely," I groused. Lidocaine or not, my slashed arm hurt. "Maybe you should take up embroidery. I hear it's relaxing."

"Knitting."

"What?"

"It's knitting that's supposed to be relaxing, Lena, not embroidery."

"Hmph."

On an ER-humor roll, Dr. Margaret Mannon called over to the other ER doc who was working on Mother Eve. "Hey, Jeff. Isn't Ms. Jones here ready for her Frequent Flyer discount?"

"She's still got one shotgun wound to go before she qualifies," Dr. Jeff answered.

Unamused, I sat up and looked across the blood-spattered room toward Sergeant Sylvie Perrins, standing next to Dr. Jeff. Sylvie was gloating down at Mother Eve, whose right wrist was currently attached to the gurney via a shiny pair of handcuffs. Sylvie loved arresting people.

"I called Jimmy and he's on his way," she informed me. "Figured you couldn't drive like that, your Jeep being a stick and all."

"You think she's good for it?"

"Huh?" Sylvie looked puzzled. "Who's good for what?"

"Mother Eve. Good for the deaths of Megan Unruh, and Ford and Doreen Laumenthal?"

Sylvie put a finger up to her lips. "Shh. Baby's trying to sleep."

Mother Eve muttered something, but it was unclear because she'd obviously been given twice the amount of painkillers I had. Once she drifted back to sleep, Sylvie answered, "Well, we're still working on that. But I'm hoping she is."

I also wanted to believe that Mother Eve—a.k.a. Priscilla Marie Heywood Stahl—was our killer. After all, she had a long criminal background and tonight had attempted to kill me. But something about it didn't feel right.

"You have got to be kidding me," Jimmy said when he caught me heading for the corral the next morning, my left arm swathed in bandages.

One of Jimmy's faults—although they weren't many—was that he tended to hover. In the past, whenever I'd been hospitalized with a workplace injury, gunshot or stabbing, he'd stayed by my hospital bed until the nurses threw him out. And that was when we were just friends and business partners. Since we'd moved beyond mere friendship, I foresaw a life of being hovered over, and I didn't know how I felt about that. Comforted? Suffocated?

"Exercise is good for me," I told him, grabbing the saddle horn. "Besides, Adila looks lonely."

He put his hand on top of mine. "How much blood did you lose last night?"

"I bled worse when I got my ears pierced."

"I'm not going to let you lift that saddle."

"I can always ride bareback."

"Not on that horse, you won't."

After comparing the value of total independence to sensible health precautions, I slipped my hand out from under his. "Then saddle 'er up, Pardner."

He was still grinning when we rode toward the rising sun.

As October in the desert tends to be, the morning was flawless. The summer heat had long disappeared, and the winter rains lay months in the future. The only thing lacking was color, which we wouldn't see until spring, when the various species of cacti blossomed—red, pink, orange, and on the stately saguaros, startling snow-white with bright yellow centers. But you can't have everything, can you? I contented myself with the muted greens of sage and the soft golden glow of the caliche soil, relishing the fact that the desert's subtle beauty helped me ignore the ache in my stitched forearm.

"…and so I told him there was nothing we could do about it." Jimmy's voice intruded upon my sylvan reverie.

"Huh?"

"You didn't hear a word I said, did you, Lena?"

"I, ah, caught the part about there being nothing we could do about it."

"You agree, don't you?"

Ahead of us, a covey of top-knotted Gambel's quail scattered out of the horses' way, seeking shelter under a creosote bush.

"I always do, don't I?"

There was silence for a moment, broken only by the sound of the horses' hooves, the singing of a cactus wren. Then Jimmy rode up beside me, a rare expression of irritation on his face. "Did you hear the part about him wanting you to call him?"

Time for the truth. "Okay, okay. I wasn't paying attention. What am I supposed to agree with and who wants me to call him, and why?"

The irritation softened into concern. "Is your arm hurting? Do you need to go back to the Emergency Room?"

"I'm fine, but I repeat, who am I supposed to call?"

Jimmy studied me carefully, then seeing no evidence of pain on my features—I'm careful about that sort of thing—he relaxed. "Harold Slow Horse. He's not taking the news about Chelsea very well."

I frowned. "What news?"

"About her marriage."

"Her *what*!?"

He reined Big Boy in front of Adila, bringing her to a halt. "How long have you not been listening to me?"

In the ensuing silence, Adila took the opportunity to nip Big Boy on the neck. He squealed and nipped back. Adila responded in kind, and next thing you know, we were in the middle of a horse brawl, not the kind of fight you want to get involved in on a nice October morning. At least bringing the horses' back under control gave me time to collect my thoughts.

When the two animals finally settled down, I said, "I'm sorry I wasn't listening, but I was, ah, thinking about something else." *Like how much my arm hurt.* "So tell me. What's all this about Chelsea getting married?"

"In a candlelight service last night, apparently. Right afterwards, she called Harold to give him the news, told him he should be happy for her, and to top it off, emailed him a picture of her arm in arm with New Hubby."

"I bet that went over well."

"Like the sinking of the *Titanic*."

"So what does Harold want from me now?"

"The name of a good lawyer."

"Why?"

"He wants to sue New Hubby for alienation of affection."

Wincing, and not from physical pain, I asked, "What's New Hubby's name? And where the hell did she meet him? She's been up at Kanati for over a month, so…" I stopped. "Oh, hell. She married someone from there, didn't she? Please tell me it wasn't Roger Gorsky!"

"His name is Adam, and here's his picture. Somewhere in his forties, it looks like. Kind of handsome in a way, if you go for skinny blond men." With a wicked grin, he leaned over and handed me his cell phone so I could see.

Chelsea in a bridal veil.

And then it all came back.

I was four years old and it was my wedding day.

Of all the little girls among The Children of Abraham, Golden Boy had chosen me for his bride. Everyone said it was a great honor, but if it was, why was Mom crying? And why was Daddy so angry it took two men to hold him back?

As Mom ran to Abraham's tent to tell him that I was too young, two of the older women, one fat, one skinny, dressed me in a white dress—so much lace!—and covered my face with a white veil that made everything look foggy.

"Beautiful clothes for a beautiful bride," the fat one said.

"But I can't see the world anymore!"

"From now on Adam will do the seeing for you."

"Nobody can see the world for someone else. We've each gotta see it for oursels."

She frowned. "Who told you that?"

"My mom."

The two women looked at each other. "Helen, again," Sister Skinny said. "She's nothing but trouble. I told Abraham he was making a mistake with her."

Sister Fat made an ugly sound. "Abraham never makes mistakes."

Sister Skinny blushed. "Oh, that's not what I meant. Of course he doesn't. It's just that his ways are like God's, sometimes difficult to understand." Then she turned to me, lifted my veil so she could look me in the face, and said, "Your mother was wrong."

I wanted to say my mom was never wrong, but I remembered her last night, crying and crying, and saying she'd been so wrong, so wrong.

Deciding I didn't want to get married, I grabbed the veil away from Sister Skinny and threw it to the ground. Then I started to take off the white dress. It didn't feel pretty anymore. But when I tried to walk out of the tent, Sister Fat grabbed me and slapped me in the face. "You'll do as you're told, Little Miss Snot."

They dressed me again. I wanted to cry because my face hurt, but I didn't want them to know anything about me, how I was feeling, how scared I was of the way Golden Boy looked at me, how everything was getting so awful that Mom cried all the time, how Daddy wanted us to leave, how…

"She's ready," Sister Skinny said.

"About time, too," Sister Fat muttered.

I tried to escape again, but it didn't work. They just grabbed me and dragged me out of the tent to the clearing where Abraham and Golden Boy and the others were waiting. My mom was there, too. A couple of big men stood next to her, almost as if they were guarding her, which was silly. Mom didn't need to be guarded. She could take care of herself. At least that's what she always told Daddy.

I looked around for Daddy, but he wasn't there, just Mom, who kept yelling, "No, no! No, no!" until Sister Fat leaned over and slapped her like she'd slapped me.

"That was mean!" I yelled, running over and slapping Sister Fat on her big fat butt with both of my hands. She reared around and raised her hand to me and…

"Stop it!" Golden Boy commanded. "If you touch her I will have you killed."

Sister Fat put her hand down.

"That's stupid," I told him. "You can't go around killing people even if they are slappers."

He gave me a startled look, then began to laugh.

An hour later, after Abraham said some fancy words about a whole lot of things, Golden Boy and me were married.

Looking back, I don't think I had a wedding night. At least, I can't remember one, because after that day, everything changed.

Everything.

Chapter Twenty-four

"Lena, what's wrong?" Jimmy's voice broke through the memory of gunshots and screams.

It took me a minute to catch my breath, but once I did, I turned to my partner with a quickly formed lie. "Oh, nothing. I thought I recognized Chelsea's new husband, but after a closer look, realized I was wrong."

He frowned. "You sure?"

"Absolutely." It would be a long time, if ever, that I'd be able to share that pain with anyone, even Jimmy. And to a certain extent, I hadn't really lied, just told a partial truth. I didn't know the man pictured on Jimmy's cell phone. How could I? The last time I had seen Adam Arneault, not counting that quick glimpse at Kanati, was thirty-five years ago, when he'd been my own "husband" in a cult known as The Children of Abraham.

When my name had been Christina.

It had all come back. The wedding. The sacrifice of the first-borns. Taking another little girl by the hand and running with my parents and the other children through the woods.

The chasing voices. The gunshots. The deaths.

My father and baby brother on the ground, bleeding into the earth.

Small bodies tossed into a mineshaft.

Sitting next to my mother on the old school bus until our ride ended with another gunshot.

Then darkness, awakening weeks later in a desert city where I knew no one, not even myself.

After taking a few seconds to calm down, to make certain I wouldn't begin screaming, I said, "You know, after thinking about it, I've realized Harold has a point."

"What point? Suing Chelsea's husband for alienation of affection?" When he laughed, the tribal tattoo on his forehead appeared to wink. "This isn't Victorian England, and alienation of affection isn't going to fly in any twenty-first-century courtroom. Arizona doesn't even have an alienation law."

I waved my good hand in a dismissive gesture. "Oh, I don't mean the lawsuit, because of course that's nonsense. But in his own way, Harold's as addicted to Chelsea as she was to drugs. Maybe if we got a little more information about this...this *Adam* person, we could use it to break through Harold's denial and wean him away from her." Sometimes psychobabble comes in handy, for instance, when you're trying to keep someone from noticing that you're lying your head off.

"Lena, please tell me you're kidding."

"I've never been more serious."

"So how do you plan to do this? Through one of those terrible interventions?" Not being a fan of the method, he made a face. "Look, I'm not saying you're wrong, because, yeah, to a certain extent you're right. Harold is somewhat addicted to the drama Chelsea brings into his life—he's an artist, remember, and they're all prone to drama—but you can't force enlightenment on someone. Especially not someone like Harold, who loves that silly woman so much he can't see straight."

If the science of neurolinguistics is correct, when a person looks up and to the left, he or she is remembering something. I couldn't be certain, but it was even money that Jimmy's own leftward eye movements were caused by remembering the years I had chased after shadows while ignoring the light in front of me.

And now it was too late.

I reached across my horse and took Jimmy's hand. "People grow. It just takes some of us longer than others."

He smiled.

Tender moment over, I pointed Adila's nose toward home. Big Boy duly followed. "There's something I need to take care of," I told Jimmy. "But after that, I'm driving out to Kanati again."

"To talk to Chelsea?"

"Yep." *And to someone else.*

"Well, since I've probably used up my allotment of bossiness for the day, I won't forbid you to go—not that you'd obey—but please drive carefully. Morning rush hour is rough on I-10, and you're still not as rough and tough as usual. That arm of yours…"

"*No problemo*, Kemosabe. And don't worry about my arm; it's fine. I have to take care of some stuff at the office first, so by the time I make it onto the I-10, the traffic will have eased up. But maybe you could feed the horses and help Wolf and his apprentices get started on the house before you come in?" I was proud of how steady my voice sounded.

"Will do."

When we dismounted back at the trailer, I gave him the kind of kiss that should have made him suspicious, but given his pure Pima heart, it didn't.

The drive to Desert Investigations only takes fifteen minutes from the Rez, but due to the shock of recognizing Chelsea's new husband as my own childhood "husband," I almost didn't make it.

After running straight into the bathroom, I held my hair back and knelt in front of the commode and lost breakfast, heaving and heaving, until nothing but bile came up. It took a while. Finally staggering to my feet, I scrubbed the commode and tile surround to within an inch of their lives. Then I sprayed the bathroom down with Lysol Fresh Linen disinfectant, adding a few spritzes to the outer office, just to be safe. I didn't want Jimmy to suspect anything was wrong, because if he did, he would do something to keep me from doing what I had to do.

Now that Desert Investigations smelled like clean laundry instead of sick PI, I sat at my desk, turned my computer on, and did some more research on Arneault, Pichard, and Theron, Kanati's parent company. By the time Jimmy walked in, all I'd come up with was the same old superficial hype along the lines of "Kanati changed my life."

"Smells nice in here," Jimmy said, when he arrived and was grinding up Jamaican Blue Mountain beans for the morning brew.

"Coffee beans always smell nice."

"I meant that new air spray you bought. Clean Sheets, is it called?"

"Fresh Linen. It, ah, smelled a little stuffy in here when I arrived, so I thought I'd try it out."

"Good choice."

With coffee on the way, Jimmy went back to his desk, while I poked around the Internet, this time trying individual names. I had no luck, because the clumsily translated versions of the Frenchmen's bios contained little of importance. Maurice Abraham Arneault, deceased, was described as an American-born dentist with an interest in Edgar Cayce. René Alain Pichard, also listed as deceased, had been a clothing designer who wrote a weekly astrology column for *Le Figaro*. Gaston Baptiste Theron, another dead guy—not a long-lived lot, apparently—had at one time been a Franciscan monk. A decade before his death, Theron left the Franciscan order, spending his remaining years as a "seeker of Truth," or at least that's the way his official bio described it, capital "T" and all. There had to be a backstory connecting all this to what was going down at Kanati, but my own computer skills were less sophisticated than Jimmy's.

"How you coming along on that research into Adam Arneault?" I called across the room.

"Slowly," Jimmy said. "I got derailed onto the Sanders Brothers investigation. Remember them?"

In my rush to find out more about Adam, I had forgotten one of Desert Investigations' newest clients. Not used to being rich, brothers Derek and Brian Sanders had cashed out their start-up and invested everything into a fund run by Dobbs & Calhoun Financial Services, a shell company that had taken their money and vanished. The police hadn't been able to help, and neither had the FBI, once it was discovered that "Shane Dobbs" and "Carl Calhoun" were pseudonyms for Vasily Minkorski and Shasha Grivanov, and that the two were now safely ensconced on Russian soil. Appeals to Vladimir Putin had gone unanswered.

"You can't even give me a few minutes?" I asked.

"Not at this point. Ever try to hack a holding company with an address in the Cayman Islands? They say it can't be done, but I'll blast through if it's the last thing I do, so if you don't mind…" With that he ducked behind his computer and continued typing.

When Jimmy was like this, nagging at him was fruitless. I was on my own. The problem was, with my computer skills being less than a tenth of his, I felt hopeless. Then I remembered Jimmy once explaining how to access the Dark Web.

It took three tries, but I was eventually able to log onto one of the Dark Web's most nimble search engines. Once there I found a forty-year-old article that had originally been microfiched and translated from *Chercheurs*, a magazine that specialized in the occult. In it was an interview with Adam's father, Maurice Abraham Arneault, wherein he discussed his reasons for returning to the States after having lived in France for ten years. I had to endure a page and a half of Arneault's quasi-religious gobbledygook before the interviewer pared him down to then-recent events.

CHERCHEURS: "But let us now address the fact that you are leaving France. People are saying…"

ARNEAULT: "People say a lot of things. They are also saying that after the tragedy in Quaydon, the reorganization of The

Divine Temple of the Holy Cross widened the breach between
its two factions, and that is absolutely untrue. I remain a loyal
member of The Divine Temple of the Holy Cross, which I assure
you has been unfairly smeared by lies in the press. Yes, there was
a schism. Considering our differences there had to be, but those
responsible for the tragedy are no longer with us to explain how
it happened. Let me assure you that the current members of
The Divine Temple of the Holy Cross were not responsible for
the personnel failures that led to those deaths. But that is water
under the bridge, is it not? Yet the outcry has been such that I
must resign from my partnership here. So I am moving to the
United States, where freedom of religion remains a sacred right
of all its citizens. Although my father was a French citizen, I was
born in Oklahoma, and thus enjoy dual citizenship. Do not you,
as a natural-born Frenchman, who himself has lived abroad in
Morocco and Spain, find it natural to wish to return to one's
homeland? And in my case, I also find it natural to desire to
elevate the souls of my countrymen and bring them back to the
most holy teachings of God."

Elevate. So Adam's father had used that word, too.

CHERCHEURS: "But those deaths, Monsieur Arneault.
Since you were the person who oversaw the property in Quaydon
where the deaths occurred, do you not feel in the least responsible?"

Unfortunately, Arneault had apparently refused to answer the
question, and the rest of the article was filled with more religious
gobbledygook. Having little interest in religion myself, I started
speed-reading through it to the end, which I found unsatisfy-
ing. Something seemed to be missing. Then I remembered that
newspaper articles were written in what journalists refer to as
"pyramid" style, with the most important information up front,
the details coming later. So I scrolled back to the beginning of
the article. Only then did I realize I had begun reading on page

28 of the magazine, which had no headline or byline, just the words "Continued from page 27." But there was no page 27. In fact, there was no page 26, either, or page 25, or any page before that. Whoever had transcribed the article had either skipped the magazine's first twenty-seven pages, or those pages had somehow become lost. The only way I was able to tell when the magazine was printed was by its issue date on the bottom left of each page.

Using the same search engine, I typed Quaydon+tragedy+ Divine Temple of the Holy Cross, pressed Enter—and hit gold.

MASS ASSASSINER DANS LE CULTE DE QUAYDON, screamed the headline in *La Vérité*, the French version of an underground newspaper. I hit the "translate" link and read, *Mass murder in Quaydon cult.* The subhead told me, "Only *La Vérité* brings truth to the cover-up!"

According to *La Vérité*, six months before *Chercheurs*' print date, fifty-three bodies, almost half of them children, had been found dead at the church's center on the outskirts of Paris. All were members of The Divine Temple of the Holy Cross.

After several months of in-fighting, the Divine Temple of the Holy Cross had split into two sects, one led by Maurice Abraham Arneault, the other by René Pichard and Clément Theron. The group headed by Pichard and Theron believed the story about God ordering the biblical Abraham to sacrifice his firstborn son was a parable, not a news account. Arneault's group believed the Bible should be taken literally. After all, the Bible was God's holy word, and you can't cherry-pick Scripture, they claimed.

Four months later, the Pichard and Theron group apparently changed their minds and adopted their former members' beliefs. But unlike the other group, they also decided they should act on those beliefs. From what the police and other investigators discovered after being summoned by a neighbor who'd heard gunshots, the carnage began with the sacrifice of Laurent Pichard, René Pichard's firstborn son. Using the end of an iron cross, the elder Pichard, surrounded by his inner circle, had ritually stabbed his three-month-old son to death on the sect's altar.

La Vérité reported that the first murder passed unnoticed by neighbors, but a few days later, the other killings began. Those *were* noticed, but by the time the police were alerted, fifteen inner circle members had died from poisoning, thirty-eight more from various other causes, including gunshot, smothering, and bludgeoning. All, with the exception of five infants still in swaddling blankets, were wearing white ceremonial robes at the time of their deaths. Each adult male lay on his back near his white-clad wives—the sect was polygamous—but the children, eighteen in all, were grouped together.

In the interviews that followed, Arneault claimed he'd known nothing about the impending death ritual, saying that after the original schism, his group—now called *Les Enfants des Abraham*, or The Children of Abraham—had severed all ties with The Divine Temple of the Holy Cross.

"This entire made-up story of a ritual slaughter is ridiculous," he'd told *La Vérité*. "And it certainly had nothing to do with me or Les Enfants des Abraham. When René Pichard had a nervous breakdown, some unfortunate things happened, but neither I nor any of my people were involved. We may believe what we believe, but in practice Les Enfants des Abraham follows the laws of modern society."

"You lying son of a bitch," I whispered. "You *murdering* son of a bitch!"

Once I had calmed down, I resumed reading, and discovered that because of the incendiary nature of the story, press coverage of the ritual murders had been squelched. The official cause of the deaths had been attributed to carbon monoxide poisoning. Unlike the rest of the French press, *La Vérité* continued to report the rumors that Arneault had been seen in the vicinity of the "death house" at the time of The Divine Temple of the Holy Cross tragedy. At the end of the article was a blurb noting that

Arneault had ultimately been cleared of any responsibility. The French court accepted the testimony of several people, each one a member of Les Enfants des Abraham, who swore that their leader had been having dinner with them at the time the killings took place.

I believed *La Vérité*'s version, because at the age of four, I had witnessed Maurice *Abraham* Arneault and his golden-haired son—commit mass murder.

35 years earlier

Helen hardly remembers the ride in the old school bus from the Flagstaff forest to Phoenix, but when the bus she's on turns down another city street, she realizes this might be her last chance to save Christina. Abraham wants her child dead. The only thing that has kept her alive so far are the protests from her daughter's twelve-year-old "husband," the young killer Christina calls Golden Boy.

But what can Helen do? Christina, silent since last night, sits on her lap, her eyes as blank as the bright sky above the bus. She and the child are so tightly packed in, neither can move. Abraham has forced them to sit between Brother Steve and Brother Joseph, two of his most trusted followers. Both are armed, and as they proved in that bloody forest meadow, they will kill on demand.

As the bus trundles slowly a past a hospital, Helen gets an idea. They are sitting in the long seat that faces the bus's exit. Out of the door's glass panels she can see that the sidewalk in front of the hospital is crowded with white-clad nurses, men carrying lunchboxes, Hispanic women strolling along with their beautiful, dark-eyed toddlers. If she can somehow get Christina off the bus and into that street, those people will surely help her.

Out of the corner of her eye Helen she sees Brother Steve's gun. She recognizes it as a revolver, the same kind of gun her own father owned. When she had turned thirteen and blossomed, he started taking her into the woods behind their house for target practice, saying, "A young lady needs to know how to protect herself."

She hadn't done a good job of that, had she? Liam is dead, along with little Jamie, and as soon as they reach the promised new settlement in California, Abraham will most certainly kill Christina. Probably Helen, too, not that she cares anymore. At this very moment Abraham is telling his golden-haired son how necessary more killings are because Helen is no longer a faithful follower. She is an *apostate*, and neither apostates nor their children should be allowed to live and spread their poisonous lies.

Pretending to wipe dust from her thigh, Helen studies Brother Steve's revolver. The holster has no cover flap, leaving the pistol's handgrip within easy reach. She looks back out the window to see the hospital growing smaller in the distance. She knows she should plan her next move more carefully, but the sidewalk ahead is less crowded, and she can already see the green sign that says I-10 - LOS ANGELES.

It has to be now.

In one lightning move, Helen tears Christina's clutching arms away and yanks the pistol out of Brother Steve's holster. Screaming "I'll kill her myself!" she aims as best she can at the glass panel above the door. At the same time she kicks her daughter in the chest, slamming her against the exit door.

But a split second before Helen pulls the trigger, Brother Steve hits Helen's arm, knocking the gun downward...

...and the bullet finds Christina instead.

Chapter Twenty-five

I managed to hold myself together until just before nine, when Jimmy received a call from Wolf Ramirez. The tribal elder was asking so many questions that Jimmy turned to me and said, "I'd better get back there. They've run into a plumbing problem. Want to come with me? Or do you still plan on driving to Kanati?"

Part of me wanted to return to the Rez with him and forget all about Maurice Abraham Arneault and his son, but the screams of the dying were too loud to ignore.

"Sorry, still gotta make that trip. Have fun." My smile must have resembled a death's head grin, but concerned as Jimmy was about the house, he didn't notice.

"Oh, yeah, plumbing's always fun." He gave me a quick peck on the cheek, and left.

Once I lessened my control I began to shake again, but not from fear.

From rage.

Kanati's Adam was the murdering spawn of a man who had killed dozens. The apple hadn't fallen far from the tree, had it? I now even understood why three bodies had been dumped so far north from Kanati—one in Scottsdale, one on the Rez, and the other further north on the Beeline Highway. The man revealed in those old newspaper accounts hadn't been stupid, and neither was his son. By dumping the bodies of their dead many miles north of Kanati, Adam Arneault had purposely implicated EarthWay. Given its parasite-friendly dietary beliefs, the back-to-the-land commune made the perfect red herring. But it wasn't Adam himself who had told me about EarthWay; it was Gabrielle, whom I'd begun to trust.

Unable to keep my mind focused, I turned off my computer and put the CLOSED sign on the door. Then I went upstairs.

The familiarity of my apartment, ragged though it remained after Snowball's tender administrations, calmed me. I eased myself down on the sofa and took a few deep breaths, feeling my stomach muscles unclench. I didn't understand everything yet, but so far I had figured out this much. Despite her obvious talent, Megan Unruh had been raised by a cold-hearted woman who couldn't even love herself, and the resulting lack of confidence made Megan the perfect mark for any group offering salvation. As for Ford and Alene Laumenthal—my poor Reservation Woman—the couple had been working their way through the waning commune system until they found Kanati, which they'd believed to be the pot of gold at the end of the rainbow. Ford had been the leader in their misguided search for salvation, Alene his whither-thou-goest follower.

But I couldn't figure out why—despite Kanati's gourmet meals—those people had died of starvation.

Now that I was calm enough, I made a couple of phone calls on my cell, getting voice mail each time. As I waited for the call-backs, I busied myself by packing what remained of my life here into banker's boxes; if I didn't return from Kanati, at least Jimmy wouldn't be stuck with the job.

While working, I listened to *John Lee Hooker On the Road*, the live blues album that included my father playing backup on his Gibson dobro. Of the few things I could remember about him, that one event shone most brightly. My mother had taken me to the nightclub where Hooker was playing, and my father had been asked to perform along with the blues legend. I remembered sitting on my mother's lap when he and Hooker launched into "Boogie Chillen," which segued straight into "Boom Boom." The pride on my mother's face had stayed with me throughout all these years.

Ignoring the lump in my throat, I folded another shirt and put it on top of the others. How had I wound up with so many black tees? And why, once they'd become too ragged to wear, hadn't I thrown them out?

Easy answer. As alike as those tee-shirts might look to a casual observer, each was unique and bore a particular memory. The shirt I'd bought at the old Sears store, for instance. I'd been wearing that when a killer had dumped me in the desert and left me there for dead. The shirt from JC Penny? I'd been wearing it when Jimmy first walked through the door of Desert Investigations and applied for a job. I folded that one even more carefully than the others.

Now for the final carton.

I fully unpacked that box because I wanted a final look before duct-taping it closed.

I wanted to see the photograph of my blood-stained blue dress, the newspaper headline...

CHILD SHOT IN HEAD REMAINS UNIDENTIFIED

I wanted to touch these artifacts again and draw strength from them.

As my murdered father's dobro sang through the apartment's stale air, I hugged the photo of the dress to me.

And thought about vengeance.

The first call-back came in just after ten. It was Pete Ventarro, from the Medical Examiner's office. "It's her," he said.

"Who?" My mind was a hundred miles away, maybe two hundred, in a forest glen littered with small bodies.

"The gal you sent me a sketch of the other day when I was

so busy. People have been calling her Reservation Woman, but yeah, she's Alene Laumenthal, the wife of the also-deceased Ford J. Laumenthal. The mother was just here and ID'd her. She's taking her daughter's body back to Wyoming for burial as soon as the ME releases it."

I closed my eyes in relief. No pauper's grave for my girl. Granted, she wouldn't be buried next to her bully of a husband, but he hadn't deserved her anyway.

"Thank you, Pete," I whispered.

"Hey, is something wrong?"

"Not anymore."

"There's, ah, one more thing." Pete sounded embarrassed, which wasn't like him.

"Which is?"

"Since you're the one who found her, the mother wants to meet you. And she wants to see where her daughter was, um, found."

"Dumped, you mean." I felt my anger rising again at the thought of her alone in the desert, tossed like a sack of garbage.

"Dumped, yeah, but I didn't put it that way to her, because I wanted to, you know, ease the blow as much as possible. Not that it would make any different in the long run, because, you know, well…" He cleared his throat. "So could you, I mean, I know it's unusual, but I'm thinking it would…"

There are times when vengeance has to take a backseat, and this was one of them, because even the dead had a right to compassion. Maybe somewhere someone had done the same for my mother.

"Yeah, Pete. I'll do it."

Forty minutes later I met the widowed Faye Chambers at the Airport Comfort Inn. She was waiting for me in the lobby, a sweetly plump woman with permed brown hair, wearing a plain black dress. Her faded eyes were rimmed in red, and her hands clutched at a manila folder.

Before she let me lead her to my Jeep, she wanted me to see her daughter as a living, breathing person, not as the lifeless husk she'd had to identify. I sat next to her for as long as it took while she opened the folder and showed me the pictures of Alene as a baby: "She was such a good baby, never cried." Alene as a toddler: "Always getting into things but you couldn't get mad at her, you'd just laugh." Alene as a kindergartener: "Her teacher said she might grow up to be a musician because she would play the class's xylophone by ear and get it right the first time." Alene as a teenager: "That's her prom dress, she insisted on picking it out by herself and I was nervous about that because you know how girls can be, but look at her here, the dignity and grace." Alene the week before she'd left home: "She looked so full of hope that day."

Starvation-shriveled Reservation Woman had not been beautiful, but the Alene in the photographs was. Her skin glowed, light shown in her clear blue eyes, her smile dazzled. "She was a catalog model, you know," Faye said. "For *The Plus-Sized Beauty*."

Faye took out the company's catalog and flipped through the pages. There was Alene wearing a dusty rose evening gown, looking like a princess. There was Alene dressed in a red, white, and blue sailing costume, ready to board a yacht. There was Alene, curvy and irresistible in a sleek black swimsuit.

"I was so proud of her."

I squeezed Faye's hand. "You had a right to be."

"But when she met that man, he made her feel bad about herself."

"Sometimes it goes like that."

Faye's back, which had been bowed, straightened. "All right. I'm ready to go see the place now."

Still holding her hand, I led her to the Jeep.

A half hour later we stood at the spot where I had found the woman I'd known only as Reservation Woman. The Pimas had memorialized her with a white cross. The ground was covered in freshly planted flowers, and the cross shadowing them was looped with colorful strings of beads. I had added a necklace of my own, beads of multi-colored quartz interspersed with small bits of turquoise. We desert people would never forget Alene's brief sojourn among us, and would always pay homage to her spirit.

"It's so beautiful," Faye whispered.

"Just like your daughter."

Chapter Twenty-six

The next morning I was getting ready to lug the packed cartons down to my Jeep when I received the call-back I'd hoped for yesterday. Gabrielle.

"Our Adam, he has agreed to meet with you, *mon amie*, sometime between lunch and dinner," she told me. "And yes, I bear even more good news. He has invited you to attend with us the morning meditation. That is a great honor, you understand, because only members of Kanati are allowed to attend."

"Then I'll see ya in a jiff." Acting jovial wasn't easy, but somehow I managed it.

Oblivious to my deceit, she laughed. "How I love your quaint Americanisms!"

What else besides quaint Americanisms had Gabrielle learned since she'd been in the U.S.? How to starve people to death? I did some quick math in my head, and realized she might have grown up in The Divine Temple of the Holy Cross, which had morphed into the quasi-rehab facility known as the Kanati Spiritual Center. Then it occurred to me that Gabrielle's own parents could have been part of the murder/suicide pacts in Quaydon, leaving only their daughter to carry on The Divine Temple's deadly work.

Was the sad story she'd told me about a friend in the fashion industry dying from anorexia true? Or was it just another of her lies?

I felt my rage rise again. "Here's another Americanism for you, Gabrielle. I'm locked, loaded, and ready to rumble."

Not understanding, she laughed again.

Before leaving for Kanati I made a quick stop at Gary's Gun Shop to load up on hollow points for the .38. At times like this I regretted not having already bought the Glock 17 I'd been checking out, but you can't see into the future, can you? I'd had enough trouble seeing the past.

Still, my .38 could do the job.

Foregoing my strap-on holster, I stashed the revolver in my tote bag, covering it with tissues and a couple of granola bars. Then I wrote Jimmy a note and left it on his desk downstairs.

Just in case.

Never had the drive to Kanati seemed to go so slowly, but an hour later the Jeep arrived at the guard shack in front of the former movie set. The sun shone brightly overhead while Ernie gave me a cheery smile and an "Always glad to see ya, Lena." Then he caught sight of my arm. "Hey, what happened?"

"Accident."

"Car?" He shot a worried look at the Jeep's unmarked bumper.

"I fell in the shower."

In my suspicious frame of mind, I suspected everyone, and wondered if friendly Ernie knew about The Divine Temple of the Holy Cross, and the Arneault family's murderous history. But chances were, only a few of Kanati's higher-end officials did know: Adam, Gabrielle, and the people walking around with the heavily beaded headbands. That was the way cults worked. The big dogs kept everything secret until the sheep had been brainwashed into believing that the murder of innocent children was part of God's holy plan.

After assuring Ernie that I was fine, I parked the Jeep and walked through the gate into Kanati.

This time, the Old West storefronts behind the stockade looked as phony as Kanati's Elevated belief system. The name

Hotel OK Corral wasn't funny anymore; it was dreadful. This was a place that promised a better way of life, but was a cover for a death-worshipping cult no better than Jim Jones' People's Temple and its cyanide-laced Kool-Aid, or Shoko Asahara's Aum Shinrokyo and its sarin gas. They all dealt in death, not spiritual awakening.

The first person I ran across in Kanati was Roger Gorsky. He was carrying a box loaded with clay pots to one of the picturesque storefronts. Since his wares were so ugly, I couldn't imagine they'd be popular with tourists. Come to think of it, I'd never seen any tourists at Kanati; the place was too far off the I-10. No matter. The cute Old West buildings were lies, anyway, because the real Old West hadn't been romantic; it had been brutal.

As I passed Roger, he gave me a nod. I noted with interest that two new beads adorned his headband, meaning he'd been promoted to four. *Nvgi*, as the Kanatians called it in their uninformed Cherokee. *Sowo, tali, tsoi, nvgi, hisgi, sudali, galiquogi, tsunela, sonela, sgohi*. One through ten. But even Gabrielle's bead collection had been halted at *sonela*, nine, as if she wasn't quite part of Kanati's elite. And if not, why not? What lie had she refused to tell for Adam? And yet I remembered the gentleness of her hand when she'd traced the scar on my forehead, the compassion in her voice when she'd said, "Your *maman* did not mean to shoot you, Lena Jones."

I remembered the long scars on Gabrielle's own wrists, her own pain.

Putting my own compassion on hold—did death merchants deserve compassion?—I continued across Kanati's wide plaza, past the storefront declaiming RUSTLER'S ROUNDUP SALOON, past the HOTEL OK CORRAL spa/massage parlor, past all the phony Old West storefronts until I reached the huge lodge that housed Kanati's dining area and administrative offices.

I didn't see Gabrielle when I walked in, but I did see someone else I needed to talk to. Chelsea, Adam Arneault's new blushing bride. She was covering the long luncheon tables with white table-cloths that must have cost a pretty penny. Kanati may have been phony from the get-go, but at least it wasn't a third-rate phony.

"Hey, there, Chelsea," I said, making certain no trace of my rage leaked into my voice. "How come I didn't get invited to the wedding? And why in the world are you working on what should be your honeymoon?" *Smile, smile.*

Chelsea cast me a bewildered look. "Why shouldn't I be working? Kanati teaches that work frees the soul."

Arbeit macht frei. Work sets you free. That was the sign the Nazis hung over the gate to Auschwitz, pretending that just as long as its prisoners worked hard, everything would be fine, just fine. I remembered that the people at The Children of Abraham had always been busy, too. Chopping wood, building shelters, working in the garden. When you're busy, you don't have time to think.

"Work frees the soul, huh?" I said to Chelsea. "I didn't know that."

She stopped smoothing the linen tablecloth long enough to deliver a mini-sermon, straight from a phony prophet's playbook. "Working together promotes a sense of harmony. Keeping our hands busy teaches us that Truth and Elevation can be found in the smallest of tasks." Looking back at the table again, she added, "And as for you not getting a wedding invitation, only Kanatians were allowed to attend. Say, what's wrong with your arm?"

"It had an argument with a knife. By the way, Harold was pretty upset when you sent him that text. Why'd you do it?"

With a vacuous smile, Chelsea smoothed the tablecloth again, but there were already no wrinkles left in it. Did the Kanatians iron their sheets as well as their table linens? "After what he pulled with that damned de-programmer, he's lucky I didn't press charges."

So it had been revenge, then. There sure was a lot of that going around.

I faked my own smile. "Let me see your wedding ring."

She thrust her left hand forward. A plain gold band, just like the gold bands worn by Alene Laumenthal and Megan Unruh. Just like the gold band the ER docs had to cut off me when I was only four years old.

"Pretty," I said. "Doesn't marriage to Kanati's Head Honcho count for more than one lousy bead on your headband?"

She let the snipe at her new husband slide. Instead, she flushed with pleasure. "I'm being awarded eight more beads tonight in a special ceremony. That means I'll be eligible to try for *sgohi*! There is no higher honor in Kanati!"

Hearing that, some of my anger vanished, replaced with concern. Whatever that final damned bead represented was dangerous. "What do you have to do to get that remaining bead?"

Her eyes danced with an edgy joy, she said, "*Have* to do? No one is ordered to do anything here. Whatever we do, we do willingly."

She was so "up" it was a miracle her feet still maintained contact with the floor. For a moment I thought it might have been drugs, but then I decided not. I was looking at religious mania in its purest form. Trying to sound soothing, I said, "C'mon, Chelsea. We're friends, remember? You can trust me. How do you get to, uh, *sgohi*?"

"I can't tell you. It's a secret rite." She looked proud, and a little bit scared.

I was scared for her myself, suspecting what horrible secret that final bead represented. But from past experience I knew nothing was to be gained by attempting to reason with her when she was like this, so I just patted her on the arm. "Well, good luck. Have you seen Gabrielle, by any chance? I need to talk to her."

"Are you thinking about joining Kanati? She told me you sounded quite excited about coming up here today."

Another forced smile. "More excited than you can possibly imagine."

"Gabrielle's in the kitchen. There was some sort of screw-up in there this morning, and Adam asked her to handle it."

After telling Chelsea I'd see her later, which was doubtful, I headed toward the kitchen. Before I got there, the double doors opened and Gabrielle emerged. For once she didn't look serene. Strands of her chestnut hair had come loose from her chignon, and a pink bra strap peeked out from the short sleeve of her Kanati shirt. The cross expression on her face lightened when she saw me.

"Oh, my, but that was a fast drive!" Then she saw my bandaged arm. "What…?"

"Workplace injury. Did I get here in time for Adam's meditation?"

Her smile was my answer, and a few minutes later I filed into the big meditation teepee, hand-in-hand with a possible murderess. Gabrielle, along with all the other female Kanatians, hid their hair under white scarves. The men were more decorative, with long stoles vaguely reminiscent of Messianic tallit prayer shawls. But instead of being white and decorated with blue Stars of David, these were blue, and in keeping with Kanati's phony Native Americanisms, boasted embroidered white buffalos. I've always loathed it when people co-opted someone else's religion, but I knew there was something more horrific than religious plagiarism going on at Kanati.

"Your arm?" Gabrielle asked. "Does it hurt you?"

"Not at all. It's just a scratch." I had long-ago learned never to show weakness in dangerous situations.

"That is a long bandage for a scratch."

"Just an over-zealous nurse."

A strong scent of sage smoke filled the air, and since the teepee only had one large opening at the top, and two smaller ones for the entrance and exit, I was a bit concerned about the lack of oxygen, but both tent flaps were kept open, and the ensuing cross-breeze felt fresh. As we took our seats on the large pillows, a flautist played something that sounded vaguely Navajo, while the drummer—the elderly man I had hoped to interview—delivered a slow, steady beat. In an obvious attempt to keep the ceremony from becoming overtly sexist, an attractive soprano dressed in a flowing white robe sang "Amazing Grace" in what sounded to me like flawless Cherokee.

The pre-meditation service, although a bit hokey, was no stranger than others I had encountered. To my relief, the wooden altar was too small to be used for sacrificing chickens or virgins, large enough to hold only a jumble of pseudo-Native American trappings. Feathers, drums, and a carving of a white buffalo encrusted with white beads. Speaking of beads, the soprano wore five on her headband, which from what I had been led to believe, denoted good spiritual progress. She also had a nice voice, even though with her sandy hair and gray eyes she looked more Swedish than Cherokee.

Once the last Kanatian had entered, I did a quick head count. Eighty-two, including me, too many people for such a small space. As I eyed the tent opening on the other side of the teepee, the music stopped. Even the drum fell silent. The entire room assumed an air of expectancy that was as tactile as a touch.

Then he was there.

Adam.

Golden Boy, who at the ripe old age of twelve had shot my father and infant brother to death, and who as a grown man, led a cult responsible for at least three more deaths.

"*Tsalagi!*" Adam said in a voice so low I shouldn't have been able to hear it but that somehow managed to reach the farthest rows in the teepee. "Peace!"

Dressed in a loose white robe not all that different from the soprano's, the serial killer was thin to the point of gauntness. Sharp cheekbones shadowed concave cheeks, and his mouth, which I remembered as being full, had dwindled to a thin line. With his bowed head and prayerful hands he appeared harmless, but I knew better. I touched the tote nestled between my knees, reassuring myself that my .38 was still there.

"Close your eyes," Adam/Golden Boy murmured, his voice slightly accented from his years in France. "Take a deep breath, then relax. Let the White Buffalo speak to your innermost being."

The old drummer began to beat a rhythm I recognized as a healthy heartbeat.

Clever. But of course, the Arneaults had always been clever.

I looked down and pretended to meditate.

For the next half hour Adam's followers relaxed into what appeared to be a semi-conscious state. I didn't, having no desire to converse with a white buffalo. But there was nothing I could accomplish right now, surrounded as I was by eighty-plus people who believed they were in the presence of a miraculous bovine. I had to wait for my appointment with the madman.

Finally, a quickening of the drumbeats announced the end of the meditation. When I opened my eyes, Adam was gone.

"Was that not wonderful?" Gabrielle said, her face ecstatic.

I looked around and saw the same expression on everyone's face. "It was something, all right."

"The best is yet to come. A personal audience with Adam himself!" Hooking her arm around mine, she led me from the big teepee and toward the lodge, her eyes glittering with adoration.

"He looked pretty thin, though, don't you think? Like he's been ill."

She shook her head. "Like most men of holy nature, Adam fasts on a regular basis."

"With a cuisine like Kanati's?"

"Do you not see? That is the whole point!"

No, I did not see, but having other things on my mind, I let it go. If I'd stayed safely in my office and merely called the authorities, all I could offer them were nightmares about a mass slaughter somewhere in Arizona or New Mexico. As for Adam Arneault's connection to those old killings or the contemporary deaths of Megan Unruh and the Laumenthals, I had nothing there, either, just a hodgepodge of memory and suspicion. Under such iffy circumstances, the authorities were useless. Without probable cause, they couldn't even get a search warrant. And yet I knew Adam's skewed world was readying itself for a fresh set of victims.

Execution was the only answer. I had come close to it once before, when a serial child molester was grooming his next victim, but someone else had lifted that burden from me.

This time there was no one left to do that for me. To save lives, I would take a life, but not before I asked Adam Arneault one final question.

"Are you excited, *mon amie?*" Gabrielle asked.

Forcing a smile, I answered, "You can't imagine."

But I felt like molten lead had been poured down my throat.

35 years earlier

It is all over. Despite Helen's attempt to save Christina, her daughter had still died.

As had Liam.

And Jamie.

All her fault.

Nothing matters to Helen anymore, nothing.

Except revenge.

The loud chaos in the bus rises as she jerks the hot barrel of the .38 away from Brother Steve and shoots him in the head.

And after him, Brother Joseph.

Two more to go.

As Abraham, who has risen from his seat on the bus, stares open-mouthed at her, she shoots him in the neck, and with satisfaction, watches a fresh spurt of blood.

Now it is time for Golden Boy, Abraham's twelve-year-old son, the killer of Helen's husband and baby boy. He must pay for his crimes, too.

But as Helen stares into Golden Boy's terrified eyes, she realizes that she can't kill a child, no matter what he has done. Too many children are already dead, their bodies thrown down into that dark mineshaft.

Liam. Jamie.

Eager to end her pain, Helen angles the gun barrel toward her mouth.

"No!" A woman's voice rises above the screams, and Helen is tackled by two women, women she'd believed paralyzed with grief over their own murdered children.

"Please let me!" Helen screams as Sister Bonita, a burly mother of two now instead of three, wrestles the gun away as Sister Jessamine, now mother of none, rams her head into Helen's stomach.

Helen falls to the floor of the white bus.

Defeated again.

Chapter Twenty-seven

Adam Arneault's office was on the second floor of the big cedar lodge, tucked away in the back as if trying to hide. Which he was, of course. His entire Elevated life was a lie, and liars don't like to be found out, so he had hidden himself inside a phony community where people had no idea who he really was or what he had done—*was still doing*.

My father, shot to death.

My baby brother, shot to death.

Megan Unruh, starved to death.

Alene Chambers Laumenthal, starved to death.

Ford Laumenthal, starved to death.

And probably others I didn't yet know about, because serial killers can always be counted on to kill again and again until someone stops them.

The living spaces people create for themselves always contain "tells," so as soon as Gabrielle left me in the empty office, I studied my surroundings. I wasn't surprised at the number and quality of books lining the floor-to-ceiling bookcase, because most cult leaders read a lot. The problem was, they misinterpreted what they read. Adam's bookshelves contained tomes by Descartes, Kant, Nietzsche, Sartre, Diderot, as well as several different translations of the Bible. Plenty of room for misinterpretation there. I also saw books on various Indian tribes, from the Anasazi to the Zuni, with the most titles given over to the Cherokee.

Otherwise, the décor was pretty much what I'd expected from a white man who thought he represented America's indigenous people. Navajo rugs on the floor. Leather sofa with cowhide throws (casting couch for future wives, perhaps?). Wooden desk with carved Native American images as authentic as a cigar store Indian. A weirdly out-of-place ergonomic chair behind the desk. Hanging on the wall across from the bookcase, an oil painting of a white buffalo. The buffalo had eyes as dark and depthless as licorice jelly beans.

The room had no windows, just another door to my right, but it was closed, like the door Gabrielle had exited. Executive washroom, or something else? The door gave me a bad vibe, so I skipped the comfort of the cushy leather sofa and stood in front of the bookcase, slipping my hand into the tote. The revolver was still there, its handle nestled against my palm. With a pistol in your hand, you're never alone.

From the great room below, I could hear laughter as Adam's followers enjoyed their superb Le Cordon Bleu lunch. I wondered how many of them realized what went on behind Kanati's closed doors. A select few, probably, because such knowledge was too dangerous for clueless people like Roger Gorsky and Chelsea Cooper-Slow Horse. As for Gabrielle…

My thoughts were short-circuited by the sound of a nearby toilet flushing, then water running from a faucet.

I drew the .38 at the same time the bathroom door opened, revealing Adam Arneault standing there. Up this close he appeared even more skeletal than he had in the big teepee. He had been twelve years old to my four when his homicidal father "married" us, which made him around forty-seven, but he looked older. Participating in mass murders ages a man.

Adam smiled when he saw the .38. "Still the brave one, aren't you, Christina?"

"Where is she?" I asked, centering the barrel on his heart.

His smile remained in place. "Do you mind if I sit? After my long fast, I feel quite weak."

"I don't care if you hang yourself, as long as you answer my question. Where is she?"

"Where is who?"

"*My mother!*"

Unfazed by the .38, he walked over to his desk and sat down in the ergonomic chair. Sighed. Maybe he had a bad back from carting all those corpses around.

"What makes you think I know where your mother is?"

"If anyone knows, you do. Is she here?"

"I haven't seen that bitch since the day she murdered my friends."

"My mother never murdered anyone."

A moment of rage passed across his face, then disappeared when he remembered he was supposed to be Elevated. "Your mother is a murderess, Christina."

"Even if that were true, which I doubt, it was nothing compared to the slaughter your father initiated."

"An unfortunate blunder in an otherwise glorious reign."

"You're calling the mass murder of innocent children a *blunder*?"

"My father was simply obeying the god of his understanding. There was no malice involved, therefore no murder."

"Killing in the name of religion is permissible, then?"

He shook his head. "Not for religion, for an ideal. And yes, killing in order to pursue an ideal has always been permissible. When governments do it, it's called war. They even hold parades to celebrate its glory, Christina. Oops, sorry. You're going by the name of Lena now, aren't you? Why is that?"

Because at the age of four, with all my injuries, I couldn't pronounce my real name, that's why, and the social worker attached to my case thought he heard me mumble "Lena." Determined not to be lured away from my primary purpose, I skipped the history lesson. "Tell me exactly what happened that day. The last time I saw my mother she was on the old school bus taking us to a new compound."

"I'm surprised you remember that. You were what, four years old? Five? We thought you were dead, killed by your own deranged mother. But here you are, alive and well, and every bit as beautiful as I remembered." Bracing himself against the desk, he stood up and took a step forward, closing the distance between us.

With the bookcase at my back I could only move to the side. I didn't want to kill Adam until he told me everything I needed to know, but I wasn't going to let him put his hands on me.

"Stop right there," I told him.

He complied.

"I was four. Tell me about that day, step by step, what happened after…"

"After your mother shot my father and two of his closest friends? Ah. You didn't know about that, did you? That's right, you were gone by then, fallen into the street. But even if I tell you, I'll gain nothing, because you're going to kill me anyway, aren't you? Like your mother, you are a great believer in revenge."

"I won't kill you if you tell me where she is," I lied.

He chuckled. The chilling sound had nothing in common with the innocent laughter dancing its way up from the great room below. The Kanatians had probably reached the dessert course. The aroma of cinnamon wafted up the stairs. Clafoutis aux Poires?

"Oh, Christina, you always were a bad liar. But all right, because what do I have to lose? Either way, I'm dead. So here's the way it went. Thanks to your murderous mother, Brother Steve and Brother Joseph were dead, and the rest of the Believers were spattered in blood, wailing at your mother's display of evil." He paused, his eyes unfocused as he looked back down the decades.

"Move it along, Adam."

Snapping back to attention, he said, "Such impatience! Remember what old Ram Das said, 'Be here now.' But whatever. Back to the bus. Despite the discord around him, Brother

Jonathan drove onto the freeway, speeding toward New Place in California, toward the land of milk and honey, toward…"

The revolver felt heavy in my hand, and I realized what was happening. Adam's words had fallen into a rhythm designed to lull me into inattention, the same rhythm used by Kanati's elderly drummer during their meditations. "Skip the travelogue and get on with it," I snapped.

"You have such marvelous focus! No wonder I loved you." Admiration gleamed from his lunatic eyes.

Not as patient, I assumed the firing position, one leg in front of the other, both hands grasping the .38. My damaged left arm protested, but I didn't care. "Adam Arneault, you die on the count of three. One. Two…"

He blinked. "Ah, yes. You want to know what else happened on the bus. Well, of course I'll tell you, because we are past the need for secrecy, aren't we? By the time we made it to California, Sister Bonita had taken control, and that's when I learned a lesson that has guided me to this very day. *Never underestimate a woman.* Sister Bonita made Brother Jonathan pull into an abandoned rest stop and dump out the bodies of Brother Steve and Brother Joseph, which if you don't mind me saying, was a disrespectful way to treat fallen soldiers. Women, you know. Always driven by emotion." He waved his skeletal arms. "As for your mother, she was thrown out, too. Once the mess was off the bus, we were on the road again."

The *mess*? Two dead men and my mother were a *mess*? "What happened to your father's body? Same thing?"

An odd expression crossed his face. "No one would ever treat God's holy prophet in such a despicable manner. As soon as we arrived at New Place, we erected a monument to his memory. Where—and I'm certain this will please you—the coyotes sing him lullabies."

"Lullabies? For a child killer?"

Impatience flickered across his face. "You still don't understand, do you? Death doesn't exist. It's only an illusion. But to an extent, I must agree about the children. Their transition to the next phase of life—especially my older brother's—was unnecessarily messy." He shuddered. "All that blood."

My trigger finger itched. "Where are The Children of Abraham now?"

"In the wind. New Place welcomed us with open arms at first, but Nature abhors a vacuum, and soon there was squabbling, people vying for control." He shook his head. "Then there was more blood and Sister Bonita and many of her followers disappeared. You've been around long enough to know how these things go. After that second round of depravity, Brother Gaston, who had been with my father since the days of The Divine Temple of the Holy Cross, suggested that those of us in the original group return to France. So we did. End of story. Today New Place is covered in dust."

"Brother Gaston?" I remembered the old man I'd seen on my first trip to Kanati. He'd been hobbling around on two canes, but wore a headband loaded with status beads. More recently I'd seen him pounding a drum during the meditation service.

That odd look again. "Brother Gaston reached the highest level of Elevation many years ago, and we all remember that moment with great fondness. The wisdom I gained from him kept me from repeating my father's mistakes, so at Kanati, there is no forced sacrifice. Children are not even allowed on the property, let alone serve as sacrifices. Are you not proud of your husband's compassion, Christina?"

"You're not my husband, you jerk. Marriage to a four-year-old girl isn't legal, so stop with the bullshit and tell me what happened to my mother or get gut-shot."

All color left his face. "Your mother probably killed herself at that rest stop!" In an imploring tone, he added, "But how would I know? I wasn't there!"

One liar can recognize another. I smiled. "Do you know how much a gut shot hurts? You'll die in agony. Slowly."

"Please, I...I won't..."

The bookcase at my back suddenly swiveled open, knocking the .38 from my hands. Before I could reclaim it, one of Adam's burly bodyguards emerged from the hidden alcove with an enormous Taser X2.

The prongs hit me in the neck.

Once I was down, he kicked me in the head.

I felt nothing after that.

35 years earlier

Helen stands alone at the boarded-up rest stop.

The bodies of Brother Steve and Brother Joseph lie half-hidden in the underbrush, but Helen pays no attention.

Her eyes are dull, unseeing. She cannot hear the passing traffic on the interstate, or the mockingbird that serenades her from a nearby tree. The buzzing of cicadas as they call to each other goes unnoticed. She sees nothing, hears nothing, knows nothing. The world that existed before this moment is no more.

She stands there unmoving for hours, but toward evening, a California Highway Patrol cruiser leaves the highway and pulls up beside her.

"Ma'am, do you need assistance?" the trooper asks.

But Helen can neither see nor hear him.

"Ma'am? Are you... Oh, *shit!*"

Helen's sins have silenced her.

She does not speak again for twenty-two years.

Chapter Twenty-eight

"...so you see, Christina, while I am not truly *of* this world, I remain aware of its dangers. Thus the alarm button on my desk. Thus my clever bookcase. Thus the escape hatch in my bathroom."

A blurry Adam Arneault stood above me.

I was lying on the ground and my head throbbed so badly I had trouble focusing. I ached all over—my head, my hips, my shoulders, my everything. Even my fingers hurt, especially the one on my left hand, which felt as if someone had tied a memory-jogging string around it too tightly and then forgot to take it off. When I tried to pull my hand up so I could see it better, I realized my hands had been tied behind my back.

Blinking away the spots dancing in front of my eyes, I surveyed my surroundings.

I lay in a dimly lit square room built from unpainted cinderblocks. The cement floor was unpainted, too, and had a drain in the middle. The lodge's basement? I hoped not, because three of the room's other inhabitants needed immediate medical attention. Two frighteningly thin young women wearing white robes lay unconscious on nearby pallets. Both were brunettes and looked so much alike they could have been twins. A similarly garbed woman, blond but as skeletal as the brunettes, sat slumped against the wall. As Adam spoke, her eyes tracked him with adoration.

"Look well upon these courageous women, and do not fear following in their footsteps." When he bent down and kissed the still-conscious blonde on the forehead, she moaned in appreciation.

"Behold my love for you, Monica," he murmured to her. "You are truly worthy to be my bride."

"Lo…Love you," she whispered.

My mind was still muddled, but I'd caught the word *bride*. Was the white robe she wore a wedding dress? Was I here to witness a wedding? But what about the other two white-clad women? Bridesmaids weren't supposed to wear white, everyone knew that. I looked down, hoping to find myself dressed more appropriately, only to discover I wore a white robe, too. What the hell?

I shook my head, which made it hurt even more but the pain helped clear my mind. Adam Arneault was flanked by two male acolytes so muscular I suspected steroids. Strangely enough, the elderly man I'd seen during my earlier visits to Kanati, was here, too. Instead of propping himself up on canes, he now sat in a wheelchair.

"Do you not realize the great gift you are about to receive, Christina?" Adam droned on in a sing-song voice. "I, the hand-picked prophet of the one true God, am awarding you the highest honor a woman can have, and yet you appear unhappy."

Adam's self-celebratory words didn't quite manage to cover the ragged breathing of the other women. My vision had become sharp enough for me to see that all three wore simple gold wedding rings, but unlike me, their hands and feet remained untied. Each bore the gaunt face and swollen belly of advanced malnutrition, yet judging from the response of the blonde, they had done so voluntarily. Starving their way into Adam's good graces. Was this what Chelsea had let herself in for?

As Adam moved closer, I could see the jaundiced pallor of his skin. He was starving, too, but his eyes were lit with an unholy fire. "This is the final Elevation, my beloved, where you undertake your own personal vision quest. Here you will purify your body and enter a higher plane, as have other brave souls before you. The Cherokee, the Arapaho, the Cheyenne—so many others. They were spiritual warriors. Like myself, they fast, understanding that we must deny the delights of this Earth in order to be worthy of the White Buffalo's teachings. These courageous women beside you, they understand."

I know crazy when I see it, and I was seeing it now. "Just to get another plastic bead for their Dollar Store headbands?" I spat. "In two more days they'll be dead. And by the way, you jackass, the Native Americans fasted for only four days, not weeks. What you're doing here is murder!"

Before he could respond, the old man in the wheelchair muttered, "*Elle ne peut pas être rachetée.*"

Adam raised his hand in admonition. "She can't be redeemed? You give up too quickly, Father. You always did. With my help, my beloved Christina *can* be redeemed. Love such as mine carries within it the strength of holy salvation for others. All she needs now is to complete her vision quest."

The old man laughed. "Oh, grow up. The only thing that bitch needs is a bullet in her head." His English was unaccented, his smile chilling.

Father, Adam had called him. *Father.*

I jerked my head toward the old man. "What church allowed you be a priest?"

"The same church your apostate mother belonged to."

For a moment I couldn't react. This old man knew my mother? I peered at him more closely, studied the shape of his head, saw what appeared to be an old bullet scar on his neck.

He couldn't be. But he was.

Abraham.

Maurice Abraham Arneault, the deranged prophet who thirty-five years earlier had ordered the killing of all firstborns in *Les*

Enfants des Abraham, The Children of Abraham. The man who had ordered his son to finish off my father and baby brother.

Before I could find my voice, Adam said, "I must apologize for my father. He is almost ninety now and has been in constant pain for decades, pain caused by your mother's attempt—a failed attempt, thanks be to the White Buffalo—to shoot him to death." He raised his eyes reverently to the room's ceiling.

"Thanks be to the White Buffalo," his acolytes chanted.

Abraham sneered.

Focusing on me again, Adam said, "You still misunderstand, my beloved. These precious ones," he made a sweeping motion with his hand, "are in the process of learning that the sensuality of Earthly love is our worst enemy. The love of beauty, the love of a caress, the love of beautiful music, the love of fragrant blossoms, and especially the love of good food—these carnal urges pave the pathways to Darkness. Ah, I see the confusion in your eyes. Kanati provides all these pleasures, does it not? But of course it does! Because what avails a person if he only renounces the things he does not love?"

I thought I heard Abraham mutter "Bullshit." The old man may have been evil, but he was no fool.

Adam shot his father a withering look, then turned his maniacal gaze toward me again. "And now, my beloved Christina, now that you are returned to me I offer you the gift of Elevation, so that you may join with me on that Heavenly Plain as my One True Wife." He raised his arms and addressed the ceiling again. "Oh, great are the gifts of the White Buffalo!"

Throughout this bizarre sermon, Adam's henchmen had been gazing at him with the same adoration as had the woman slumped against the wall. "Great are the gifts of the White Buffalo!" they chorused.

This time Abraham spoke so loudly there was no mistaking his words. "What crap."

My throbbing head prevented me from feeling worshipful, too. "You're all crazy."

Adam bent down and caressed my face. I tried to bite him, but he was too quick.

"We are not crazy here at Kanati, Christina. We are Elevated beings."

I looked at the red plastic bucket in the corner. "So you're going to Elevate me how? By waterboarding?"

A gentle smile. "There is no suffering unless you choose to interpret your vision quest in that way. We are not savages. You will be provided with enough water to ward off dehydration, and your sanitation needs will be cared for in a most civilized manner."

He pointed to the bucket. On the opposite side of the room I spotted a gallon jug of water sitting on the floor; next to it was a Styrofoam cup.

Abraham growled at his son. "Stop wasting your time on the bitch. Just roll me over there and let me at her. I still have enough strength in my arms to finish her off."

Pointedly ignoring him, Adam continued, "Furthermore, Christina, your condition will be checked on every six hours, so never fear abandonment. Your continued safety during this trial is most precious to me."

I refused to let him see my fear. "How long is this endurance contest supposed to last?"

"Until you are Elevated beyond all physical desires, as I have been. When you are purged, you will enter into *Gaivladitsosv*, the Cherokee word for Heaven."

"Sane people call it death." Staring at the unconscious women, I said, "Surely these women are Elevated enough already. They're nothing but bones."

His eerie smile never wavered. "To educate you is a privilege, Christina. As you pass through the many stages of your trial, you will learn that only I—a man who regularly endures them all yet still remains on this Earth to fulfill my most holy mission—only *I* can judge when a person has been completely cleansed, thus redeemed. Sisters Vera and Zoe are almost, but not quite, ready.

Sister Monica…" Here he gestured toward the blonde slumped against the wall, "She will be ready in another week, perhaps. She can still speak."

A dreamy look entered those curiously flat blue eyes. "Christina, did you know there is a man in India who for years has not eaten so much as one grain of rice? *His soul is so pure that he takes all his nourishment from the air!* That is the level of purity we at Kanati strive for." The madman's eyes focused on me again. "Remember, the thing you call 'death' means nothing. It is merely a portal to the Dwelling Place of the White Buffalo. With initiates such as these faithful wives," he waved a bony hand at them, "entering into that exalted place is a voluntary act, something they *choose* to do."

"I'm not volunteering."

"As your husband, I…"

"Stop calling yourself that! You're no more my husband than that…that *thing* over there." I jerked my head toward Abraham.

"Insult me though you will, you and your sister wives will be honored at the Welcoming Rite, where after Elevation, you will all be awarded the final jewel in your crown."

I remembered Gabrielle's explanation as to why her headband only held nine beads, not ten: that she was too cowardly. "Gabrielle couldn't tough it out, could she?"

His smile flickered. "Total Elevation is not for everyone. Gabrielle came close, but failed. Yet I did not let her die, did I? I made her useful. But your courage is indisputable, as I hope will be the courage of your friend Chelsea, who will be joining you soon."

"You leave Chelsea alone!" As foolish as the woman was, I didn't want to see her harmed.

"And throw away her one and only chance for redemption? Oh, I think not." His voice sank to a near whisper. "I wish for you all to stay with me on this Earthly plain, and help me share the Kanati gospel with the entire world. Then there will truly be peace on Earth."

"You know what, Adam? You're every bit as crazy as your father."

The gentle smile finally disappeared. "My father is the sanest of us all."

As soon as the cell door closed behind Adam and his cohorts, I got busy.

To enable my access to the red bucket, one of Adam's guards had untied my feet while his buddy threatened me with another shot from the Taser, so although my hands remained bound behind me, I was able to move around more or less freely. I wriggled my way over to blond Monica, who during Adam Arneault's sermon, had lost consciousness. After I knelt down and butted my head against her bony thigh, her eyes fluttered open. "Is…is this the Dwelling Place of the Whi…White Buffalo?" she whispered.

"Not yet. Help me get out of here." I flipped over so she could see my bound hands. "You need medical attention."

Unwilling or unable to help, she closed her eyes again.

Had Reservation Woman died like this, still believing? Or had she, with her final breath, seen the lie?

"You must have suffered so much," I whispered to her across the miles.

But pity wasn't useful. Only action was. Recognizing that Monica was a lost cause for now, I moved over to the other two women and did more head-butting. "Vera! Zoe! Wake up!"

Nothing but raspy breaths. Both appeared comatose.

All three of these deluded women would surely die unless I could figure out a way to alert the authorities. Desperate, I wriggled around the tiny cell, looking for something I could use as a weapon. Three men, one of them carrying a three-shot Taser X2, against one unarmed woman were lousy odds.

But I found nothing I could use in the scrupulously clean room.

Even the sewage bucket was empty, more proof the three women sharing the cell with me were shutting down physically.

However, while I was looking at the bucket, I got an idea. First, though, I would need to free my hands.

The softness against my wrists assured me my bindings weren't zip-ties but some sort of rope. An exercise rope from Kanati's gym, perhaps? I tugged at it for a while, which made my damaged left arm start bleeding again, but whichever of Adam's guards had tied me up had done a good job. Plan A having proved impossible, I started on Plan B.

No skilled carpenter had designed this room, just a do-it-yourselfer in a hurry. The cinder block walls and concrete floor were useless, as was the unvarnished wooden door, which appeared a mere afterthought. The similarly unpainted doorjamb was bolted into the wall, leaving an ugly surround of rough cinderblocks. A nasty piece of work, but as I studied it, the sloppy workmanship began to look beautiful.

I backed up against the roughest corner and slid down, keeping my hands pressed against the cinder blocks. As soon as I was on the floor, I felt around for a useable edge. When I found one, I started scraping my bound wrists up and down, back and forth, sometimes grating skin against cinder block instead of rope. Every now and then, to take my mind away from the pain burning through my left arm, I talked to the other women.

"Still hanging in there?" *Scrape, scrape.*

No answer, not that I'd expected any.

"So how'd you hear about Kanati?" *Scrape, scrape.*

No answer.

"But you've got to give Kanati points for its cuisine, don't you? The Chicken Basquaise is superb." *Scrape, scrape.*

No answer, but at least they were still breathing.

Conversing with people who don't converse back grows tiresome, and my meager collection of small talk soon ran out. To keep my mind off the pain in my wrists—the fierce grating had shredded the skin on both—I remembered Jimmy's strong but gentle hands, his everlasting patience. I remembered him building our lovely little house to create a safe place for us in a dangerous world. I remembered the note I'd written, telling him how much I loved him, how much I wanted his…

But thinking about Jimmy made me choke up, so I turned my mind to Ali and Kyle, who were somewhere out there in the Arizona wilderness, holding fast to their love for each other. I even managed to think about Chelsea without anger, because Chelsea was Chelsea, and couldn't help being what she was. As the pain in my wrists increased, I thought about Reservation Woman, real name Alene Chambers Laumenthal. This made me think about her unpleasant husband Ford, who had dragged her from commune to commune until he found the place that would kill them both. As my anger rose again, I shifted my thoughts to Megan Unruh and her brokenhearted paintings of body parts. But I found I couldn't think about her without thinking about her mother, a woman whose aloof manner concealed a great emptiness. Then, most distressing of all, I thought about my mother's screams as I fell out of the bus and onto the Phoenix street, where…

The rope fell away from my hands.

I was free.

After standing up—I was shaky and both my wrists were bleeding badly—I ripped at the hem of my white robe, and halted the blood flow with makeshift bandages. While doing that, I discovered the cause of the pain in my ring finger. A wedding band, probably put on there by damned, delusional Adam while I was unconscious. I tugged the nasty thing off and threw it in the corner.

Time to help the other women.

Ignoring my own thirst, I filled the Styrofoam cup with water and went from woman to woman, lifting up their heads, wetting their lips, their tongues, their gums. Since they were unconscious, I was careful not to let any water trickle down their tracheas. No point in trying to rescue them if they drowned during the attempt.

"Stay with me," I murmured. "Just stay with me."

Vera, at least I think it was the twin named Vera, moaned.

"Do you know where you are? What's happening?"

She fell silent.

Determined not to let sadness overwhelm me, I patted more water onto her lips. "We're getting there, Vera, but in the meantime, don't enter any tunnels, and for God's sake, stay away from any white light you happen to see."

After doing the best I could for the three of them, I drank the rest of the water in the cup. Filled it again. Drank that. Repeated the process, drinking and drinking until I sloshed. Within minutes Mother Nature came calling. I relieved myself in the bucket, then drank more water. *Every six hours*, Adam had said. When they'd undressed me, they left me my Timex, and it showed I'd been in this cell for almost three hours. Three more to go. It took mere minutes to take the wire handle off the bucket. I bent the ends together, creating a narrow loop at the top, then with the help of the rough cinder block walls, honed the loop into an approximation of a point. Not the best prison shiv ever made, but it would serve my purpose. Satisfied, I drank more water.

Peed again.

Who should I use the shiv on first? Maurice Abraham Arneault, who had killed children in the name of God? Or his son Adam, who had continued his father's murderous work, albeit in a less bloody manner?

Whoever I ran into first, I decided.

I drank more water.

Peed again.

I kept repeating the process until I heard footsteps in the corridor outside. Then, ignoring the pain in my wrists, I picked up the bucket, which was now half-full of urine, and stood to the side of the door.

"You gals wish me luck," I whispered to my unconscious roommates.

When the door opened, I hurled the bucket of urine into the two guard's faces. Their reaction was exactly what I'd hoped for. Both men instinctively raised their hands to rub their burning eyes.

This gave me time to deliver a bloody karate chop to the wrist of the guard carrying the big Taser, followed by a knee to the groin.

He dropped the Taser.

I snatched up the Taser and did unto them what they'd done unto me. Since they were both drenched in urine, it worked especially well. But I didn't take time to admire my handiwork. While the men were still unconscious—or dead, maybe?—I relieved them of their two-way radios, cell phones, and keys, then grabbed my handmade shiv and left the cell. Once outside, I locked the bastards in with the women they had helped starve.

I found myself in a short hallway that ended in two choices: a staircase to my left, a wheelchair-friendly ramp—guess who for—to my right. My blood-spattered white robe had no pockets in which to tuck anything, so I dumped most of my trophies onto the ground. Entangling my homemade shiv in my long hair, I hurriedly hit 9-1-1 on one of the guards' phone. From the tone in the dispatcher's voice, I wasn't certain she believed me, so as soon as I finished with her, I called Detective Sylvie Perrins.

"Do what you have to do, but make sure they send out several ambulances," I finished, after telling her everything I'd told the 9-1-1 dispatcher. "The women are in the lodge's basement, which is accessible through a fake bookcase. And, uh, Sylvie?" I looked down the hallway. Saw what I hadn't wanted to see. "There's a second cell down here. And I hear moaning coming from it."

Sylvie had no trouble believing me, but being a cop, she bowed to the snail-slow workings of the law. "For shit's sake, Lena, don't do anything you'll regret. You need to…"

"Bye."

Armed with my homemade shiv and the Taser X2—it had

one cartridge left—I climbed the staircase on my left, praying it would lead me to Adam's office, where I hoped I'd find him.

I had one last job to do.

The staircase ended inside a cabinet in Adam's bathroom, which meant that the paranoid monster had built two escape routes. The good thing about this was that it enabled me to creep out of the bathroom without making a sound. Before he realized what was happening, I was an arm's-length away from my one-time "husband."

"Surprise!"

He looked up in shock. "Christina, I…"

With great satisfaction I delivered the X2's final shot.

When he stopped writhing, I knelt on his chest and held the shiv to his throat, pressing just hard enough for a thin line of blood to trickle onto the carpet.

"Like how this feels?" I asked.

"Don't! You…"

"Did you ever wonder how your older brother felt when your father carved out his heart?"

"But I didn't…" His entire body shook.

He was almost ready. I pressed the shiv in further so that the run of blood thickened.

My voice trembling from a bottomless well of grief, I whispered…

"Where is my mother?"

This time he talked.

And a fat lot of good it did me.

Chapter Twenty-nine

Jimmy, standing next to my hospital bed, looked like twenty miles of bad road himself. But he had given into my pleas and, despite doctor's orders, had brought the morning newspaper. There was so much red on the *Montezuma County Gazette*'s front page, the newspaper looked like it was bleeding.

STARVATION CULT LINKED TO 4 DEATHS!

If the headline had been any bigger, it wouldn't have had room for the photograph of Adam Arneault and his henchmen being led, handcuffed, into the Montezuma County Jail, with Maurice Abraham Arneault following close behind in his wheelchair. And it wouldn't have been able to show the photographs, taken in happier times, of Megan Unruh, Doreen and Ford Laumenthal, and Vera Worthington.

Vera, one of my cellmates, died of a coronary on the way to the hospital, but Sylvie had slipped me the information that Zoe, Vera's twin sister, might make it. Same with Monica. In fact, Monica lay in the room next to mine at the Montezuma County Hospital. When she regained consciousness, would she be glad to be alive, or bereft that her attempt at Elevation had been halted?

As for me, I wasn't happy about being here, but the stitches in my left arm had been torn apart during my escape and needed re-suturing, and while freeing my hands, I'd somehow managed to grind several pieces of cement deep into my wrists. The wounds were infected.

"Have another drink of water," Jimmy said, noting the perspiration on my face.

"I've had all the water I can stand, thank you very much, but I'd love a Tab. Or a Coke. Diet Coke. Coke Zero. Whatever it's called these days."

"But water is…"

"Do I need to remind you how I got out of that cell?"

He sighed. "There's a soda machine in the cafeteria. Be right back."

Moments after he left, Sylvie sidled in with a smirk. "Don't you look lovely today!"

"Up yours."

"I see your sweet personality's returned, too. And to add more sweetness to Ms. Sweet, I've brought you a gift."

"Something other than water, I hope."

"Yeah, I heard about that." Snickering, she took a copy of the morning's *Arizona Republic* out of her briefcase. "For your literary edification."

The *Montezuma County Gazette* may have devoted one and a half pages to the raid on Kanati, but the *Republic*, as befitting any Pulitzer-winning newspaper, had given it six. They had even traced Kanati's origins back to Europe's Divine Temple of the Holy Cross and the mass murders in Quaydon, France.

I read so fast the words blurred together.

"…after Maurice Abraham Arneault was severely wounded, the group known as The Children of Abraham fell apart, with many of its former members returning to France, Switzerland, Canada and other countries of origin. Several years later, Arneault's son Adam emerged as the organization's new leader. Due to his personal magnetism, the younger Arneault was able to reorganize the group, giving it a new mission. Adam Arneault called his new group 'Kanati,' a Cherokee word for God. He combined his father's teachings with a hodgepodge of various Native American traditions, cobbling together a belief system which at first glance appeared to stress physical, mental and spiritual health.

A closer look, however, revealed that the basic tenet of The Divine Temple of the Holy Cross remained in place—salvation through sacrifice. In Kanati, this led to the starvation deaths of at least four of its members.

There have also been rumors, as yet unsubstantiated, of a mass grave in northern Arizona, where members of Abraham's original group are buried."

So now I knew. For whatever reason, my mother and father had joined the American branch of the deadly Divine Temple of the Holy Cross. Their mistake resulted in the murders of my father and baby brother. Sick at heart, I asked Sylvie the question that had been gnawing at me for two days. "Did Adam say anything else about my mother? Did Abraham?"

I had never seen her look so unhappy. "Wish I could tell you, Lena, but the Feds and the Montezuma County Sheriff's Office aren't telling me everything. Thankfully, I arrived at Kanati while the big roundup was still going on, and overheard a couple of deputies talking about two French nationals locked in the cell next to yours. You know anything about their backgrounds?"

"Just heard them moaning, that's all. But what about Gabrielle? Did she know how bad things were?"

She shook her head. "Never got a chance to talk to her. But those French guys, the youngest was only sixteen, for Christ's sake. Word is, he might not make it."

We stared at each other for a moment, both of us feeling like hell. Teenagers were so easily led. While lying in my hospital bed I'd done some math. My parents had probably been teenagers themselves when they first became involved with The Children of Abraham, way too young to understand what they were signing up for.

"Do you know where Abraham is now?" I could hardly bring myself to say the old demon's name.

"Not specifically, just that everybody in Kanati is being held pending further investigation. In the Arneaults' and their body-guards' cases, that means a jail cell, but I don't know about the others, like your friend Chelsea. Hell, the whole county's crawling with lawyers."

"Chelsea's not my friend."

"Yeah, yeah, tell me another one."

"Forget her. What I need..."

Before I could finish, Jimmy came through the door carrying a can of Coke Zero. I couldn't understand why he looked so unhappy until I saw what was following him.

Two men in black suits.

Chapter Thirty

Being interviewed by the Feds is never fun, especially when they've already done their homework and know who and what you are. In my case, the "what" meant being one of only three known survivors of The Children of Abraham; the other two were Maurice Abraham Arneault and his skeletal son Adam.

Since I'd been only four years old when the slaughter happened, there wasn't a lot I could tell the Feds about those last days—just that Maurice Abraham Arneault, mimicking the deranged behavior of his biblical namesake, had called for the sacrifice of all firstborns. My mother and father attempted to rescue some of the children, but failed. As a result, my father and baby brother had been shot and killed by Adam Arneault, whom I had known only as Golden Boy. I remembered seeing the bodies of Abraham's oldest son and all the other murdered children, tossed into a mine shaft, but its exact location was a mystery to me. As for my mother, the last time I saw her was when she shot me in a failed attempt to help me escape.

The only thing Adam had been able to tell me about her was her first name: Helen.

After a few frustrating hours, the black-suited men left, even more tight-lipped than they'd been upon their arrival. I couldn't tell if the look on their faces was anger or sorrow.

But the Feds weren't my only visitors that day. The other two were more surprising, and considerably more welcome.

I had been dozing when I heard someone enter my room. Expecting a nurse, I opened my eyes to see Ali and Kyle leaning over my bed. Considering the fact that the two had been hiding out in the Arizona wilderness for almost two weeks, they looked pretty good. Maybe that was because I was looking at them through a godmother's nonjudgmental eyes.

"This morning we found a newspaper in the waste bin near where we'd been camping and read what happened." Ali.

"So we drove up to see if you were alright." Kyle.

"I'm fine and dandy, but you two won't be once your parents get hold of you." I hated the wobble in my voice, but at least they had the decency not to call me on it.

Instead, Ali leaned over and patted me on the shoulder. "They've promised not to kill us."

"So you've already been in touch."

"Pay phone in the hospital lobby," Ali said. "Mom's driving down to get us."

"You realize your stunt probably cost her the election."

Ali shrugged. "Eggs and omelets."

"What?" My eyes felt hot. Probably something in there.

"You know, to make an omelet you have to break a few eggs."

"People aren't eggs, you brat."

"Sticks and stones."

By sundown the kids were back with their parents and I was sitting in front of the firepit on the Pima Rez, delivered there by Sylvie while Jimmy followed in my Jeep. Given my bandaged arms, I wouldn't be driving for a while. As I watched the flames flickering, I tried to forget the gaunt faces of the three starving women in the cell, and the indignation of Kanati's true believers while being herded into police vans. The authorities hadn't even made an exception for Ernie the gateman, just herded him in with the rest of the others. Chelsea, whose flightiness began my interest in the group, had been one of the first to be arrested.

She'd become so enraged at not being allowed to undergo her own starvation ritual that she head-butted a deputy.

"I'm never speaking to you again," she'd spat at me, as an officer zip-tied her hands behind her back.

"I'll hold you to that promise," I'd replied, wondering who or what she would glom onto next? Whatever, I was well out of her life.

Sylvie, although not officially part of the case, promised to keep me updated on the rumor mill, especially where it concerned Gabrielle. While Gabrielle must have known that some Kanatians didn't make it through the starvation ritual alive, I saw her as another victim of the Arneaults. I remembered the tenderness with which she'd touched the scar on my forehead, the long scars on her own arms.

"Thinking deep thoughts?" Jimmy asked, over the crackle of the fire.

"People don't ever seem to learn, do they?"

"Sometimes they do. Here. Thought you might like some barbeque after all that bland hospital food." He handed me a plate of spareribs.

I managed to gnaw my way through a few of them. When I finally put the plate aside, I said, "Adam Arneault didn't know much more about my mother than I already did."

"Maybe he knew enough."

"Those bastard murderers left my mother at a rest stop. She'd have been just another hitchhiker back in the day when highways all across the U.S. were cluttered with them."

"He remembered her first name was Helen."

"How many Helens are there in the U.S.? Tens of thousands? Millions?"

"I'll see what I can do. In the meantime, have another rib. It'll make you feel better."

I did, but it didn't.

"There's something else we need to discuss." Jimmy's voice sounded grim.

When someone delivers a statement like that, in a tone like that, bad news is certain to follow. "I'm not ready for anything heavy," I told him.

"Whether you're ready or not, here goes. That was a nice note you left me before driving down to Kanati to get yourself maybe killed, but it wasn't enough. I'm through being an adjunct to your life."

"*Adjunct?*"

"Don't pretend you don't know what I'm talking about. If you're not involved in one cause, you're involved in another, then another. And whatever's going on, I'm always the last to know. Sometimes living with you feels like living with a ghost."

I felt a surge of panic. Was he breaking up with me? Jimmy had been my rock for years, the one person I could count on, no matter what. We'd been through hell together, and it had only made our partnership stronger. Then I had a moment of insight. I had been thinking about our *working* partnership, not our personal one. He was right.

"Oh, Jimmy, I…"

He held up his hand. "Let me finish."

I bit back what I wanted to say, that I loved him, that I couldn't imagine life without him.

"That kind of behavior has to end, Lena. From now on, I want you to include me in everything you do, whether it be the office billing or the hunt for your mother."

"But she…I'll never…"

The hand came up again. "I'm not finished."

This time I noticed his calluses. He'd been working harder on the house than I had. Same with our relationship.

"I'm going to find your mother for you, but when I do, you have to realize something."

"What?" My voice was no more than a whisper. Here it came. The end of us.

"You have your way of looking at the world, and I have mine.

I may have been raised by a white family, but I'm one hundred percent Pima, with everything that entails. This means something you're probably going to find scary."

I steeled myself, prepared ready to hear the Pima version of goodbye.

"Your mother will be *my* mother, too."

With that, he handed me another barbequed rib. "You don't have to say anything now, just start thinking about how our relationship needs to change, no matter what we find out about her. I'm through being left behind. From now on, you're going to have to include me in every aspect of your life, even when it goes against your instincts."

I stared at the fire, red and gold against the indigo sky. Sparks from the burning embers rose toward the Milky Way, which astronomers estimated was comprised of a billion stars. Maybe even more.

Chapter Thirty-one

Two weeks later my left arm was still stiff, but my Appaloosa mare reined in her fiery heart as if she understood and ambled across the desert with the mildness of a child's first pony. This was our first solo outing since I'd been injured, and it felt freeing to leave the ever-hovering Jimmy and Big Boy behind for once.

"Just us gals, right, Adila?"

She flicked her ears in acknowledgment.

The air was crisp, no more than sixty degrees, and the desert smelled fresh after the night's thunderstorm. Ahead of us stood the old ironwood tree I'd given up for dead, but it was hanging in there as if hoping to survive through another season. We'd lost one of the great saguaros, though. It had been split apart by lightning, its skeleton scattered along the desert floor. A reminder that nature could be cruel as well as kind.

As could people.

Maurice Abraham Arneault and Adam Arneault, along with their strong-armed cronies, had been charged with multiple counts each of aggravated homicide, and were now awaiting trial. Abraham, too old and feeble to care what happened to him anymore, had admitted to a long-ago massacre in a nameless forest, but he could no longer remember the exact spot it had taken place. Whether New Mexico or northern Arizona, trees all looked the same to him, he told the authorities. More charges against the old demon were pending. As for Gabrielle Halberd, who had given an interview to the *Arizona Republic* claiming she knew nothing about people dying during Kanati's trial-by-starvation, she had been charged with three counts of negligent homicide. Her future appeared as bleak as our one-time friendship, but once the dust cleared, I might be able to bring myself to visit her in whatever prison she wound up in. Not much would happen to the rest of the Kanati folk. Freedom of religion, and all that.

I tamped down my anger and concentrated on Adila's steady hoofbeats. We kept our slow pace for another half hour until we reached the necklace-draped white cross. Today the memorial for Reservation Woman had a family of Gambel's quail for company. The mother stood guard as the adolescents pecked around the brush for insects. I waited until they moved on before dismounting and paying my respects with a Pima prayer Jimmy had taught me.

> *Do you hear me?*
> *Do you hear me?*
> *Away off the wind runs*
> *Away off your travels*
> *Through the sweetly flowered fields*
> *To the home of your mothers.*
> *Oh, desert woman, do you hear me?*

Finished, I remounted just in time to see a horseman galloping toward me, his long black hair streaming out behind him.

I tensed, expecting bad news. Jimmy wasn't the hurrying kind.

"What's happened?" I asked, as he reined in Big Boy next to Adila.

His deep brown eyes squinted against the rising sun. "I found her."

I glanced down at Reservation Woman's memorial. Surely there was some mistake. "But Alene's mother already took her body back to Wyoming. Don't tell me it was the wrong one!"

Jimmy flicked a look at the cross, noted a new rope of beads, nodded in appreciation. "I'm not talking about Alene Laumenthal."

"Who, then?"

He took a deep breath. "Remember that new search app of mine?"

I frowned. "Not really. You've always got a new…."

Suddenly Big Boy danced away from my horse as she tried to bite him. Then a small breeze came up, rattling the new beads on the white cross, which made Big Boy shy again.

"Better control your horse," I warned Jimmy. "He's about to back into a cactus."

"Woman, you are so…" He gave a sigh of exasperation as he brushed his long hair out of his face. "Can I talk now?"

Big Boy flinched. Yep, the cactus had stung him. Horses. Never a dull moment. "What did you want to tell me, Jimmy?"

"I found your mother."

Chapter Thirty-two

It took more than an hour to drive from LAX to Chino, California, and the California Institution for Women, where my mother—Helen Stocker Grant—was serving a life sentence for multiple homicides. She had been transferred there thirteen years earlier, after spending twenty-two years at Camarillo State Mental Hospital.

I had talked to the warden, Dr. Wanda Bosham, over the phone last week. Before speaking with me, she'd done considerable homework, but for once the past had been on my side. A graduate of Arizona State University, the warden and I turned out to have an acquaintance in common: Detective Sylvie Perrins, whose mother had been in the same sorority as Dr. Bosham. The warden wasn't optimistic about a face-to-face meeting with my mother, though.

"For the past ten years your mother hasn't allowed any visitors, not even the standard church-affiliated kind," she'd said when we'd first talked on the phone. "Several people had turned up claiming to be relations, but who were in actuality reporters or true crime writers in search of a story, so…"

"I'm coming anyway."

"It's your funer…" Although gruff-sounding, Dr. Bosham wasn't without compassion, and had stopped herself before completing *funeral*. "Well, you might be in for a big disappointment, is all I'm saying. I'd like to spare you that."

"I've handled worse."

A long silence. Then, "Yes, I guess you have, Ms. Jones."

Chino was a small city with a curious past. One of the original Spanish land grants, its ranching and cropland remained largely intact. The oddity had crept in during the twentieth century, when it acquired three prisons—the California Institution for Men, the California Institution for Women, and the Heman G. Stark Youth Correctional Facility. Most of the guards at these institutions lived in the area, rubbing elbows with dairy farmers and ranchers, not to mention the gun enthusiasts who began flocking to the place once the city's Prado Olympic Shooting Park hosted the shooting events at the 1984 Summer Olympics.

I was fine with the city itself, and even finer once I'd driven through it and entered the farmland on the other side. But when the first guard tower of the California Institution for Women appeared on the horizon, my heart beat faster. At least Jimmy wasn't along to witness my onslaught of nerves. After a long conversation, he'd agreed his presence might complicate the world of prison bureaucracy, and so he stayed in Scottsdale to mind the store. But there was another reason I was relieved he hadn't accompanied me: I'd always preferred to do my falling-apart in private.

From a distance, the one hundred and twenty acres of the California Institution for Women complex looked like a particularly ugly community college enduring financial difficulties, but as I grew closer and began to ignore the surrounding farmland, its true purpose became obvious: keeping the guilty away from the innocent. Assuming, of course, that every woman found guilty in a court of law had actually committed the crime she'd been charged with. Given the high cost of good criminal defense attorneys these days and the zero bank balances of most female defendants, that assumption was iffy.

No old-fashioned, high-walled complex at CIW, just a sprawling collection of low-rise buildings and cottages surrounded by razor wire, some of it electrified. A few severely trimmed trees set far back from the main fence softened its utilitarian appearance somewhat, but razor wire was razor wire. Just looking at it sliced your skin.

This was where California's high-profile female killers were housed. In the past, the inmate list had included Patricia Krenwinkel, Leslie Van Houten, and Susan Atkins, all members of Charles Manson's demented "family." But the prison had also housed more upscale killers, such as San Diego socialite Betty Broderick, who'd murdered her ex-husband and his new wife, thus gaining a best-selling book about her exploits, as well as a TV series. In such cases, the razor wire was well-earned.

Not wanting anything to go wrong at the last minute, I had taken care to read the lengthy dress restrictions for prison visitors. No clothing that resembled the clothing prisoners wear, such as blue denim and chambray, orange jumpsuits, muumuus (not that I would ever have worn such a garment), or anything the custodial staff might wear, so no forest green pants, tan shirts, or camouflage. And no halters, bare midriffs, sheer or transparent clothing. No skirts, dresses, or shorts that exposed more than two inches above the knee. No wigs, hairpieces, extensions, or hats. No clothing that exposed the breast, genitalia, or buttocks area.

My usual black-on-black ensemble was acceptable.

Warden Bosham had done her best to cut through the standard red tape and procured a visitor's pass for me, but getting inside the prison was a test of anyone's endurance. After being waved through the outer gate, I parked my rented Corolla in the visitor's lot and joined the long line in front of the Visitor Processing Center.

I wasn't surprised at the number of children in the line. Every other visitor had at least one child in tow. Most of the inmates were mothers, just as most inmates in the men's prisons were fathers, thus visiting days were family days. Still, it tugged at my heart to hear so many toddlers crying out for their mommies.

An hour and a half later, when I finally reached the head of the line, my ID was checked by a redheaded guard with a bad sunburn who reminded me vaguely of Ernie at Kanati. No relation, though, unless guarding killers ran in the family.

Younger and less jovial than redheaded Ernie, this guard took his time. While I waited for him to check my previously filled-out visitor's pass on his computer and decipher the fine print on my Arizona's driver's license, a brisk breeze came up, carrying with it the scent of alfalfa and something else. I looked up at one of the guard towers, and saw a dark-haired man holding a rifle. He was singing an old song about a woman who kills her lover.

> *Bring out your long black coffin,*
> *Bring out your funeral clothes,*
> *Johnny's gone an' cashed his checks.*
> *To the graveyard, Johnny goes.*
> *He was Frankie's man,*
> *But he done her wrong.*

Given the song's current setting, it made me shiver. How many of the women here were responsible for their lovers' deaths?

"Who are you here to see?" The guard's voice, seemingly coming from afar.

"What?"

"I asked, who are you here to see?"

Irritated by my long wait, I snapped, "Can't you read? It's on the form."

No answer.

The silenced stretched between us long enough that I began to worry. Recognizing that I wasn't the person in power here, I finally said, "Helen Stocker Grant."

He looked up from studying my ID. His eyes were brown, not the expected blue. "Grant, hmm?"

"Helen Stocker Grant."

Sighing, he typed a few more keys on the computer, then

handed me back my license and visitor's pass. "Good luck, Ms. Jones."

He let me in.

Thirty-five years earlier, a California highway patrolman had found my mother covered with blood at an abandoned rest stop. A few yards behind her lay two gunshot victims: Steve George Garabaldi, 37; and Lester Eagan Westerly, 29. Subsequent testing traced the blood spatter on her to each victim, the angle suggesting she had been standing less than two feet away from each man as she fired. Ballistics tests also tied the empty .357 Mag revolver found lying at her feet to the bullets in the men. Her prints overlaid Garabaldi's, proving that although he had at one time handled the weapon—it was legally licensed in the state of New Mexico—she was the last to hold it.

When taken into custody, my mother had made no statement. She had remained silent while meeting with the defense attorney provided by the court. Eventually, Elmo Harris Krycheck, M.D., the state-appointed psychiatrist, declared her as being in a rare dissociative fugue state that in her case, led to catatonia. Considered too mentally ill to be tried in a court of law, she was sent to the Camarillo State Mental Hospital for treatment. More than two decades later, and the veteran of several sessions of electroshock therapy, she began speaking again.

She pled guilty to four murders, although the bodies of two of her victims—her daughter, and a man she called "Abraham"— were never found.

Pictures of Helen Stocker Grant were sprinkled liberally through the newspaper articles Jimmy dug up, beginning from the first time she had come into public attention thirty-five years earlier, when she appeared to be little older than my goddaughter, to ten years ago when a true-crime writer who claimed to be a relative managed to take a picture as Helen came through the visiting room door. In the earlier pictures, she had my face. In the last, her face was lined with age and despair. But despite the damage done to her appearance over the years, I think I would still have recognized her.

After that last dishonest snapshot—the true crime writer was denied further visits to the prison—my mother had refused all visitors. As if reverting to her former catatonic state, she stopped speaking, even to fellow prisoners. From what the warden had told me, Helen Stocker Grant's voice could now only be heard when she was recording audiotapes of books for the blind in the prison's "Voices from Within" program. One of the books she recorded was Maya Angelou's *I Know Why the Caged Bird Sings*.

Given all those children in line to visit their mothers, grand-mothers, or aunts, I wasn't surprised to see the toys in one corner of the visiting room I was ushered into. There was even an area where, for a small fee, you could have your photograph taken with your imprisoned loved one. Maybe if things worked out...

I turned in my visitor's pass to another guard, and he relieved me of my driver's license and other ID. While I fidgeted, he called my mother's housing unit to advise her of a visitor, and to come to the waiting room. I took a seat at one of the many small tables, and watched as several corrections officers roamed between them, eyes alert for inappropriate behavior.

Ten minutes later my mother was a no-show.

Fifteen minutes.

Twenty.

Thirty.

I sat there for a full hour while around me other visitors reunited with their loved ones. Partner with partner, sister with sister, mother with child. Sobbing. Laughing.

My own mother never showed.

After calling Jimmy and telling him what happened, or rather what hadn't happened, I spent the night at the motel in nearby Norco. The next day, I returned to the visitors' area. When she no-showed again, I flew back to Phoenix and ran into Jimmy's welcoming arms.

I repeated the same routine the next weekend.

And the next.

Each time I took the same Southwest flight from Sky Harbor, rented what looked like the same white Corolla, reserved the same motel room, filled out the same visitor's pass, stood for hours in the same line, saw the same faces. I felt nothing anymore. You know what they call you when you keep making the same mistake over and over again while expecting a different outcome? They call you crazy, that's what.

On my fourth Sunday visiting the California Institution for Women, I sat across from Lindie Sullivan, who three years ago had knocked over a Circle K to feed her heroin habit, then shot herself in the leg on the way out of the store. She was laughing at the jokes told by Trevor Puente, her ex-husband. Not all reunions were as happy. On the other side of the room, JoBelle Gudreax, doing time for three counts of arson, sobbed on the shoulder of Jane Graham, who'd come to tell her she was marrying someone else.

As for me, I wasn't the crying type. Besides, this time my wait was made less onerous by Marie Lopez, who had burned her abusive husband to death. She was reading a book of nursery rhymes aloud to her great-granddaughter. Marie had just moved on to Humpty Dumpty when Officer Matt Hill approached me. He was the same redheaded guard who had wished me luck during my first visit. Since then, I'd learned that he had two children under five and his wife was battling breast cancer.

From the serious look on Matt's face, I figured he was about to deliver an order from the warden for me to stop coming, to stop wasting everyone's time, to go back to Arizona and forget about the sorrows at the California Institution for Women.

Instead, he whispered, "Brace yourself. She's on her way down."

"She?"

"Your mother."

Ignoring my trembling knees, I stood up. I wasn't certain if I could even talk. Should I tell her I'd missed her, even though I could hardly remember what she looked like? Tell her it was okay she'd shot me because that bullet had freed me from The Children of Abraham? Should I lie and tell her my years in foster care had been a fourteen-years-long banquet of joy?

Ten minutes later, the door separating the visiting room from the inmate units opened, and two correctional officers I didn't recognize walked through. Between them was a lean gray-haired woman, her face twisted in anger. She obviously expected to tell another journalist to get lost.

"I...I..." Thirty-five years of separation had stolen away my voice.

Her blue eyes narrowed, she strode through the crowded room to me, then stood so close I felt her breath on my neck.

"You're not my daughter," she hissed. "Christina's been dead for years, and I'm the one who killed her, so you stay away from..."

She fell silent.

Stared at me.

Stared at my pale yellow hair: hers. My high cheekbones: hers. My straight nose: hers. My strong jaw: hers. My green eyes: my father's.

She lifted an age-spotted hand.

Touched the scar on my forehead.

Whispered, "My baby?"

Then she slumped to the floor.

Chapter Thirty-three

Thirty-five years of institutional life hardens a woman, but not enough to make her numb when her daughter rises from the dead.

Matt Hill was the first officer to reach her, but I already held my mother's head in my lap. She hadn't fallen too hard. Wilted, really.

"Step back, Lena," Matt ordered. "Let us take care of this."

I gently lowered my mother to the floor and stepped back.

As the other corrections officers worked to keep everyone else calm, Matt spoke into his radio, requesting medical assistance. Looking up at me, he added, "She had a coronary last winter."

The prisoners had fallen silent, some of them out of sympathy, the others enjoying the free show. Then the door burst open and three more staffers rushed in carrying a stretcher. The noise started up again, with inmates calling out suggestions. Some of their comments revealed surprising medical knowledge, although one harsh-voiced woman screeched, "Let the old bitch die. Even Hell be better than this place."

I ignored them as Matt led me off to a tiny room I hadn't noticed before, sat me in a chair, and said, "I'll be right back."

Thirty minutes later I was still staring at the blank wall when he returned carrying a plastic glass of cold water. "She's going to be fine. Just a moment of shock, what with…well, you know."

"When can I see her?"

"Drink that. You're in shock yourself."

"When can I see her?"

"The warden says for you to come back tomorrow. Ten o'clock. That'll give your mother a day to process this."

"Tomorrow's Monday. Not a visiting day."

"It will be for you, Lena. For now, go back to your motel and rest up. But drink that first. I don't want another fainting woman on my hands."

"I don't faint."

"Hmph."

I drank the water.

As soon as I made it back to the motel, I went to the front desk and asked Sophia, the friendly desk clerk, to add another week to my stay. That accomplished, I got the motel's fax number and went to my new room. The old one had already been booked.

Then I called Jimmy and told him what had happened.

"Want me to fly out there now?"

"Not if it would mean closing Desert Investigations on Monday, our busiest day, and it would."

I told him what I needed.

After a long silence—so long I began to worry—he agreed.

Ending the call, I looked at my old Timex. It was six minutes after four. *Seventeen hours and fifty-four minutes before I could see my mother again.* I couldn't sit around the motel doing nothing, my nerves wouldn't let me. So I changed into my running shoes, then walked over to the lobby to ask Sophia for directions to a good running trail. Earlier, she'd wanted to know if I felt okay, and now she repeated the same question.

What was with everyone's sudden concern for my health? I was fine. Perfectly fine. Never better. The fact that my right leg kept wobbling, the heel doing a rickety tap dance on the tile floor meant nothing. Absolutely nothing.

Sophia looked me up and down. "How fit are you?"

"Very fit."

"That's what they all say. But maybe some diversion would be good for you, so how about the Pumpkin Rock Trail? It's not far from here, and makes for a pretty rigorous sprint. One and a half miles, all uphill. It overlooks some nice scenery, too, if you're into the desert kind. That sound okay?"

"I'm good with deserts."

She drew me a map. I snatched it up and ran out the door.

Seventeen hours and forty-five minutes to go.

Pumpkin Rock's parking lot, well away from town and out in Norco's scrubland, was empty. I locked the Corolla and began running.

Sophia had described the trail well. Surrounded by not much more than dirt, rocks, and scrub, it meandered up the hill toward a series of rock formations. The arid sparseness resembled the Sonoran Desert so much that I felt almost at home. The only jarring note was the smell. Unlike the herbal scents of the Pima Reservation, the air here smelled musty and acidic at the same time, probably because of the nearby cattle ranch and the ever-moving freeway. I didn't mind. My brain was so busy with the things I wanted to say to my mother that I didn't even care when a rattlesnake slithered across the path.

Don't bite. Don't bite.

I ran past the snake, past a curious steer, then past something small and brown and furry that scampered into the weeds at my approach.

Just passing through.

I ran away from my thoughts and toward whatever.

I ran.

I ran.

When I reached Pumpkin Rock, I wasn't the slightest bit tired. It was easy to see why Sophia had sent me here, but I remained too jumpy to appreciate her attempt at humor. The giant boulder was about three times the average person's height and almost perfectly spherical. Local wags had painted it bright orange and drawn on a jack-o-lantern's face. Mr. Pumpkin leered at me as, without pausing for breath, I whirled around and began running back down the trail.

Sixteen hours and thirty-seven minutes to go.

After returning to my car, I checked the other map Sophia had drawn me and headed for L.A. Fitness just off I-15, where the toned ash blonde at the counter issued me a guest pass. This enabled me to spend two hours on the Nautilus machines.

Fourteen hours and six minutes.

Muscles aching, I stopped by for a carnivore-N-carb reload at In-N-Out Burger, then made my way back to my motel room.

Thirteen hours, fifty-two minutes.

There wasn't much on TV, just so-called reality shows, an *NCIS* rerun, and a piece of HBO fluff about a book club where none of the Hollywood-looking women ever seemed to read. They all had great hair, though, and I received a few makeup tips to make myself look younger, not that I wanted to. In my business, experience trumps looks.

When the last woman in the book club had found cheap and easy everlasting love, I turned off the TV. What to do now? Unable to come up with anything more reasonable at the moment, I decided to rearrange the furniture. My motel room was ugly, but I'd chosen it for its nearness to the prison, not its charm. Everything was either solid brown or solid orange except for the carpet, with its pattern of orange flowers on a deep brown background. Oh, and the coverlet, which featured broad brown stripes on an orange background.

Ugh.

I eased the visual monotony by dragging the brown tweed chair away from the orange-curtained window and placing it against the brown opposite wall. Then I moved the faux wooden desk to the window. The desk lamp had an orange shade, which blended well with the orange drapes. Now I had my choice of looking at solid brown or solid orange, as long as I didn't look at the carpet or the bed.

Still feeling antsy, I did some pushups. Despite my weak left arm, I managed thirty. Then I showered again.

Nine hours, fifteen minutes.

After toweling dry, I slid naked underneath the cool sheets— white, thank God—and turned off the light. I lay there in the dark for what seemed like an eternity, then turned the light back on and looked at the clock.

Eight hours, six minutes.

There would be no sleep for me tonight. On my way back from L.A. Fitness, I'd passed an all-night Walgreens, so I threw on a clean tee-shirt and jeans, drove as slowly as I could to the drug store, and limped in. I browsed the magazine and book section, grabbed a Sue Grafton—sainted be her name—a Lee Child, and a Stephen King horror-a-thon, along with a copy of the latest issue of *Guns & Ammo*. Thus fortified, I took them to the cashier.

"Doing a little light reading?" the cashier cracked. Well past retirement age, he sported a hairdo so thick and black I suspected it was either dyed or a wig.

"It's for my mother."

His silver eyebrows almost touched his low hairline. "She must be some woman."

"Buddy, you have no idea."

Seven hours, forty-six minutes.

Almost two hours later, having speed-read my way through the Jack Reacher shoot-em-up—*six hours and eleven minutes*—I developed a desire to talk to someone who didn't kill for a living. Jimmy was the logical person to call, but it was only eight minutes after four a.m., and he needed to be alert when he opened Desert Investigations tomorrow morning—make that *this* morning—in case some dumb judge had let Mother Eve out again. My left arm still throbbed from the pushups.

Sylvie? Like me, she suffered from insomnia, but if she'd finally been able to drift off, it wouldn't be friend-like to wake her again.

Then there was Juliana. With the election only one day away, she would be wide-awake, too, but just in case she wasn't…

Deciding there was no one I could decently call at this time of night, I picked up Grafton's *Y Is for Yesterday* and began to read. Since it was Grafton's final book, I'd been putting off the pleasure, hardly able to say farewell to Kinsey Millhone, but as the time to see my mother grew nearer, nothing short of that sad goodbye would suffice.

I tried to slow down my reading pace for Kinsey's last stand, but with three hours and eight minutes still to go, I turned the final page.

Then I showered again, put on the same tee-shirt and jeans, and sat by the window, waiting for the sun to lift over the hills.

It took forever.

Chapter Thirty-four

"I didn't sleep, either," was the first thing my mother said to me when I walked into the private visiting room.

"I...I..."

I began to sob.

She stood up and enfolded me in her arms. "There, there, baby. There, there."

Chapter Thirty-five

After you get through bawling your head off, what do you say to a woman you thought was dead? What do you tell her about your life? About the foster homes you'd endured for fourteen years, the beatings, the rapes?

You don't even bring it up, that's what. You pretend your life in foster care was easy because you don't want to break her heart all over again.

She wanted to know, though, so instead of telling all of the truth, I told her about Reverend Giblin, the foster father who taught me how to tell the difference between hope and delusion. I told her about the couple from the Philippines who taught me how to dance. I told her about Madeline, who showed me that all the beauty of the world can be contained in one small canvas.

Then my mother told me about her life, the life that had stopped after she'd shot me.

"After that, what else was there to live for?" She pulled another tissue from the box Matt had left for us. "Liam was dead, little Jamie was dead, and with you dead, too, what was the point? It was all my fault anyway." She blew her nose again, this time drawing a spot of blood.

As for me, I was all cried out. "How could it be your fault? You had no way of knowing what was going to happen."

"Liam kept telling me something was wrong with Abraham, with the whole setup, but I wouldn't listen. Abraham had promised us an egalitarian society, a place where we'd raise our own food, and cause no harm to any living being. We would create a world where there was no hunger and no sorrow. I bought into the whole thing. Every time Liam wanted us to leave, to go back home and make up with our folks—they'd been against our getting married so young—I talked him out of it. I was afraid that if we went back there, they'd get our marriage annulled. What happened later, it was all on me."

Annulled? "How old were you when you and my dad married?"

"Not quite seventeen. Liam was only a month older than me, but we'd known each other all our lives. I was pregnant with you, so we lied to the preacher about our ages. He was half-blind and couldn't see our forged marriage license."

She'd been a year and a half older than my goddaughter.

As she told her story, I took heart in the fact that although her eyes were red from weeping, she looked healthier than yesterday. Her hair was brushed to highlight more blond than gray, and her skin, although sallow from so many years behind bars, was now tinged pink. Pink was also the color of the private meeting room walls, where prints of baby animals, fawns and bunnies warmed it even further. But the chairs and table were standard prison fare: metal, and bolted to the floor.

I wanted to ask her so much, why she hadn't spoken for more than twenty years, where her mind had been during that time, but she was so eager to learn about me that I held the rest of my questions back. After completing my heavily censored biography of Lena Jones, Private Eye, I finished with, "So I'm presently living on the Pima Reservation with Jimmy, two cats—Snowball and Mama Snowball—and two horses, Big Boy and Adila."

I showed her the pictures the corrections officer had allowed me to keep this morning while going through processing.

"That horse. White with black spots?"

"Adila's what's called a leopard Appaloosa."

"And such a kind face she has! I'll bet she's sweet."

"Not exactly."

Those blue eyes met mine. "'Sweet' would be too easy for you, wouldn't it?"

I thought back over my life, at the few things I'd actually revealed. "You may be right."

She stubbed a short-nailed finger at another picture. "Him. The Indian. You say he's Pima. What's he like?" She gave me another sharp look, then said, "Never mind. I can already tell from the expression on your face."

"What expression?"

"The kind that makes you look even more beautiful than you already are. He's good to you, isn't he?"

Heat rose to my face. "Yes."

"Your father was good to me, too. We Stockard women know how to pick our men."

"In my case there were, ah, some missteps along the way."

"There usually are." It was the first time I'd heard her laugh. "But you're okay, right?"

I took her hand. "Yes, I am. Now."

When the corrections officer—this time it was redheaded Matt Hill, came in and said our time was up—I looked at my watch, certain he was wrong.

I'd been talking to my mother for four hours.

It felt like five minutes.

The faxes I'd asked Jimmy to send had already arrived at the motel when I returned, freeing me to start calling. It took seventeen different conversations before hitting pay dirt in the guise of Theo Morrison, Attorney at Law. Then I called U.S. Senator-elect Juliana Thorsson, who against all odds—and the wishes of my goddaughter—had won the election by a wide margin. Arizonans love their gun-toting broads.

"I need your help," I told her.

"You've got it."

Four months later, Danielle Devlin, the governor of California, commuted my mother's life sentence to time served.

That same afternoon, as I was putting on my boots to join Jimmy in a celebratory ride across the Rez, my cell phone rang out the first notes of John Lee Hooker's "Boogie Chillen." It was Burt Eisweirth, the sheriff of Coconino County. An old friend from our Scottsdale PD days, said he was calling to alert me that two cavers exploring an abandoned mine near the Humphrey's Peak area had discovered human remains in one of its shafts.

"The remains aren't much more than bones, and there looks to be twenty-something, ah, skulls, most of them small. Since you're on record as reporting…"

Twenty-something. "Were they shot?"

"Looks like it."

"Children?"

Since he was having trouble with his throat, he couldn't answer right away, but when he did, he gave me the answer I'd long been expecting. "Yeah, except for one, an adult male."

It was my turn to have throat trouble. Damned desert pollen. "Any identifying features on the adult? Billfold, belt buckle, whatever?"

"Nothing like that, but he, ah, he had red hair. Just like you wrote down on your report."

I closed my eyes. Remembered my father's bright red hair gleaming in a sunlit meadow, remembered him strumming his guitar and singing "Michael, Row the Boat Ashore" with a group of children.

"When can I come up there?" I finally managed to ask.

"As soon as you want, Lena. You've been waiting a long time for this."

I cleared my throat. "I'll call you back in a couple of days. I need to go somewhere else first."

Then I put the phone down very, very carefully, and went out to the corral to tell Jimmy that the lost were now found.

Chapter Thirty-six

Helen

As the prison gate closes behind me, I can see my daughter. She is standing next to a man with long black hair.

Jimmy.

He is even handsomer than she said he was, and his smile is genuine.

I take a moment to inhale the clean March air. Although Chino is many miles inland, it still holds a hint of the Pacific, which I have never seen. Christina—I haven't yet gotten used to calling her *Lena*—has promised to take me to it before we leave for Arizona.

"I'm ready," I tell her, although the day is so bright it hurts my eyes.

My baby takes me by one hand, her man by the other.

"Let's go home, Mother."

The End

Acknowledgments

Twenty years ago, Lena Jones came to me in a dream, asking me to tell her story. At the time, I was a reporter for the *Scottsdale Tribune*, covering events that ranged from politicians' preachments to the escape of two girls from one of Arizona's many polygamy compounds. Those girls' mindsets—they believed their self-described "prophet" Warren Jeffs had a direct pipeline to God—reminded me of Guyana's Jim Jones, who convinced more than nine hundred followers to drink his deadly Kool-Aid. When I researched polygamy cults for Lena's adventures in *Desert Wives*, I also looked into David Koresh's Branch Davidians in Waco (from seventy-six to seventy-eight dead), Japan's Aum Shinrikyo (thirteen dead, thousands injured), Switzerland's Ordre du Temple Solaire (seventy-four dead), and Marshall Applewhite's San Diego-based Heaven's Gate (thirty-nine dead).

While *Desert Redemption* and its characters are fictional, the emergence of apocalyptic cults is unfortunately real. Too many gullible followers continue to believe madmen's ravings and drink the Kool-Aid.

Desert Redemption—as with all the Lena Jones novels—could not have been written without the input of the Sheridan Street Irregulars; blessings to those brothers- and sisters-in-arms. Blessings, too, to Barbara Peters and Robert Rosenwald of Poisoned Pen Press, who ushered Lena into the world. On the civilian side, Judy Par, Marge Purcell, and Debra McCarthy gave, and gave, and gave.

Any mistakes in these pages are my fault, not theirs.